ROBYN CARR

FORBIDDEN FALLS

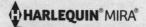

HARLEQUIN® MIRA®

Recycling programs
for this product may
not exist in your area.

ISBN-13: 978-0-7783-1697-8

Forbidden Falls

Printed in U.S.A.

Praise for #1 *New York Times* and #1 *USA TODAY* bestselling author Robyn Carr

"An intensely satisfying read. By turns humorous and gut-wrenchingly emotional, it won't soon be forgotten."
—*RT Book Reviews* on *Paradise Valley*

"This book is an utter delight."
—*RT Book Reviews* on *Moonlight Road*

"Strong conflict, humor and well-written characters are Carr's calling cards, and they're all present here....
You won't want to put this one down."
—*RT Book Reviews* on *Angel's Peak*

"This story has everything: a courageous, outspoken heroine, a to-die-for hero and a plot that will touch readers' hearts on several different levels. Truly excellent."
—*RT Book Reviews* on *Forbidden Falls*

"Carr has hit her stride with this captivating series."
—*Library Journal* on the Virgin River series

"The Virgin River books are so compelling—I connected instantly with the characters and just wanted more and more and more."
—#1 *New York Times* bestselling author Debbie Macomber

Also available from Robyn Carr and Harlequin MIRA

Thunder Point Series
THE HOMECOMING
THE PROMISE
THE CHANCE
THE HERO
THE NEWCOMER
THE WANDERER

Virgin River Series
MY KIND OF CHRISTMAS
SUNRISE POINT
REDWOOD BEND
HIDDEN SUMMIT
BRING ME HOME FOR CHRISTMAS
HARVEST MOON
WILD MAN CREEK
PROMISE CANYON
MOONLIGHT ROAD
ANGEL'S PEAK
PARADISE VALLEY
TEMPTATION RIDGE
SECOND CHANCE PASS
A VIRGIN RIVER CHRISTMAS
WHISPERING ROCK
SHELTER MOUNTAIN
VIRGIN RIVER

Grace Valley Series
DEEP IN THE VALLEY
JUST OVER THE MOUNTAIN
DOWN BY THE RIVER

Novels
FOUR FRIENDS
A SUMMER IN SONOMA
NEVER TOO LATE
RUNAWAY MISTRESS
BLUE SKIES
THE WEDDING PARTY
THE HOUSE ON OLIVE STREET

Look for Robyn Carr's next novel

available soon from Harlequin MIRA

This book is dedicated to my daughter and best friend, Jamie Lynn. Thank you for being your wonderful self. I'm so proud of you.

One

Recently ordained minister Noah Kincaid was surfing the Internet, killing time, when quite by chance, he happened to find a church being auctioned on eBay—in some little place he'd never heard of—Virgin River. He laughed at the very idea, but was intrigued. He'd been waiting patiently for an assignment to a church of his own and thought it couldn't hurt to take a look at the place himself. If nothing else, it would be a good excuse to get out of town for a day and see something different. He'd heard Northern California was very beautiful.

The first thing that struck him was the overwhelming beauty of the mountains, redwoods and rivers. The town was a little washed out and the church was a wreck, but there was a peacefulness and simplicity there he couldn't dismiss. Or forget. It seemed uncomplicated, fresh.

No one really noticed him in the little town; the local men he'd seen either had hair shorn in military fashion or ponytails and beards, just like the fishermen Noah had worked with over the years. He fit right in—he wore scuffed boots, his jeans were almost white with wear, ripped here and there, his denim shirt was thin on the elbows and frayed around the collar and cuffs. His black hair was too long and curled over his collar; he planned to get it cut the second he was assigned a church of his own. But for now, he fit right in, looking like any other laborer after a hard day's work. He was fit and toned like the local Virgin River men; years of working on a fishing boat and dockside, dragging nets, hauling in tons of fresh catch will do that.

The church had been easy to locate and he hadn't needed a key to get inside—it was boarded up and appeared to have been abandoned for years, but the side door wasn't locked. The place had been stripped bare and filled with years of trash, probably litter from transients who'd taken shelter there at one time or another. Almost all the windows had been broken before being covered over with plywood. But when he got to the sanctuary, he discovered a stunning stained-glass window, boarded from the outside to keep it safe. It had been left untouched.

Afterward, he had driven the neighborhoods in town, which hadn't taken long, had a cup of coffee at the only eating establishment, snapped a few digital pictures and left. When he got back to Seattle he contacted the woman who was auctioning the church on eBay, Hope McCrea. "That church has been boarded up for years," she said in her gravelly voice. "This town has been without religion a long time."

"You sure the town is in need of religion?" Noah asked her.

"Not entirely sure," she answered. "But it could damn sure use some faith. That church needs to be opened up or razed to the ground. An empty church is bad mojo."

Noah couldn't agree more.

Despite being busy at the college where he taught,

Noah couldn't get Virgin River, or that church, out of his mind.

He took the idea of buying the church to the presbytery and found they were already well aware of its existence. He showed them his digital pictures and they agreed, there was great potential. Placing a minister there appealed to them; the population was just the right size to build a congregation and it was the only church in town. But the renovation, not to mention the accoutrements, would put the costs too high. There was no way they had the budget. They thanked Noah sincerely and promised him he would get his own church real soon.

What the presbytery didn't know was that Noah had recently come into some money. To him, a small fortune. He was thirty-five and since the age of eighteen had been slaving and studying. While attending the university, he'd worked on boats, docks and in fish markets out of the Port of Seattle. A year ago his mother had passed and, to his surprise, had left him a hefty portion of her inheritance.

So, he offered to lighten the presbytery's financial burden by taking on the renovation costs of the church as a donation if they would see fit to assign him as the pastor. The proposal was an appealing one for the Presbyterian church.

Before closing the deal, Noah called his closest friend, and the man responsible for talking him into the seminary in the first place. George Davenport thought he'd lost his mind. George was a retired Presbyterian minister who had been teaching for the last fifteen years at Seattle Pacific University. "I can think of a thousand ways for you to throw away that money," George had said. "Go to Las Vegas, put it all on red. Or finance your own mission to Mexico. If those people needed a pastor, they'd go looking for one."

"Funny that church is still standing there, useless, like

it's waiting for a rebirth. There must be a reason I happened to see it on eBay," Noah said. "I've never looked at eBay before in my life."

After much debate, George conceded, "If it's structurally sound and the price is right, it might work out. You'd get a big tax write-off with the donated renovation cost, and a chance to serve a small, poor congregation in a hick mountain town that doesn't get cell-phone reception. Sounds perfect for you."

"There is no congregation, George," Noah reminded him.

"Then you'll have to gather one, son. If anyone can do it, you can. You were born to do it, and before you get all insulted, I'm not talking about your DNA. I'm talking about pure talent. I've seen the way you sell fish, I always thought there was a message there. Go—it's what you want. Open your doors and your heart and give it all you've got. Besides, you're the only ordained minister I know who has two nickels to rub together."

So Noah inked the deal with the presbytery and hoped his mother wasn't spinning in her grave. Truth be told, she'd always quietly supported him when, years back, he had been determined as hell to run *away* from the ministry. She had good reason. Noah's father was a powerful, semi-famous televangelist—and a cold, controlling man. Noah had run away while his mother could not.

If someone had told Noah seventeen years ago, when he fled his father's house at the age of eighteen, that he would one day be a preacher himself, he'd have laughed in their face. Yet here he was. And he wanted that church. That wreck of a church in that peaceful, uncomplicated mountain town.

Several weeks later Noah was in his fifteen-year-old RV, which would be his home for a good long time, towing his twenty-year-old faded-blue Ford truck. En route to Northern California, he called George's office, placing the call from his cell phone before the signal was lost in the mountains and tall trees. "I'm on my way into Virgin River, George."

"Well, boy—how does it feel?" George asked with a deep chuckle in his voice. "Like you pulled off the sweetheart deal of the century, or like you'll be dead broke and out in the street before you know what hit you?"

Noah laughed. "Not sure. I'll be tapped out by the time the church is presentable. If I can't drum up a congregation, I could be back in Seattle throwing fish before you know it," he said, referring to an old job of his working the fish market on Seattle's downtown wharf. He'd literally thrown large fish across the market. It had been like theater and it was where George had discovered him. "I'll get started on the improvements right away and trust the presbytery won't leave me out in the cold if no one shows up to services. I mean, if you can't trust the church…"

That comment was answered with George's hearty laughter. "They're the last ones I'd trust. Those Presbyterians think too much! I know I wasn't keen on this idea at first, Noah, but I wish you well," George said. "I'm proud of you for taking a chance."

"Thanks, George. I'll keep in touch."

"Noah," George said soberly. "Good luck, son. I hope you find what you're looking for."

It was the first of July when Noah rattled into Virgin River and pulled right up to the church. Parked there was a big old Suburban with the wheels jacked up and covered with mud. Standing beside it was a tiny old woman with wiry white hair and big glasses, a cigarette hanging from her lips. She wore great big tennis shoes that didn't look as if they'd ever been white and, although it was summer, she had on a jacket with torn pockets. When he parked and got out of his RV, she tossed the cigarette to the ground and stomped it out. One of Virgin River's stunning beauties, he thought wryly.

"Reverend Kincaid, I presume?" she said.

From the look on her face, Noah assumed she was expecting someone a bit more refined. Maybe someone who dressed in khakis and a crisp white button-down? Shiny loafers? Neatly trimmed hair? Clean shaven at least? His hair was shaggy, his whiskers itchy, and he had a healthy bit of motor oil on his jeans, a result of a stop a hundred miles back when he'd had to work on the RV. "Mrs. McCrea," he answered, putting out his hand.

She shook it briefly, then put the keys in his palm. "Welcome. Would you like a tour?"

"Do I need keys?" he asked. "The building wasn't locked the last time I was here. I looked it over pretty thoroughly."

"You've *seen* it?" she asked, clearly startled.

"Sure did. I took a run down here before placing a bid on behalf of the Presbyterian church. The door wasn't locked so I helped myself. All the presbytery really needed from you was the engineer's report on the building's structural competence. I gave them lots of pictures."

She pushed her oversize glasses up on her nose. "What are you, a minister or some kind of secret agent?"

He grinned at her. "Did you think the presbytery bought it on faith?"

"I guess I didn't see any other possibility. Well, if you're all set, let's go in to Jack's—it's time for my drink. Doctor's orders. I'll front you one."

"Did the doctor order the smokes, too?" he asked with a smile.

"You're damn straight, sonny. Don't start on me."

"I gotta meet this doctor," Noah muttered, following her.

Hope stopped abruptly, looked at him over her shoulder as she adjusted her jacket and said, "He's dead." And with that she turned and stomped into Jack's bar.

Noah had only been in town a couple of days before the need for cleaning supplies sent him in the direction of Fortuna. The narrow, winding mountain roads led him toward the freeway, and he marveled that he had managed to get his RV to Virgin River at all, especially while towing his truck. He wasn't quite halfway to Fortuna before he had his first lesson in how dramatically different mountain life was from life in the city, the campus and the Seattle wharf.

He spied a motionless animal by the side of the road and by pure coincidence there was a wide space on the shoulder just ahead. He pulled over and got out of his truck. When he was within a few feet, he realized it was a dog; perhaps some family pet. He went closer. Flies were buzzing around the animal and some of its fur looked shiny with blood, but Noah detected a slight movement. He crouched near the dog, whose eyes were open and tongue hanging out of its parted mouth. The animal was breathing, but clearly near death. The condition of the poor beast tore at his heart.

Just then, an old truck pulled up and parked behind Noah's vehicle and a man got out. Noah took him for a farmer or rancher; he wore jeans, boots, a cowboy hat, and walked with a hitch that suggested a sore back. "Got a problem there, bud?" the man asked.

Noah looked at him over his shoulder. "Dog," he said. "Hit by a car, I guess. And a while ago. But it's alive."

The rancher crouched and took a closer look. "Hmmph," he grunted. He stood. "Okay then. I'll take care of it."

Noah waved away the flies and gave the dog's head and neck a stroke. "Easy now—help's on the way." He was still stroking the dog's neck when the man's boots came into view beside him, as well as the business end of a rifle, aimed at the dog's chest. "Might want to move back, son," the man said.

"Hey!" Noah shouted, pushing the rifle away. "What are you doing?"

"I'm going to put that poor creature out of its misery," the man said in a tone that indicated he found the question ludicrous. "What else you gonna do?"

"Take it to a vet," Noah said, standing. "Maybe it can be helped!"

"Buddy, look at that dog. It's emaciated, pretty much starved. That animal was half-dead before a car hit it. Wouldn't be right to leave it to lie here, dying." He aimed again.

Again Noah pushed the rifle away. "Where's the nearest vet?" he asked. "I'll take it. If the vet can't help it, he can euthanize the dog without blowing it apart."

The rancher scratched his chin and shook his head. "Nathaniel Jensen is off 36, just this side of Fortuna, but he's a large-animal vet. He's got dogs, though. If he can't help, he can give you the name of someone who can. Or put it down for you. But, buddy, that dog isn't going to make it to the vet."

"How do I get there?" Noah asked.

"Turn left off 36 on Waycliff Road. You'll see a sign for Jensen Stables and Vet Clinic, and Dr. Jensen. It's only a few minutes down the hill." He shook his head again. "This could all be over in thirty seconds."

Noah ignored him and went back to his truck, opening the passenger door. He returned to the animal and lifted it into his arms, which is when he discovered it was a female. The blood was dried and didn't soil him, but flies buzzed around the injury and he was pretty sure he'd end up with maggots on his clothes. He was about halfway to his truck when the rancher said, "Good luck there, buddy."

"Yeah," Noah grumbled. "Thanks."

Dr. Nathaniel Jensen proved to be a friendly guy just a little younger than Noah and he was far more helpful than the old rancher had been. He looked the dog over for about sixty seconds before he said, "This looks like it could be Lucy. Her owner was a local rancher, killed in an accident up north, near Redding, months ago now. He was hauling a gelding; killed him and the horse. They never found his dog, a border collie. She might've been thrown and injured. Or maybe she got scared and bolted. Oh, man, if this is Lucy, I bet she was trying to find her way home."

"Does she have family who will take care of her?"

"That's the thing—old Silas was a widower. He had one daughter and she married a serviceman, moved away more than twenty years ago. Silas's ranch and stable sold immediately. The remaining animals—horses and dogs—were sold or placed. I don't think the daughter was even back here for the sale. I could call around, see if anyone knows where she is. But that could take time old Lucy doesn't have. She didn't take on any of her father's other animals. And we don't even know if this is—"

"*Old* Lucy?" Noah asked.

"I didn't mean it like that. She's not that old. Three or four, maybe. Silas had a pack of ranch dogs. Herders. But Lucy was a favorite and went everywhere with him. She's a mess."

"Can you do anything for her?"

"Listen, I can start an IV, treat her for a possible head

injury, find the source of bleeding, clean her up, sedate her if she needs it, run some antibiotics, transfuse her if necessary—but you're looking at a big expense that Silas's only daughter might not be willing to pick up. People around here—farmers and ranchers—most of 'em aren't real sentimental about their dogs. They wouldn't spend more than the animal's worth."

"I'm beginning to understand that," Noah said, pulling out his wallet. He extracted a credit card and said, "I don't have a phone yet—I just got here and there's no reception for the cell. I'll call in or stop by. Just do what you can do."

"Nothing wrong with just letting her go, Noah," he said gently. "As banged up as she is, that's what most people would do. Even if she pulls through, there's no guarantee she'll be much of a dog."

He stroked the dog's head and thought, *No guarantee any of us will be much of anything, but we still try.* "Be sure to give her something good for pain, all right? I don't want her to be in pain while you see what can be done."

"You sure about this?" Nathaniel asked.

Noah smiled at him. "I'll give you a call tomorrow afternoon. And thanks."

The next day, Noah learned that Lucy had a few cracked ribs, a couple of lacerations and scrapes, was malnourished and infested with tics and maggots, and had a systemic infection. She might recover, Dr. Jensen said, but her condition was poor. If she did get stronger, Dr. Jensen insisted she should be spayed. So on top of everything else, poor Lucy was going to have a hysterectomy. He gave Nathaniel Jensen the phone number for the bar next door to the church, in case something came up. It turned out Doc Jensen knew the owner, Jack.

Noah soon discovered that Virgin River's Communication Central was located right next door to the church—at Jack's Bar. Jack was a very nice guy who seemed to know everyone and everything. He quizzed Noah briefly about his denomination, education, what plans he had for the church, and that was all it took for the entire town to be informed. Noah had expected some rude jokes and at the very least some good-natured ribbing about being the pastor who bought an old church on eBay, and he hadn't been disappointed. But it also seemed the people in town were relieved to learn he was an ordained minister, since he looked pretty much like an out-of-work lumberjack; all the thin white scars on his hands and forearms from work on the boats and docks undoubtedly set him up as a man who did hard, physical labor.

Noah explained that the building officially belonged to the church but that it would be governed by a group of church elders once they were functional and had a congregation. Ownership would hopefully, in time, pass to the congregants, as they amassed and grew and gathered the funds to support it. His plans? "How about a low-key, friendly place for people to gather, support each other, worship together?" Noah had answered. "No revivals or animal sacrifices till we're all better acquainted." And then he had grinned.

Not only did Jack give him good press, which Noah appreciated, but in short order Jack began to feel like a friend. Noah checked in daily at Jack's, usually having at least a cup of coffee, and through Jack he met many of the locals. And Jack's phone was the hotline to the veterinarian. "Nate called in, Noah," Jack reported. "That dog of yours is still hanging in there. Doing better."

"She worth more than my truck yet?" Noah asked.

Jack laughed. "I saw that old truck, Noah. I suspect

she was worth more than that when you scraped her off the road."

"Funny," Noah said. "That truck gets me where I'm going. Most of the time."

Jack's partner and cook, known as Preacher, invited Noah to jump on their satellite wireless-Internet connection so Noah could use his laptop for e-mails and research on the Net, but cautioned him against buying anything else Hope McCrea might be selling.

When he wasn't cleaning out the church or getting himself settled in town, every other day Noah visited Lucy at Jensen's Stables and Vet Clinic. Since the weather was warm, Nate was keeping her in an empty stall and Noah would spend an hour or so just sitting on the ground beside her, talking to her, petting her. By the time she'd been there a week it was apparent she was going to pull through. After ten days she was walking around, if slowly. "Don't show me the bill," Noah said to Nate Jensen during one of his visits. "I don't want to cry in front of you."

There was no parsonage for Noah to call home, but he was comfortable in the RV and he had the truck for getting around the mountains. He did a little door-knocking, letting the folks know he was new to town and planned to get that church going. He had hoped some volunteers would materialize to help with the cleanup, but he refrained from asking and so far no one had offered. People seemed extremely friendly, but Noah thought they might be holding off a little to see what kind of minister he stacked up to be. There was a good chance he wasn't what they were looking for at all, but only time would tell.

He'd collected enough cakes and cookies for a bake sale. The women in town had been dropping by, bearing sweets and welcoming him to the neighborhood. Even though Noah had a scary-powerful sweet tooth, he was getting a little tired of feasting on desserts. He even gave a passing thought to holding a bake sale.

Another thing Noah did was visit the nearest hospital— Valley Hospital. He called on the sick and bereaved. Preaching might be his job, but bringing comfort was his calling.

Since there was no hospital chaplain, they relied on the local clergy to visit, so Noah just asked a hospital volunteer to point him toward anyone who might need a friendly visit. She looked him up and down doubtfully; he was dressed as usual in his jeans, boots and flannel shirt… He wore the T-shirt without holes. If he hadn't had a Bible in his hand, he had the impression the volunteer would have seriously questioned him. Clearly, the pastors hereabouts must spruce up a bit before visiting the patients.

His first client was an elderly man, a real sourpuss, who eyed the Bible and said, "I ain't in the mood."

Noah laughed. "Since I can't fit the Bible in my pocket, why don't you tell me what you'd like to do. Talk, tell jokes, watch some TV?"

"Where you from, boy?" the old man asked.

"I'm from Ohio originally, most recently from—"

"No! I mean, what religion you from!"

"Oh. Presbyterian."

"I ain't been in a church in fifty years or more."

"You don't say," Noah replied.

"But when I was, it sure as hell wasn't Presbyterian!"

"I see."

"I was born Catholic!"

"No kidding?" Noah said. "Well, let's see." He dug around in the pocket of his jeans. He pulled out a rosary. He dangled it. "You have any use for this?"

"What the Sam Hill is a Presbyterian fella doing with one of those? You using those now?"

"No, we're still sticking to the basics, but I'm a pretty all-purpose preacher. You want it?"

"I won't use it," he said defiantly. "You can leave it, but I won't use it."

"Sure," Noah said. "So, what's that you got on TV?"

"Andy Griffith," he answered.

"All *right!* I love that show. You ever see that one when Barney had the motorcycle with the sidecar?" Noah moved into the room and took the chair beside the old man's bed, draping the rosary across his arthritic hands.

"I seen it. You see the one where he locks himself in the cell?"

"Didn't he do that every few weeks?" Noah asked with a smirk. "How about when Aunt Bea accidentally got drunk? You see that one?"

"Otis, the town drunk, now there's a character," the old fella said.

It took a while, but he learned this man was Salvatore Salentino, Sal for short. They went over their favorite episodes for a while, then Sal needed assistance to the bathroom, then he wanted to talk about his old truck, which he missed like crazy since being put in a nursing home. Next, he spoke about his grown daughter who'd moved out of the mountains and rarely came back. Then he got onto how much he hated computers. Finally, he asked Noah if he'd be back this way anytime soon because he was returning to the nursing home in a couple of days. "I could stop by there if you'd like me to, Sal," Noah said.

"Can if you want," the old fella said. "But don't get the idea you're going to turn me into some goddamn Presbyterian!"

Noah smiled and said, "Good grief, no. I just haven't had anyone to watch Andy with in a long time."

* * *

There wasn't much to salvage in the old church. The pews had been removed, the appliances in the church kitchen ripped out, the pulpit, altar and baptistery gone, not an accessory in sight—all sold off when the church had closed its doors. There was, however, that incredible stained-glass window at the front of the church. It was an amazing, valuable work of art.

The first thing Noah had done when beginning the cleanup was borrow a ladder from Jack and tear the plywood off the outside of the church. The daylight revealed a far larger and more beautiful stained-glass window than he imagined a poor church could afford, and he was surprised it hadn't been removed and sold or transported to another church. When he stared up at it, it gave him a feeling of purpose, of belonging. It was an image of Jesus, white robed, arms spread, palms out and accessible. On his shoulder was a dove. At his feet a lamb, a rabbit, a fawn. In the setting sun the light caught the eyes of Christ and created a beam of light that shone down into the church; a path of light in which he could see the dust motes dancing. He had no prie-dieu kneeler, but he would stand in front of that beautiful creation, hands deep in his pockets, staring up at the image and repeat the most beautiful prayer he knew. The prayer of Saint Francis of Assisi. *Lord, make me an instrument of your peace....*

By his third week in Virgin River, Lucy had been released into Noah's care. Dr. Nathaniel Jensen gave him Lucy's bill, and Noah folded it in half, stuffed it in the pocket of his Levi's and refused to look at it until he had Lucy home. When he looked at the statement, he grabbed his heart. "Really, I should be able to drive you," he said to the dog. Lucy licked his hand. "Remind me to keep my eyes on the road when I'm driving through the mountains," he said.

Lucy was still a long way from being a frisky pup—she was on a special recovery diet, along with vitamins and antibiotics. She was a black-and-white border collie, maybe a bit of something else in the mix, and she had the most beautiful, large brown eyes that could look very pathetic and sad. Noah purchased a soft dog bed that he carried from the RV to the church office to accommodate her lingering aches and pains. Preacher agreed to fix a special chicken-and-rice meal for her twice a day, since Noah's cooking facilities were a bit restricted in the RV. Lucy could manage the three steps up to the bar porch, where she took many of her meals, but she had a terrible struggle getting up the stairs to the church office. Noah usually ended up carrying her.

What with the community outreach, caring for Lucy and the slow progress on the church cleanup, Noah realized he was going to need some help. So, once the phone line was installed, he advertised for a pastor's assistant. He fielded many more calls than he expected, but once he'd answered a few questions about hours, pay and benefits, most of the callers said "they'd get back to him." The duties weren't typical—there would be cleaning and painting, as well as setting up an office—and he guessed the callers found the work too hard. He made appointments for three women who hadn't bothered to ask questions. With Lucy settled on her pallet beside the old desk that had been left behind, he prepared to interview the first round of candidates.

The first was Selma Hatchet, a portly woman of sixty who walked with a three-pronged cane. "You the pastor?" she asked.

"Yes," he said, rising. "Pleasure to meet you, ma'am.

Please, have a seat," he said, indicating the chair that faced his desk. When they were both seated, they proceeded to visit a bit. The lady had raised a family and a couple of grandkids for her working daughter, done a great deal of volunteer work, and had been quite involved in the Grace Valley Presbyterian Church for the past twenty years.

"Mrs. Hatchet, this position will evolve into secretarial work, but right now it's going to be a very physical job. I not only need help organizing an office and library, but scrubbing, painting, spackling and probably a lot of heavy lifting. It might not be what you're looking for."

She stiffened and lifted her chin. "I want to do the Lord's work," she said tightly. "I'll willingly carry any load the Lord entrusts me with."

Noah briefly wondered if Mrs. Hatchet thought he had workmen's comp for when she threw out her back or took a tumble off a ladder. "Well, that's admirable, but in this case the Lord's work is going to be dirty, messy and the only praying will probably be for Bengay."

He saw her to the door with a promise to be in touch.

The next applicant looked physically better suited to the hard work ahead and she was more than willing to pitch in, no matter how difficult or dirty the work. Rachael Nagel was in her midforties, a rancher's wife who'd done her share of lifting and hauling, but she was a little scary. She had that pinched look of disapproval and began questioning him before he could get a word in edgewise. "You're not going to be one of those liberal preachers, are you?"

Liberal was just about his middle name. Noah's father was all about fire and brimstone, hell and damnation, and was probably the main reason Noah was not. "Um, I've been considered liberal by some, conservative by others.

Tell me, Mrs. Nagel, do you by chance play the piano or organ?"

"Never had time for anything frivolous with a ranch to run, but I raised seven children with a firm hand. I can make sure the doctrine of the church is followed to the letter."

"What a wonderful gift," he said. "I'll be in touch."

"You oughtn't keep a dog like that in the church," she pointed out. "You're gonna end up with problems."

"And where do you suggest I keep her?" he asked.

"Since you don't have land, you could get an outdoor kennel. Or tie it to a tree."

Noah knew right then Mrs. Nagel wouldn't work out.

His third applicant was Ellie Baldwin. Noah was sitting behind his desk when she walked into his ramshackle office. He paused before managing to get to his feet to greet her. She looked young, early twenties at best. And tall—almost six feet—without her shoes and hair. Most of that six feet was legs, which were sticking a long way out of a short flouncy skirt, her feet slipped into high-heeled sandals. She had very big hair, a ton of coppery curls that were streaked with gold and that fell to her shoulders and down her back. Not only was her yellow sweater tight and revealing, but a little bit of her purple bra was showing at the low décolletage…on purpose. This was a look he'd been seeing for a while—this showing of the bra, a push-up bra no less. He couldn't deny it was a lovely sight, but he didn't usually see this immodest style in a church.

She had a crinkled-up piece of newspaper in her hand. "I'm looking for Reverend Kincaid," she said.

"I'm Noah Kincaid. How do you do?"

"You're—"

"The pastor. And you must be Miss Baldwin."

Her eyelashes were thick with black liner and mascara,

her cheeks rouged, her lips red and glossy, her nails long and painted blue with sparkles, and a glance down those long legs revealed the polish on her toes matched her fingertips. She smiled at him when she came into the room. Then she turned away abruptly to take the gum out of her mouth, though he couldn't tell where it went. But the image of her smile was immediately tattooed on his mind—it was beautiful. Also hopeful. But what was she thinking, coming to a job interview in a small-town church dressed all honky-tonk? And he thought, *Aw, Jesus. Why me?*

He stuck out his hand, hoping a wad of gum wouldn't be left in it. "How are you?"

"Fine, thanks," she said. "Have you filled the job yet?"

"I have a couple of promising applicants. But let's talk about the job," he said. He had a twinge of guilt—no way could he, a single minister of thirty-five, hire someone like this. People would never understand. Or worse, they'd assume they *did* understand. This interview was going to be a waste of time.

"Awww, is that your dog?" she asked, smiling down at Lucy.

"Meet Lucy," he said. At the sound of her name, she lifted her head.

"Is she really old? She looks very tired."

"She's recovering from a bad accident. I found her by the side of the road and, presto, I became her new owner," he said. "The job," he went on, "isn't limited to office work. As you can see, there's a lot of renovation and repair going on here. This church won't be ready for a congregation until some very heavy and very dirty work gets done. A couple of months' worth, at least."

She nodded. "Right," she said. "Fine."

His eyebrows lifted. "If you don't mind me saying so, you look kind of fragile for that kind of work."

She laughed and her whole face brightened. "Is that so? Well, this fragile girl has cleaned up a lot of dumps and lifted more than her share of heavy stuff, Your Reverence."

He cleared his throat. "It's Noah. Please. I'm not the pope."

"I know that," she scoffed. "I was being funny."

"Ah. And so you were," he admitted. "So, not only do I need an office set up and some appointment, phone, and calendar management, but also help with moving furniture, painting, cleaning, et cetera."

"Got it," she said.

He leaned forward. "Ms. Baldwin, why do you want this job?"

"Isn't it a good job?" she asked. "There wasn't much to the ad, but it sounded like a decent job in a decent line of work."

"Sure. And you're drawn to this line of work because…?"

"I need a change. Something a little more secure. Less stressful."

"And your last or current job is…was…?"

"Dancer. The hours don't work for me. I have kids. They're with my ex right now, but I'd like a job I can do while they're in school. Y'know?"

"But do you have secretarial experience?"

"For when we're done plastering and painting and moving furniture? Sure. A lot. I have a list of previous jobs," she said, pulling a pretty tattered, folded piece of paper out of her purse.

He glanced at it. He didn't see dancer on there but, without asking, he suspected he knew what kind of dancer. Just the way she was dressed, decidedly not churchy, suggested way too much. But, she had also worked for a real estate broker, a property manager and a "Lawyer?" he asked, surprised.

"Uh-huh. Nice guy. I did a real good job for him. You can call him—he'll tell you. He said he'd write me a letter of recommendation anytime I ask."

"And you left that job because…?"

She looked away a bit uncomfortably. "He liked my work, I promise. But his wife wasn't real crazy about me. But call him!" she said, looking back at him. "I did a good job there."

The girl had worked everywhere. Everything from a loading dock to a convenience store. "How could you do all this stuff?" Noah asked, perplexed.

"Two jobs," she shrugged. "Office work during the day, for the experience and benefits. Then a second job, part-time, at night and on weekends. I worked at a convenience store at night till it got held up, then I cleaned business offices with a cleaning crew. I have a lot of experience."

"Loading dock?" he asked, glancing up from her résumé.

"For a big retailer. It was kind of temporary, till I could get a job that didn't break all my nails." And she smiled at him. "I don't think there's anything you could throw at me that I haven't done."

"Great," he said. "Can I keep this?"

She looked a little panicked. "Could you just copy down stuff? Names and numbers or whatever you want? I had to go to some trouble to make that up and I only have the one copy."

"Of course," Noah said.

"I should probably get copies," she said. "I don't have a computer, myself. A friend helped me do that up."

"No problem," he said. And he made a point of copying some things off the page, though he had no intention of following up. When he looked up at her again, it was difficult not to notice that chest. He couldn't escape the feeling those boobs were going to poke his eyes out. "Tell me something—any chance you play the piano or organ?"

"Organ? No. But my gramma taught me the piano, and hymns were her favorite. I could manage, probably. If I had time for a little practice. It's been a while."

"Church hymns?"

She grinned. "It's what I grew up on, believe it or not."

"Really?" Noah said, intrigued. Then he found himself just staring at her for a long, mesmerizing moment. "Um," he started, collecting himself, "where do you live, Ms. Baldwin?"

She leaned forward, and her boobs nearly fell out of that tight sweater. He could feel his eyes bulge and his hands itch with temptation. "Ellie is fine," she said. "I mean, if I don't have to call you Your Reverence, you can call me Ellie. I have a place in Eureka right now, but I'd like to get my kids out of there. I'd like to move them someplace small and friendly where they can grow up safe, you know?"

"Do you mind me asking, how old are your kids?"

"Danielle is eight and Trevor is four." She smiled proudly. "They're amazing. Beautiful and smart and... Well," she said, straightening. "Of course I'd think that. They're also very healthy. I shouldn't be missing work because they're sick or anything."

He was speechless. "You don't look old enough to—" He stopped himself. It was none of his business.

"I started the family too young, I know that. But I'm sure glad I have them."

After a moment of silence he said, "Yes. Absolutely. Well, listen, you have some very good qualifications here. Can I get back to you?"

Her face fell. "Yeah," she said. "Sure." And then she stood. "I wish you'd take it kind of serious. I need the job. I've looked everywhere for a job I can do while my kids are in school and it's hell, you know? Sorry—you probably don't say hell…"

He felt a smile tug at his lips. He almost said, *Hell if I don't.*

"Really, I could do just about anything," she said. "I'm a very hard worker."

"You're very qualified," he said with a nod. "I'll be in touch." He stuck out his hand.

Eyes downcast, Ellie took it limply. "Thanks," she said, looking totally disheartened.

Two

While Ellie made her own way out of his office and the church, Noah stayed behind his desk. He hadn't really expected to immediately find someone he could hire, anyway. In fact, he thought the search would probably be long and difficult. But the last thing he'd expected was to interview someone who could do the job, and do it in a push-up bra and short skirt. *Whoa,* he thought. He was actually having a reaction. He shifted in his chair to get comfortable, trying to ignore his body's response. Nature was a practical joker.

Reflecting on the past several weeks and remembering Ellie's dejected posture as she left the interview got Noah thinking. When his wife, Merry, died a few years ago, the grief bit hard and the adjustment was terrible; marriage really worked for him and the loss was devastating. Merry's death left him a thirty-year-old widower, just about the last thing he ever envisioned for himself. For a year he felt like a pebble banging around inside an empty tin can and then, with George's encouragement, he headed for the seminary.

Noah had nurtured a lifelong aversion to the ministry

because of his father whom he considered a mean-spirited hypocrite. Jasper Kincaid was a semifamous preacher who had his own cable television mission in Columbus, Ohio. Big-time church, big-time money, big-time fame and power. But Jasper had treated his wife and son with indifference, and that was on a good day. They were too often the objects of his anger and recriminations. No way was Noah ever going to follow in those footsteps.

"Stop judging how everyone else treats their faith and study your own," George had counseled. "It took a bloody ton of it to get where you are today."

Indeed. While still a teenager, Noah had fled his Ohio roots and headed for the Pacific Northwest. He worked as a laborer anywhere he could get work, but fell in love with the fishing industry, with the ocean and the livelihood it offered. While he worked, he also studied— sometimes as a part-time student, sometimes full-time.

His mother, too loyal and kindhearted to ever defy his father, stayed in touch and even visited. She wanted to give him money to assist with his education, but Noah refused. His mom met Merry only once and, for the first time in his life, Noah saw his mother weep with happiness that Noah should find a young woman so full of love and joy. Only two years later, his mother came, alone, to Merry's funeral.

Noah and his father had spoken only once in the past seventeen years and that was at his mother's funeral a year ago. He had no desire to reconcile with Jasper. He considered it a matter of survival.

Noah had been at his desk about an hour, trying to write up a schedule for himself but doing nothing but thinking and remembering, when he looked at his watch. Three o'clock. There wouldn't be a crowd at Jack's at this time of day and he thought maybe a cup of coffee was in order. He gave Lucy a pat on the head and promised to be back soon.

When he walked into the bar, he was surprised to see Ellie Baldwin seated at a table not far from the empty hearth. A cup of coffee sat in front of her, her hands were folded in her lap and she gazed out the window. Instead of looking brassy and sexy, she looked a little lost. Noah lifted a hand in her direction, but she was deep in thought and didn't even notice him. So he went up to the bar.

"Hey, Noah," Jack said.

"What's she doing here?" Noah asked.

Jack shrugged. "Disappointed, I think. But what are you gonna do?" Jack put a mug in front of Noah and poured coffee without being asked.

"Disappointed?" Noah asked.

"She said she didn't get the job."

"I said I'd get back to her about that," Noah said.

"Maybe that's not what she heard, Noah."

"Hmm." He took a sip of coffee. "How about two slices of pie, right over there."

"Sure thing," Jack said.

Noah migrated to Ellie's table. He stood there until she looked up at him. Oh, man, he was in trouble. Her eyes were red rimmed and wet, her mascara a little smeared. *Grant that I may not so much seek to be understood as to understand.* "You mind if I join you?" he asked.

She straightened and her eyes immediately cleared and narrowed. She was one tough customer. "Knock yourself out," she said coolly.

He pulled out a chair and set his coffee cup in front of him. "You seem upset, Ellie. Was it something I said?"

"It was something you didn't say," she replied.

"Oh? What was that?"

"You're hired," she said.

"I thought I should give all the applicants a fair shot."

"Are you kidding me? I sat in my car outside waiting for my turn. I saw the other applicants—all two of them. One could barely get up the stairs; not a good bet for moving furniture. The other one had such a mean schnobble, she could break glass with her face."

"Schnobble?" he asked.

"What my gramma used to call a sourpuss. Now, *that's* a church lady, all right—if you're looking for one as mean as a junkyard dog."

He laughed before he could reel it in. "Who knew you were checking out the competition." Jack brought the pie, put it in front of them and got the heck out of there. Noah lifted a fork. "Pretty accurate, too. But I told you I'd get in touch."

"If you do, it'll be to say I didn't get the job."

He was quiet a moment, then he said, "Have some pie. Nobody makes pie like Preacher."

"Preacher? You made the pie?"

"No, the cook—he goes by the nickname Preacher. That could lead to problems." He nodded toward the plate. "Try it."

"Thanks," she said. "I'm not hungry."

"Give it a chance, you'll be amazed. And between bites, tell me why I don't get the benefit of the doubt."

Slowly, reluctantly, she took a bite of blackberry pie. She chewed and swallowed, but clearly the ambrosia of Preacher's pie was lost on her. After one bite, she put down the fork and her hands went back into her lap. Noah had to concentrate to focus on her eyes. That cleavage was killing him. "No hard feelings," she said quietly. "I haven't had much luck in the job market lately. I think it's made me a little cranky."

"Well, what are you looking for?" he asked, digging into his pie.

"Anything proper," she said. "It's like I said, it's for my kids."

"And they'll benefit from their mom having a *proper* job?"

She chewed on her bottom lip for a moment. "Look, it's kind of personal—my kids are going through a hard time. I don't think I should talk about it. No way I want people to know all that stuff…"

Noah considered this for a second and against his better judgment he said, "If you feel like talking about it, Ellie, you can trust me with a confidence."

"How can I be sure of that?" she asked with a lift of one eyebrow.

He sat back and smirked. "I'm a minister. I took Secret Keeping 101."

"But you're not *my* minister," she reminded him. "It's all pretty messy."

"And of course I never hear anything messy in this job," he said sarcastically. "I don't mean to pry. I was just offering you a chance to—"

"I lost my kids," she blurted. "My ex-husband filed for custody and got it. It shouldn't have happened, but it did. I was dancing in a club where some of the girls take off their clothes sometimes." She shrugged. "Not sometimes—all the time. They think the more they're willing to take off, the better the tips, and that was usually true." She swallowed and looked away, her eyes threatening to fill again. "My tips were about average."

"You were an exotic dancer?" he asked.

She looked back at him. "There was nothing exotic about it."

Truthfully, she looked like someone who'd be more

than comfortable taking it off. Noah was hardly shocked; while he was working his way through seminary, he had a casual little ministry down on the docks. His best customers were bums, strippers, homeless people, addicts and others.

"Are they okay with their dad?" Noah asked with as much sensitivity as possible.

The question got an instant reaction out of her. Her face became angry and hard, erasing some of the youthful beauty buried under too much makeup. "He's *not* their dad. He was their stepdad for less than three months, and this isn't about giving them a good life, it's about holding them hostage. He wants me, that's what he wants. I dated him for quite a while and I thought he was a nice, normal guy, but he's not. He's weird, abusive, mean and controlling, so we got out.

"After we left him, I found myself a real nice setup— I rented half a duplex next to a great lady who could keep the kids at night while I worked. I needed the sitter, she needed the extra money and we had a good arrangement. She was super to the kids, they hardly knew I was gone. I fixed dinner and left at six, she got their baths, read with them and put them to bed, then she'd nod off on the couch till I got home. It was one of the first times I could afford both the rent and the babysitting on just one job. But Arnie wanted us back. He doesn't like it when things don't go his way. Taking my kids away from me was the only thing he could think of. He's one of those people who has to be in charge all the time. In control."

Noah's fork was frozen in midair. After all that, all he could say was, "Abusive?"

"Mean," she said. "He doesn't hit, but he's real rigid, demanding as hell and says hurtful things. You don't like what's on your plate, you go to bed hungry after you're called a whole bunch of names. You don't snap to attention, and you're called stupid and idiot. Don't rinse the dishes and wipe the table just perfect, you go to bed without stories or playtime. There's no TV in the house, no talking at the table, no playing outside unless an adult is standing over you. No sleeping together—that's *dirty*." Her eyes watered. "Trevor is only *four!* And even when I did manage to get a place where they had their own room, they were always crawling in with me! It's what kids *do!*"

Noah couldn't move. She was pushing some buttons he didn't feel like having pushed. He started hearing his father's voice. *What do I ask of you besides respect and decency? You have to learn discipline and restraint for your own good before you're completely lost! No dessert/football/summer camp/TV/friends/et cetera et cetera et cetera!*

Her voice lowered and calmed. "Danielle is only eight, and she's expected to make sure everything is perfectly tidy and clean. And if it isn't exactly how he wants it, which she's just too young to do, he calls her names and takes away privileges." Her laugh had a hollowing. "They're not things I call privileges—like dinner? Like reading before bed? A privilege? I call it a necessity. How's Danielle going to grow up smarter than me if she doesn't get to *read?*"

Noah cleared his throat. "And this is better for them than a mother who dances for a living?"

She shrugged and looked down for a second. "It was the kind of dancing I did, I guess." But she met his eyes when she said, "I don't see the problem. It's not like I took the kids to the club. It's not an illegal place."

"And the judge awarded custody to their stepfather?"

Her lips curved in a cynical smile. "The judge isn't such a good tipper, either," she said.

Noah felt sick. He put down his fork. "How did the judge figure in this, Ellie? Did you know him before?"

"He came into the club sometimes. He asked to buy me dinner a few times and I said no—he's an old man! And besides, we don't date customers. I explained that, but he wasn't happy with the answer. But he fixed me, didn't he?"

"Did the judge tell you that if you found a 'proper' job, you could have custody again?"

"No," she said, shaking her head. "He said he couldn't, in good conscience, leave the children in the hands of a stripper when there was a better alternative. All he knows about Arnie is that he's a principal for a private school. He doesn't know the real Arnie. The real Arnie can have a mean mouth on him. The judge said this was just temporary—he'd look at the custody again in ninety days." She glanced away. "Eighty-two and counting."

"Are you seeing your kids?"

She nodded and that's when things fell apart for her; she couldn't keep the tears back. One big one rolled down each cheek. "Every Saturday, just during the day. They can't even spend the night with me. They've never been away from me before. I've never spent a single night away from them since they were born, except to work! Do you know the only reason why I haven't done something like snatch them and run? Because Arnie is obsessed with winning, with having his way. I believe he'd hunt me down and have me locked up. And that would be even worse for the kids than this."

Noah's pie sat untouched, as well. He didn't feel so hot. "Have you tried to get help, Ellie? Like legal aid?"

"Sure," she said. "They were very nice to me. But there's not a lot they can do with the decision at this point. Their advice was to try to find an acceptable job.

They said they'd go back to court with me, maybe even sooner than ninety days, and they'd make sure I got my kids back. And make sure Arnie didn't get any visitation—we were only married three months and they're not his kids. Once I have my kids back legally, I'm running for my life. I'll go as far as I have to go. I'll change our names. I'm never letting something like this happen to them again. I made a lot of mistakes… I know I'm not the best mother—the *best* mother wouldn't dance for strange men. But I love my kids. I take as good care of them as I can and I love them. And they are, for *God's* sake, going to be able to read before bed!"

He smiled at her. "I think that's something a good mother would insist on."

"I try. I do everything I can. What else you going to do? It's really hard when you have to work two jobs. At least at the club, I didn't have to have a second job to make ends meet. And it was a job I could do while they were asleep."

"Ellie, do you mind if I ask—how old are you?"

"Twenty-five."

Well, she said she had them too young, he thought. "Where's their biological dad?"

She shook her head and heaved a defeated sigh. "Oh, what the hell, you're not giving me that church job anyway. A church job would really kick ass, but—" She took a breath. "This is all part of that Secret Keeping 101, right?"

"You bet."

"I got pregnant in high school and then my boyfriend got killed in a motorcycle accident before we could even get married. It took me a long time to pick up the pieces and then I made my second big mistake—Trevor's daddy went to prison when I was just barely pregnant. Robbery.

He had a cigar lighter that looked exactly like a gun—how about that? He decided to play a joke on a store owner and ask for the bank deposit. We don't have any contact at all and never will. And then, as if I couldn't be smart even once in my life, I married Arnie Gunterson."

"Wow," Noah said. "Why'd you marry him?"

"Come on, he didn't act crazy when I was getting to know him. He was real nice. And he offered me something I'd never had before—a chance to live in a real house and stay home to take care of my kids. He treated me careful, with respect. He never even tried anything, he was saving himself for marriage—remind me never to fall for that one again! I didn't know there was anything wrong with him. I mean, I knew he wasn't *fun*. But the last fun one, Chip, was a laugh a minute, all the way to jail." She took a breath. "Honest to God, I don't even know why Arnie wants me. I wasn't married to him for three days before he started acting all jealous, asking every day if I talked to any men, acting as if he didn't even really like me. But he wanted me there, in his house, taking orders. And I don't take orders very well. I must have been like a bad dream to him and he still wouldn't let me go.

"But you know what? I'm going to figure this out. I'm going to get on my feet, get my kids back, and we're going to be fine. There have been three men in my life, one of 'em dead and two of 'em too lousy to talk about, and that's the total number of men there ever will be until I drop dead. How's that? I don't care what it takes, I'm getting ahead of this. My gramma always used to say the stuff that doesn't kill us makes us stronger. Pastor Kincaid, meet Hercules Baldwin."

Right away Noah's thought was, *You might've sworn off men, but I bet they haven't sworn off you—not with that face and body.* Shew. He was starting to feel a little warm. *Let me seek to understand rather than to be understood. Where there is despair, let me offer hope. And dear God, could you please get her to cover up that cleavage for a while?*

"Look, Your Reverence, I just need a job like this for ninety days. That's all. Maybe even less. I just have to convince the judge I'm a good mother, that I have a proper job, and then I'll get out of your hair."

"You know the judge shouldn't have been able to take them from you without a pretty exhaustive investigation, right? You know he overstepped his authority, right? Did the legal-aid people explain all that?" Noah asked her.

"That the judge went his own way on this because he *could?*" she asked. "Oh, yeah, I know he was just screwing with me. And it was also explained that challenging him right now could drag things out even longer—it would make his decision more of an issue than the custody. And believe me, I don't cut him any slack here, but he doesn't realize what he's doing to the kids by giving Arnie control any more than I did when I married Arnie. I'm sure he didn't think it would be horrible for them. That's no excuse for ignoring some real important rules, like giving the kids a lawyer of their own... That isn't going to happen twice, I promise!"

He thought for a second, studying his pie. He looked up. "Ellie, I'd like to ask you a question and I don't think there's a way to do it that won't be offensive. I apologize for that. Could there be any other possible reason the judge chose your ex-husband as the guardian?"

"Like?" she asked, as if confused.

He shrugged. "Problems with the law? Parenting problems? You know..."

Her eyes narrowed. "I don't drink or smoke. I don't

do drugs. The only law I ever broke was not getting my license tags renewed on time because I didn't have the money. I have a potty mouth, but not in front of the kids…I hardly ever slip. I don't leave my children alone, and I've lost jobs when the sitter stood me up. I can't give my kids everything I want to, but I take care of them the best I can."

"You understand, I can't even consider you for the job unless I ask."

"I can do your stupid job," she said defiantly. "And you can bet I'll do a damn good job. No one has *ever* complained about my work. I work *hard.* I always do two days' work in one, just in case one of the kids gets a fever or something and I have to call in sick to stay with them. I swear to God, if there's one thing I'm not, it's lazy!"

"You know, Ellie, the pay I'm able to afford is low. Very modest," he said. "There are some benefits, but they're not the greatest."

"I figured," she said with a shrug. "I don't care about that."

"How would you make that work? You obviously need money."

"I'll make changes," she said. "Give up the duplex. Find one room somewhere. I don't need a house when I can't have my kids overnight. We've lived in one room before and we could do it again." She shrugged. "Cozy. We just curl up and tickle and laugh and play and—" Again her eyes misted over. "I'll manage whatever life throws at me. That's what I'm used to doing."

"The church job—it's not a piece of cake," he said. "I need help with heavy jobs. You saw the place. I have to fix it up before I even get to the preaching part."

She flashed him a smile. "Sounds like fun. More fun than listening to a lot of bible beating."

"At least I'm not going to have to work at getting you to come out of your shy little shell," Noah said, and she laughed. "You're in a tight spot. You need just under three months to get back to the judge and for me to find someone permanent. We could try it. But it's not going to be easy." *On either one of us,* he thought.

"Do I seem like someone who knows what to do with easy?"

He smiled and shook his head. He knew better; this was a bad idea. But the kid deserved a break, didn't she? He dared a glance down from her eyes. A tremor ran though him. She sure didn't look like a church secretary. But then, he didn't look like a preacher. "You're out of work right now?" he asked.

"I quit the day the judge gave Arnie the kids. I have to find something right away."

"Tomorrow's Thursday. If you want to start then, you can. But like I said, it's dirty work. Do you have…ah… Jeans? Sweatshirts? Some shoes that aren't high heels?"

"Sure," she said, beaming. "Cool. I haven't been in a church in *years!*"

"No kidding? I'd never have guessed. Well, people will have certain expectations…"

"Okay, no swearing. I'll be totally polite. And I'll leave my pasties and G-string at home." Noah went completely red and she burst out laughing. "I don't have pasties and G-strings. That club? It wasn't that bad."

"Just out of curiosity, what was your part?" he asked.

"Well," she said, rolling her eyes upward. "That's the interesting thing—sometimes a certain costume or look does more for the guys than being totally naked. The two most popular outfits were the cheerleading costume and the candy striper's costume. The men—they really go for pompoms." Ellie looked at Noah. "Hey—are you all right?"

"Fine. I'm fine," Noah said weakly. He'd been in his share of strip clubs, but not for a while. And he hadn't had much female companionship lately, either. Until today, he hadn't realized how much he missed that. "Now, try that pie."

"Thanks," she said. "Are you just doing this to be nice?"

"Pretty much. Are you conning me?"

"Out of a job that's really hard and pays practically nothing?" she asked. "Why? So I can steal and hock a crucifix? Please. If I could figure out how to con someone, I'd go after that judge. What a jackass he turned out to be. Oops. Sorry. I'm going to have to work on my language, huh?"

"Probably," Noah grumbled.

After finishing their pie, Noah and Ellie stood, shook hands, and she left. Noah took the empty plates and cups over to Jack at the bar.

"She seemed a lot happier when she left than when she came in, if you know what I mean," Jack said.

"She assumed she wouldn't get the job at the church," Noah said. "Not exactly church-secretary material, I guess."

"I guess," Jack said. "Nice-enough girl, though."

"She needs a job," Noah said.

"That a fact?"

"What she needs is a break. And it turns out she has all the qualifications."

Jack grinned. "I couldn't help but notice."

Noah sat on a stool. "Better give me a beer…."

"You bet. What's your pleasure?"

"I'm flexible."

Jack drew him a cold draft. "You gave her the job, didn't you?"

"I did," Noah admitted.

"Whoa, this is going to be fun."

"For who, exactly?" Noah asked.

Jack laughed at him. "I only talked to her a minute, but she seems okay, don't you think?"

"She could be a little rough around the edges for a church job."

"Ya think?" Jack asked with a laugh. "So could you, Noah. But you're an old softie. You sure she's not just using you?"

"At eight dollars an hour? Come on. I'm going to have to pray for forgiveness all night for taking advantage of her."

"Well, there's a point."

"But we're going to have to do something about those… Maybe a shawl? A nice big, concealing shawl?"

"I don't know, Noah. How about a tarp?"

"God help me." Noah took a drink of the beer. "Jack, it's been a real trip, getting to know you and the town. But when the locals get a load of the pastor's assistant, I'm going to be run out on a rail."

"Easy, Noah. This is Virgin River. We like things a little on the interesting side. You'll manage."

Noah took another drink of his beer. "Let's hope so," he muttered.

For her first day of work at the church, Ellie chose to wear something conservative. She dressed in overalls with a white, sleeveless tank top underneath that laced up the front. She slipped into sneakers, pulled her plentiful, curly, copper-colored hair up in a clip, lined her lips and eyes and off she went to Virgin River.

"I'm here," she yelled as she walked into the church.

"I'm in the basement," Noah yelled back.

She clomped down the steps, jumping off the bottom

step. Noah was patching cracks in the unfinished cinder-block wall, a plasterer's hawk with a mound of wet cement in one hand, a putty knife in the other. Lucy lay not far away on her bed, lifting her head and wagging her tail as Ellie came down the stairs. Noah smiled at her, then his smile froze. He looked her slowly up and down. And again.

"What?" she demanded hotly, hands on her hips.

"Nothing," he said, turning away.

"No. What? What's the matter?"

He turned back slowly, put his tools down on top of the ladder and approached her. "I don't know how to say this. I think it would be in the best interests of both of us if you'd dress a little more…conservatively."

She looked down at herself. "More conservatively than *overalls?*" she asked.

He felt a laugh escape in spite of himself. He shook his head. "Ellie, I've never seen anybody look that good in overalls before."

"And this is a bad thing?" she asked, crossing her arms over her chest.

"It's provocative," he tried to explain. "Sexy. People who work around churches usually dress a little more… What's the best way to put this…?"

"Frumpy? Dumpy? Ugly?"

"Without some of their bra showing, for one thing."

"Well now, Reverend, just where have you been? Because this happens to be in style. And I'll do any work you give me, but you really shouldn't be telling me what to wear. The last guy I was with tried to do me over. He liked me well enough when he was trying to get my attention, but the second I married him, he wanted to cover me up so no one would notice I *had* a body!"

"The husband?"

"The very same. It didn't work for him and it's not going to work for you. You didn't say anything about a dress code. Maybe I'll turn you in to the Better Business Bureau or something."

"I think you mean the Equal Employment Opportunity Commission. Or maybe you should go straight to the American Civil Liberties Union." He stepped toward her. "Ellie," he said, using his tender but firm minister voice. "I'm a single man. You're a very beautiful young woman. I would like it if the good people of Virgin River assumed you were given this job solely because of your qualifications and not because you're eye candy. Tomorrow, could you please wear something less distracting?"

"I'll do my best," she said in a huff. "But this is what I *have,* and there's not much I can do about that. Especially on what you're paying me."

"Just think 'baggy,'" he advised.

"We're going to have a problem there," she said. "I don't buy my clothes baggy. Or ugly. Or dumpy. And you can bet your sweet a…butt I left behind the clothes Arnie thought I should wear." She just shook her head in disgust. "I don't know what you're complaining about. You know how many guys would rather have something nice to look at than a girl in a flour sack? Guess you didn't get to Count Your Blessings 101." She cocked her head and lifted her eyebrows.

"I'm counting," he said. But his eyes bore down on hers seriously. He was not giving an inch. "Just an ounce of discretion. Do what you can."

She took a deep breath. "Let's just get to work. Tomorrow I'll look as awful as possible. How's that?"

"Perfect. Why don't you get started by sweeping up in the kitchen. It's large enough for a dozen people to work in there together—it's a big room. The appliances are all gone, but it's going to have to be cleaned up before I can put down new flooring and paint. It's accumulated a good ten years of dirt. Some of my household things are being delivered in a few weeks. After I get the walls patched, textured and painted, and put down flooring over the concrete, I can store my shipment and other things down here while we work on the upstairs."

"Sure, fine. Are there supplies somewhere?"

"Already in the kitchen."

"I'm on it, Rev," she said with a salute, turning on her heel to march off toward the kitchen, treating him to a little skip and fanny wiggle on her way.

Noah grimaced. He looked down at Lucy, who lifted her head and wagged her tail—maybe in sympathy, so he gave her a pat on the head. That went well, he thought. He'd offended Ellie and judged her all at the same time. He already knew she was forced to pinch pennies and couldn't buy new clothes for a job of cleaning and painting. Besides, the absolute truth was, she was a pleasure to look at. And frankly, you could see more skin and curves on prime-time TV. So what was he afraid of? That stodgy church ladies were going to get uptight, seeing her around town, knowing she was helping him work on the church?

The girl's having a hard enough time, going up against a judge who is, himself, a patron of the very strip joint he condemns her for working in. She was taking a low-paying church job just to gain enough credibility to get her kids back—credibility she shouldn't need. Any woman her age willing to work more than one job to afford the most rudimentary stuff of life, having never been separated from her children before except to work, should be plenty convincing.

For a second he wondered if he'd been sucked in by

her lost soul. "Pah," he scoffed aloud. Ellie didn't seem at all lost. She was a fighter, and that impressed him. He barely knew her and he already admired her. Plus, it was good that she was sassy; she shouldn't let anyone tell her what to wear.

He was right about one thing, however. She was distracting, even when she wasn't in the same room. It wasn't just the visible edges of her bra. Her thick, curly hair, pulled up and cascading down, her creamy skin, sultry, deep brown eyes, full lips, teasing smile, long legs, narrow waist, perfect hips and nice round booty— all that added up to an appearance that couldn't help but bring sex to mind. And it reminded Noah that he'd been on a serious sex diet for the past few years. Not exactly a starvation diet, but still…

He climbed back up on his ladder and continued to patch the walls while Ellie worked in the kitchen. And while he worked he thought a lot about what had brought him here to this run-down church in Virgin River.

He thought back to something his mom used to ask him from time to time. "What are your goals, Noah?" she had asked.

"I will never be a minister, Mom. Never."

After a long period of silence, she said, "I'm relieved. I think your father and I have thoroughly ruined you for that."

As he continued to repair and patch the walls, Noah smiled at the irony—he was embarking on a career he never thought he would have. It was a shame that his mom and Merry weren't here to see this. They had always supported him and he knew the irony of his current situation would not have been lost on them, either.

Even though it had been a few years since her death, Noah still missed Merry sometimes. Their couple of years together had been magic. She had been such a free spirit; she made him laugh, brought him wisdom and optimism. She was edgy and fun—she took chances and encouraged him to do the same. Merry was a committed soul who cared deeply and loyally about her "causes," as he called them, and all the people in her life. After she was gone he made a point of remaining in touch with her family. Her parents and siblings were a great support to him even as they contended with their own grief.

The whole idea of considering going back to the seminary came from George, who described it as a combination of dredging the soul for the innermost spirituality, personal faith, teaching, counseling, community and theater. Only George could come up with a combination like that. "You've had those leanings anyway," George had said. "Just check it out."

"But I will never preach," Noah said.

"Not that many ordained ministers do," George said with a shrug. "They're therapists, minister to sick and needy folk, teach—there are more options than I can list. But along the way you might find out a thing or two about yourself. No harm there."

In short, Noah was convinced. During his studies, he found out he was meant to try to hold a group of believers together in faith, to lend a hand, to communicate, to educate, to bring hope. To be a friend. There was only one thing that was required of him that he could not do—and that was to forgive his father.

Just last year his mother passed. She had slipped away in the night, having had a stroke at the age of seventy. Noah attended the funeral, even though he hated the idea of seeing his father. But it was the only time in Noah's life he could remember having the last word with his dad.

Jasper said to him, within the hearing of many others,

"Do you see what leaving the family and the faith did? It killed your mother."

Without missing a beat, Noah replied, "You should be aware that Mother and I have been in touch ever since I left home. She visited twice even though I wouldn't come back. She was always there for me and we loved one another profoundly. The truth is, I think *staying* with you was what killed her."

The shock on his father's face was priceless; and the insult bit Jasper deep. It had obviously never occurred to Jasper that his wife would keep secrets from him. Maybe it was just that he paid so little attention to her, he was unaware that she kept a close relationship with her son. The reading of the will hammered Jasper with a few more home truths—Inez Kincaid had brought a trust fund to her marriage to a poor preacher who was ten years her junior. Her personal wealth had helped Jasper build a big following, televise his services, evangelize and collect members. She willed half of the fund to Noah. Jasper had expected to receive all of it.

And now Noah was going to run through a great deal of his inheritance fixing up this old church.

He looked in the direction of the kitchen. Another free spirit, he admitted to himself. In a completely different form.

There was a crash, a splash, and Ellie said, *"Fuck."*

Lucy came to her feet and Noah looked up. "Very funny," he said to God. "That kind of thing isn't going to go over well." Then he walked to the kitchen, Lucy beside him.

He stood in the doorway and watched as Ellie used the rag mop to try to capture the flood that resulted from a tipped bucket. But that wasn't where his focus was—he frowned and looked at his watch. The morning had passed without him even realizing it. He'd been completely lost in thought. And while he'd been thinking of his past and patching wall cracks, Ellie had been working like a demon.

The huge, restaurant-size kitchen almost glowed. The floor had been swept, mopped, and was being mopped again. She'd done some things that had made an enormous difference—the high windows were cleaned and spotless, the frames scrubbed of dust, spiderwebs and dirt. The countertops were scoured and disinfected. The cupboards were washed out with their doors standing open. The few remaining kitchenware items that had been abandoned were washed and drying in a dish drain she'd found; all four deep sinks were scrubbed clean, the faucets shining. The room didn't look like new, but it was clean and fresh and ready for painting and flooring.

She squeezed her mop, straightened and wiped a hand across her forehead, pushing up a curl that just bounced back to hang over one eye. She blew out of her lower lip to cool her face, making that curl flutter in her breath. "Let me guess," she said. "You heard me say *fuck*. Sorry. I'll try not to say it. But I bet if you'd dumped a big pail of nasty mop water on your clean floor, you would have said *fuck*, too."

He laughed and just shook his head. "Maybe. It looks good in here, Ellie. Who knew you could do something like this with long, blue, sparkly fingernails."

"I figured you meant for me to clean it, so I cleaned it."

"It's fantastic. I bet you're hungry. It's after one."

She got a very strange look on her face, as though a thought just came to mind or she'd forgotten something. Then she just continued mopping. "Nah, I don't think I could eat. I really pigged out on pizza last night and I'm still stuffed."

"I'm going next door for a sandwich. Come with me."

"Nah, go on. I'll just finish up here. If I do a good job, maybe you'll let me out of here early or something. I have to get looking for a new place to live."

"You can leave whenever you've had enough—you've done an incredible job. I've been chipping away at the dirt in this place for weeks and it looks like you conquered it in no time at all."

She straightened again. She pushed that curl back. Her neck and chest were damp with perspiration, which made her look even sexier. She smiled almost shyly. "I cleaned office buildings and sometimes houses for cash—under the table. One of my many second jobs. I don't think it was listed on that sheet of jobs."

"Résumé," he corrected, then damned himself for being so uppity. Why couldn't he just accept her the way she was?

"Résumé," she agreed. "I got some great tips from the girls who had more experience than me. Clean is good. Fast and clean makes more money."

He laughed with genuine pleasure. "You've been in the trenches," he said with appreciation. Admiration. "Come on—let me buy you a sandwich. If you're not real hungry, Preacher will make you half, but it's your first day working for me. My treat—come on."

Three

For someone who had stuffed herself on pizza the night before, Ellie seemed to have no trouble packing away a very large chicken-salad sandwich and some of Preacher's potato salad. Noah doubted the pizza story. He picked up their plates and carried them to the bar, and when he returned he said, "Jack's bringing chocolate cake."

Her hands were on her flat belly. "Oh, man, I couldn't…"

"Just a bite or two," he said. "So—you said you were raised on hymns. Tell me about that. I mean, if you want to."

"Sure, I'll tell you. I grew up with my gramma. What a peach—you'd have liked her. My mother wasn't… isn't…very stable. When I was born, she was clueless, so my gramma took over and my mother left and I stayed. When I was seven, Gram started teaching me to play the piano. It was a real old piano and about the only thing worth a dime in the house, but we had a neighbor guy who kept it tuned. Gramma hummed gospel tunes all day long and she loved it if I could figure out one of those old-time hymns. 'The Old Rugged Cross,' 'Amazing

Grace,' 'Great Is Thy Faithfulness…' 'Course, I would have rather played Elton John, John Lennon or Billy Joel, but for her I tried."

"Where was your mother?" he asked just as the cake arrived.

"Jumping from man to man," she said, lifting her fork.

"Were there more children?"

"No." She laughed. "She figured out that much. When I got pregnant in high school, my gramma must have been scared to death that I was just following in her footsteps. I wasn't really, but it must have looked like I was."

"Well," he said patiently, "what were you doing?"

She sighed. She shook her head. "Trying," she finally said. "Trying my hardest. I got pregnant at sixteen. I was three months pregnant with Danielle and trying to throw together a fast, cheap wedding to my nineteen-year-old boyfriend when he was killed. It wasn't his fault, either. His family sued the driver of the car that killed him, and they won. They were supposed to set something aside for Danielle, but I guess it slipped their minds." That last was delivered with a dubious look on her face. "By the time she was three, I'd gotten my GED and had finally stopped feeling sorry for myself long enough to meet someone I liked—a guy who made nighttime bread deliveries to the convenience store when I worked there. Like some kind of curse, I was three months pregnant when he pulled that stupid robbery stunt."

Noah chewed on the cake and this history for a second. He had a million questions, but the one that popped out was, "You didn't have any intuition about him, that he was capable of a felony?"

"Ha, he *wasn't.* He was an *idiot.* He was out with his friends, drinking. Twenty-two, drunk, and he thought he was funny—putting his lighter that looked exactly like a revolver—into the hardware-store owner's chest and saying, 'Hand over the money.' The store owner was going to drop off his deposit for the night when my dipshit boyfriend decided to be cute. Didn't quite work out for him, though. I guess the judge had no sense of humor. He was convicted. Did time."

"Did?"

"He's either out by now or due to get out."

"Can't he help you with his son? With the kids?" Noah asked.

"Oh, please. No, he can't. And besides, I'm not going back that way. In fact, I'm not going *back*. Period."

He smiled at her. "Have you always been this stubborn? This strong willed?"

"Uh-huh. For all the good it's done me."

"So—where did the husband come in? If that's not too personal?"

"Nothing personal about it, Rev. I was a working mom with two little kids and two jobs. He was new in the area and came into the real estate office, looking for something to rent or buy. I was the office manager. Our agents didn't find him anything, but he kept coming back, was real nice, real friendly. I thought he was a stand-up guy. Trevor was only two, my gramma had died a year before, and I was having a real hard time holding everything together. I didn't rush into anything—I made him act nice for six months. I didn't have much time to date, but I never had a single date alone with him—if he asked me out for dinner, I told him the kids went where I went, and that wasn't a problem for him. He did a lot of talking about wanting to be a family man and just hadn't found the right woman yet. I took that as a good sign." For a moment she looked away and couldn't connect eyes with Noah. "I knew I didn't love him, but I was so tired," she said softly.

"So scared I wouldn't be able to take care of my kids with my gramma gone. My kids saw more of the babysitter than they saw of me."

She looked back at Noah and said, "I married him and quit my job because he wanted to take care of us. It didn't take two days before I knew I'd made a big mistake. He insisted I dress real dowdy and awful. He had *rules*. He needed to be right about everything. Ridiculous demands. He started trying to get me to give up my independence on the first day! He wanted me to sell my car, and he took his computer to work, out of my reach. He doled out money for food… It was terrible. And I wouldn't play along, which made him so frustrated and angry. I mean, I knew in two days it was a bad deal, but I gave it almost three months. Then I packed up our stuff while he was at work, picked up Danielle from his private school, and we were history. I went back to an old boss, the lawyer, to draft a divorce petition. That gave poor old Arnie the impression I had a rich, classy lawyer. I didn't ask for anything, so he couldn't contest it. I just wanted out."

"He didn't fight it, then," Noah said.

"Not legally. But he threatened me. He said if I went through with it, he'd be my worst nightmare. We had been divorced for about nine months when he made a case for custody. There's where I wasn't too smart—I couldn't see how he had a leg to stand on. He wasn't their father, we'd lived with him less than three months, and I didn't think I needed any help keeping my own kids. And, like I said before, I'd never done better for myself workwise. I had a good job, made good money, was taking good care of my kids. That club is totally legal. Maybe it's not tasteful, but it's *legal*. Most of the women dancing in there are single moms. That judge—he had it out for me. Maybe I should've let him buy me dinner."

Noah's eyes narrowed and he glowered. "He didn't want dinner."

"Yeah, that's why I said no," she said.

"You were blindsided," he said.

"Yeah. There's so much I don't know. I should have called my old boss again. I did call him afterward. What a nice guy. He said there wasn't much he could do for me, but gave me the name of a friend of his who worked for a legal-defense office that did charity work. He called them for me, and that brings us to today. Hey," she said, "this is still part of the silence pact, right?"

"Absolutely, Ellie. I don't gossip."

"Because I'm not ashamed of anything, but I'm not stupid. All the stuff I've screwed up? I'm bound to be judged pretty hard by people who don't know me. But it's not even that—it's the kids. I don't want them judged because I—"

"Don't worry," he said. "Our conversations are private." He concentrated for a minute on the chocolate cake, which didn't get as much appreciation as it deserved.

Noah had a lot of experience counseling people who were down on their luck, many of them actually in need of food and shelter. He'd seen worse than what Ellie was going through, but just the same he was mighty impressed by her toughness, her fearlessness. She wasn't dependent on him for anything. All she needed was a job chit to take back to that crooked judge in eighty-one days, collect her kids and get on with her life. Meantime, he'd help her any way he could. He was glad he'd taken a chance on her.

"I'm not embarrassed I had that job, you know," she said, lifting a bite of cake to her mouth. He lifted his eyes to hers. "The owner of the club—he's a great guy who liked to take good care of his girls. And the funny thing was, the ones who didn't mind getting right down to cracks and nipples weren't always the most popular ones...."

One end of Noah's mouth lifted in a half smile. Ellie laughed.

"I guess I'm a little too straightforward for you, huh?" she asked. "Thing is, all I had to do was wiggle around with those pom-poms or the white nurse's hose held up with a garter belt and I did just fine. I think Madonna wore less on stage half the time than I did in that club. The people were usually nice, the customers didn't give us any trouble. 'Course, we had a plus-size bouncer, just in case. It was just work. It paid the bills. It's not something I wanted to do forever. I was always on the lookout for something better."

"You shouldn't have lost your kids over that job," he said. "Worst case, they should have been left with you with visits from Child Welfare. They would have seen in no time that the job wasn't damaging to the children. That was crap, what happened to you."

She just looked at him for a long moment. Then very quietly she said, "Thanks. I guess coming from you, that's saying something."

"Coming from me?" he said, lifting one dark brow.

"You being a minister, and everything. I know you don't approve of that kind of place—or of the women in it."

He gave a shrug. "Ellie, I don't have an opinion about your last job. There's plenty about it to admire," he said.

"Like?"

"Like a mother who would do just about anything to take care of her kids."

"Well, be real clear about that, Rev. If I hadn't lucked into that job, I *would* have done just about anything. When it comes to the kids, I'm all out of false pride."

Soon, he thought, I'm going to see her kids. And I bet I see something remarkable.

"Do you ever want kids?" she asked.

"I did," he said quietly. A bunch of them, if possible.

And so did Merry—she wanted them right away. "I think this little town church is going to be my kid for a while."

"Sometimes I think the deal I got with Arnie was just what I deserved. I married him because I thought he was safe for me and the kids. He seemed all right, he made a decent living, he was okay that I had children while a lot of guys run for their lives when they find out you come with kids. I wasn't attracted to him, I wasn't in love with him. So maybe that's what I deserved, huh?"

Noah didn't have to consider it. "Never think that," he said. "No one deserves cruelty of any kind. Not on their worst day."

Just then, the door opened and Mel came into the bar. She went first to Jack, lifting herself up to lean over the bar and give him a kiss. Then she turned and looked at Noah and Ellie. "Mel," Noah called. "Got a minute?"

She walked over to their table. "Mel Sheridan, this is Ellie Baldwin. She's helping out in the church for a while."

"Nice to meet you," Mel said, putting out her hand. "Jack said there was someone new in town. How's it going over there?"

"It's my first day, so it's looking pretty ugly," Ellie said honestly.

"Well, it's not my first day, but Ellie got more done this morning than I've managed in the last week. She's a whirlwind."

"Good for you. Very cute top, by the way."

Ellie looked down, then lifted an eyebrow toward Noah before she said, "Thanks. Target. Under twenty bucks."

"Really? I need to get over there one of these days. They usually have good buys. So, Ellie—where do you live?"

"I'm in Eureka now, but I have to find something

closer—I can't afford the gas. Would you happen to know of anything? Nearby?"

Mel pulled up a chair. "I can sure ask around. What are you looking for?"

"My kids are with my ex-husband right now, so all I need is a bed and a roof. Really, one room would do it for me. Something cheap, but not scary. His Holiness here doesn't exactly pay a lot."

Mel laughed. "I know one thing that qualifies as cheap and real nice, but I think it might flunk the scary test. Right at the end of the block, nicest house down there, Jo Ellen and Nick Fitch have a great one-room efficiency over the garage. I don't think they've rented it out in a long time. Jo Ellen's a doll, a very nice lady. But she's married to a groper."

"Is that so? How serious a groper?" Ellie asked.

"The first time I met him, he treated me to a major butt grope while I had my back turned."

Hearing this exchange, Jack put a cup of coffee in front of his wife and used the pot to refill Ellie's and Noah's cups. "Mel drop-kicked him," Jack inserted. "It was a beautiful sight. I think that's when I really fell in love with her."

Ellie grinned widely. "What did you do to him?"

"I got lucky, that's all. I took a little self-defense course in college, I didn't think I even remembered any of it. But he snuck up on me and I just reacted. I threw him an elbow in the gut and then under the chin. One little swipe behind his heels and he was flat on his ass. Sorry, Noah—I meant to say *butt. Butt*'s okay, right?"

Noah looked up at Jack. "The women in this place are rougher on the language than the men."

"Tell me about it," Jack said. "We now have a swear

jar at home. David's college education will be paid for and we'll have a trip to Bermuda by the end of the year."

"I might have to put a swear jar in the church," Noah said.

"I could teach you that move," Mel said to Ellie, taking a sip from her cup.

"Thanks. I have some moves of my own, too. So, this guy—is he dangerous? Or just frisky?" Ellie asked.

"I don't think he's dangerous, but I couldn't guarantee it," Mel answered. "I'd hate myself forever if you came to any harm from him. But, as the gossip goes, he's been slapped down by several women in this town. Too bad Jo Ellen hasn't hit him over the head with a big club. I can't believe she puts up with that behavior. Really, she's such a nice person."

"Nick might have ideas all the time, but I think he's only frisky when he drinks," Jack said. "His problems usually come up during a party. Most of the time, when the town gets together, they do it here, they have food and drinks, and Nick loses his head."

"It's out of the question, Ellie," Noah said. "You can't even consider it."

"It could work," Ellie said. "Mel, would you be willing to introduce me to them, be there when I ask about the room? I'd have to have a look at him, too. See if I think I could take him."

"This isn't happening," Noah muttered.

"Sure," Mel said. "I'm positive he's still scared of me. I know he's been slapped, but I hold the sole distinction of taking him down."

"And she put a boot on his chest to hold him down while she threatened his life," Jack said. "I'm telling you, I almost exploded with lust. I had to marry her."

Ellie sipped her coffee. "Well, I'm bigger than you are," she said to Mel. "And I have Mace."

"We could try starting with a firm warning," Mel suggested.

"You can't be serious," Noah said. "You'd rent from a guy who's a known molester?"

"Okay, let's be totally straight here—is this just an idiot who gets stupid and cops a feel? Or has he left a trail of wounded victims in his path?" Ellie asked.

"So far as I know, he's a laughingstock," Mel said. "But there's no guarantee that wouldn't escalate. Luke Riordan has some cabins on the river—vacation rentals. Also one-room efficiencies with kitchenettes, but I'm sure they're more expensive. And from what I hear, he's done a brisk summer business—full or almost full all the time with early reservations for hunting season."

"I'm on a tight budget," Ellie said.

"No reason to be afraid of Nick," Jack said. "I could take you down there and introduce you, threaten to sic my wife on him if he steps out of line."

"I bet one knee in the nuts straightens him right out," Ellie said.

There was a strange sound from Noah, something of a growl. "I don't like this idea at all. If this guy got fresh with you, I'd have to deal with him. That wouldn't be good."

"Horsefeathers," Ellie said. "I can take care of myself."

This wouldn't be the best time to bring up the fact that she was having a tough time doing exactly that—taking care of herself. And in almost exactly twenty-four hours Noah was already feeling the urge to deck the imbecile who would dare put a hand on her. It had been years since he'd been in a fight; it wasn't nice for ministers to fight. He was supposed to counsel and pray his way out of tight spots.

One corner of his mouth lifted. Actually, he was competent in a fight. Didn't bother him in the least to engage, as long as it was fair.

Noah looked over at Ellie. She hadn't completed her first day of work and already she was complicating his nice uncomplicated ministry.

Right at the end of the main street in Virgin River was a beautiful two-story home, freshly painted a pale yellow with white trim, just like three other houses on the block. But this one was large and pampered—it looked almost new. The porch was wide, the lawn was lush and green, summer flowers grew thick and healthy along the walk and tall trees shaded the house from the summer sun. It had white shutters and rocking chairs on the porch. The driveway went around the side of the house to a detached two-car garage. There was a staircase on the outside leading to the room upstairs.

Mel had called Jo Ellen, learned the room was available to the right person and had set up an appointment. Noah would not be left behind, and so it was that the three of them stood on the porch of the lovely house and rang the bell. Jo Ellen Fitch came to the door with a smile on her face, but the second she saw Ellie, she gasped and covered her mouth with her hand. Then she shot a pleading look at Mel, which Mel completely ignored. Even dressed in overalls, no makeup, and her hair pulled up, Ellie was a striking young woman. She had a beautiful face and a drop-dead-gorgeous body that she made no attempt to downplay.

"Hey, Jo," Mel said. "This is Ellie Baldwin, who's looking for a room. And this is Reverend Noah Kincaid. You might have heard about him—he's the new minister, fixing up the old church. Ellie works for him and needs a place to live. So, what do you think? Want to show her the room?"

"Ohhhh, Mel," she said miserably.

"You can make up your mind about me later, Mrs.

Fitch," Ellie said, taking charge. "First things first—let's see if I like the room. How about that?"

"Sure," she said a bit nervously. She opened her front door, keys to the room in hand, and began to lead them toward the garage. Then she stopped suddenly and turned. "Oh, I apologize. How do you do, Reverend Kincaid? Miss Baldwin. This way." When they entered the room, Ellie went into a kind of daze. It was perfectly lovely—a double bed with two bedside tables against one wall, a small bathroom with a tub and shower, and on one wall a minirefrigerator, two-burner stove, microwave, sink and a few cupboards. At the foot of the bed was a chest. A comfortable chair and ottoman sat in the corner. There was no closet, but rather a large armoire for clothes. It was finer than anything Ellie had ever lived in. In her life.

"We don't have a TV in here or anything," Jo Ellen said.

The bed had a yellow floral comforter and lots of fat, decorative pillows. There was a picture of a meadow and barn over the bed, a full-length mirror on the bathroom door, a reading lamp behind the overstuffed chair. Ellie sighed. She fell in love with the room at once. "Does that phone work?" she asked.

"It does," Jo said. "It's a private line."

There was the sound of a car in the driveway, followed by the slamming of the car door.

"Are there some plates and glasses?" Ellie asked. "A couple of pans?"

"Yes, some. Not much. And towels. This is kind of a one-person room."

"What a coincidence." Ellie laughed. "I'm exactly one person."

"Nothing extra comes with the room," Jo said. "No housekeeping. You're on your own. There's no washer or dryer. I mean, it's not a bed-and-breakfast—you'd have to take care of all your own needs. Meals, laundry, that sort of thing."

There were feet on the stairs.

"I understand. There's probably a coin laundry somewhere nearby."

The door opened and Nick walked into the room. "Well, I thought there was company here." He smiled.

Ellie smiled back. He was probably her height, wasn't all that bad looking and he was fit. His salt-and-pepper hair was still thick, his brows heavy and graying. He wore a short-sleeved shirt—light blue—with a bad tie that he'd loosened, nice dress jeans and boots. His eyes glittered approvingly and he smiled at Ellie.

Jo Ellen cleared her throat and made introductions; everyone shook hands. "How much is the room, Mrs. Fitch?" Ellie asked.

Jo Ellen opened her mouth to speak, when Nick interrupted her. "Honey, is a hundred a month too much?" Nick asked his wife.

"We usually—"

"How does that sound, Ellie?" Nick asked her.

"Very reasonable," she said. "If you find me acceptable."

"There won't be a problem, if you work for the preacher, here," Nick said.

"How soon can I move in?"

"It's ready when you are," he said. And he slipped an arm around his wife's waist and gave her a squeeze. "Right, honey?"

"Thank you," Ellie said. "I didn't bring any money or checks with me today. Can I settle up with you tomorrow?"

"That would be fine," Jo said, clearly not happy.

"Oh, thank you. I think this will be perfect for me."

"If you're sure…"

"Oh, I'm sure," she said. But when she looked between Mel and Noah, she saw doubtful expressions. Their expressions could have to do with that lascivious gleam in Nick's eye. "I'll see you sometime tomorrow, Mrs. Fitch."

"Sure," Jo said, standing aside so everyone could go single file down the stairs. Noah followed Mel. Nick held the door open for his wife, then for Ellie.

"Oh, Mr. Fitch—can I talk to you a second?" Ellie asked.

"Of course, sweetheart," he said.

She spoke to him at the top of the staircase while the others descended. They all stopped at the bottom while Nick listened to Ellie and actually seemed to back away from her. But she was smiling the entire time, smiling with a glow. Then she grabbed his hand in both of hers to shake it vigorously, and hurried down the stairs to join the others.

Everyone said their goodbyes. Nick and Jo Ellen went into their house while Noah, Ellie and Mel began walking back toward the bar and the church. "You sure about this, Ellie?" Mel asked.

"Absolutely, it's going to be great. I love the room. The price is terrific, I'm going to save a ton in gas, I can walk to work. And I'll be close enough to sneak away from the reverend here and catch a nap."

"You got a glimpse of Nick," Mel said.

"I did. He agreed I'll be totally safe in that room."

Mel lifted a brow. "I didn't see his lips move, actually."

"Trust me," Ellie said. And then she walked on. "It's going to work out perfectly." When they got to the bar, Mel said goodbye. "Thank you so much, Mel," Ellie said, waving.

Noah walked Ellie to her little PT Cruiser that sat in front of the church. "What went on while you two were out of earshot?" he asked Ellie.

"Oh, Your Righteousness, you probably don't want to know. What if it makes you an accessory to the crime or something?"

He sighed heavily. Impatiently. "Just lay it on me, Ellie."

"You sure?"

"I'm sure. Come on. You smiled the whole time."

"Yeah, that part wasn't so easy. I wanted to smack him just from the look in his eye. I said, I know about you, so don't try anything. My boyfriend is a six-foot-five-inch bouncer in a mean bar and my father is a judge, and if you even exhale within twenty feet of my boobs, I'm going to have your nuts on a platter. And then I'm going to call my boyfriend and my father."

Noah was speechless for just a second, but then he burst out laughing. "You didn't!"

"Of course I did. I think that's called a preemptive strike. Isn't that what it's called?"

"You're out of your mind," he said, laughing in appreciation.

"I got that room for a hundred bucks a month. And it's a *great* room."

He shook his head. "You think that threat will hold?"

She peered at him, lifting a corner of her mouth and an eyebrow at the same time. "That bouncer? He's a friend. I babysat for him and his wife a couple of times. He'd come out here and scare the bejesus out of that imbecile if I asked him to. But before we even get to that, Mr. Nick has a date with my knee. And I know how to do that."

Noah just chuckled and shook his head.

"I just want that room. It's the best room I've ever seen. My gramma and I slept on a pullout sofa together my whole life. The only thing that could make that room prettier would be if my kids came with it."

Noah sobered. Two sentences hit him in the gut—she slept on a pullout sofa bed her entire life? With her grandmother? They must have lived in one room. And her kids? It must have been so traumatic to leave her children with a guy she knew didn't love them. When they got better acquainted, he meant to ask more about that. "So," he said. "When will you move in?"

"Oh, right away. I'll bring money and my stuff tomorrow. It'll just take one trip. Can I have a little time in the morning to unload the car? I'd like to do it when Mr. Hands is at work. I plan to avoid him."

"What about the duplex?" he asked.

"That nice lady next door owns it. She'll let me go without a problem. She understands my situation. She's on my side."

"You can move in one trip?" he asked, looking at her car.

She turned to look at him. "Noah, the kids have their clothes and toys with them. I have very little to move. Believe me, I live a one-trip existence."

"My car is full of stuff," Ellie said to Noah when she arrived at the church the next morning. Then she crouched in front of Lucy, grabbed her head in her hands and kissed her snout, receiving a lick in return. "Morning, girlfriend. You're looking better every day." Then to Noah, "If it's okay with you, I'd like to take an hour to tote it up the stairs to my new residence. I just want to wait until Mr. Fitch has gone to work."

"Ellie," he asked, "did you leave anything behind? Or in storage somewhere?"

"Nah, that's it. I travel light. So, what's on the schedule for today?"

He tried not to let it show that he felt something cinch in his chest at the very idea she could fit all her worldly goods in the little PT Cruiser she drove. Up until he married, while working and going to school, he'd had next to nothing, but that was different. He liked having a light load; it was all part of the changes he wanted to make in his life. But Ellie had a family! What about her grandmother's house, her grandmother's furniture—the pullout sofa and piano? But asking about that would have to wait. He said, "Well, I'd like you to get started painting the bathrooms today, if you think you can do it."

"Of course I can do it. I should probably change clothes. Around nine, I'll go move my stuff, but I'll wait till later to put it away. I'll grab something old and ratty to put on and get started. You have the paint?"

"Some yellow, some white, some blue. Can you work with that?"

She made a face. "How were you planning to use them? One blue bathroom, one yellow, white trim? Because that's very boring."

He looked at her long fingernails. Today was hot pink with sparkles. He looked down—she was wearing tennis shoes, but somehow he knew her toes matched her nails. Against his better judgment he said, "Use it any way you like."

"Good deal. Do you have any masking tape? Any caulking?"

"Yes, why?"

"Straight lines and edges. Just out of curiosity, how'd you settle on those colors?"

"They were on sale," he said.

She shifted her weight to one foot. "Have you ever actually *had* a church before?"

"Not exactly."

"Listen, I'll make something work with those colors. Even though they're pretty dorky colors...."

He had a fleeting thought that this was not the woman to be lecturing him about good taste in *anything*. "Aren't you the least bit afraid I might take that personally? Maybe I'm sensitive about the colors I picked."

"No," she said, tilting her head and peering at him. "You're not gay."

He smiled at her. "You sure about that?"

And she smiled, her hands on her hips. "Obviously. Or you'd have chosen more interesting colors."

He sighed heavily. He watched her walk toward the upstairs bathroom in her shrink-wrap jeans. He squinted. He followed, Lucy ever at his side. She had a tattoo peeking out of the back of her low-rise jeans, right in the small of her back. "I...ah...have an old painting shirt you can throw over your clothes, if you'd like. Would that help?"

"Sure, thanks. After I get my stuff out of the car, I'll put on my old sweats. You have all the supplies for me to get started?"

"Stacked outside the bathroom in the hall."

"Super. I'll start up here and, when I'm done, I can move it downstairs. Let me check it out, make sure you have everything I'll need." She knelt on one knee, checking out the supplies, showing more of that tattoo, but he still wasn't able to make out what it was. She looked over her shoulder. "Noah, can you round up the masking tape and caulk? And get me a screwdriver and hammer, please?"

"Screwdriver? Hammer?"

"I'm going to take the door and mirror off. Open paint cans."

"By yourself?" he asked. "Want me to help with that?"

"No. Just get me what I need."

"Sure," he said. But he stood there, his eyes riveted on that tattoo.

She looked over her shoulder again. "It's called a tramp stamp," she said. "I got it when I was fifteen, to be cool."

"I know what it's called. I just can't make out what it is."

"It's vines in the shape of my name, and I'm not showing you any more of it. Let's get this show on the road, huh?"

"Right," he said, going off to his toolbox. And he thought, *I'm taking orders from her. Why am I not the least bit surprised?*

After he delivered what she asked for, she completely ignored him, so he took Lucy to his office. He heard Ellie humming, moving around the drop cloth, pounding at the hinges to remove the door. She didn't ask questions, nor did she need any help with the heavy door or with the mirror over the sink. He could hear her peeling off strips of masking tape for the borders. Completely self-sufficient and low maintenance. That's what a good pastor's assistant was, whether painting or managing the office. Now, that *did* surprise him.

Before sitting down to make a renovation list, Noah decided to tour the old building once more. The church was large but simple. Upstairs was a sanctuary that could hold about three hundred people. There were large double doors at the east end of the church that opened onto a foyer. From here, four wide stairs led up to the sanctuary level and a wider foyer—wide enough for a staging area, as for the gathering of a bridal party. Large interior double doors opened to the aisle, which led toward the stained-glass window, then two more steps led up to a deep stage that had room for the altar, the pulpit, a couple of choir pews. Up here Noah would find room for the piano that had been Merry's.

There were doors to the right and left at the front of the church. To the left was the pastor's office—a room large enough for his desk, shelves and filing cabinets plus a big round table for meetings. Outside that office, the stairs led down to the basement and a side exit door. On the other side of the sanctuary was another room of equal size that could serve as a secretary's office and library. Right next to that room was the upstairs bathroom. Just a sink and toilet, of course, but it had taken the strain off his RV bath facilities. They seemed to be in perfect working order, even though they hadn't been used in years. And that was it—no classrooms. But the basement could be divided with movable panels.

Noah went to his office and set about making a list of things to talk about with the local builder. Paul Haggerty was a friend of Jack's and was going to work on the remodel. That big basement room with a kitchen would make a great community hall, once finished. Right now the walls were plain cinder block and needed texturing. The ceiling was stained from mystery leaks that should be checked out before new ceiling panels were hung. The floor was hard, cold concrete and could use a subfloor covered in tile.

The sanctuary was in pretty good shape, if a little beat up. If he rented a sander, he could finish the hardwood floors himself, but the ceiling was much too high and would require scaffolding.

He had ordered pews, an altar, a pulpit, a baptistery and a new desk for his office. The pews were an extravagance—they could make do with folding chairs. But the pews would be beautiful; he wanted them and there was enough money. Once done, the sanctuary would be breathtaking. And while Noah would enjoy doing all the work himself, it was his mission to get the church open for business as soon as possible. Paul could undoubtedly help with that.

Maybe while Paul was handling the walls and ceiling of the sanctuary, he could be painting the offices. He and Ellie, he thought. He heard her faint humming. She seemed completely capable. If the bathroom didn't end up painted in stripes or polka dots, he might ask for her input on colors for the offices.

She popped her head into his office. "I'm going to run home, unload the car, change into painting clothes and come back. If you don't mind, I'd like to take you up on that offer of your old shirt."

"You bet. I'll have it here when you get back."

Less than an hour later, she was back wearing sweats and a tank top. It seemed everything Ellie owned fit snugly, without a pleat, gather or wrinkle to spare or rattle around in. Fitted to that extraordinary body with those incredibly long legs Ellie managed to make old sweats look sexy. She'd had two children— how'd she manage her flat stomach and high, full breasts? Surgery? Somehow he couldn't imagine her spending money on plastic surgery if she didn't even own a couch.

He handed her one of his blue work shirts, already decorated with a little old paint. He was very happy to see her put it over her sweats and tank. Then he observed with some consternation that she looked every bit as pretty and sexy in that oversize shirt. Thank goodness she got right back to work. Humming. Sometimes actually singing, too softly for him to make out words, but it was very pleasant. Every once in a while Lucy meandered from his office to the bathroom and Noah would hear Ellie say, "Hey there, girlfriend. How's it going? Bored?"

Around eleven in the morning, he checked on Ellie. In just a couple of hours, she had taped off all the edges and was almost done trimming the baseboards in white. When she heard him in the doorway, she looked up from her place on the floor and a coppery curl fell over her forehead. He couldn't help but smile at her—she looked cute as the dickens with her hair piled on top of her head and drowning in his shirt. Besides, there wasn't a bubble or streak on those baseboards. It was perfect.

"Are you extra happy today?" he asked.

"I might be," she said, smiling. "I talked to my kids last night and gave them my new phone number. I'll talk to them tonight and then tomorrow I'll pick them up at eight in the morning for the day. I'm thinking of showing them my new apartment."

"That's right, tomorrow's Saturday. Your day off."

"Seventy-nine days to go."

"You're doing a very nice job there, Ellie."

"Thanks. I know how to paint. I have a knack."

"Lucky me. I'm going to put that talent to good use. Listen, I have some errands to do. I might not be back before you're through today. I'm going to leave Lucy in the RV. I want you to help yourself to the lunch fixings in the refrigerator in the RV. There's sandwich stuff and fruit, bottled water and soda."

She wiggled around to her knees. "You don't have to do that, Rev. Really."

"I know I don't have to, but it seems only fair. I could either raise your pay to eight twenty-five an hour or offer you lunch. I went with the lunch idea."

"You're actually a very nice guy, aren't you?"

"Ellie, I'm a man of God. Don't you expect nice?" Then he grinned.

"Does God know you're throwing his name around to impress people?" she asked.

He laughed. "The RV is unlocked. Take a nice long break. Would you mind letting Lucy out to do her business? And try not to get paint on my dog or my La-Z-Boy."

"You have a La-Z-Boy? Oh, brother. You're *certainly* not gay...."

"How did they sound when you talked to them?" he asked. He hadn't planned to ask, but it popped out. "The kids—how did they sound?"

"Well, fair. Not happy. They were a little emotional. They want me to come and get them right now and they're having a real hard time understanding why I can't. But they didn't sound scared or hurt or anything. And I was as nice to Arnie as I could manage—I told him I was working things out so the judge would be happy with my job, and that I had a new place that was small but perfect. He was a jerk, but he promised to take good care of the kids. 'They're in better hands than they were, Ellie,'" she mimicked. "School starts soon and he goes to his office every day, getting ready for classes to start, and takes them with him. The school secretary keeps an eye on them. They miss me, but they're safe. I think."

"This must be very tough for you."

"Yes, it is, but I'll have them tomorrow. I'll be able to see how they're really doing." And then she smiled at him.

Four

The only plan Noah had for Saturday morning was to take life slow and easy. While Ellie was with her kids, the church would be quiet. He began the day with a leisurely cup of coffee, checked his e-mail, listened to his stomach growl. "Is that you or me?" he asked Lucy. He heard it again. "Okay, me. We should think about breakfast." He looked at Lucy. "I'm talking to a dog."

Lucy looked at him with questioning eyes.

"Let's go to Jack's," he said. And Lucy followed obligingly.

While Lucy had her breakfast on the porch, Noah had his at the bar. He sat beside a local rancher and commiserated on the price of fuel, visited with Preacher for a while and discussed next week's menu ideas, listened to Jack brag about the great progress his young protégé, Rick, was making as he adjusted to a prosthetic leg. Then he took his coffee out to the porch to soak in a little of that sunshine.

One of the best things about having a dog, Noah had realized, was that she usually drew a crowd, and that meant he got to know a lot of people. Noah had noticed the majority of dogs around these parts were herders, working dogs. One of his favorite visitors was young Christopher, Preacher's son. Chris had a pup named Comet, a border collie by the looks of him and, at a few months of age, was already almost as large as Lucy. Since dogs weren't allowed in the bar, Chris and Comet visited with Noah and Lucy on the porch.

Around noon, Noah finally ambled back over to the church, intending to take his good old time with the newspaper. He got set up in the church office, glanced at the lists on his desk before spreading out the weekend edition. He could, of course, help out with the painting of the bathrooms, but he didn't want Ellie to think her work was less than adequate, so he gave up on that idea and got back to the sports pages.

He heard a sound and cocked his head to listen. There was movement in the church, so he went off to investigate, but Lucy beat him to it—she was already looking in the doorway of the upstairs bathroom, tail wagging.

There was Ellie, wearing his long, oversize blue work shirt, painting the top half of the bathroom walls yellow. She must have heard Noah approach, but she didn't say a word. She didn't even turn to look at him. And she wasn't humming. She was working that paint roller with a vengeance.

"What are you doing here?" he asked.

"Painting," she said.

"What about the kids?"

She stopped and looked at him and her expression was at once furious and completely broken. "He wouldn't let me have them."

"What? Why?"

She lowered the roller to the pan on the floor. "He wouldn't let them speak to me on the phone last night and wouldn't let them come with me this morning. He said they had misbehaved and were grounded. They were disrespectful to him by complaining to me that they wanted to leave. My God, they're *babies!* They want their mother! When I told him we had a court order, he told me to take it to the judge."

"Ellie, did you call the judge?"

She rolled her eyes before leveling them at him. "A— the judge is not on my side, and B—he's not around on Saturdays."

"How about the police?"

"The police? Now come on, Rev. Do the police get into stuff like this?"

"I don't know. I've been in situations in the past where they have, though not in this state. He has to turn over the kids on your scheduled days. He's been ordered by the court. He's in contempt. He could go to jail. Or at least be fined or something."

"Oh, your lips to God's ears. Listen," she said, "I'm pissed as hell about this, plus my kids are all torn up. I left them crying and begging and clawing for me with Arnie holding them back and threatening them. But I'm afraid of him, you know? Afraid he'll take it out on them or something."

Noah thought for a second. Then he said, "Wait a minute—did he suggest you resolve this problem by moving back in with him?"

"Not exactly, but he did say we could've been a family if I hadn't been so impossible. That's not true, by the way. I tried—for two months and twenty-six days. He's the stubbornest, most unreasonable man I've ever—"

He grabbed her hand. "Come on," he said, pulling her out of the bathroom.

"What the hell…? What are you *doing?*"

He stopped right at his office door and slowly unbuttoned the paint-splattered work shirt that she wore. "We're gonna go get your kids. It's your day."

He hung the shirt on his office doorknob. He looked at her low-cut, sleeveless T-shirt, her tight jeans. He sighed. Well, this was Ellie. No doubt this had *always* been Ellie. And he was in a position he'd never been in before in his life—he liked her just fine the way she was. The fact that he worried about the judgment of others made him furious with himself.

"I have to rinse my roller, my pan…"

"No time. Let's go," he said.

"Noah," she said, pulling back. "If the paint dries on the roller…"

"I'll get you a new roller tomorrow," he said. He crouched and looked deeply into Lucy's eyes. "You stay here. Take a nap. No painting." Then he pulled Ellie out of the side door of the church. "If you're right, and it sounds like you are, he wants *you* back. Ellie, do you think he cares about your kids? Do you think he wants them, on any level?"

"The kids annoy him. He doesn't do things with them, like play or read or anything. He wants them quiet, neat, invisible. All kids annoy him. Really, he's the last person who should be the principal of an elementary school…."

"Private school, you said."

"Yeah, private. More money there, he said."

Noah's brain was working. Maybe a small private school wasn't so picky about things like credentials, and past work problems. Noah wondered what Arnie's employment history would reveal. "He's punishing you, Ellie. Don't buckle. Let's go get your kids."

"What are you going to do?" she wanted to know.

"I'm going to do to him what you did to Nick Fitch—

but I'm going to do it in a pure ministerial, manipulative and threatening kind of way." He grinned. "We'll have to take your car so we have room for the kids. I'll drive. Now, where are we going?"

Noah pulled into a neighborhood in Redway, just north of Garberville. The houses were a lot alike in shape and size, but were painted a variety of colors. Most had two stories with dormer windows, porches, detached garages and front walks. Some boasted pampered lawns and summer flowers, some weren't quite so well loved. They were all what Noah would consider small—maybe three bedrooms, as well as attics and basements. They were all nestled into tall trees.

Noah drove very slowly because kids were playing in the street. There were a few riding their bikes around in circles while a group in the center appeared to be playing kickball. A couple of parents were busy with the usual Saturday chores—cutting the lawn, digging in the garden, washing the car.

"It's that house," she said, pointing. "There's a black SUV in the driveway."

"Are your kids out here?" he asked. As he drove slowly down the street, the legion of kids separated to let his car pass.

"No. Arnie doesn't let them play outside unsupervised. And he doesn't have time to supervise, so they never had a chance to make friends."

"Do you have any idea what I should expect?" Noah asked.

She took a breath. "He's a chameleon, Noah. He fooled me for quite a while. The school secretary worships him, she thinks he's a kind, devout man, who's strict and doesn't put up with bad behavior, but he's beyond strict. He can be nice when it suits him. His favorite saying is, 'Speak softly and carry a big stick.' His other favorite is, 'Children should be seen and not heard.' By now the neighbors hate him because he's antisocial and wouldn't allow the kids to interact with their kids. He'll probably be very nice to you, but don't fall for it."

Like that's new to me, Noah thought. A lot of people treated him with deference and extreme politeness when they'd prefer not to talk to him at all. They were talking to the minister, not the man. Not only that, but his father had been that kind of man—a charmer at church and a demon at home. That experience gave him an edge—he knew exactly what he would be dealing with.

"If there's no TV in the house, what's he doing in there?"

"He's on his laptop all the time. *All* the time. He carries it around with him. When I got too close and might see what he was doing, he'd close it. My babysitter, from the duplex? She said he might be playing games. You know—real complicated games that have other people online from all over the place? Or maybe he's looking at dirty pictures. Lord, I have no idea. But that's what keeps him busy all the time."

"Interesting," Noah said. "I'm on my laptop a lot, too. But you can read over my shoulder anytime and just get bored to death." He pulled alongside the curb at the front walk. "Do me a favor and stay in the car, for right now at least."

"Why?" she asked, already out of her seat belt.

"Because I'm going to give him a chance to preserve his manhood, which will be hard for him to do in front of you. Let me try reasoning with him."

"Oh, you better watch out."

"I'm not a naive goody-goody, Ellie. Ministers deal with more dysfunctional people than strippers do, believe me."

"I bet you're right," she agreed.

"Stay in the car and don't ruin my show." And with that, he got out and strode purposefully up the walk.

It shouldn't have surprised him that his knock was not answered. He rang the bell, he knocked again, he rang and knocked and hoped it was becoming increasingly obvious that he wasn't going to stop. Finally the door opened and the man standing there looked completely composed and not in the least ruffled. Ellie hadn't mentioned he was a big, ugly guy. Oh, man, how Arnie must have lusted after Ellie! This was not a guy who had a long line of women waiting to hook up with him.

Arnie smiled without showing any teeth and there was a slight tic in his jaw.

"Arnie Gunterson?" Noah asked, putting out his hand.

"*Arnold* Gunterson," he said. "Normally when people don't answer the door, they're either not at home or not interested in company."

"I'm Reverend Noah Kincaid, and I knew you were home because your car's in the driveway," he said, his hand still out.

Arnie burst out laughing, but there was not an ounce of humor in his eyes. "Reverend?" he asked, looking Noah up and down. So what if he was wearing worn jeans and a plaid flannel shirt over a waffled, gray, long-sleeved T-shirt? "Reverend of what? The church of hope and BS?"

Noah tried to ignore him, though it did briefly cross his mind to get that haircut and some of what he always called "town clothes." "Forgive me for being so determined, but it is imperative I speak with you before calling the police department," Noah said.

"Why would you go to the police? Is it against the law not to answer the door?"

Noah finally pulled back his hand. Arnie was six feet or so and broad shouldered, but he was thick around the middle. He looked about forty years old and had an awful big head. His light brown hair was going thin, but it was neatly combed back from a long, wide forehead. His face was slightly flushed, suggesting he had high blood pressure or had been holding in some anger. Noah glanced at the hands that hung at Arnie's sides; they were loose and relaxed. "Not at all, Mr. Gunterson. It's against the law to defy a court-ordered visitation agreement. Miss Baldwin is in my car. She's my employee, she works for the Virgin River Presbyterian Church now. And while she was willing to let the matter go, I thought it was important for her to see her children, and I insisted on stepping in."

"You shouldn't have. The situation is under control."

Noah laughed indulgently. "Unfortunately, that's not true," he said. "She needs to see the kids and, from what she told me about her attempt to pick them up this morning, they need to see her. I am sure we can work it out. If we talked about it."

Arnie's eyebrows came together in a frown. "Is that what you thought? Well, the kids are having time-out. We had talked about how they would behave if they wanted a special day with their mother. No crying, yelling, complaining or throwing fits. No *begging*. They haven't been with me very long, so acting appropriately is new to them. Their mother never bothered to discipline them. Or take care of them at all, for that matter. I'm sure they'll be on their good behavior by next weekend, but I thank you for your concern." He backed into the house and attempted to close the door in Noah's face.

But Noah's hand came out fast, hitting the door and preventing it from closing. "But see, that's not in the court orders—concessions, loopholes and time-outs. I have a copy if you've lost yours," he lied. "You have custody for ninety days until the judge revisits the issue, and your ex-wife has a visit every Saturday from 8:00 a.m. to 6:00 p.m. It's a legal document, Mr. Gunterson. At the very least, I'll get us an escort from the police or sheriff's department. But if we have to haggle over this more than five more minutes, I'll get help from the police. And I'll be in court Monday morning with Miss Baldwin and an attorney. Because you can't do this to her or the children. It's cruel. We have to work it out. Or fight it out."

Arnie smiled meanly. "Well now. I guess she's got you under her spell."

Noah returned the smile and met his eyes. Noah was determined to set a good example by his behavior, but nothing would have felt better than dragging this son of a bitch out of the house and beating the crap out of him. *I could wipe the floor with him; he's totally out of shape,* Noah thought. *He's just a big fat bully.* Yet all Noah said was, "Entirely."

Arnie chuckled. "You're going to pay for that. See, Ellie has a very strong tendency to stretch the truth. She's not usually honest with the facts. Believing what she says usually carries a big price. You just have no idea."

If there was one thing Noah had figured out in only a couple of days, Ellie was *painfully* honest. She could have come up with much more flattering tales about her predicament than she had. "I'll probably pay a visit to the judge anyway, just to assure him that Miss Baldwin has herself a good job with the local church, has a nice little apartment right on the same street for very affordable rent and has already collected some well-respected friends around town. I might let that go another week or two, depending. You could sweeten the pot by letting the kids pack an overnight bag." Noah glowered at Arnie meaningfully. "Since they missed most of the day with their mom, and all. Mr. Gunterson, knowing how *decent* and fair-minded you are, wouldn't that be a generous gesture on your part? The judge would have a hard time believing you're just a cruel, vindictive bastard if you did something nice like that." And then Noah smiled. Meanly.

Arnie was speechless for a moment. "You really don't know who you're dealing with, do you?"

Noah let out his breath slowly. Unfortunately he did. He grew up with one of them. "I just thought we'd both be happiest if we negotiated. Met each other halfway. Because if we go head-to-head, physically or legally, I'm going to win. Trust me. Now—give the kids a break here."

"If I do that, it'll take me all week to get 'em back into shape."

Noah pushed the door open a little more, pushing it against Arnie. "Watch that, Arnold," he threatened. "You're already on thin ice here. You're not going to get away with anything. You treat those kids harshly and it's going to come back on you so hard, you'll never forget it."

"Like it's my fault they haven't been raised right?"

"I said, go real easy on them. And I mean it."

"Are you threatening me?" he asked coolly, totally unafraid.

"You're damn straight. Now, get the kids. I'm getting tired of trying so hard with you."

Arnie seemed to think about this. Then he said, "You sure you're a preacher?"

"Complete with two master's degrees, a ton of money and a load of local influence." He faced him down squarely. Noah was just a hair taller than Arnie, but his arms and shoulders were strong, his neck thick, his chest hard, and while Arnie had that generous spare tire, Noah had a six-pack. He looked Arnie in the eyes easily. And there was only one, maybe two lies in what he had said, and he considered them small ones. His money did not amount to a lot after spending on the church, and he thought maybe his influence went as far as the local bartender. Period. But what the heck. These were innocent children. And no matter what Ellie had done for a living, this bastard was *bad.* Yet there was nothing about Ellie that was bad. Just nothing.

Noah's little secret was—he had a bit of a temper. It didn't take all that much to push his buttons—especially over matters of injustice. He'd been trying real hard to be one of those turn-the-other-cheek kind of guys, but it wasn't going that well. Injustice like this ranked right up there as something that made him fighting mad. And he was damn sure going to research Arnold a little further.

"Stay out here," Arnie said. "I'll get the kids ready. And don't ever pull this again or you'll be sorry."

Noah wanted to slap back many retorts and threats. But he said nothing. He stood. And stood. And stood. He cast a glance over his shoulder at Ellie, waiting impatiently in the car, confusion and anxiety all over her face. It was a good ten minutes before the door opened again.

Arnie appeared alone in the doorway. He looked behind him and said, "Stay! I said stay!" as if the kids were dogs in training. Then to Noah he said, "She can keep them overnight if she'll get them back by four tomorrow afternoon."

"We can do that. I'll make sure of it. And I'll come along to bring them home, just so we're sure we're all on the same page here." From the look on Arnie's face it was pretty clear that he understood the subtext of Noah's comments.

"So, you're sleeping with her?" Arnie asked.

Noah was momentarily stunned. "Did you seriously ask me that?" he said, shocked. He shook his head and laughed unhappily. "You know, she's my employee. People can respect and help each other without there being a sexual agenda. Did you know that?"

"Not with Ellie," he said. "She's a tramp."

Noah ground his teeth, his eyes narrowed and his fists clenched. He was seconds away from the happiest moment of his life, when he broke this guy's nose. But there was a miracle. He didn't move at all, and simply said, "Let the kids go to their mother now."

Arnie stepped back, gave his head a nod and let the kids past. "Mind your manners," he called after them, and his voice was controlled, civil, as though he meant well. It made Noah's head spin. It was just as Ellie had said, this guy had two sides—both of them creepy.

The children each carried small backpacks for overnight, and they tried to walk slowly, until they were halfway to the car, until Ellie's door came open, and then they lost control and broke into a run. Ellie fell to her knees and they flung themselves into her arms.

There was so much kissing and hugging and crying, it made Noah nervous. He saw that Arnie watched for a moment, then closed the door. He heard the dead bolt slide. "Come on, let's get out of here," Noah said, trying to shepherd them into the car. "Kids in the back, seat belts, come on, let's go."

"In the car, kids," Ellie said. "This is Reverend Kincaid, my new boss. This is Danielle and Trevor."

"Noah," he said. "Just call me Noah. Come on, let's get outta here, huh?"

When he was behind the wheel, his brain went into overdrive. Would Arnie call the police and insist the kids had been kidnapped by a small-town preacher? Would they suffer even more when they were returned because Arnie felt he had lost ground? What could happen to these kids a few weeks down the road? Was there any way to assure their safety? How would Ellie survive if something happened to them and she felt it was her fault?

Noah listened as Ellie and the kids discussed the situation. "He said we were good enough today so we could spend the night. But we have to be back by four."

"Did he?" Ellie asked Noah. "Did he say they could stay over?"

"He said we have to mind our manners and behave if we ever want another visit. Mommy, I *have* been doing my manners," Danielle said. "I've been doing my please and thank-yous, I've been keeping Trevor from crying at night."

Noah thought furiously, that son of a bitch let them think they had *earned* their visit by being "good."

"Oh, baby," Ellie said, tears in her voice. "Trevor, have you been scared?"

He nodded piteously and reached for his mother, the seat belt holding him in place.

"It's okay, Trev—you're very brave," she told him, holding his hand. "Did you bring your books?"

He shook his head. Danielle said, "We didn't get to bring them. We only have two now. Arnie said they keep us from paying attention."

"No, they don't," Ellie said. "That's not right. How upside down is that? A school principal who doesn't want kids to read? Okay, here's what we'll do. When we get back to my new place and drop Noah off at his church, we'll go to the bookstore at the mall in Eureka. We'll buy books for you to keep at my house. And there's a library in town— they have books for children. Every week I'll get new ones for you to look at when you have Saturdays with me."

"I'm going with you," Noah said.

"Huh?" Ellie asked.

"I'm going to take you and the kids to lunch, or early dinner, or whatever it is, then to the bookstore for books."

"You don't have to do that, Noah," she said. "We'll manage."

But no one could manage against that big, mean cretin. "And then, we're going to get some legal help. Right away."

It took a long time for the tension from the escape to wear away, but it did. Noah asked the kids where they most wanted to go for lunch and they picked McDonald's. Ellie said, "That's a big treat. We couldn't do that a lot."

"Well, today it's my treat," Noah said.

"This is… Well, I wish you wouldn't do so much. I'll buy. Let me buy. I don't want to owe you so much."

"Get over it," he said shortly. "I want to do this."

She leaned closer to him. "And I don't want to be a charity case, Rev."

"You're not. You're a friend. Let it go at that."

"How'd I rank friend so quick?" she asked him.

"You're kidding, right? You cleaned the kitchen. Painted the bathroom. Nice job, too. Just looking at how you paint your nails, I was afraid. I was very afraid."

And she laughed. "That's good. We'll get along fine if you stay a little on edge like that."

Children are almost too resilient sometimes, Noah thought. They were so excited to be having McDonald's, they perked right up and forgot all the stuff that had them anxious and scared in the car. He delivered their orders while Ellie found a booth. Of course, she sat on one side with the kids, an arm around each one, and they talked about a trip to the bookstore. She promised to read to them a little bit and buy them two books each.

Noah wanted to buy them ten books each. And

clothes—they were growing out of theirs. For a guy who couldn't seem to work up any excitement about his own wardrobe, he was surprised to be angry about the state of theirs. Couldn't Arnie, who claimed to be the better parent, do something about that? Apparently Arnie had no talent beyond disciplining and punishing. Noah wanted to make a big run through Target and make sure the kids had clothes and shoes that weren't too small, too worn and too scuffed. He knew Ellie's funds were limited, but what about the big shot who was going to do better by them? But he kept his mouth shut; it wasn't his place and he'd been pushy enough.

At the bookstore he told her to take all the time she wanted—hours if she felt like it. "I want to graze, myself," he said. "I can be happy in a bookstore forever. Just relax and enjoy yourself."

Noah picked up book after book, reading the jackets, skimming first pages, but unlike his usual bookstore crawls, he couldn't keep his mind on all the choices. Every so often he'd wander over to the children's section. He saw them cuddled close to their mother while she read. The next time he checked, he saw Danielle close to her mom while Trevor pillaged the stacks for the next book. Then he peeked and saw Trevor on her lap while Danielle sat nearby, reading her own book. The last time he looked, Trevor was asleep on Ellie's lap while she read to her daughter.

If the judge saw this, would it matter? he asked himself.

Noah wasn't only watching Ellie and her children or browsing for books—he was also people watching. He wandered through the mall a couple of times. He'd been out of the mainstream of life for quite a while; he was either working in the fishing trade, attending the seminary or teaching at a conservative university. The students and staff were pretty buttoned down, more right wing than left. They certainly hadn't looked Amish—there were plenty of tight and ragged jeans, short skirts, but they didn't push the limits much. He'd been in a monastery, of sorts, where the culture was cautious. He had probably stood out the most, refusing to wear the standard V-neck sweater or herringbone jacket to teach in. As a professor he looked like he looked right now—very casual. He had acquired a suit for his wedding, and he wore it again for Merry's funeral. He didn't like the idea of suiting up for future church services.

But here, in the bookstore and mall, there were hip young women, mothers and otherwise. He saw bare midriffs, pierced belly buttons, tattoos poking out of low-slung jeans and a rose on the top of the rise of a breast. He hadn't seen much body art at his teaching job, but it was popular around the docks and he had even acquired his own tattoos while working as a fisherman. Ellie's clothing might be a little racy for a church lady, but by contemporary standards, she fit right in. Well, except that it was hard to find anyone as beautiful, or as sexy.

And why wouldn't a woman with those assets—height, figure, thick hair, ivory skin—want to look pretty? Sexy? Her means might be slim, but in her own way she was making the most of what she had.

He smiled and admitted to himself that he found Ellie a lot of fun. Edgy and authentic and full of delightful mischief. Seeing her with her kids gladdened Noah's heart.

When they were finally back in the car, each child hanging on to two books, he said, "Well, anyone hungry?"

"I'm stuffed," Ellie said. "Kids? Hungry?" They shook their heads. "We'll just head home, Noah," she said. "Thanks for asking. That's very nice."

It was only 5:00 p.m. They'd had their McDonald's at two—they'd get hungry. Ellie hadn't been planning on an overnight visit. "I bet you could use a run by the grocery store before going home, to stock up for your sleepover," he said.

"Do you mind? I'm sure you have to get back to Lucy and I can just head out after I take you back to town."

"Don't be silly, Lucy is fine. She probably has that second bathroom painted by now. We'll stop at the store on our way home. You'll need something for tonight, after the hamburgers wear off. And breakfast. As for tomorrow—don't take them back to Redway without me. I want him to know there's some scrutiny. That you have backup. Let me take you there."

"But, Noah, it's Sunday. You probably have things to do. Don't you have religious things to do?"

Yeah, he thought. *I have to stand in that empty church and remember what community really means. What shoring up your friends and neighbors is all about. What the real blessings are—they're small of stature, they're young, they're innocent and they have to be protected.* "I'm free all day, but I won't interfere with your family time. I'll be ready to take you in time for your deadline."

"Mama?" Danielle asked from the backseat. She pronounced it "Mumma." "Can we stay with you now?"

"Just for tonight, angel. Arnie thinks he can do a better job, and so does the judge, and we have to give him some time."

"But, Mama, he doesn't do his manners," she said. "He doesn't like us very much."

"Sweetheart, all we can do is go along for now. The judge said ninety days, and we're getting through it, then it will work out. Try not to let your feelings be hurt when he doesn't mind his manners. Just do your best. And please, baby, please know that I will never ever be disappointed in you. I'm proud of you every second. We'll all do our very best and soon it will be over." She smiled at her daughter over her shoulder. "My gramma used to call it 'Go along to get along.' That's what we have to do—go along for now. Pretty soon, we'll be together. Forever."

Danielle sniffed a little. "Oh, Mama," she said. "It's hard not to let my feelings hurt."

"I know, Danny. But when we don't have a choice, we have to be tough. I know how strong you are. You can get through this. And then, when it's over, I'll hold you and cuddle you every night."

"Oh, Mama," she said softly.

"I love you, Danielle. I'm proud of you for trying so hard." But when Ellie said that last, her voice caught. She shook herself. "Well, having to be strong is no big deal to us, huh? Because we're very strong! We love each other, and it makes us very strong. Right?"

"Mama," was all the little girl said.

"I know it's very hard," Ellie said. "I know, honey. It's very hard for me, too. I miss you so much it makes me want to cry. But I'm trying to be as brave as you. I'm so proud of you."

Noah thought he might have to pull over to the side of the road, put his head down and have a bone-deep cry himself. When he pulled into the grocery-store lot, he forced himself to let her be the parent, to be independent and do her own shopping. He offered to keep the kids while she went into the store, but of course she couldn't be separated from them for a second. They returned a few minutes later with only two shopping bags, but she must have indulged the kids, because they were happy again. They chattered about little pizzas, popcorn, cereal, juice and milk.

He dropped them off right at the back stairs to her rented room and watched them clamber up. Just as he was about to walk back down the street, Jo Ellen Fitch came out on her porch. She watched Ellie and her children go up the stairs. To Noah she said, "She didn't mention kids. I'm not really set up for kids here."

When Noah looked at her, his expression was grim. "Gimme a break. It's overnight, that's all."

"Where do they live?" Jo asked.

"They're with her ex-husband right now. She only sees them on weekends. Try to be nice about it. They mean everything to her."

"Of course I'll be nice about it," she said, sounding affronted. "It's just that—"

"It's very hard for her, so let's all be generous," he said.

"Of course," Jo Ellen said. "I didn't mean—"

Noah took a breath. "I'm sorry, Mrs. Fitch. It's been a rough day for them." *For me,* he thought. "I know you'll be very kind to them. Thank you."

He thought he should probably go someplace quiet and just pray until he fainted or lost bladder control, but instead he collected Lucy and went to Jack's. He leashed Lucy while she ate, and he went into the bar, his throat dry and aching. He asked for ice water.

"Anything to eat or drink with that?" Jack asked him.

"Not yet, thanks," Noah said. And then he sat, pondering the water in his glass, thinking. He'd been close to more than one difficult domestic situation in his career, especially as a counselor. Some of them had been more dramatic than Ellie's, frankly. But this time it felt personal. Just listening to Danielle in the backseat of his car, her voice barely controlled, "Mama…" It tore his heart out.

"You getting hungry?" Jack asked him a while later.

"Nah," he said.

"Having trouble with the cleanup next door?" Jack asked, obviously trying to pin down the reason for Noah's unusually quiet mood.

Noah lifted his eyes to Jack's face. "I have a situation."

"No kidding," Jack said. He nodded to Noah's glass. "You haven't downed that water yet. And you don't have much to say, either. Which is a first."

Noah took a breath. "You know just about everyone around here, right?" he asked Jack.

"I've been around long enough to know plenty of people."

"I have an issue to resolve. It's not a confidence, but I really can't talk about it."

"Hey, I didn't mean to pry," Jack said.

"It's just that it's… Well, it's a custody issue. I'm trying to puzzle it out."

Jack lifted his eyebrows. "You divorced?"

"Nah, it's not my issue. It's a friend's."

"Ah, I see. Hard to know how to help, I guess."

"That would be it," Noah said. "I feel helpless. That's my least favorite feeling."

"You haven't had enough time around here to make your connections, figure out who's going to be useful to your work," Jack said. "That helping-people line of your work, I mean. I'm sure you're good for some mighty powerful praying, but sometimes a man has to know who's gonna pass him the ammunition."

Noah had to chuckle. "You hit that right."

"Friend of mine had some serious custody concerns a couple years back. There was a woman he was interested in and she was running from a dangerous ex. She had a kid with her and nowhere to turn. But my buddy had been fishing with this judge from Grace Valley and they were tight. That old judge—named Judge, by the way, like his folks knew the day he was born where he was headed. Anyway, that tough old bird, he didn't like domestic violence. Irked him right down to his toes. He helped. So did my little sister, Brie—she's a lawyer. She's dealt with more than her share of domestic situations, not to mention her own divorce. She lives right next door to me and Mel. The judge and my sister helped my buddy out."

"Really? And is the woman safe now?" Noah asked.

"I'd say so." Jack smiled. "My buddy married her, had a baby with her. Everything got sorted out."

"That's good to know. Maybe I ought to go see this judge. Or talk to your sister. Maybe someone has some advice."

"First off, why don't you go back to the kitchen, have a chat with the other Preacher around here while he slices and dices. He might head you in the right direction so you can help Ellie."

"Ellie?"

"Noah, everyone seems to like you fine, but you don't have all that many close friends yet. If it isn't Ellie and it isn't me, the person's not from around here." He gave the counter a wipe. "Go talk to Preacher. He's real good at confidences. He'd have his tongue cut out before he'd give up your secrets, but he's candid about his own. And he knows everything. He gets on that computer of his and gets himself an education about every issue under the sun. He's one smart critter. And awful helpful."

"Think he'd mind? Even if I can't really discuss the particulars of this problem?"

"Noah, most folks around here would jump in to help a neighbor, but Preacher is one of a kind. He might be built like a refrigerator and look scary as hell, but he's the sweetest man I know. He'd do anything in the world to help. Go on back. Then I'll give you some dinner."

Five

Noah didn't see Ellie all day on Sunday and didn't expect to. The way they had left it, he was planning to drive with her to take her kids back to Redway to their stepfather's house. He was hoping that if she had support, it might modify the jerk's behavior.

But that wasn't the way it worked out. He walked down to her rented room at three that afternoon, but she wasn't there. Her deadline for getting her kids back was four and her car was already gone. He waited around awhile in case she came back looking for him, then at close to four he went back to his RV. At six he and Lucy grabbed a bite to eat at Jack's, hung around for a while, then walked down the block just to see if her car was back yet.

It wasn't. He worried briefly that she hadn't taken them back to her ex-husband's house at all. Frankly, if he were Ellie, he might not have. The temptation to flee must be overwhelming. He went back to his RV, knowing he wouldn't sleep all night without knowing.

At nine, he walked down the street again, but this time he left Lucy behind. The summer sun had set and people turned in early in this little town, but her car was not yet parked in front of the Fitch house. There was a single light on inside the big house and an outside light at the top of the garage stairs, but her room was dark. Noah sat on the stairs that led to her rented room and waited.

About thirty minutes later, he heard the engine of her PT Cruiser as she came into town. She pulled up in front of the house and parked. He heard the car door slam; her feet were quiet and slow on the driveway that led to the garage.

Deep in thought, she didn't see him until she was about twenty feet away. She stopped. He stood. The light from the top of the stairs illuminated him. Still sheathed in semidarkness, she approached another ten feet and stopped again. Finally, in a very soft voice that didn't sound like Ellie, she asked, "What are you doing here?" She took a couple more steps toward him. She looked different. Oh, the clothes were Ellie—tight jeans, snug top. But her makeup was gone, her big hair pulled back severely into a ponytail. She looked so young. Sweet. And so vulnerable.

"I was waiting for you," he said. He came down the steps and stood in front of her. "I wondered how it went. If everything was okay."

"It's okay," she said in a voice that sounded weak and beaten. "They'll be all right."

"Was it terrible? Were they very upset?"

He saw her shake her head and there was only silence for a moment.

"Ellie," Noah said, "did you get them back on time?"

She nodded. She bit her lower lip, looked down and didn't say anything more.

"Did he give you any trouble?"

She shook her head. Then she said, "Well, there was

the usual. He told them to go to their rooms, get ready for bed and stay there. Ready for bed, at four o'clock. But I made sure they had eaten before I took them back, so if he doesn't give them dinner, they won't be hungry. Then again, if he does give them dinner and they can't eat it, there could be a different kind of problem. I couldn't tell him, though…that they'd eaten." She sniffed and wiped at her nose with the back of her hand. "He seems to be always looking for ways to get to them and it would be just like him to give them a big dinner and insist they eat every bite, even though they can't. But there's not much I can do to control that. He'll do what he'll do."

"You've been crying."

"Some," she admitted.

"Since four o'clock?" he asked, an ache creeping into his chest. When she didn't answer him, he said, "I was worried about you. About you and your kids."

"I never thought about that," she said. "That you'd worry. I went to my friend's house. Phyllis—the lady who owns the duplex. I just wanted to talk to someone who understood the whole mess."

He gave her a moment. *Where there is despair, let me offer hope…* "That probably helped." He saw her nod. "Would you like to talk about it now?"

"I'm pretty worn out."

"Would it help to pray about it?" he asked. "I could—"

And she laughed a little, shaking her head. "If it's all the same to you—"

"Sometimes it really does help," he said.

"Not today," she said. Then she sniffed. "Look, I'll be fine in the morning. I just need some rest. I'm sorry if you were worried."

"I didn't mean to put that on you—I have no business

waiting for you to get home. You're an adult. I can't explain—it's just that I felt for them. The kids. And you—I just wanted to know you were okay."

"Well, I'm okay, Noah. And the kids will get by. We talked about how we had to accept the way things are for a little while longer. We sang songs all the way to Redway in the car, just to keep their minds off things. I only had to put up with Arnie for three or four minutes, just long enough for him to tell me I'd better remember who's calling the shots here." She groaned in the back of her throat. "Maybe I should go back to him. Could I do that? Stay with him for the ninety days so I could watch over the kids? Then leave with them after the time's up? Legally? Could that work?"

Noah felt a surge of anger rise up in him at the very thought of Arnie touching her, putting his hands on her, telling her what to do. In that instant he knew he'd lose his mind if she did that. "You can't do that," he said, and then he asked himself who he thought he was to tell her what she could do. "Arnie might trip you up somehow, make it worse. You're doing what the court asked. Um, listen, I did some checking this afternoon—there's a woman lawyer in town. Jack—the guy who owns the bar—his sister is a lawyer and she lives here."

She sighed heavily. "I can't afford a lawyer."

"She might be willing to talk to you for free. If you explained. If you told her the cheapskate preacher doesn't pay worth a damn. I mean, maybe she can't build a case or go to court on your behalf without a fee, but—"

"Noah, stop. I've talked to lawyers…"

"I could give you a loan. Long-term. Interest free."

She tilted her head. "Don't do this," she barely whispered. "Leave me some pride. I got us into this, I'll get us out."

"Ellie, there's no shame in a helping hand…."

"I just need some rest. I didn't sleep at all last night. Once I have some sleep, things will look better in the morning. I'll be able to think straight."

Noah pulled a rumpled piece of paper out of his pocket and held it toward her. "Well, sleep on this. Her name is Brie Valenzuela. I just met her. Very nice woman." He shrugged. "According to Preacher, the cook, she's been known to help neighbors. She helped him once."

"But they all know each other."

"Just take it. It's Mel's sister-in-law, Ellie."

She took the paper and said, "You didn't tell them all about—"

"I didn't tell anyone anything. I just said I had a friend with a difficult custody situation that, as far as I could tell, was diabolical. I said I knew someone who could use some help."

"They'll all figure it out," she said, her voice tired.

"That's not the most important thing," he argued.

"I have to go to bed now. So I can work in the morning."

Helplessly, he said, "Is there anything I can do to help? Right now?"

"Yeah, boss. You can let me get up the stairs and shake this off. This isn't your problem."

Oh, but it was, he thought. It wasn't that he took on pain and suffering like an addict. He barely knew her and yet he was completely enmeshed in this crisis; his throat ached from remembering the sound of the children's voices when they were in his backseat. "You're right," he said. "I'm sorry to get in your business. Sleep well."

He walked around her and down the driveway. "That's nice, though," she said to his back. "Nice to have someone care. Thanks for that."

* * *

Noah found himself wondering why Ellie hadn't slept last night. He would have imagined having her kids with her, so close, all in one big bed, would have given her comfort, peace of mind. Was she completely wigged out with stress? Fear? Confusion?

Where there is sadness, let me bring joy....

Noah realized with some embarrassment that he wanted to hold her and comfort her, whisper all the right words that would bring her peace of mind. He wanted to be the one to get her through this. To rescue her. To put his arms around her, protect her and bring contentment where there was fear and pain. Hope. He would show her hope where there was hopelessness. *For it is in giving that we receive....*

But this was *not* his job. He was not her minister. He was her boss.

He shook his head, trying to shake away the impulse that was all wrong for the circumstances. It was just that he'd been too alone for too long. It wasn't just since Merry had passed, it was before and after that. There had been women, but nothing lasting, no one to whom he could really give himself except for that all-too-brief time he had his wife. He needed to get beyond that.

Ellie would probably be happier with a hundred-dollar bill than an offer to pray with him. Why didn't he know that? He'd always known things like that! Anyone who could go to skid row with a Bible in one hand and a grocery sack full of peanut-butter sandwiches in the other knew when it was appropriate to offer spiritual assistance and when it was time to just be a friend.

He'd gotten himself in deep. And fast. Well, that happened to counselors, he knew that—it was a hazard of the profession. But he had fallen into her problems like a drunk into a shot glass. He took them on, worried them to death, worked at finding a solution. He liked happily ever after, even if he didn't exactly have an acquaintance with it right now.

He would have to separate himself from this situation, be objective, remember his job, his particular skills, his role.

He'd better back off, before he did more harm than good.

Come Monday morning, Noah had a headache. He'd tossed and turned, suffering through deep thoughts that ranged from his spiritual commitment and his job here, to Ellie and her problems, to missing Merry. He wished he had a woman in his life, he thought. Talk about hopelessness. Nothing can keep you up all night like worry and self-pity.

But when he finally made it to the church office at eight in the morning, he heard movement and soft humming. When he went to the upstairs bathroom, he found Ellie painting away, the little bathroom almost done. She wasn't wearing makeup this morning. Her hair was clipped in the back, but fell in a shiny curtain down her back—she'd straightened it somehow. Instead of her tight jeans, she wore some khaki things that tied right below the knees. And his painting shirt. She looked about fifteen.

She turned and smiled at him. "Morning," she said. "Sleep in?"

"This is my usual time," he said.

She laughed. "Yeah, I know. Just giving you crap. I slept like a dead woman last night and thought I'd get an early start."

"You did?" he asked, rather stunned. When last he'd seen her, she was a crying wreck. *He* hadn't slept. And she'd been part of the reason.

"I did. I was worn out. But then I woke up early and thought, why not just go for it. I didn't bother fixing up at all—I figured no one would see me but you and the paint." Then she smiled again.

"You seem in a very good mood," he observed.

"*So* much better. Really, you can't let yourself get tired out. It's bad all around."

"What kept you from sleeping the night before? Worry? Upset?"

"No," she said, laying her roller in the pan. "Oh, I'm worried. I try not to let that take over, since worry isn't going to help anything. But I had my kids with me." Her eyes lit up. "I snuggled them all night, listened to all their sleeping noises, smelled them fresh out of the shower, and just couldn't shut my eyes no matter how hard I tried. Knowing I wouldn't see them for a week and probably wouldn't get another overnight, I—" She shook her head. "Like a stupid ninny, I was up all night just holding them and watching them sleep. No wonder I wasn't any good at taking them back on Sunday."

And he thought, wait a minute! *You have all the same problems! Nothing has improved just by sleeping!* What the hell…?

"Are you all right?"

"I have a slight headache," he said.

"Did you take something?" she asked.

"No. It'll probably pass."

"Then you must want to have a headache. Right?" she asked, lifting her pretty eyebrows.

"You actually look better without makeup. Without the big hair. And you're not six feet tall, after all."

"Please!" she admonished. "Nothing you say is going to make me look like some Amish woman. Besides, all that curly hair is mine—I'm stuck with it. Sometimes I straighten it, but it's way too much trouble. And I know it would make your life easier if I was really butt ugly and asexual, but I'm here to work, not make your life easier."

He tilted his head. "Excuse me, but isn't the job of a pastor's assistant designed to make the pastor's life easier?"

"No, Your Worship. It's to *assist*. And I am. And I will. And I will look good if I can, thankyouverymuch. So why the headache? Drink too much last night?"

"Think too much, more likely. Listen, you don't have to tell me if it's none of my business, but how are you so well adjusted after just a little sleep? You were kind of…kind of…"

"Messed up over the kids last night?" she finished for him. "Yeah, I know. I admit, it gets to me. And no matter how well I sleep, I *hate* it. This shouldn't be happening to them. I mean, it shouldn't be happening to me, either, but I can take about anything. It's them hurting that tears me up. I think people who hurt children are going to burn in hell."

"Ah. You believe in hell?"

She tilted her head and smirked at him. "Why wouldn't I? I'm closely acquainted."

Take that, he thought. But instead of following his own advice and staying out of it, which kept him awake all night, he crossed the line again. "You going to talk to that woman lawyer? Brie?"

She shrugged. "If the time seems right. Really, my biggest worry is that if I get in Arnie's face anymore, try to upset his temporary win here, he'll get worse."

"Maybe that would be a good thing to talk to the lawyer about," he suggested. "Because while you're painting and leaving him alone with his temporary win, he could be plotting his next move."

"Like I said, I'm not ruling it out. And believe me," she said, stooping to pick up her paint roller, "the first thing I'll tell her is I can't afford her because my boss is a hopeless tightwad." She winked at him. Then her grin faded and she said, "Jesus, you look miserable. You have bags under your eyes. You might want to drop the macho-man deal and pop a couple of aspirin."

"You're not the only one with worries, you know," he said defensively.

"Baby, everyone has worries. The rich have as many as the poor. The healthy as many as the sick. It's a worrisome deal, this life business. You have to learn to mellow, not stay up all night feeding it."

"Well, you sure shook off your funk pretty well. Maybe I'm just not as good at it as you are."

"Hanging on to it a little, are you?"

"Not because I like being worried," he said. And it was damn tempting to point out to her that she and *her* problems started the whole thing.

"Ah," she said. She rolled more paint onto the wall. Then without looking at him, she said, "Must be a payoff in there for you, bud."

"Knock it off, Ellie."

"There's a trick to letting it go, in case you're interested."

He took a deep breath, an impatient breath. "Lay it on me."

"You can't try. Trying is a struggle and doing is an act. You can't witness the act of *trying,* but you can see the results of *doing.* Trying brings on stress because not only do you have the problem, but now you have all this frustration with it not going away just because you want it to. It's kind of like being told not to think of pink elephants—impossible. What you have to do is stop. You say to yourself, this is over for now. I'm done for now. Take your mind to another place and concentrate on that peaceful place. Deep breaths. Go limp. Put your mind in another state. It takes practice, but it gets easier, over time."

"Thanks, Scarlett," he said with a laugh, not believing a word. He tried to imagine counseling a completely stressed-out person by telling them that all they had to do was not try to let it go, and it would go. Although he did admit to himself that he had used that technique, or something similar, in the past with some o his clients.

"My gramma used to say, you can only feel one feeling at a time. For example, you can't feel trust and fear together. If you want to trust but you're afraid, fear is still in charge. If you trusted, there wouldn't be fear. She also used to say, you have to listen to what you feel—feeling fear could be a warning, right?"

He knew this theory. Fear and faith cannot coexist. He'd used that a hundred times, too. But he had never counseled *her*. Her grandmother had. "Well, I guess I'm not as good at it as you are. If I have a problem, it tends to haunt me for a while."

She looked at him, lifted one thin, light brown brow and said, "Oh. Sure. So, how's that working out for you?"

Enough! he thought. No twenty-five-year-old stripper was going to counsel him! But he said, "What else did your grandmother say?"

She got a very happy look and turned to him, roller at her side. "Don't make love to your problems—they'll never give you back the satisfaction you give them. And, troubles aren't worth the paper they're written on, but that doesn't mean writing them down won't help you get a fix on 'em. And, God respects you when you work, but he loves you when you dance. That last one might've gotten me into some trouble."

Good God, he thought. This was like listening to Grandma Pyle's wisdom on *The Andy Griffith Show!* "I won't be around until later today," he said briskly. "I have errands. I'll be gone most of the day."

"She also used to say, 'If Jesus walked the earth today, he wouldn't be hanging out with Billy Graham. He'd be found with drug addicts and prostitutes and the like.'"

That one stunned Noah still for a moment. He'd always thought that himself. "Need anything before I go?" he finally asked.

"I'm good," she said, rolling away. "I'm sure I'll get started on the downstairs john while you're gone. Take aspirin, Noah. Don't be stupid."

"If I don't see you when I get back, I'll assume you worked as long as you could."

"Okeydokey."

"Will you please give Lucy a spin over the grass for her potty break and leave her in the RV when you quit for the day?"

"Of course. Want me to get her dinner at the bar before I leave?"

"Nah, I'll be back for that. That's almost the best part of my day."

With that, Noah left the church and got into his truck. It really pissed him off that she was doing so well this morning. Not that he wanted her to be in pain—of course not. But he was the professional—he was supposed to be telling her how to cope, not the other way around. Her grandmother had some very sage advice. And, he *wasn't* doing as well as she was…even with her problems! So one of them was not a particularly good role model, and he feared it was him.

And that *really* pissed him off.

* * *

As Noah pulled around to the front of the church, he saw Mel Sheridan loading a box into the back of the Humvee with another one sitting on the clinic porch. She lifted a hand and gave him a wave, so he pulled up alongside. "Need a hand there?" he asked.

"Thanks, but it's not heavy. Where are you headed?"

"I thought I'd run over to Grace Valley and visit with Harry Shipton, the pastor there."

"I know Harry. We always called Harry when we needed a minister. Now I guess we won't have to do that anymore."

"I hope not," he said.

"Are you in a hurry? I mean, do you have an appointment with Harry?"

"No," he said. He shrugged. "I called him and said I'd drop by this week and he said that'd be great. Why?"

She walked over to his open window. "How would you like a private tour of some interesting and little-known parts of the area?"

"Cool. I'd like that."

"You'd have to keep some secrets. Are you any good at secrets?"

"Gimme a break!" he said, insulted. "I'm a minister!"

"Yeah, well, that's not saying you don't have a big mouth," Mel said.

"And what if I swear to God?"

"Jack's trying to get me to stop swearing, but go ahead, if it floats your boat. I just have something you might be interested in, but you can't tell. If you tell, my life is going to be too miserable to describe."

"You have a problem you'd like to talk about?" he asked hopefully. Right about now he'd like to feel as good at counseling and giving comfort as Ellie's grandmother.

"No, nothing like that. Tell you what, follow me out of town…if you feel like it."

Nothing could stop him now. "I'm right behind you."

Mel loaded the second box, jumped in the Hummer and pulled out of town. Noah was right on her bumper. They drove for about twenty minutes, out Highway 36, then turned off on a side road that wound up and down a big mountain, and then Mel pulled over at a wide space in the road. Noah pulled up behind her. She stepped out of the Hummer and beckoned him with a wave of her hand. "Leave your truck here and come with me."

He did as she asked, getting in the front seat of the Humvee. "Where the devil are we going?"

"When I first got to Virgin River, I was working with old Doc Mullins. He died last year and Cameron Michaels came down from Oregon to work as the town doctor for at least a year. Mullins was an ornery old coot, but I loved him. Anyway, I came from the city—from L.A.—and there were things he tried to tell me about life in the mountains. For that matter, Jack tried, too. Some things I just had to learn for myself. You a city boy, Noah?"

"Pretty much. I grew up in a suburb of Columbus and went to college and seminary in Seattle."

"Where I came from, working in an urban trauma center, when we treated indigents or vagrants, we called social services and just handed them off. I never had to worry about what had become of them after that transfer. The doctors called it 'buff 'em and turf 'em.' Treat the patients as well as you can for your specialty, then hand them off to another service—someone else's turf—and then it's their problem. Things are very different around here—except for the larger cities, there aren't facilities for dealing with poverty and homeless people. Virgin

River doesn't have anything to offer, and neither do the surrounding small mountain towns."

"You have homeless here?" he asked. He knew that except for the successful ranches, farms and vineyards, most of the community lived a lower-middle-class existence, but he hadn't seen any stark poverty or homelessness.

"Boy howdy," she said. "I think you should see for yourself. I doubt there's much you can do about it, Noah. They sure won't cotton up to you bible beating them. They might torture you for that. Or just plain go to sleep. But you should know about mountain life. There are lots of poor people out in these mountains who aren't homeless, people who homesteaded, and once they sold off their quotient of lumber, had nothing left but a mountain full of forty-foot trees and very little income. If they homesteaded, they're probably elderly and often sickly, but they're not real fond of doctors, either. I get a little slack, being a nurse-practitioner. We look in on them when we can."

"I guess you have to know the area pretty well," he said.

"More than half of our population is rural," she said. She turned off onto what appeared to be a hidden road. Narrow, all dirt and washboard, obviously very seldom used.

"It's not all charity work in our practice," she said. "In fact, we're doing better all the time—there are more insured and paying patients every year around here, but there are still people in need who don't have the means. It's all part of the territory, Noah. I get a lot of food at the clinic as patient fees. After Cameron and I go through it and see what we can use, most of the really good stuff goes over to Jack's. Preacher cooks it, bakes it, freezes it, cans it…and they always serve people who serve the town—"

"He's been real good to me that way," Noah said. "I

won't take advantage, but I'll take the occasional piece of pie off his hands...."

"Well, it all shakes out even in the end. There's always stuff left at the clinic—milk and juice real close to going bad, cheese with a few moldy spots I can cut off and, depending on the season, there might be some produce. And then there are the casseroles that are half eaten. Stuff that can't be used at Jack's but can fill a belly. The boxes in the back have food in them. There's just one problem...."

"What's that?"

"Jack has absolutely forbidden me to do this. As Doc Mullins did before him. So, I'm trusting you."

"Oh, great. Secrets between husband and wife."

"I don't see it that way," she said. "They are confidences kept by a medical practitioner in this town. You can rest assured that when you come to me with a medical problem that you might find personal and perhaps embarrassing, Jack will never know about it."

"Well, there's a comfort," he said. Like when would that happen? When he finally had constipation? The drip?

"Well, Jesus, Noah—would you tell about my spiritual struggles?"

"You have some?" he asked almost hopefully.

"Not that I recall," she said with a shrug. "We're almost there. I'd like you to please stay in the car. You're new around here. They don't know you. It might make them skittish."

"Who?"

But before Mel answered, she pulled into a clearing. And there was a camp. Surrounding a bald spot within the trees were tents, a couple of old vehicles—one up on bricks without wheels and one that could be functional— one old dilapidated trailer, some furniture that looked as if it had been pilfered from a dump, some tarps stretched over the furniture to keep the moisture off. And a few men standing around who looked for all the world like hill-billies. They had a pot over a fire and that was it.

Mel jumped out, opened the back of the Humvee and hauled out a box. She put it onto the hood of the Hummer and waited. An old man with a gray beard that reached down to his chest ambled forward. He was skin and bones and real shaky. He nodded a little as Mel spoke to him. She reached inside the box and pulled out a large white plastic jar and held up one finger. She shook the jar and held up that one finger again, in emphasis, and the man nodded.

Noah watched in fascination. And then, although he had been told to wait in the car, he got out. Mel glared at him briefly, but didn't say anything. Noah stayed beside the passenger door, minding his own business. Then, braving her reproach, he went to the back of the Hummer and got the second box, bringing it slowly and cautiously around to the front of the vehicle.

"Anyone sick or hurt?" Mel asked the man.

He shook his head and she handed him the box.

"That's good to hear. You know where I am if you need anything medically."

He nodded without speaking and took the box off her hands. By the time he was on his way back to his tent, another man came forward from behind the old trailer. Since Noah was holding the box, he went straight to Noah.

"How are you today, brother?" Noah asked pleasantly. And the man merely nodded, not making eye contact. "Can you think of anything you need, besides the food in the box?" Noah asked. No response. "Coats? Blankets?" At that, the man lifted his beady gaze and connected with Noah's eyes. "Ah," Noah said. "Coats and blankets. That makes sense. I'll look around, see what I can find."

The man broke his gaze and merely accepted the box, taking it back where he'd come from. The entire transaction lasted under five minutes. They got back in the Hummer and Mel backed around carefully, heading down the bumpy road. "Well, you don't follow instructions very well, do you?" she asked.

"I don't know what came over me," he lied. He wasn't about to be kept back. He felt right at home. "How many of them are there?"

"Only a few now. Six or seven, maybe. The faces change—people wander in and out, stay awhile, move on. Sometimes I'll actually spot a woman. One of the men had an adult daughter with him for a while. There were more before, in a camp closer to town, but Jack and his boys ran them off."

"Why?"

"Well, it was complicated. Some drug farmer set up in their camp and there was a caretaker watching the grow who was a dangerous felon. We had an altercation—he put a knife to my throat and wanted narcotics from the clinic. Jack killed him. I mean, it was totally self-defense, you understand. It was down to me or him and Jack wasn't at all attracted to him." She turned to Noah and smiled. Then her smile vanished. "I'm sorry. I shouldn't joke. The man was going to kill me. After it was over, Jack rounded up his friends and they ran off all the old boys. He said if they couldn't keep the dangerous element out, they had to move farther away, so the town wouldn't be at risk. Turns out they didn't go that far. If they weren't on restricted land, Jack might've run across them while hunting."

"But *you* found them?"

"About a year back one of them came into the clinic. He had a nasty, infected laceration that needed debriding, antibiotics, and dressing. I told him if I knew where he'd settled, I could bring him some leftovers to eat sometimes."

"What was in that jar you showed the man?"

She laughed. "Expired prenatal vitamins. Might keep him going one more week in his life, but what the heck. The thing is, Noah, I wanted to save them. Get them bottled water at least, if not placement in some facility with clean sheets. But the fact is, this is either what they want or serves what they think they need. There's undoubtedly some addiction or mental illness at root there—alcoholism, bipolar, war disability, anything is possible, although I don't know that any of them have been evaluated. And since nothing will change it, no harm comes from a little decent food. Those old boys exist on fish and squirrel. And in the winter they almost freeze. But they won't go to town, won't go to a shelter. They know they can get help in Eureka. But they are not interested."

"And if Jack finds out?"

"He's going to make a big stink. He might run them off again. Or see if he can get some law enforcement to do it. He has a point—if they're too close to town and open to dangerous types settling in with them, that could be a big problem. But I have a point, too—it's not against the law to be homeless. They're not hurting anyone, as far as I know. If they break the law, they'll have to go, I suppose."

"Is that the only group like that you know about?" he asked.

"The only one around here I know about, but June Hudson, the doctor down in Grace Valley, she keeps an eye on an impoverished settlement near that town. She's given medical treatment to some of them. There are several families in her shantytown—some of them actually keep animals—mules, goats, chickens, like that."

"Lord," he said. "I've seen some people real hard put,

but for some reason I didn't expect it here. I guess I thought homelessness was only in the inner city, and near the docks."

"I can relate, I was likewise naive. There are lots of folks living in isolated cabins out in the hills. If we know about them, Cameron and I try to keep track of them. We'll often go together, but he just became the father of twins and has been a little scarce around town lately."

"Mel," he said quietly, "you're a missionary."

"Nah. Just doing the people's work."

"That's what a missionary is. It's not all about bible beating," he said with a grin. "You have to fill their bellies before you can expect to peek into their hearts. Are you and Cameron the only ones who know about them?"

"The exact location, maybe, but probably not. Jack knew about them when they had that old camp nearer town and he just ignored them. Until there was trouble."

"Does he have a problem with you going out to isolated cabins to check on people?"

"Sometimes someone will tell me there's no smoke coming from a neighbor's chimney, or that someone is bedridden and could use medicine, and often Jack will take me and wait in the car. Jack's been known to split logs for an old-timer who can't hoist his ax. Sometimes Cameron and I go together. I have to be real cautious. Some people really don't want to be disturbed. Some could be unstable. Even violent. Believe me, I don't venture foolishly. And don't you, either."

He smiled at her. She knew. There was a reason she had taken him, shown him and told him. Because his was also the people's work. What she didn't know was that his father was a wealthy, somewhat famous televangelist, who made a lot of noise about helping the needy and yet had never managed to get his hands dirty. He consorted

mainly with rich people. In his stable of friends were poli-
ticians, government honchos, police officials, philanthro-
pists. Anyone who could protect him in the clinches and
make him richer.

In Noah's stable of friends, so far, there was a bartender, a stripper, a cook and a midwife.

For the first time in a long time, the flavor of his life
tasted good in his mouth.

Noah's trip with Mel to the vagrants' camp in the forest presented many possibilities to a man whose soul
was fed when he could feed people. His visit to Grace
Valley to spend some time with Harry Shipton, a heck of
a nice fellow, had been likewise illuminating. They spent
two hours together and Noah learned Harry was not just
a Presbyterian minister, but also divorced and a recovering compulsive gambler. Even though he'd swindled
some local friends, the whole town had welcomed him
home after his treatment program. Here, in this little
burg, Harry had found the truest sense of forgiveness
and community.

Harry then gave Noah a tour of the town and lunch at
the Grace Valley Café. Noah met Dr. June Hudson and
her partner Dr. John Stone, and June's father, the former
town doctor, Elmer. He had an invitation from Elmer to
go fishing and get an education about a few things those
Virgin River men didn't know and couldn't learn. "No
matter what they say, I've always outfished them. Bunch
of liars, that's what they are," Elmer told him.

Grace Valley was a precious little town of quaint clap-
board houses and delightful people, but when he'd
brought up the subject of rural poverty, June and Harry
had been quick to fill him in, in detail, about their special
cases. On the surface, some of these mountain towns

looked to be thriving and healthy, but there was an underside, hidden in the trees, of both marijuana growers laying low under the law and impoverished families that June, John, Harry and a few others tried to look after.

A few days later when Mel Sheridan pulled into the vagrants' camp, Noah was seated around a weak fire with the boys, Bible in hand. Four of them sat on overturned buckets and there was a stack of army blankets beside one of them.

"Well," Mel said, approaching. "Didn't take you long to make yourself at home."

"We were just talking about Jesus in the garden of Gethsemane," he said, standing. "These guys aren't the first in history to look for answers in solitude. So—what's in your pantry today?" he asked with a smile.

Six

Noah had a couple of phone calls to make that he'd been putting off for more than a week. Mrs. Hatchet and Mrs. Nagel. He had to tell them he'd hired someone and thank them for their interest in the job. Mrs. Hatchet said, "Yes, I know. It's all around that you hired some pretty young thing."

"As it happens, she is both pretty and young, but she was hired because she has office experience and is capable of helping with the heavy work that has to be done around here. I'm sorry it didn't work out, Mrs. Hatchet, and I'm very glad I got to meet you. And I'll look forward to seeing you again."

She merely grunted and hung up.

"Mrs. Nagel," he said when he called the next woman. "Reverend Kincaid here. I just wanted to let you know that I—"

"Hired that young slut," she snapped into the phone.

"*Excuse* me?" he said, shocked and affronted.

"I'm glad I'm not going to work for you if that's the kind of man you are!"

"I see," he said calmly. "I'm sorry it didn't work out."

She gave a derisive snort before disconnecting without saying goodbye. "Whew, dodged a bullet there," he muttered into a dead phone.

Noah spent the next week door-knocking in the more rural areas of Virgin River, introducing himself and inviting people to a church that would be refurbished and open for business in a couple of months. He'd also been to Valley Hospital twice. He was now known among the volunteer women and before he even asked, he was directed to a patient who had had no visitors. While he carried a Bible and introduced himself as Reverend Noah Kincaid, he wasn't there to pray or preach unless asked. All he did was visit. He sympathized, comforted, consoled. He also laughed, shared favorite jokes, straightened linens, fluffed pillows and even gave assistance to the bathroom.

Merry had died at home, in his care. During her brief illness and chemotherapy he'd spent countless hours at the hospital. While she was reading or dozing as the chemo IV or transfusion was running, he'd make the rounds and visit with staff, patients and gathering families. He hadn't even realized he'd found a mission there. But people welcomed his friendliness and it filled a place in him. It fulfilled him.

On his way back to Virgin River, he visited the nursing home where Salvatore Salentino was living. When he stood in the doorway, the old man said, "Well, here you are again. I guess you won't give up till you convert me."

Meanwhile, Ellie and Lucy were making progress on the cleaning and painting. Ellie had finished two bathrooms and was getting to work on the kitchen. And Lucy, for all her infirmity, was getting up and down the steps like a pup…and following Ellie everywhere.

On this particular day, Noah made it back to the

church a little before three because he had an appointment with Paul Haggerty. He heard the water running downstairs and found Ellie bent over the sink, cleaning her painting gear. "I'm back, Ellie," he announced.

She glanced over her shoulder. "Boy, you have a ton of messages. The phone was ringing all day. It's a shock I got anything done around here. Why's that phone ringing all of a sudden? You run an ad for some kind of soul-saving special or something?"

"Messages?" he asked with trepidation.

"Yeah. I wrote 'em down and left 'em on the desk."

"You answered the phone?"

"What did you expect me to do? Let them all think there wasn't any minister in this town? Besides," she said, turning around to face him, "I'm supposed to assist. Right?"

He swallowed. "Um. I have a meeting with Paul Haggerty, the builder. Off the top of your head, do you remember any—"

"Well, a woman named Shelby MacIntyre wondered if you could perform a wedding in a couple of months. She's hoping there will be a church by then. Gloria Tuttle called from Valley Hospital. She's seen you around there visiting people and thought you should call her—she's one of the nurses and can tell you about patients who might want you to visit them. You're gonna wanna watch Gloria, Rev—she wants to jump your bones. She asked if you were married and when I said no, she giggled. Some old woman named Hope, who sounds like a man, called and asked how things were going and I told her we were doing our best." Then she grinned. "And there were others. A lot of 'em just want to call back. And there were hang-ups—maybe you got a number that was used too recently. Do you usually get so many calls? I can't remember the phone ringing once last week."

"What did you say?" he asked.

"To who?"

"Whom," he said, and then he almost kicked himself. "To Miss MacIntyre, for example."

She studied his face for a second and then, with a hand on her hip, she said, "I said, 'You're damn skippy he'll do a wedding—he needs the work!' What do you think I said? I took her number and told her I'd have you call her back. The same to all of them. Except the nurse—I told her she was scraping the bottom of the barrel, going after your hot pants." Then she smirked.

"You're a pain in the butt," he said.

"Yeah, so says the pot to the kettle. You thought I wasn't *smart* enough to know how to answer an office phone. I've worked in offices!"

"I know this," he informed her.

"Ah, you thought I got those jobs because I have—"

He put up a hand to stop her. "I never thought a thing," he said.

"Boobs," she finished insolently. Then she winked while she chewed vigorously on some gum. She cracked it for good measure. "I'm going to get this stuff cleaned and get out of here. I'm totally shot," she said, turning back to the sink. "Can you manage now?"

"I'll muddle through. By the way, thank you."

"For?"

"For taking messages. I appreciate it."

She grinned over her shoulder. "No problem, Your Worship. You have a good day?"

"I did," he said.

"What do you do at the hospital?" she asked.

"Visit."

"Visit?"

"There are people who don't get company, people

waiting around for someone to get out of surgery, people waiting for someone to die. It's the kind of place where a friendly face and a few kind words go a long way."

"People you know?" she asked, turning back toward him.

He shook his head. "I don't have a congregation. They're complete strangers. But that doesn't matter."

"Aw, Noah. That's nice."

"I've been trying to tell you, I am nice."

She dried her hands on a towel. "Yeah. Watch out for Gloria, toots. I think she's looking for more than *nice*."

Ellie walked back down the street from the church to her rented room, feeling that good kind of tired that comes from having worked hard and done well. She was down to sixty-seven dollars until she could pry some church money out of the fierce grip of her cute boss. Oh, how she wished he was ugly, stupid or gay, she thought for the hundredth time. Why couldn't he just be gay? That would make life so much easier.

But he was *not* gay. Rather, he had waves of testosterone rolling off him. There was that build, for one thing— powerful. And that thick hair that fell over his collar, itching for her to run her fingers through it, and the burning blue eyes, the hands… Oh, God, his *hands!* When she got up close, and if he had his sleeves rolled up, she noticed a map of tiny white scars that marred the backs of his hands and forearms. When she knew him better, she was going to ask about the scars, maybe twenty of them, but she suspected he got them when he was doing whatever he'd been doing to make his palms callused and rough. He'd only touched her a couple of times, just guiding her in a gentlemanly fashion, but she felt his rough hands. You don't get those in a pulpit.

Thinking about Noah made it difficult to remember that there would never again be a man in her life. Ever, ever, ever. She'd been hurt by men too often. Okay, there hadn't been many, but the three major contenders had been totally horrible. Death, prison and weirdness. If there'd been even one lucky break where love was concerned, she might consider another stab at it down the line a bit, but not likely. She had already proven she didn't know how to pick a man, and it was doubtful she could start now.

But he was very attractive, the preacher man. Six feet, ink-black hair with a lock that fell over his brow sometimes. Expressive dark brows over the most beautiful blue eyes she'd ever seen. And lips that just screamed Come to Papa. Then there was that smile. Or, all those smiles—the one that indulged, the one that mocked, the one that burst out of him before he could stop it. He couldn't hide the fact that for a devout sort of guy there was some bad boy in him that he was barely keeping under control. His smile came with dimples that almost brought her to her knees. Six feet of delicious man with strong shoulders, long legs and big, hard hands.

Yeah, he could get her in trouble.

But then, if she was realistic, he was a *minister.* No matter how he set her on fire, he was puritanical and pure, right? Life was just too short to forgo that playful, naughty edge. She didn't want to be in the missionary position for the rest of her life, anyway. He'd probably make love with his black socks on. And his T-shirt. Lights out, covers up, in and out real quick, no screaming. Dull and boring.

Oh, that's right, she forgot, she thought with a laugh. She was giving up *all* positions. No men, no sex, no more heartaches or headaches. But it would be easier on her nerves if he were just a little homelier.

She wondered if she should be grateful he even inspired thoughts of sex; it had been so long since she'd even been tempted. She had all but forgotten what tempted felt like. Long before Trevor was born, and it was a miracle Arnie hadn't killed it altogether.

Ellie stopped her daydreaming and realized she was almost home. When she got to her new address, she found Mrs. Fitch raking leaves and pine needles out of the flower bed in front of her porch. "Hey there, Mrs. Fitch. How's it going?"

Jo Ellen looked at her. "Fine, Ellie. Are you off early today?"

"Kind of. The reverend has an appointment and I've been starting at the crack of dawn all week. I was painting by five this morning."

"He's got you painting?" Jo Ellen asked.

"Mrs. Fitch, there's not a dirty chore in that old trash heap of a church that I'm not doing. While we get it pulled together, anyway."

"You must be exhausted."

"I feel good," Ellie said with a smile, rolling the ache out of her stiff shoulders. "Nothing like some good old hard work. You should see the bathrooms— they look great. I can tell Reverend Kincaid can't figure out how he got stuck with me, I am so *not* a churchy person, but I'll tell you what, it was his lucky day. The stuff that has to be done around there? Painting, cleaning, organizing? Heck, I've had to make do so much of my life, that's what I know best—making something decent out of a mess. Lots easier than computer programs."

Jo Ellen leaned on her rake and laughed. "Would you like some iced tea?"

Ellie ran the palms of her hands down her pant legs.

"Oh, gee, I'm a mess. I probably smell like paint and sweat, besides."

"Better than me—I smell like compost. Why don't I bring us some tea out here to the front porch. Just for a little break."

"That's awful nice of you. Thanks." *Gosh,* Ellie secretly mused, *I thought she didn't like me. I thought I had tricked her into renting me that room.*

Jo Ellen was a plain woman in her fifties, but she had a softness that made her pretty. Her hair was light brown and strung with gray, which gave it a dull appearance, and she pulled it back in a simple catch at the base of her neck. She didn't wear makeup, which made perfect sense while gardening, but then, she hadn't worn it when she first met Ellie, either. Her eyebrows had a nice arch, which made her expression pleasant. But what Ellie noticed about her for the first time, was that her complexion was clear and her skin tight and smooth. There was a little bit of sun on her cheeks and nose from her afternoon of outdoor work. And her smile, which Ellie hadn't seen much of the first day they met, was lovely.

When Jo Ellen returned with two glasses of tea on a tray with a few cookies, Ellie said, "My gosh, Mrs. Fitch, this is just so nice of you."

"It's nothing, sweetheart. And call me Jo Ellen. Or Jo—that's what my friends call me. It occurred to me that I hadn't visited with you at all since you moved into your little apartment. You've been there a couple of weeks already! I didn't want to bother you while you had your children with you, but now that you're on your own again, I want to at least make an effort to get to know you a little bit."

"I hope that's okay. About the kids," Ellie said. "Honestly, I didn't think I'd ever get to have them overnight.

It's a mess, this custody business." She sipped her tea. "Do you and Mr. Fitch have children?"

"I'm afraid not," Jo said. "I'll be honest with you—it's one of the greatest disappointments in my life. I don't have too much else to complain about, but I really wanted children."

"Oh, I'm sorry. I wish you had. My kids are the center of my world."

"It must be hard for you to be away from them."

"It's all a terrible misunderstanding, and I'm going to get it straightened out as quick as I can. When they're back with me where they belong, I'll move—I won't try to keep them here with me. I know you didn't intend that room for more than one person anyway. But don't worry, Mrs.... I mean, Jo—I won't leave you owing rent. I promise."

"I'm not worried, Ellie. That room hasn't been let in a year or more. It's nice to have someone use it again. And I happen to like children."

"It's a wonderful room," she said. "If I'd had a room like that growing up, I would've felt like a princess. I *love* it."

"I decorated it myself," Jo Ellen said.

"Have you lived around here all your life?"

"Since I got married," she said. "I met Nick when he was in the air force, stationed in Florida, and fell madly in love, married him, and when he got out of the service we moved here. He's from these parts."

"Oh, gee—is your family back in Florida?"

"Just a sister, her husband and my nieces. We don't see too much of each other. But I have friends here now. Women friends. This is a good little town." She laughed. "Real little."

"I like it," Ellie said. "The only thing that would make it better for me is if I had my kids with me."

"And where are you from?"

"Eureka. I grew up and went to high school there."

"And is your family nearby?"

"There's no one except the kids," she said. "My grandmother raised me alone and she died a couple of years ago. That's it. No brothers or sisters."

"Are your parents dead?" Jo asked cautiously.

"No, no. My mother is kind of a whack job…. Okay, not kind of—she's pretty nuts. She had me when she was real young, never would say who my father was, and just left me with my gramma. She's all over the place, traveling, constantly moving. She visited now and then when I was growing up, sends postcards sometimes, but when my gramma died, I couldn't even find her. I haven't heard from her in a long time and, really, that's okay. The last time she visited, my daughter was totally confused about who she was. They knew my gramma as gramma and my mother was horrified to think *she* was a grandmother! She pretty much ran for her life."

"Oh, what a shame. I'd love to have a daughter with children."

"Well, like I said, she's pretty nuts. But I'm not, I swear. Well, I have been known to marry stupidly, but I'm working on that."

"It's amazing how much we actually have in common," Jo said. Ellie went alert, wondering if Jo was about to tell her how *she'd* married stupidly. But she said, "Two women, transplanted to this little town, with no real family."

Ellie almost said, *But you have Mr. Fitch!* But then, she'd met Mr. Fitch, so she didn't say it. Instead she said, "Tell me about Virgin River, Jo. I hardly know anything about it, but I really like it."

An hour later, after talking and laughing and asking

each other questions, Ellie headed for a long soak in the tub and Jo finished raking up her flower beds. Ellie wanted to get to her room before crossing paths with Nick; she thought it best to give that man a wide berth. And if she wasn't totally mistaken, Jo felt the same way.

But before they parted, they made a date to have lunch together next week. Jo offered to make them sandwiches to eat on the back patio when Ellie took her break from the church. Ellie felt a rush of unexpected warmth coming from the woman, a feeling she welcomed.

Noah met with Paul Haggerty for a couple of hours, discussing what Haggerty Construction could do to help out with the renovation in the church. Noah had a lot of ideas about how he could save money by doing some of the work himself, like installing the basement flooring, refinishing the sanctuary floor, putting new glass in the windows, painting the offices, texturing and painting the basement walls.

"The first thing you have to do is paint the outside, Noah," Paul said.

"I thought maybe I could put that off, concentrate on the interior first."

"Nope," Paul said. "No one will see the inside if you don't spruce up the outside. You can't expect to draw a crowd if it looks like the same old broken-down church. In renovation, even do-it-yourself renovation, you want to start with what people see first."

"I never thought of that. I guess you're right."

"I'm right. Here's what I'm going to do for you, Noah," Paul said. "I'm going to get some measurements and get an itemized bid ready for you—one that shows the cost of a complete remodel, from ceiling to floor, including the outside. The big issue is going to be time—

if you're in this project, we can't get started until you're done sanding in the sanctuary and replacing window glass. We can't have sawdust in the paint, or scratch it up during window replacement. If you look at the numbers and decide you still want your own hand in it, I'll be happy to loan you a sander and other equipment, no charge. But, if you want us to do the whole remodel, we'll get in and out of here pretty quickly. While we're at it, we'll check all the plumbing and wiring and roof, at no extra cost to you. And I'll give you my best church price. And my best church scheduling."

"That would be great," he said. "That'll give me some good choices."

"I can deliver the bid by next week. Now, I have to measure."

So while Paul got about the business of measuring, Noah went to his office and began returning the phone calls he hadn't gotten around to earlier.

He spoke first to Shelby MacIntyre and set up a time to visit with her and her fiancé, Luke, to get the details regarding her upcoming marriage. He had a couple of other calls. One woman wondered when he'd be set up for a baptism or should she take her new grandchild to Harry in Grace Valley, and another wondered if he'd have a position for a choir director when the church was functional. And, last of all, he phoned Gloria Tuttle at the hospital. She had left all her numbers: work phone, home phone and cell phone.

"How are you, Reverend Kincaid?" she asked cheerily.

"Very well, thanks. So, I understand you're a nurse at Valley Hospital?"

"That's right. I saw you on one of your visits and a volunteer told me you stop by now and then. Your church is in Virgin River?"

"It is, but we're still in development. It's an old church and needs a lot of work. I'm trying to get it back in shape while I get to know the town. Meanwhile, I try to make a few calls at the hospital and nursing home."

"Aw, that's so thoughtful. Would it help if I could point you toward patients who don't have visitors? Or who seem particularly lonely?"

"You don't have many long-term-care patients at Valley, do you, Gloria?"

"Well, we're small, and critical-care patients are sent to larger facilities, but there's almost always someone who could use cheering up. Why don't we meet for coffee at the hospital the next time you're over this way."

"That would be helpful, thank you," Noah said. "I won't be back over there until at least next week. I have commitments here in town and a lot of work to do on the church. When will you be working?"

"It doesn't matter," she said. "I live close to the hospital and can dash over for coffee whenever it's convenient for you. Do you have my cell number and home number?"

He repeated the numbers for her.

"Then I'll look forward to hearing from you next week," she said.

They chatted for about fifteen minutes, but Noah had known within thirty seconds that Ellie was absolutely right. Gloria was interested in him. Well, at least in checking him out. He'd seen a number of nurses at the hospital, of course, but he had no idea who she was.

He supposed it was too much to hope that Gloria would ring all his chimes.

Noah liked women, rather more than he probably should. He'd never considered himself indiscriminate; however, it had never taken all that much to get him interested. And dating was a good idea, he knew that. But he had a real healthy libido. He happened to think sex was one of the best things in life. That hadn't gotten in his way when he was throwing fish and studying, but since entering the seminary, women who were attracted to him had their eye on an entirely different thing. They were setting themselves up to be Mrs. Minister, and he had entered a whole new territory. Every word or gesture, every affectionate move was translated into how it would contribute to their future together. He could hardly take a woman out on a first date without her imagining he wanted to get married. He had to use caution. And caution just didn't appeal to him. He'd talked with his best friend and mentor, George, about this.

George was now seventy. He was divorced from a first wife, a second had passed on, and he wasn't exactly indulging in lengthy or lonely grief. George had lady friends. Quite a few, in fact. "Even if you have no interest in another marriage, you should be seeing women, at least casually," George frequently told him.

"What for?" Noah asked.

"Because it rounds you out as a human being," George always answered. "You're a single man, not a hermit. You should have friends of both genders."

"What for?" Noah asked again. "I'm not into long, platonic courtships. It's painful."

George had sighed enviously. "God, how I wish I was young again."

So he would have coffee with Gloria at the hospital. They would talk and he would be friendly and kind. And she would offer to cook him dinner, poor lonely bachelor that he was, and he would wiggle out of it to keep from leading her on.

And then, although there were other things he could

be doing, he fired up the laptop and got online. He had a satellite dish on the RV, but the wireless connection he was using came from the bar. Jack invited him to make use anytime; since he installed the satellite for the TV and Preacher's computer, most of the town jumped off their connection.

Noah searched for Arnold Gunterson on Google. The only thing he came up with was his position as director of Brightway Private Elementary School. The school had a small Web site where the bios of the board of directors were posted, but the staff was only listed by name. A further search didn't turn up any Arnold Gunterson in Northern California. A statewide search turned up one other man by that name in La Jolla, and he was eighty-nine years old.

Arnie no doubt had degrees that qualified him, prior experience that proved him capable of his position, a résumé that he could give to parents of prospective students. But, he wasn't likely to give that information to Noah, not after what had passed between them.

Noah decided he'd have to find a moment to quiz Ellie on what she knew about her former husband. And then he'd figure out a way to learn about this guy's past. Because if he knew anything, just based on Arnie's behavior, he knew Arnie had a past.

When Ellie rented her small room over Jo's garage, the last thing she expected was to make a new friend. Her plan had been to be an invisible tenant—she knew Jo was nervous about her being on the property and she thought she knew why. Nick Fitch could be a problem for his wife; he had a reputation. And Ellie did not want to be part of the problem.

However, Jo invited her to lunch, then invited her

again and again, and Nick was never around for these lunches that were dedicated to women-talk. In a little over a week of lunches, Ellie felt closer to Jo than she had to a woman friend since her grandmother's passing. But when Jo pressed her for details about how this ex-husband, this stepfather, could gain temporary custody, Ellie fibbed. "I don't have much," she said. "I just don't have the means Arnie has. I rented a small place in a so-so neighborhood while Arnie has a house in a nice neighborhood. Plus, I worked nights in a bar while Arnie's trump card was being principal of an elementary school. I sure wish I knew how he managed that job—he's not patient with kids at all." She so hoped Jo wouldn't hate her when she learned the truth, which she inevitably would. Ellie just wasn't ready to reveal it yet, though she already felt great affection and trust for Jo.

"The bastard," Jo said. "Where you work has nothing to do with the kind of mother you are."

"Well, it worked for Arnie," Ellie said with a nod. "But I think we're doing all right at the moment, the kids and me. He's letting them talk to me on the phone every night and I haven't had another problem on the Saturday visits. He always gets in my face a little bit, but I never let him see me sweat. I did tell him a small lie, though. I wanted him to think he was being watched, so I said that I'd told the court where I was working and that I'd have letters from real upstanding, proper people saying I'm a good person and decent mother."

"Oh, my darling," Jo said, running her fingers across Ellie's hand. "And you will! We'll all write letters for you, if that's what it takes."

Ellie laughed. "Jo, I don't know many people. I've been scrubbing, painting, hauling trash and answering the phone."

"Is working with Noah going well?"

"It's okay. Sometimes he's a pain in the butt, but he's fair and even funny. It's busy every minute, especially when he's away from the church, which is a lot of the time lately. I run from cleaning or painting to the office to grab the phone, back and forth. There have been a lot of hang-ups, by the way. I don't know what to make of that."

"Your ex, possibly?" she asked. "Checking to see if you really work at the church?"

Ellie shrugged. "I suppose it could be. But wouldn't one call do it? Maybe it's that nurse from Valley Hospital who's chasing my boss."

"Oh?" Jo said. "Do tell?"

They talked for a while about the nurse, about the fact that Noah was a pretty good-looking guy, and then moved on to discuss about everything from the price of gas to the fact that soon the leaves would be changing color as August aged and September loomed on the horizon.

"Ellie, do you think I could meet the kids sometime?" Jo asked.

"Really? You want to?"

"I would love to," she said. "I mean, if you'd share your time. I don't want to impose—I know you don't get them often. But, let's see—Saturday. The weather's cooling. We could bake! We could make cookies and decorate them. We could color and finger paint. We could—"

"Jo! You don't have kids! You don't have all that kid stuff!"

Jo smiled patiently. "Just tell me which Saturday. I'll be ready."

Ellie was silent for a while. "Can I ask something personal?"

"You can ask me anything, Ellie."

"Why didn't you have children? You and Mr. Fitch?"

"Nature's mystery," she said with a shrug. "We were both healthy and normal, but I didn't conceive."

"Did you consider adoption?"

And that's when Jo dropped her chin, and her gaze. "Nick wouldn't hear of it. He said if he wasn't having a baby of his own he wouldn't have someone else's, not knowing where it came from." And then she lifted her gaze and met Ellie's. Just that little piece of information changed Jo's eyes and Ellie knew there was so much more to the story.

Ellie frowned and shook her head. "But adoption isn't that mysterious or secretive. Oh, there might be one or two hidden things, but that's a risk even when you have your own—that some little-known relative, or someone generations back contributed something you weren't even aware of yourself."

"I know," she said. "But that was the end of it as far as he was concerned."

"I'm sorry," Ellie said softly. "Both of mine were total accidents. And it hasn't been easy—but maybe I'm the lucky one. Of course, I have no husband, no father for them, no partner…"

"Nick made that decision a long time ago," Jo said. "Things haven't been the same between us since."

"Oh, Jo," Ellie said. "Oh, the son of a—"

"It was me," she said. And then she was quiet.

"Look, it's not my business… You don't have to—"

"I drove him crazy, trying for a baby. Then I was getting into my late thirties, it wasn't happening and I wanted to adopt a baby, but he wouldn't even talk about it. He was adamant. I've never really understood. Oh— he tried to get me to understand that the whole idea of raising someone else's child just didn't work for him, and he was getting older and ready to give up on the idea. He was happy without kids. At least happy *enough*. The truth is, I've never forgiven him for that. For depriving me of that one chance to raise children."

Ellie reached for her hand and just held it for a minute. Finally, in a very soft voice, she said, "Jo, that was a long time ago. Can't you work through that now?"

"I gave working through it a serious try—for a couple of years I was a foster parent. And it should come as no surprise, within five minutes I was attached to the children I kept. And the ones I got weren't easy kids, either, which almost proved Nick's point. Then I was depressed when they left." She laughed a little and averted her eyes. When she looked back at Ellie, she said, "These things get so complicated. I was angry, he was confused by my anger and maybe hurt by it, I was unforgiving and cold toward him, he didn't treat our marriage with the same respect… It didn't take long for us to fall into a routine where we get along, but there's nothing special between us anymore. There hasn't been for twenty years. We keep separate bedrooms."

And he flirts and gropes, Ellie thought. "Oh, man," Ellie said.

"Don't feel sorry for me," Jo said. "I couldn't stand it. Now," she said, brightening purposefully. "There's still plenty of time in my life to enjoy friends and their children! If you feel like spending a Saturday just hanging around here, playing, having fun—I would absolutely love it."

"You're sure?"

"Ellie, having you around has been so good for me. When I first saw you, all I could think was that you'd tempt Nick and I'd be embarrassed again, like I've been so many times. But it didn't work that way. Instead, we got close, you and me. Two women with odd pasts and a lot to overcome. I find myself telling you things I haven't talked about in years. It would be a privilege to meet your kids, to have all of you for the day."

"And Nick?" Ellie asked cautiously.

"If he isn't the most polite person on earth, I will shoot him in the head."

Ellie laughed at her. "Wow. A little fight looks good on you. Okay then," she said, giving her head a nod. "Next Saturday it is."

Ellie realized that despite the struggles she'd encountered along the way, wonderful people had always happened into her life. Her grandmother had been her angel. Her first love, Jason, had given her joy, and his loss was her heartache, but Danielle had her father's sweet disposition and bright eyes. And Chip might be a big dumb loser, but Trevor was a gift.

Her boss at that club had been a real stand-up guy who watched out for his employees. A couple of old bosses still helped her when they could, like the lawyer she'd worked for. Her neighbor in the duplex had been there for her in ways she could never repay; a trusted babysitter was priceless. Noah, without a doubt, had given her a big break, at some risk to his own reputation.

And then, unexpectedly, there was Jo.

Saturday came and while Jo hadn't gone overboard, she had been ready to show Danielle and Trevor a good time. There was chilled cookie dough, ready to roll, cut, bake and decorate. The kids finger painted at Jo's big kitchen table. And there were books to read in the hammock strung between two huge trees.

Nick was at home, and while he wasn't underfoot, he did make his presence felt between cutting the grass and watching sports on TV in the den. He joined them all for a nice lunch on the patio and joked with the kids in an affable way. To Ellie's surprise, after what Jo had told her, it seemed they actually had a very good rapport. And what a loss that he hadn't tried parenting—he was good with the kids, too.

Ellie got to thinking—this couple got derailed in their marriage over an issue major to both of them, and they had lost the ability to compromise. Ellie's children had come while she was so young, and in such a shocking, scary way, she had never had to endure the frustration that some other women went through. In fact, before now, Ellie had never known any women friends who wanted children passionately and, for whatever reason, couldn't have them. The closest she came to really understanding the plight was a movie—*Steel Magnolias*—in which Julia Roberts's character risked her life to have a baby. That bespoke a desire so primal, so desperate, it was small wonder it could mess up an otherwise good relationship.

From the way Jo and Nick both interacted with the children, you'd never know they hadn't been parents. And they seemed good together, as well; positive and even affectionate.

It began to fall into place for Ellie. She wasn't sure, but it was possible that Jo and Nick had once enjoyed a strong and loving marriage. Then they had a standoff over adoption and went to separate bedrooms. Whatever their arrangement was—he worked and paid the bills and she managed the home—there was at least some residual fondness there. But now Nick was flirting with other women and in a very wayward and foolish way, making passes. Could he be lonely? Hungry for both affection and some bolstering of his self-esteem?

"This has been such a fun day," Jo said to Ellie. "You

know, I have friends in this town, plenty of them, but I don't think I'm as close to some women I've known for twenty years as I am to you. There's something different about having you here. If I'd had a daughter when I wanted one, she would probably be about your age. She might have children like Danielle and Trevor. I hope that isn't too presumptuous of me, saying that."

"Oh, Jo, that's so sweet! If I could choose the kind of mother to have, it would be someone like you. Someone kind and stable and a friend I could depend on." And she thought maybe Jo's eyes had misted a little when she said that.

So there it was—Jo and Nick had parted while staying under the same roof, and the bitterness from their individual wounds had resulted in Nick's bad behavior and sullied reputation, and Jo was lonely and unable to hold her head up in her town.

If they wanted to, Ellie wondered, could they unravel their twenty-year-old quarrel and rebuild? Was it possible?

Seven

When Paul and Vanessa Haggerty decided they wanted to settle in Virgin River rather than Paul's home of Grants Pass, Oregon, he set up a part of his family's construction company in Virgin River. It had proven a positive choice for them, but it did require that Paul visit his father and brothers for a company business meeting about once a month. Vanni and little Matt, now eighteen months, were almost always with him, but this time she wasn't free to go—she was helping her cousin Shelby plan her wedding. So Paul decided to drive up on Thursday and come back on Friday afternoon rather than spend the weekend away from the family.

When he arrived at the office, his brother North shook his hand and said, "Hey, perfect timing. I just hung up with some lawyer by the name of Hanson. Does the name Terri Bradford ring a bell?"

The past came rushing back to Paul. "It does. Why?"

"Seems she died recently. Car accident or something. The lawyer called because there's a will."

"Died?" he asked, stunned. "A will?"

"That's what he said. Apparently she left you something. You know, in the will."

Paul was stunned and speechless. Dead? Terri was young, pretty, fun—it was just wrong, her being *dead.* "I can't imagine why she'd leave me anything," he said. "Did he say what it was? Really, I didn't know her that well."

"How *did* you know her?" North asked. "I mean, you don't have to tell me if it's personal. But—"

"It's not personal. I went out with her a few times before I married Vanni. You know—back before Matt died in Iraq and all that. It was pretty casual between us."

Except, it hadn't been quite that tidy. True, Paul had dated Terri a few times before Matt was killed in Iraq. Also true, it had been casual. She was a real pretty single girl and Paul had had no one in his life. He had been carrying a torch for Vanni, but she was married to his best friend, Matt, and pregnant with their child. But then Matt was suddenly gone, the baby was born with Paul's assistance, and Paul was all messed up in grief and guilt and regret…and hopeless love for Vanessa. In just that state, looking for someone to talk to, someone who might understand, he'd spent the night with Terri.

Then began a real mess. Terri told him she was pregnant with his child and Paul had been prepared to take care of her, but ultimately Terri admitted the baby wasn't his after all. Medical tests proved that to be true and they parted company amicably. He even offered to help her anyway. He had liked Terri; she'd been very sweet to him when he was in a bad place in his emotional life.

"Why would she leave me anything?" he thought aloud.

"Here's the lawyer's number," North said, handing him a piece of paper. "Give him a call and ask him. Then let's get everyone around the table and look at the company's last month's performance. Huh?"

"Yeah," Paul said.

The lawyer, Scott Hanson, wouldn't reveal anything over the phone. He said he'd prefer to see him in person to explain Terri's will. That was the usual protocol, he explained. Hanson gave him an appointment for the next morning so there would be plenty of time for Paul to get back to Virgin River before dinnertime.

When he talked to Vanni that evening, he told her about this unexpected development. "Oh, Paul, that's just awful that she would die so young," Vanni said. "What about her child?"

"Honey, I never spoke to her again after she told me the baby wasn't mine. I don't even know if she kept the baby. And I can't for the life of me guess what she would want me to have."

"Some memento of time you spent together?" Vanni asked. "When you dated?"

"I can't think of a thing," he said. "I don't feel connected to Terri. Just enough to be sorry she lost her life so young. Whatever she left me, I'll just ask the lawyer to give it to her next of kin."

"Paul, you don't have to do that on my account. I wasn't jealous of her before and I'm certainly not jealous of her now. Just be polite and thank the man. Then get home—we have a baby to make."

Vanni had just decided, to Paul's great happiness, now that little Matt was eighteen months old, she was ready to get pregnant again. Paul thought of little Matt as his own, but the idea of a baby carrying his own DNA would thrill him.

Paul had once been to the law office where Terri worked, but he'd never met her boss. It turned out to be Scott Hanson, also the executor of her will. After the introductions, Paul sat facing Scott's desk. "Let me skip the suspense, Paul. Terri had absolutely no way of predicting she would suffer an accidental, premature death. It was a traffic accident. But, Terri was savvy when it came to the law, and given her family situation, she made sure her affairs were in order."

"Her family situation?" Paul asked.

"Her mother has advanced MS and her parents have been divorced since Terri was a toddler, she had almost no contact with her father. Last time he came up in conversation, she had no idea where he was. And she was the single mother of an infant daughter."

"Ah," Paul said. "I knew she was expecting."

"She wants you to be the child's guardian. She'd like you to adopt her."

Paul's face was frozen in shock. His mouth stood open and his eyes were huge. "But…" He cleared his throat. "But, it's not my child."

Scott Hanson took a breath and folded his hands on his desk. "I apologize for the shock. And for the irregularity. When preparing a will and living trust for a client, it's customary to request guardianship from the adult you have in mind for the job. When I asked Terri about your willingness to take this on, she said you were a good man, would be a good father, had offered to help her even though she wasn't carrying your child, and of all the people in her life, you were the only one who came to mind. The fact that she hadn't gotten your consent to be so named was irrelevant to her as she only set up her will as a far-fetched precaution. Of course, she expected to live to be an old woman. She was in excellent health and of sound mind. She also fully expected to meet the right man one day and give Hannah a stepfather who would always be there for her. And who, of course, would replace you as guardian in the will." He took a breath. "Obviously she thought you would never know how highly she regarded you."

Paul scooted forward on his chair. "What do you know about our relationship?" he asked Hanson.

"Really? Hardly anything at all. That you were friends. That you were close."

Paul was shaking his head. "That's a stretch. We dated a few times. I mean a *few*. She tried to convince me it was my baby, but she knew all along it wasn't and before that whole thing went too far, she admitted it. What about the father?"

"According to Terri, the father bolted. There's a name on the birth certificate, but Terri collected documentation from him indicating he wasn't interested in any relationship with his child so that Terri would be free to have that future 'right man' adopt her daughter."

"We should contact him," Paul said. "Because things have changed. She's dead."

Scott Hanson leaned forward. "That's an option. You can certainly do that if you want to. But it's been my experience that people with that level of disinterest don't make good parents. I urge you to think about the baby. About Hannah."

"Mr. Hanson, I can't do this! My wife and I have been married just over a year. She was widowed when her husband was killed in Iraq and I've been a father to her son. He's a year and a half and we've just decided it's time for another child, one of my own. I can't do this. I can't take on the child of a woman I hardly knew."

"I understand, Mr. Haggerty. Believe me. I knew this outcome was a strong possibility."

"Then what will happen next?"

"Foster care for now. She'll be available for adoption

and I can handle those details. She's a beautiful, healthy little girl and there's a trust for her care and education—liquidation of Terri's personal effects and life insurance money. She'll find a family."

"A family with an eye on a trust?" Paul asked, lifting a cynical brow.

"It's not a lot, as money goes," Hanson said. "Almost a hundred grand. That's either a good college education or averages less than five thousand a year to help defray some of the costs of raising her. As a father I can tell you, it's a pittance."

"She'd be better off with no trust," Paul grumbled. "How can you tell whether the couple who wants to adopt her has their eye on the money?"

"Lots of ways, actually. She's a beautiful, healthy baby under a year old—I imagine a couple who's been in the system looking for such a baby for a long time will apply. Someone who might otherwise find it difficult to adopt."

Might otherwise find it difficult rolled over in Paul's mind. Could a couple with health issues find this to be their lucky day? Could a couple with financial problems see it as a windfall? Aw, Terri, Terri, he thought in near despair. "Well, as much as I'd like to help out, this is an impossible situation for me," Paul said.

"I understand completely. Frankly, if my wife and I hadn't just put the last of four children into college, we'd consider taking little Hannah into our home—we were very fond of Terri and grew close to the baby. In fact, we've kept her since Terri's untimely death and it will be hard to part with her. But we've raised four kids, are grandparents now and have worked hard to get to this place in life. I don't think I'm up to another twenty years."

Paul judged Scott Hanson to be in his late fifties, maybe early sixties, healthy and strong. Paul was just trying to start a family, and he was sneaking up on forty. Boy, could he relate. "I understand," Paul said. "Since Terri's death, has anyone come forward asking if they could be considered as her guardian?"

"No one," Scott said.

"Isn't that odd? I mean, she was a young woman. The night I met her, there were girlfriends. I know she had relationships with young women her age and—"

"You're right, she did indeed. And one of the reasons she decided you were the person to be named was that you're in a stable marriage and earn a decent living. She talked about your values, she admired you, Mr. Haggerty. Terri's close girlfriends are single women, just getting started in life, mostly unmarried, trying to get on their feet. I didn't expect any of them to step forward. They're nice girls, but not ready for a family. In point of fact, Terri wasn't ready, either. A lot changed in her life when she found out she was expecting a child. She got real serious about her future."

"Aw, man…" Paul was remembering. Back when he wasn't sure whether Terri's baby was his, he asked Vanessa if she could accept him with that baggage, and she said, *Of course. We don't leave our babies out there without our love and protection.* When he had forced Terri to agree to an ultrasound as a means of determining the time of conception, establishing the baby wasn't his, he had seen that little mass, the fluttering heart, and his first insane reaction had been *disappointment!* He knew that without his help, she wouldn't be able to do the best possible job of taking care of that little wonder. The results of the test let him off the hook, and he felt sorry for her. Sad. It wasn't his baby after all, but it could have been. *He* had *been intimate with her.* He'd used protection, but still—he'd been with her.

"There must be family somewhere," Paul said.

"Shirttail relatives back in Missouri," Scott said. "Terri hadn't seen them since she was a little girl. That's it. There's just one more thing I have to do before we close the book on this issue and I move on to the matter of placing Hannah," Scott said.

"What's that?" Paul asked.

"I just have to introduce you to her."

"Naw. Come on now, I don't have to see her. That'll just make matters harder. I mean, come *on*."

Scott Hanson touched a button on his phone console. "We can't let it come back on either one of us, Mr. Haggerty. We have to go through the steps. Right now the idea of taking custody of an anonymous child is complicated and inconvenient. You have to see Hannah so that the human factor is involved, so that your decision is based on all the facts."

"I wish you wouldn't—"

"It's required, Mr. Haggerty," he said as he stood. At precisely that moment the door to his office opened.

A smiling young woman, presumably an administrative assistant or social worker, entered carrying a simply beautiful baby of about ten months. She had Terri's dark hair, but in large curls that circled her head. Her eyes were so big they dominated her face. Her round cheeks were pink, she had a little, rosy, heart-shaped mouth, and she lifted her hand in the air and grinned hugely, showing two brand-new front teeth. And she said, "Ma!" before her hand dropped. But her smile continued and she clutched her fat little hands together and giggled.

"Mr. Haggerty, meet Hannah Bradford," the young woman said.

"Oh, God," Paul said.

And little Hannah said, "Ha!" And then she giggled again.

Paul did the dumbest thing. He put out his big hands toward her and she fell right into them. She put her chubby arms around his neck and buried her face there, blubbering into his neck.

"Think about it, Paul. I can't complete an adoption for a couple the mother didn't know and didn't name in her will very quickly. There will be red tape, it'll take weeks," Scott said.

"Will you take her home with you?" Paul asked.

Scott shook his head. "I'm afraid my wife and I have family commitments. We could squeeze Hannah in, but it would be complicated with the kids, grandkids. But I'll make sure Hannah gets quality foster care...."

Paul nuzzled her. She smelled heavenly. Then he lifted his head and looked at Scott. "Can I foster her until my wife and I have had a chance to make a final decision?"

The lawyer shrugged. "I don't see why not. Terri had you in mind anyway."

Paul held little Hannah close. "Vanessa is going to string me up by the balls and take strips of flesh off me with a dull blade...."

Scott laughed in spite of himself. "That would be Mrs. Haggerty?"

"Today she is," Paul answered.

"Should you call her first? Before taking Hannah home?"

"That would make sense," Paul said. "But I'm the one who owes Terri. I probably don't owe her this much, but I—" Terri tried to trick him into believing he was this child's father and it almost cost him the woman he loved. Why he thought he owed her was— "Terri was very kind to me when I was having a real hard time."

But it wasn't so much that as this precious child in his arms. Hannah. It wasn't her fault her mother was suddenly gone and the only person Terri had been able to think of was Paul.

"Let me ask you something—does Mrs. Haggerty like children?"

"She wants a houseful. I was really looking forward to starting on that."

"Did you ever discuss a possible adoption?"

"No. And we sure never talked about adopting an ex-girlfriend's offspring." Paul sighed heavily. "She's going to kill me," he muttered. Then he said to Scott, "I'm going to need a car seat. And all her stuff."

Paul was all checked out on the car-seat installation because of little Mattie. He rigged up the mirror so he could see her from the driver's seat. The truck bed was filled with her gear, from crib to high chair. He was a little rusty on changing and cleaning up a little girl baby—but he had nieces and had been roped into babysitting a few times when they were small, so it all came back to him.

He could have called Vanessa before heading out of Grants Pass to say, "She left me a child." But frankly, the whole thing scared him to death. He just made sure Hannah was dry and clean, gave her a bottle to drink as they started the trip and headed for home.

"I should've called her," he told Hannah. "That was stupid, not calling. It would have given her a good four hours to think. But see, when I thought about taking you home, it was obviously a bad idea. Just didn't fit into our family plan. All that made sense, until I saw you. Until you blew raspberries on my neck."

Hannah took the bottle out of her mouth and belched loudly.

"Good one!" Paul said, praising her. "Drink the rest of that bottle and close your eyes. It's a long drive."

"Ma!" she said loudly.

"Unfortunately, you're stuck with me. But, hey, you might try that 'Ma!' thing on Vanessa when you meet her. You're going to need all the help you can get."

He drove in silence for a while, barely hearing the soft suckling sound of Hannah finishing her bottle. In a voice quiet enough that the little girl might not have heard, he said, "Your mother was a good person. She was beautiful like you and very funny. That's why I called her the first time—she was fun. I think you got her sense of humor. And obviously she wanted the best for you. Not that I'm the best—but the way she looked out for you, in case something happened, that's what a mother who cares does—makes sure you're going to be okay." He cleared his throat. "And I'll make sure. Me and Scott Hanson— we'll make sure."

He thought he should probably rehearse what he was going to say to Vanessa, but nothing came to mind. It wasn't exactly that he took one look at the beautiful little girl and completely reversed his position. Not at all. It still didn't work into his plans for the future. But he did take one look and decided you don't just turn your back on a human being, a helpless child, and leave her to a system that may not serve her best interests. Someone had to be her advocate. And while Paul didn't think it should be him, he really couldn't think of anyone better for the job. Certainly not a biological father who had abandoned her when she was a mere seedling.

Paul pulled into a parking lot before heading into Virgin River to change and freshen Hannah, smear a little lotion on her and make sure she looked and smelled extra sweet. God, but she was beautiful. And while he carried her on his hip to walk to the trash can to pitch the dirty diaper, she put her arms around his neck and pressed her mouth against his cheek four straight times, a baby kiss that didn't quite pucker, and then she giggled.

And Paul cried.

He pulled her close and tears ran silently down his cheeks. He gulped a few times. His voice was a whisper. "See, I wasn't in love with her, but she was a very good person. She wanted you very much, even if she had to go it alone. I was almost sorry it turned out I wasn't your dad. That would've given you one more person to protect you."

And she put her lips against his cheek again.

"This shouldn't have happened to you," he said, smoothing her curls with his big, callused hand. "You shouldn't have been left with no one."

"Ma!" She put her head down on his shoulder.

"Come on, lollipop. We gotta take you to meet the family." He took a deep breath. "Brace yourself."

When he pulled up to his house, he gave the horn a toot. He pulled Hannah out of the car seat and held her on his hip. Vanessa came out onto the porch, Mattie toddling behind her.

"Guess what Terri left me?" he said.

Vanessa was stunned into total silence, staring at Paul with a baby on his hip. Mattie clung to her leg.

"Don't panic," Paul said. "Let's just talk for a few minutes."

"Oh, God," she said, her eyes as round as doughnuts. "Paul, what have you done?"

He took a breath. "The only thing I could think of at the time," he said lamely.

Vanessa turned and, taking Mattie by the hand, walked back into the house.

Paul followed, without even grabbing Hannah's diaper bag. They sat in the great room opposite each other, Mattie on Vanni's lap and Hannah on Paul's. Paul thought this was what a family-counseling session must look like when the family is at odds—separated by space, watching each other warily.

"Why?" Vanessa asked with a desperate sound.

"Why what?" Paul returned.

"Why would she leave you her *child?*"

Paul shrugged. "The lawyer said she thought I was a good person. In a stable marriage…"

"You call this *stable?*" Vanessa asked, trying to control her voice, trying not to cry. "Oh, Paul… Is this really your child and you lied to me?"

"No, Vanni, I've never lied to you about anything. She's not mine. But I told you a long time ago, I offered to help Terri. I told her if she ever needed anything, she could get in touch with me through the Grants Pass company, through my family. I did that because I felt bad for her. And we did have a relationship. Not one I'm real proud of, but we did. It turns out she died without anybody able or willing to take on this child. The grandmother's sick, the grandfather's absent, and there's no family."

"And you told her you'd be there for her?" Vanni asked.

"Yeah, well, I really expected her to call if she was a little short of cash or something.…"

"Why did you bring her home, Paul? Without talking to me first?"

Paul stiffened a little and firmed his jaw. "Because I didn't know what else to do. The lawyer who Terri worked for, who did her will and trust, he and his wife are fond of her and have been taking care of her, but they're grandparents and they've already raised four kids. Honest to God, if he'd asked to keep her, I would have walked away, knowing she was in good hands. But he's not up to it, Vanni. And she's not a stray puppy. She's a living, breathing person."

Vanni scooted forward on the sofa. "What about her biological father?"

"He doesn't want her," Paul said, instinctively pulling Hannah protectively closer. "We should talk about this, think about it, and if it's not possible for us, if it's not the best thing all around, Mr. Hanson will help us find a loving home for her. But I think we should at least try. We can talk about it and try it out a little bit."

"Why? Did you maybe care about that woman a lot more than you told me?"

He took a breath. "I don't care if this makes sense or not, but Terri entrusted this child to me. To my care. And she was a friend. And she's dead. And this little girl has no one. No one, Vanessa." He stared at his wife. "As a favor to me, will you at least think about the possibility?"

"What about a child of our own? What about that?"

"Is that out of the question? Because you said you wanted a houseful. You're wonderful at it."

"Paul, are you clueless? She's what—about nine months? Ten? Mattie's eighteen months. I had my IUD removed! I could have another one in nine months! You don't just bring home a baby under a year old and say, 'Here—add one more in diapers!' How wonderful do you think *any* woman can be at this?"

Right on cue, Hannah lifted her little hand in the air toward Vanessa and said, "Ma! Ma, Ma, Ma!"

"Oh, God," Vanessa said. And tears rolled down her cheeks because she didn't want to turn her back on this little girl any more than Paul did, but the enormity of the task was overwhelming. And the fact that the baby was Terri's didn't make it easier.

"I couldn't just walk away without even trying," Paul said.

Vanessa shook her head. "How can you love and hate the same thing about a man?" she asked quietly.

"Huh?"

"I love that you're so sensitive, so giving," she said just above a whisper. "But do you have any idea what you've done? I don't want your ex-girlfriend's child to raise and I *still* can't let you take her away now!"

"I'll help. I'll get you some help."

"We're not doing that well financially. Building in Virgin River is barely getting off the ground."

"There's a little money for her care," Paul said. "But I don't want to touch that while you're still thinking about it…"

"While *I'm* still thinking about it?" she asked, sitting forward a little. "Paul, you've made up your mind, haven't you?"

He hated that—how she could read him before he even had a chance to open his stupid mouth and put his foot in it. He shrugged and said, "I've gotten to know her a little bit. And I don't want her to be all alone." He bounced her on his knee. "I'll work out the money thing. It's not critical yet. We'll be all right. Business is fine."

"Oh, Paul," she said, and tears fell from her eyes. She blinked her eyes closed and shook her head. "Why couldn't you have at least talked to me first?"

He looked down at Hannah. "You would have said the sensible thing," he said. "The thing I should've been strong enough and smart enough to say. That this was a bad idea."

"And what would you have done then, Paul? What

would you do if I said that while we talk about this and think about this, she can't stay here?"

"As God is my witness, Vanessa, I don't have the first idea."

Paul unloaded the back of his truck while Hannah sat in the playpen with Mattie. At least there was no problem there—Mattie was a real easygoing kid and he took to her instantly. Vanessa stood guard in case there were any bad manners. Paul set up the crib but left everything else to put away later. Then he put Hannah back in the car seat and drove into town, hoping to catch Mel and Cameron at the clinic before they left for the day.

It was not yet four o'clock, but when he walked into the clinic, he found Mel talking with Cameron while Cameron was loading what looked like files into his satchel.

"Hey," Paul said.

"Well now, who do we have here?" Mel asked, coming out from behind the reception counter.

"Remember that situation I had up in Grants Pass? Before Vanni agreed to marry me? The woman who said she was pregnant?" As it happened, he had gotten advice from both Mel and Cameron at the time.

"But I thought…?" Mel shook her head, confused.

"Yeah, I escaped that one," Paul said. "Meet Hannah, Terri Bradford's baby. Terri was killed in a car accident a couple of weeks ago and it turns out she named me as Hannah's guardian, though I'm not her biological father. I just found out this morning. And brought her home."

"Whoa," Cameron said.

"Good God," Mel added.

"I have her medical records and she seems perfectly healthy," Paul said. "Cam, would you mind taking a look to be sure? For our peace of mind? We don't want to suddenly find her sick or put Mattie at any kind of risk."

"Of course."

"I feel like a freak," Paul said. "I feel like a monster. Like I'm taking a puppy to the vet to make sure the pedigree is all right."

Cam came around the counter and reached for the baby. She gave her hands a clap, grinned at him and went to him willingly. "Don't feel that way. It's for her safety and yours. I'll make sure she's up to date on shots, checkups, all that stuff."

Paul just shook his head. "I've never been around a child so sweet natured. I'm afraid the other shoe's going to drop and she's going to start screaming her head off. Since I first met her this morning, she's done nothing but smile and coo."

"Isn't that nice? How's Vanni doing with the news?" Mel asked.

"I kind of dumped this on her. I was afraid to call her, so I just brought Hannah home. Vanni's in shock. We just barely started trying for one of our own."

"Oh, boy," Cam said. "Speaking as one who hasn't slept through the night since Julia and Justin were born in June, I can imagine her hesitancy."

"Yeah, she pretty much wants me dead right now." He rubbed a hand across the back of his neck. "But what was I gonna do? Do you say no thank-you to a living, breathing, beautiful human being who needs a home? Do you say, shove her in a foster home while I think it over?" He shook his head. "This might not be the most convenient thing, but I couldn't do that."

"Thank God it was you and not me," Cameron said. "If I brought another child home to Abby and newborn twins, I *would* be dead." He jiggled the baby. "Come on, little girl. Let's look you over." He reached for the envelope that held her medical records. "I won't be long." He took Hannah to an exam room.

When Cam was not in the room, Mel took a chance. "It's none of my business, but have you been in touch with the mother all this time?"

"Not a word," Paul said, shaking his head. "Last time I saw her, she was four months pregnant and crying. She'd tried to trip me up and Cameron set us up with a doctor in Grants Pass to do an ultrasound that showed she was about a month more pregnant than I was around for. She was miserable, so sorry she'd done that to me. You know, I thought about checking on her to make sure she was okay. I thought that would be the kind thing to do, but I didn't want to set up any kind of expectations."

"I guess you didn't need to," Mel said.

"I told her to get in touch if she ever needed anything. I didn't exactly mean something like this."

"Are you planning to keep her, Paul?"

"What am I going to do? Give her away? Vanni's thinking about it. I guess if it just won't work for us, I'll get the lawyer's help to find a loving family for her. But Mel, when someone has enough faith in you to entrust you with their child, do you do that?"

"Maybe the larger question is, does anyone have the right to leave you a child to raise without talking to you about it first?"

"She didn't think it would happen," he said. "It was a car accident. She was just being cautious. Getting her legal ducks in a row. You gotta give her some credit for that."

"But still… Don't be too hard on Vanessa. I'm assuming she never even met the woman." Paul shook his head. "Lord, what a huge undertaking."

"And then again, just one more. One that actually needs us right now."

"Can I give you some advice?" Mel asked.

"Shoot. I'm wide-open."

"This is your marriage, your family. Be absolutely sure you're both of like mind. Kids put a strain on the happiest of marriages, and if it's one that came to you in a real unconventional way, you don't want any bitterness about the whole affair. I mean, you could be unhappy if Vanessa just can't take her on, she could be bitter if she takes her on because you want it so much. Think about some counseling before you make a final decision."

"That's probably a good idea," he agreed. "I'll bring that up with Vanni."

"It wouldn't hurt to show her a lot of appreciation for even considering taking in an old girlfriend's child."

"Sure. Of course. And, Mel? This is awkward, but there being no drugstore in Virgin River... Would you happen to have condoms on hand?"

She frowned and tilted her head. "Condoms?"

His face took on a red stain. "You pulled Vanni's IUD, right? She told me if I get her pregnant on top of all this, she can't be responsible for her actions."

"Oh!" Mel laughed. "Sure, I'll fix you up. But for future reference, Connie keeps some under the counter at the Corner Store." Mel went to the cabinet where she kept supplies like prenatal vitamins and brought out a box of a dozen. She handed them to Paul. "May the force be with you."

"The odds are pretty good, I'm not going to be invited to use these for a while."

Eight

Paul delivered his bids and Noah was impressed with the detail. Noah thought about it for a while and then conceded that Paul was right about having his crews do the bulk of the heavy work in the church. Noah's job was to pick out the flooring and type of ceiling he wanted for the basement, plus paint for all the remaining walls. There was still plenty that needed his hand—painting the two offices, buying appliances for the church kitchen, arranging for the delivery and installation of pews, not to mention receiving and moving in his personal shipment, which included books and an old piano.

Before Paul left the bids with him, he said, "Noah, you're actually a counselor, aren't you? Like a real one?"

"A real one?" Noah asked.

"I mean, you're not just a minister, but a— Ah, hell, what I mean is, we're not religious people. You know? I pray all the time, but I'm looking for something practical. Like marriage counseling. You know what I mean?"

Noah smiled. "I can manage that, Paul. Need a little help?"

"I do," he said, and then he explained, from the beginning, the situation with himself, Terri Bradford, his wife—and the will.

"Whoa," Noah said. "Things a little upside down at your house?" he asked.

Paul shook his head dismally. "We should have some help. There's some Ph.D. over in Grace Valley who does counseling, there's always Mel, who isn't a real counselor but she sure is smart and helpful. And maybe there's you. But, Noah, meaning no disrespect—I don't want to pray my way through this. I want to get Vanni and me what we need."

"No offense taken," Noah said. "I'm all-purpose. Let's set up a time."

In order to be prepared for when Paul had his work done, Noah had to go about the business of choosing additional items for the church. He admitted his obvious limitations and asked Ellie to help him with the selections. They spent days driving from Fortuna to Eureka and even to Redding, shopping and buying.

There was a lot of time for talk while driving and over lunch. He was relieved to learn that Arnie hadn't given her any more trouble over the Saturday visits, but was disappointed that she had so little concrete information about Arnie. "He said he grew up in Southern California, went to high school and college there, that his parents are dead and that he came here from a big private school in Arizona. I saw his framed diplomas, but I can't remember the names of the schools."

"I'm suspicious of him, Ellie. Of his past. I looked him up on the computer, but I can't find anything on him. I'll have to think about where to look next."

Ellie did have news that brought him great peace of mind. She had called Brie Valenzuela. "She's going to look into this custody thing and see if anything can be done. I *love* that woman! When I told her what had happened, she was really pissed off! I told her I'd pay her somehow, but she said I could take my good old time about it—she believed I was good for it. And she promised to discount her time for me because I'm struggling right now. She said going against judges' decisions is dicey. I guess it makes them pissy."

Noah laughed. "Does it now?"

"She's going to call Child Welfare Services and have them visit Arnie. She knows a couple of people there she's worked with before. They'll take a closer look at the way Arnie's taking care of the kids. But on paper it might not look like he's a bad parent. You know—taking away privileges when they misbehave, giving them chores, that kind of thing. The thing they won't understand is that the kids don't really misbehave. I know I sound real biased, but they're awful good kids."

Noah knew all about this sort of thing. His father looked good on paper. How can a report show the contempt in a parent's features? The narrowness of the eyes when he calls you stupid? The sheer glee on his face when he can cancel something like summer camp because you didn't curl the garden hose up right? And his father was one of the greatest men of God known in the Midwest. Kindness, humility and devotion should have been starched into his bones, but he was arrogant and cruel. How does that happen?

And how did he know Ellie was such a great mother? He didn't know how he knew, but he was sure. It was something about the way she touched the children and talked to them. They craved safety and comfort in her arms and she enfolded them so bravely, so selflessly. Their need for her, their love, it was unmistakable in their voices, on their faces. Anyone who stayed awake all night to watch them sleep, to hold them because it would be so long before she could do so again… Oh, God help him, he didn't care if she did lap dances to keep them as well as she could. At least it mattered to her that they be safe and well fed.

And then something occurred to him. "Ellie, can I ask you a very personal question?" he asked.

"Knock yourself out," she said. "It's not like I have anything private left. I've told you pretty much everything."

Still, it took him a moment. "Your job. Your dancing job. Did you like it?"

She looked across the front seat at him while he kept his eyes focused on the road. "Yeah," she said. "It was an okay job." Then she took a breath and decided to cut him some slack. "Okay, it wasn't the taking-off-your-clothes part I was crazy about. That's something you do in private for a husband or lover. I was doing it for money, and getting leered at by strange men doesn't turn me on. In fact, if you don't fight it real hard, it can be humiliating.

"But there was stuff to like," she went on. "First of all, there were some real nice girls there. They weren't all great—some were a pain in the butt. But I got kind of close to a couple of girls, and I liked the bouncer and his wife, and the owner. The owner is a good guy, always watching out for everyone. He kept a clean club, he didn't want a big hassle from the cops, so it was drug-free. If he caught anyone using or turning tricks on the side, they were *gone*. And the customers were careful because Clint, the bouncer, was a bulldog. All I had to do was wiggle around a lot and get down to a thong. And for that, I had money, protection and friends. To a girl like me— that's living large."

A girl like me? "How long did you work there?"

"Not quite three months. And before you ask, it's the only job like that I ever had. I did secretary work, waitressed, cleaned houses and offices, worked nights at the convenience store, worked on a shipping dock at a big retailer's for a while. But that club job paid the best and the hours were good for a mother. And get this—it came with benefits. I hated letting go of the benefits."

"But didn't you ever have to do things you didn't like?"

"I didn't *like* taking my clothes off," she stressed. "But, that was the job and I needed that job."

"What about things like, you know, lap dances?" he asked.

"Oh, my goodness, Your Reverence! You *know* about lap dances?"

"Don't screw with me," he said. "It wasn't easy to ask…"

"Isn't *screw* a swearword?" she taunted.

"It's on the cusp. So?"

It was her turn to be quiet for a second. "You really want to know?"

He turned and met her eyes briefly. "If you don't mind telling me, I'd like to know how it affected you. That's all."

"Well, Noah, it was like this," she said. He'd already learned that when she called him by his name, she was about to be both serious and candid. "That was also part of the job. I didn't take off the thong and they weren't allowed to put hands on me, but it was awful. I hated it. That's another thing you do for a husband or lover, a man you've given your heart and commitment to, not for a paying customer. So what I had to do was turn off my brain. Send my mind to another place. I learned to think about jets and ocean liners and hot-air balloons rather than what I was doing. And when it was over, I totally forgot about it. I scrubbed the details from my mind—the face, the smile, the smell of him, everything. And I never remember again. I do not ever once think about a lap dance."

He didn't say anything.

"Anything else about my life there that you want to know?"

"Why jets and ocean liners and hot-air balloons?"

"Because I've never been anywhere. I've never been on a trip. I've never been high up, except in a building or on a bridge. I've never traveled or had adventures. Whenever I'm in a bad place, I take a little trip in my head. My gramma used to say, 'You don't need a lot of money to live a full life—all you need is a fertile mind, some books and a good attitude. Books are free at the library, but a fertile mind takes practice.'"

He chuckled. "Ellie, your grandmother must have been incredible. I wish I could've met her."

She sighed. "She totally rocked. I miss her so much sometimes." She swallowed. "Seems unfair sometimes. Jason… My gramma… Two people I loved so much are already gone."

Noah did an uncharacteristic thing. He reached across the front seat and grabbed her hand, giving it a squeeze. Because he understood that.

Noah had several appointments the following week. One was sheer fun—meeting with Shelby MacIntyre and Luke Riordan to discuss their wedding. The second meeting was a bigger challenge for him. Paul and Vanessa needed some counseling while they tried to make a decision about Hannah. And the third meeting was a coffee date with a nurse named Gloria. He'd been putting off that last one as long as he could.

When Noah met with Shelby and Luke, he felt as if the smile was permanently frozen on his face, they were so delightful. One look told him they weren't a perfect match; Luke was considerably older than Shelby and their personalities were very different. Two minutes with them proved his first impression wrong.

"The most important thing about this wedding is Luke's family," Shelby said. "My family is already here. They're not going anywhere. But Luke's mother is a widow who's been waiting forever for her boys to settle down, and two of Luke's four brothers have been serving in the Middle East. There's a weekend in early October when we can get everyone together. If the church is going to be ready, we'd like to do it here, where we're going to make our home. And then we'll have a fancy catered dinner in a big tent in Uncle Walt's pasture beside the river, at the foot of the mountains. It sounds casual, but dinner will be served on china, there will be flowers everywhere and a wooden floor for dancing. I was for something small, but Vanni wants the wedding to be spectacular."

"I think your cousin's husband, Paul, and I can provide the church," Noah said.

"There will have to be a priest, as well. I'm not going to become a Catholic, but Luke's whole family is Catholic, and it's important to his mother."

"That's very doable," Noah said. "I've done it before. An ecumenical marriage ceremony. The priest and I will share the honor of uniting you."

"Perfect," Shelby said.

"It sounds wonderful," Noah said. "Want to talk about your vows?"

"We talked about making up our own, but we're kind of stuck. Turns out we're not so good at that."

Noah laughed. "But I am. So, I take this to mean you don't want the customary vows, but something unique. And you're having trouble getting there?"

"That's it exactly!" Shelby said.

"I'm okay with any vows," Luke said. "Just get it done. I'm ready for Shelby to get off the pill."

"Luke!" she admonished.

Noah laughed again. "I guess you'll want a cheap baptism next?"

"I'm thinking nine months from the wedding," Luke said. "Shelby's just starting nursing college. She has summers off. We should have our first in summer, if possible. Could be a push. We'll have to get rolling on that."

Shelby peered at Luke. "Our first?" she asked. "A few months ago you were never getting married and now you're having more than one child?"

"You can have input on the number," he said. "But now that you've talked me into this, I'm in no mood to wait. And it will make my mother happy if we get going on it."

Shelby looked at Noah. "I guess we'd better make it a quick ceremony, Noah," she said. "My services are being requested."

"Absolutely," he said with a happy laugh. "Quick, unique and legal. Does that sum it up?"

"Sure," she said. "When you come up with something, can we talk about it? I don't want to commit to anything that you think is totally hot and I think is really sappy."

"You got it. I'll get right to work on it. I have two church offices to paint. I come up with great ideas while I paint."

Noah's meeting with Vanessa and Paul at their home presented more of a challenge. He had requested that the children be included even though they wouldn't understand any of the dialogue. Even if they were napping, that was all right. He wanted to meet with the couple while the little ones were close at hand and on their minds, rather than removed from the home.

When he arrived, he shook Paul's hand and hugged Vanni. He met Hannah and Mattie, who were together in a playpen in the great room. He remarked on what beautiful children they were. It immediately struck Noah that they seemed to have such great rapport for babies who had only just met, rolling around and giggling, cooing and laughing at each other, Mattie pushing toys on Hannah, and Hannah knocking him down with hugs.

"Look at them," Noah said. "You'd think they were brother and sister. They even look alike."

"Mattie has his father's dark hair and eyes," Vanni said.

Paul glanced at Noah. "And Hannah has her mother's."

"Wow," Noah said. "How amazing is that? They're getting along so well. How are you two getting along?"

They seemed to look at each other cautiously. "We're struggling," Paul said. "This is very hard for Vanni. Two small children are a lot of work."

"Is it also very hard for you?" Noah asked Paul.

"Very. Hard." His elbows rested on his knees, hands clasped, and he looked down. The man was worried sick.

"Can I hear about your struggle first? If that's okay with Vanni."

"It's okay," she said. "But if Paul's honest, he'll tell you his struggle is with me."

Noah shifted gears. "Go ahead, Vanni. Talk to me."

"I butted in," she said a bit regretfully.

Noah chuckled. "Gimme a break here—I'm very good at this. Everyone is going to get a fair chance. Hit me—tell me what your biggest burden is. Then we'll get to Paul's."

She took a breath. "I resent it. And because I resent it, I haven't bonded with Hannah. And there's no reason not to—she's perfect. She's sweet and easy and delightful."

"Describe the resentment."

"How and why does this woman I've never met give me her child to raise? She might have named Paul in her will, but I've never met her. And it's not Paul who's going to take care of Hannah. At least not most of the time."

"But that's part of the problem, according to what I understand," Noah said. "She didn't ask."

"She's *dead,* Vanni," Paul said. "Doesn't she get a pass?"

"And what are you going to tell Hannah, Paul?" Vanni asked. "That you slept with her mother but didn't love her? And she's not yours but her own father didn't want her?"

There was silence while Paul and Vanni stared at each other. Noah cleared his throat. "Honestly, I don't think Hannah's going to care who Paul slept with. I don't think she's going to care who you slept with, either, Vanni. Since you never met Hannah's mother, she's going to want to know from Paul what he remembers about her. Paul will probably remember some nice things. Won't you, Paul?"

"Sure. Yeah, of course."

"She might be interested in how this came to happen," Noah said. "How she came to land in your family. Can one of you describe that to me?"

They were both quiet for a moment. Then Paul said, "Terri wanted me to be the father of her child from the first minute she realized she was pregnant. Well, maybe not the first minute, because we hadn't talked in months. She went to Hannah's biological father first and he told her she'd have to sue him to get any kind of support. But then I happened to call her, spent the evening with her and she made up her mind—she was going to try to convince me I was the father. She wanted to get married. In the end, when she admitted she'd lied about the whole thing, she said she did it because she thought I'd be a good father. She said she thought I was a good man." He shook his head. "I don't know how she figured that—I wasn't good to her. I told her I was in love with Vanni, that I couldn't marry her because I'd always be in love with Vanni."

"And when the lawyer told you Terri had named you as Hannah's guardian? How did you respond?"

"I said I couldn't do it—that Vanni and I were just starting our lives together. We wanted to have a baby together—now that's on hold."

"You've made a decision then?" Noah asked. "You'll keep her? Adopt her?"

"Not until we get more comfortable with the idea. But even though Vanni doesn't really want another child now, she doesn't want to let Hannah go."

"Is that right, Vanni?" he asked.

"I don't know," she said softly. Her voice took on some emotion. "Look at them together," she said, glancing at the kids in the playpen. "They're perfect together. And Paul adores her. But I'm scared to death—when I hold her, it's as if I'm holding someone else's baby, a stranger's baby. What if I never bond with her? What if I never think of her as my daughter? What if I'm always a little angry that her mother, Paul's old girlfriend, just gave her to Paul without checking with me first?"

"Paul, you obviously changed your mind," Noah said. "You told the lawyer no, but then you brought her home. What changed your mind?"

"I don't know," he said sincerely. "Honest to God, I don't know. Before I saw her, I knew it was a bad idea, that it would complicate our marriage, our family, and my wife and little Matt are everything to me. Then here comes this little, chubby, rosy-cheeked kid who has no idea her mother's dead, has no idea she's being *given* to a family she doesn't know. A family that doesn't want her, that considers her a total inconvenience. And she looked at me and smiled so big I thought her face was gonna crack. It just shot me in the heart. I thought I was gonna die on the spot. I just couldn't…let…any more bad stuff happen to her." He inhaled for control. "On the way home, for hours in the truck, she was so good, so sweet and quiet. I stopped to give her a change and she grabbed me around the neck and gave me sloppy kisses. Before I knew it, I was crying like a girl. She didn't even know all she'd been through. She had no idea how precarious her future was."

"See how good he is?" Vanni said. "Oh, Noah, that's why I fell in love with Paul—because he's that kind of man. What's the matter with me?"

"Don't be too hard on yourself, Vanni. It's a shock, it's an intrusion. And not a baby abandoned on your doorstep, but the child of a woman your husband had a relationship with. Add to that, Paul took one look at her and was hooked. Your adjustment is more difficult. You have to cope with the bite of jealousy, which is a burden you shouldn't be embarrassed about. I think it's pretty natural."

Paul scooted forward anxiously. "But I've told Vanni over and over, there was no reason to be jealous of Terri. Even if Matt hadn't been killed in Iraq, even if Vanni and I never got together, even if Hannah *had* been my daughter, I don't think I would've ended up with Terri. She was a good person, had lots of nice qualities, but I just wasn't in love with her. I'd have taken care of them, but I knew the way I felt wasn't enough to make a good marriage. And

Noah, it probably wasn't right for me to be seeing her, knowing that, but I never led her on, I swear."

"Easy, easy," Noah said. "Vanni's not jealous of Terri. She's jealous of Hannah."

You could have heard a pin drop. The silence stretched out.

"That can't be," Vanni finally said. "That's impossible! Jealous of a defenseless baby? I'll go to hell for that."

"No," Noah said, smiling, shaking his head. "Not in a million years."

"But that's irrational! I'm not mean enough to be jealous of an innocent child! A child who *needs* me!"

"A lot of emotions are irrational, but that's not really the case here, if you think about it. You wanted to have a child with your husband. You planned, waited until your son was a good age to space the children so you could manage, and you were looking forward to it. Paul told me—you love children, want a bunch of them. And before you even had your chance, the little babe of an ex-girlfriend needs Paul, and Paul was immediately hooked. Your husband fell in love with another woman's child.

"The thing is, this could have worked out differently. For example, if you'd been present for the reading of the will, it might've been *you* who was pulled in by her rosy cheeks and pretty smile. Her need for a loving family. But the way it went down…"

"I told him—he should have called me from Oregon. Rather than just bringing her home like he did," she said.

Noah was shaking his head again. "That might have been even harder, because Paul couldn't stop himself. He had to try. And if you'd told him no, don't accept that baby, then he would have defied you. No, I think this worked out the way it was supposed to."

"But now what am I to do?" she said, tears leaking out

of her eyes. "How can I ever bond with her if I resent her? If I'm jealous of her?"

Noah smiled patiently. "It's not going to be this way forever, Vanni," he said gently. "Your feelings aren't shameful or sinful, but predictable. They're human. You'll need a lot of reassurance from your husband, and we'll work on the issues—anger, jealousy, remorse, guilt. Paul will learn to let himself off the hook for bringing this challenge to the family, and you will learn to forgive yourself for responding in a completely understandable way. It's going to be all right. We're going to walk through this, nice and easy, and reach a conclusion that works for your marriage, your family and for Hannah. You have a wonderful, deep, committed love for each other. In the end, this is going to be all right."

After an hour with Vanni and Paul, Noah called Gloria and pushed his coffee date at Valley Hospital off to the next day. He called her and said he'd had a rough afternoon. Instead, he went to the nursing home in Eureka to watch *Andy Griffith* with Sal Salentino. An hour with Sal was like sandpaper on his emotions, smoothing down the bumps. He bought six large cans of soup at the grocery store and drove out to the transients' camp on his way home. Those old boys were starting to like him, he could tell by the way they drew near when he showed up.

He thought he'd done a decent job of reassuring Vanessa and Paul that things would work out for them, but it left him tired and feeling sorry for himself. Vanessa and Paul grappled with adjustments to a new marriage and growing family, but at the core they had health, love and passion.

Noah *missed* passion.

* * *

The next day Noah met the nurse, Gloria, during her dinner break at the hospital. She was a nice lady, but then he had expected nothing less. She was short and cute, kind of round but pleasantly so, around thirty years old. She had a heart-shaped face, lots of yellow curls that she had pulled back into a tie to keep out of her face and her work, big luminous blue eyes, rosy cheeks and full lips. Of course she was wearing scrubs to work in, but he imagined she looked quite pretty in her regular clothes. And she was very excited to meet with Noah.

They had a pleasant conversation in which it was established that she was completely available and he admitted to being widowed. Within thirty minutes she was offering to cook him dinner. And he said, "Oh, I'm sorry, Gloria. I didn't mean to mislead you—I'm seeing someone."

He had absolutely no idea why he'd said that and was enormously grateful she didn't respond with, "Who?" It was just that he knew, almost instantly, that he didn't want to have dinner with her, didn't want to date her, didn't feel that lustful tug that accompanied attraction.

People probably assumed that a man of the cloth didn't experience all the usual emotions. Maybe just the tidy and manageable ones. Noah was eternally grateful such was not the case, especially when it came to things like desire for a woman. He was so glad it didn't feel like a warm bath to want a woman, but rather like a firestorm. For Noah, when it was the right woman, it was not quiet yearning, but a desperate and hot *wanting* that threatened his control. That was definitely the best part, that it was bigger than him, that it had a life of its own, that it was more like a fire-breathing dragon than an angel of comfort. When that feeling came over him, it was so good it was scary.

He did not have that feeling for a nurse named Gloria.

Nine

After meeting with Gloria, Noah was heading back into town when he drove by the Fitches' house. He pulled up in front, parked, got out and went up the garage stairs to the apartment Ellie rented. He knocked on the door and momentarily he heard, "Who is it?"

"Noah," he answered.

She opened the door wearing loose shorts, a big T-shirt, bare feet, and was towel drying her hair. "Hi," she said. "Is something wrong?"

"No. I was just wondering… You're having the kids on Saturday, right?"

"If nothing goes haywire. Why?"

"What will you do with them?"

She shrugged. "A park, maybe. I thought about packing up some PB&J, chips, sodas, and heading to a playground for the day. Or Jo would love us to spend the day here, with her, but I don't want to take advantage. We'll play it by ear."

"How about a kid movie?" he asked. "Could I tag along? If I treat and promise not to get in the way too much?"

She tilted her head and frowned as she looked at him. "What's the matter, Noah? You look like something's wrong."

"No, no, nothing's wrong. I'm just kind of looking for something to do, and I like your kids. They're nice."

She made a face of disbelief. "Something's wrong. Why don't we just cut to the chase here and you tell me. That'll save badgering time."

"I had dinner with that nurse," he admitted. "At the hospital. Not a date. I meant it to be coffee, but it was her dinner break."

"Oh. And she's after you."

"Yup. Sort of," he said. "She'd like to make me dinner. It wasn't easy to stop her. She was almost quicker than me, and I thought I was ready for her."

Ellie laughed. "Come in—I have popcorn. You can tell me all about it."

"I shouldn't. I'm imposing."

"Yeah, you are, but you're also in the clutches of a horny nurse and I want to hear about it. Come on."

"Horny is stretching it," he told her, entering.

"Uh-huh, and let me guess," Ellie said as she closed the door behind Noah. She hung her towel over the sink. "She's kind of pretty, aggressive, works the conversation around to the next time you'll be together and has a totally futuristic tone. It goes something like, 'And when would you like to do that?'"

"My God, are you psychic?"

"For Pete's sake, have you *no* experience at all?" She sat cross-legged on her bed and offered up her bowl of popcorn. He perched on the end of the bed.

"Actually, I do have experience, I'm just not interested in Gloria."

"Why not?" she asked. "Is she ugly?"

"She's pretty," he said. "And nice. But she just doesn't start my engine, if you get my drift."

"Noah, be careful here. Don't tell me more than I want to know."

"She's boring," he said. "Nice, pretty, real determined and boring. She's exactly the kind of woman people try to fix me up with—proper and polite. I don't know what it is about being a minister, it's like people don't want me to get too excited. And also, like they think it's good résumé material for a woman to land a preacher. Or something. I don't get it."

"Good night, Nellie." She rolled her eyes. "Noah, I'm not sure it's the minister thing that makes you attractive. You're actually kind of cute."

His eyes widened briefly. "I am?" he asked, though *kinda cute* was not exactly what a man was looking for by way of praise.

"Mmm-hmm. You kind of make a girl want to shave above the knees. That was a compliment by the way."

"Is that a big deal? Shaving above the knees?" he stupidly asked.

She laughed. "Pardner, for my last job I had to shave above the—"

"Stop," he ordered. And she laughed some more. He helped himself to a handful of popcorn.

"One minute you want to hear all about it, then it offends your little sensibilities," she teased.

"They're not little," he said, opening his mouth and dropping popcorn inside. "Good popcorn," he said. "Is this microwave stuff?"

"Yup, but not bad. I love popcorn. Sometimes my gramma and I had popcorn for dinner."

"Really?" he asked. "Not real nutritious. I mean, as a meal."

"Noah, we were poor. There were times we ran a little low. But we were happy. If my gramma was worried, it didn't show. We used to giggle about ketchup sandwiches. Pickle and peanut butter sandwiches. Popcorn or rice and tomatoes."

"Rice and tomatoes?"

"A couple cups of rice, a can of stewed tomatoes, voila. Another favorite for the end of the month was soft-boiled eggs on fried potatoes. Didn't you ever have things like that when you were a kid?"

Not while growing up, he hadn't. "There were times we had pretty simple dinners, but…" His voice trailed off.

Ellie grabbed a handful of popcorn and shoved it into her mouth. "What was your growing up like?"

He took a deep breath. "Ellie, I didn't grow up poor. I grew up in a big house—practically a mansion. My father was a pretty famous preacher—he was on television. He still is—famous and on television. He was ten years younger than my mother. She inherited money, so before my father made his in the ministry, she had hers. I think it's fair to say she made him what he is."

"No shit," she said, wide eyed, fascinated. "Oops."

"Don't worry about it—I'm getting used to it. I'm an only child, my mother is dead and my father and I don't get along. But there was always plenty of money while I was growing up."

"Well, there you go," she said. "Money isn't the answer."

"No shit," Noah said.

Ellie might've grinned if Noah didn't look so serious. "So, did you always know you were going to be a minister?" she asked.

"Absolutely not. I was going to be anything but a minister. I wasn't about to follow in my father's footsteps—for a religious man, he sure had his failings. But while I was looking for some answers to questions I'd had since I was about five years old, I ended up studying religion, among other things. Go figure. I discovered parts of the ministry that had nothing to do with being on television or being famous that appealed to me in a very personal way. It took me a really long time to get there, though."

"How long?"

"I was a student forever, Ellie. I have two undergrad degrees and two master's."

"Wow. And I didn't even finish high school. Well, I got my GED later. So when did you get there? As you put it."

He chewed thoughtfully. "This really is good popcorn. I could eat this for dinner."

"Don't get distracted, Noah," she said. "When did you discover you were going to be a minister?"

"Oh, that. I was going to teach and counsel and study. Maybe get a Ph.D. in clinical psychology. I like counseling—at least some kinds. But all along I'd been doing some community service and I realized I was happiest when I was just being a good neighbor. When I was helping out, lending a hand, you know. And a minister's role is complicated, but a lot of it is helping out, acting as spiritual support. It's like a relay race, Ellie. The baton is filled with faith and knowledge and good works—like community service, food for the hungry, food for the soul, and as it's passed to me, I can run with it to the next person, who can run with it to—" He stopped to laugh and shake his head. "That's the part I gravitated to. I have a mentor professor, George. I landed in the seminary because he couldn't stay out of my business and convinced me it would make me happy."

"So you just went along with his idea?" she asked.

"Not really. It was more than that."

"Well, for Pete's sake," she said, annoyed. "*What* more?"

He thought for a minute, chewing his popcorn. "It was about God," he said. "Whenever I called out to him, he answered. Wasn't always the answer I wanted, but there was always an answer. I ignored that as long as I could."

She tilted her head in thought. "Now, that's a good enough reason," she said. Then she took one of his hands and pulled it toward her. "But these are not the hands of a preacher." She ran her fingers over the calluses on his palms and fingers, then a long fingernail over a couple of thin scars on his forearm. "How did you get so rough? So messed up?"

"I worked on the docks and on fishing boats and markets in Seattle from the time I was eighteen till I went into the seminary a few years ago. I worked my way through college that way, I wanted to get as far away from my father and his lifestyle as I could. I got most of these scars the first year or two. It was tough, physical work." He grinned. "I loved it, but I wasn't born into it like a lot of the men I worked with. It took me a while to learn, and I got hooked, grappled, cut and scraped a lot."

"Then why aren't you still there?"

He shrugged. "It was time to move on. Past time—I'm thirty-five."

She ate more popcorn. Then she thoughtfully said, "You can stop being ashamed of growing up rich now." When he looked at her in shocked surprise, she said, "If I'm not ashamed of growing up poor, why should you be ashamed of growing up rich? I think it's kind of cool. You shouldn't let that hold you back." And then she smiled at him.

"Let me ask you something," he said. "Were you lonely growing up?"

"Growing up? Oh, hell no. I probably had too many friends. Of course, they were mostly friends in the same boat as me—not a dime to spare, not going anyplace, couldn't even stay in school. But between my gramma and friends, I got by fine. Later, after I was a single mom with two jobs and my gramma gone, I was lonely all the time, but I was almost never alone. Growing up, I had friends. I always envied the girls who had good grades, cool clothes, went to lots of parties and stuff, but I wasn't ever lonely."

"Didn't all those friends of yours have parties?"

She smiled blandly. "No, Noah. We hung out. Usually around a convenience store with a big parking lot."

"You couldn't get good grades?" he asked.

"Well, sometimes I did okay, but I've had at least one job at a time since I was fourteen. Full-time babysitting, housecleaning, waitressing, you name it. I worked when I was pregnant and I worked when the babies were small and my gramma watched them. Until she died. But I've always worked—from right after school till late at night and then on weekends. There wasn't a lot of time to hit the books, know what I mean?"

He did know, but the difference was, he hadn't been the mother of two children when he'd been working and studying. "Ellie, you're smart," he said. "You're intuitive. You have common sense. I think you could do anything."

She laughed at him. "I have done anything, remember?"

"Yeah, that's right," he said, grinning back. "And now you're working for a church. God must be shaking in his boots."

"No doubt."

"Listen, I'd better get going. I'll see you in the morning." He stood up. "So, can I come with you and the kids on Saturday?"

"I'll think about it. But you have to promise to be-have."

"Thanks. That'll give me something to look forward to."

He stood in the open door and she held it a moment. "Noah? When did you stop having a relationship with your father?"

"Oh, jeez," he said, dropping his chin. "We haven't gotten along since I was a kid. He was continually dis-appointed in me."

"But when, Noah? When did you give up?"

He looked at her steadily, peering into her large eyes. How did she know the things she knew? Could her grand-mother have taught her so much about instinct? Or was she just plain an old soul? "When he didn't come to my wife's funeral," he said.

And before she could respond, he walked down the stairs and away into the night.

As Noah walked away from Ellie's apartment, he thought, that was wrong, the way that happened. That's not the way you tell a friend about your past. And he realized suddenly, Ellie had become his friend. When you ask someone if you can join them for their very limited time with their children, that's about friendship.

Yes, she was a friend now. She trusted him with her personal challenges, even if they might be embarrassing. But that was what was odd and admirable about Ellie— she might not want the town to know the details of her past, but she had no shame; she didn't waste her energy on it. For such a young woman, she was comfortable in her own skin. And then he realized with a shock of sud-den clarity, she didn't treat him like a *minister*. She treated him like a friend. A regular man.

Too often, people approached him as someone whose

approval they needed, and that was so far from his role. It not only made him uncomfortable, it created a barrier between him and friendship. And he didn't want only friends in the clergy. Ellie? She didn't much care if he approved of her. He loved that about her.

The only thing that seemed to rattle her were issues with her kids—their welfare and safety.

Noah, however, had enough shame for both of them. What kind of fool laments his sad childhood to someone who ate popcorn for dinner and slept beside her grandmother on a sofa bed her entire life? Or how about the way he dropped that bomb about Merry's death? Ellie lost her boyfriend in an accident when she was a kid herself, a poor kid who was expecting a baby. She must have been devastated and terrified. But she somehow kept on trucking, determined. Hercules Baldwin. He would have to apologize to her in the morning.

He was behind his desk in his office the next morning when he heard the backdoor open. Lucy bolted for the door to greet Ellie. When he saw her in the doorway, he said, "I'm sorry, Ellie."

But she said, "I'm sorry, Noah," at the same moment.

And then in unison they both asked, "What are you sorry for?"

"You first," she said. "Go on. My list might be longer."

"I'm sorry I told you my wife had passed away like that. That was cold. You deserved a more thoughtful explanation. She died of cancer about five years ago. She was very young and her illness was sudden. She went fast. I shouldn't have told you the way I did. What are you sorry for?"

"I'm sorry your wife died. I'm sorry your father let you down and sorry I ask such personal questions. And sorry I confront you and push the point so much. And I know I tease you and torture you and I'm very sorry that I have *way* too much fun doing that. I think I need to work on boundaries. First of all, it's not my business and second, you'll tell me what you want me to know when you feel like it. And I should show more respect for your—you know, your *position.* That you're a minister. And everything."

He laughed and shook his head.

"What's funny?" she asked.

"I ask you about lap dances, but you're apologizing to me about boundaries? I have an idea—let's just go back to being ourselves and not be sorry about any of it."

"Okay. Except that one thing—I'm sorry your wife died."

"Thank you. I'm not trying to keep it a secret, that I was married, that I'm widowed. No one asked. And then someone did—that nurse. Gloria."

"Well, I guess she had to be sure you weren't gay," she said, and grinned largely.

He grinned back. She was impossible. And wonderful.

"I'm going to get some work done," she said. "You have flooring coming real soon and there's a storage closet under the stairs that's full of dusty old boxes. I thought I'd get in there."

"You can if you want to, but I'm not going to have the flooring extended into the closet. It's a big storage area; it makes no sense to spend the money there. The boxes won't care."

"It should be cleared out anyway," she said. "Unless there's something else…?"

He was shaking his head. "Go for it. I only opened the first two boxes and found them full of rotting sheet music. Whatever is in there is probably destined for the Dumpster. After you look through it, I'll haul it over behind Jack's."

She gave him a salute and off she went. And Lucy, the traitor, followed Ellie downstairs.

Noah was supposed to be dreaming up a wedding script, paying bills, catching up on some e-mails—but he was thinking. Merry would have liked Ellie. While most wives wanted their husbands to hire unappealing women to work for them, Merry was never that way. Ellie's bold sexiness wouldn't have intimidated Merry; she was a confident woman. Of course, Noah's total devotion might've had something to do with that, as well.

And Merry wasn't one of those proper, boring types, either. She had been born and raised in Seattle and was a dangerous liberal feminist. Before they were married, she belonged to an organization working toward the decriminalization of prostitution. She'd been arrested a couple of times—once for chaining herself to a tree to protect the forest from decimation, once for picketing a federal building. She was also very involved with an AIDS hospice program. And she did volunteer work for Habitat for Humanity—she said holding a hammer made her feel *strong*.

She'd coveted breasts like Ellie's. She'd often talked about buying herself a pair. And one night she said to Noah, "I'm thinking of getting a tattoo…." So he drew one on her belly with a felt-tip pen and then they laughed themselves stupid.

What he liked best about her was her wicked and irreverent sense of humor. And her lack of inhibition with him. He never had to coax her to let go in their bed— she was a free spirit. She believed everything that happened between a man and woman who loved each other was virtuous, and also believed what took place between husband and wife was sacred, no matter how wild and daring.

And while Merry wasn't shy about voicing her opinion when she sensed an injustice, she seemed to be able to find the inherent goodness in the most unlikely characters. Noah hiring a stripper? Merry probably would have *liked* that.

"I have to come up with vows," he muttered to himself. "Unique but not sappy vows…" He pushed back from his desk and wandered into the sanctuary, gazing up at the stained-glass window. It came to him suddenly, something he would try out on Shelby and Luke.

And then he heard a loud shriek from downstairs, a bark from the usually quiet Lucy, and Noah clamored down the stairs at top speed. He found Ellie on the floor clear across the hall, her back up against the wall, hugging her knees. She looked up at him. "A rat," she said, breathless. "Behind that box. It's four feet long."

Lucy wasn't trying to get at anything in the closet. "I think you scared my dog," he said.

"The *rat* scared her, I bet."

Noah entered the closet cautiously, kicked the box, and when nothing rustled, he pulled it out a bit. Ah. Behind the box was a dead mouse. Probably four inches long at best. It was very dead, dried out, kaput. He lifted it by the tail and held it toward her. "Is this the rat?"

"No. My rat is *much* bigger. That must be its baby."

"Maybe you just got scared and it looked much bigger."

"No," she said. "There's a rat the size of a Volkswagen in there."

"Was it a dead rat, Ellie?"

"Possibly. It wasn't moving."

He went into the downstairs bathroom and dropped the thing in the trash.

"Why did you do that?" she yelled, getting to her feet. "What if he gets out of there and attacks me?"

"He's petrified. It's over," Noah said. Then he smiled at her. "I'll protect you."

"Right," she said. "So far you don't even have the real rat! What good are you?" She stomped away from him in the direction of the kitchen and came back wearing work gloves. "I hate rats," she said, pulling the box out of the closet into the hallway. She opened it slowly, cautiously pulling out what looked like wrapped bundles. She folded back some plastic, some towels. And said, "Oh my God." She lifted and turned an elaborate gold candelabrum toward Noah.

"Oh my God," he echoed, taking it. He was lifting it, weighing it. It was heavy. And while he was doing this, Ellie was opening another towel-wrapped package for its mate. "This is valuable," he said.

"It's Christmas," she said, holding up the second one, beaming.

They got busy opening boxes and found things Noah hadn't bothered to look for—even though the church building and contents were part of the sale, they weren't listed as inventory of the property. He'd assumed everything of value was gone. Yet here were valuable altar accoutrements, from candelabra to chalices to communion trays. Everything was packed carefully in plastic and linens, clerics' vestments and choir robes, neither dusty nor moth-eaten. Dishes for the kitchen, for community gatherings—over a hundred sets of plates, cups, saucers, bowls, flatware, punch bowls and glass cups. More crosses, some wooden, some gold. Hymnals, Bibles, altar linens. Tablecloths and napkins. There were boxes of candles that, thanks to the cool mountain temperatures, hadn't melted in God knew how many years. Boxes and boxes of things the church could use. They unearthed a thirty-year-old IBM electric typewriter that actually still worked. "Except there will be no replacement ribbons on this earth," Noah said. The space under the stairs was a good eight feet long and four feet wide and Noah had virtually ignored it because the first boxes contained useless paper and the rest looked water damaged, dirty and crushed—he couldn't imagine there was anything of value there.

"But this is incredible," she said, dragging a big box of dishes out of the hall and across the basement floor.

"Where are you going?"

"I'm going to put these in the kitchen so I can wash them and put them away!" she said, all excited.

Rather than paying bills or writing wedding vows, Noah and Ellie worked all day at emptying boxes. Noah took a big load of vestments, robes, altar and table linens to the dry cleaner's in Fortuna and picked up tarnish remover for the candelabra and cross. They shook dust off Bibles and hymnals and put them in clean boxes, washed dishes and put them away.

And the sun began to set, the eyes of the stained-glass image of Christ shining into the sanctuary. Noah looked at his watch. "We've been at it all day without stopping for lunch."

"I got into it," she said.

"You know what we're going to do? We're going to have a big meal at Jack's. It's time for Lucy's dinner anyway."

She looked down at herself. "Oh, no," she said. "I'm dusty and falling apart and probably look like a vagrant. I'll just go home and—"

"No one over there cares, Ellie. And for heaven's sake, you're not eating popcorn tonight! Come on!"

"*I* care, Noah! I'm just getting to know these people. I'm at least going to be put together when I go there."

"Fine," he said in a pout. "Fine. Okay. Tell you what—figure out where we're going to eat and I'll take Lucy over for dinner and get takeout. I mean, we have dishes and stuff, right?"

The smile on her face said she liked that idea. "Right."

When he got back from Jack's with three bags of takeout, he found Ellie had spread a tablecloth on the clean basement floor, set two candelabra with lit tapers on the cloth and had put out plates. A picnic. Lucy plunked right down next to the tablecloth. Noah looked at it and said, "Nice."

"Is this floor going to be too hard for you?" she asked. "Your desk is covered with stuff and there's no table in the place. We could go to the RV or picnic on my bed at the apartment."

"I like this." He put down the sacks and settled himself on the floor. He opened the first bag and pulled out two bottles of beer. From the second bag he removed cartons of brisket, mashed potatoes, creamed spinach, warm bread and mostly melted butter. He put the third bag to the side and said, "Pie."

"Were you starving?" she asked him.

"Aren't you? Because unless you're hiding the evidence, neither of us has eaten." He twisted the cap off a bottle of beer and handed it to her.

"I haven't had a beer in ages. At least a couple of years. I never drink."

"You'll probably get all loopy on me."

"Probably," she said, tipping the bottle up.

"What kind of stripper doesn't even have a beer?"

"A sober one," she informed him. "But I have to admit, this tastes very good. What kind of minister drinks?"

"Jesus turned water into wine for a wedding. He was hip. I bet they all got trashed." He lifted his bottle toward her. "To your incredible find today. Good for you, Ellie."

"And you thought I wouldn't work out," she said, toasting him. "I bet I'm the best assistant you've ever had."

"And also the only one. Want me to dish us up?"

"Good idea. Now that I smell it, I think I'm going to stuff myself." She watched him serve up two plates and it came to her he was very well trained. And she asked, "Did you ever get in trouble as a kid, Noah?"

"Depends on who you ask," he said, passing her a plate. "My mother thought I walked on water, my father was never satisfied."

"There's that father thing again," she muttered.

"The rule is, if I open the subject, you can ask questions," he told her. "My father is a lot like Arnold Gunterson. Arbitrary. Low tolerance. Rigid and unemotional. He used to ground me all the time for little stuff. The punishment never fit the crime. I'd have to give up football because I was a half hour late on my curfew—and I had the earliest curfew in town. I lost summer camp when I was about ten because I didn't curl the garden hose right."

"Holy moly," she said. She ate a forkful of mashed potatoes. "That's a little over the top."

"Well… He did trip on the hose," Noah said. "But still, that's kind of a no-TV punishment, not four weeks of summer camp. I mean, it didn't kill him or even break any bones."

She grinned at him. "Like you wished."

"He's a bastard, Ellie. My mother was a plain, sweet woman on her way to being an old maid when a poor young minister married her for her money. And made her life miserable from that moment on."

"She *told* you that?"

"She didn't have to tell me. I have no evidence, but I'm pretty sure he screwed around on her their whole marriage. He was frequently in the company of pretty, young women and it tore her heart out."

"That's awful, Noah," she said. She reclined on the floor, her long legs out to the side, her hair falling over her shoulder while she ate. "Anyone who doesn't go to his daughter-in-law's funeral would be a bastard in my book."

Noah looked down uncomfortably. "Dammit, I can't lie. That was my fault. He wasn't invited to my wedding, which was small and private, and I made sure he found out about Merry's death, but he didn't hear it from me. I had a secret agenda—if he came and was kind, I'd give him another chance. He didn't. And I didn't."

Ellie's fork was hovering in midair, her mouth slightly open. "Wow," she finally said. "Are there a lot of people you have these kind of secret deals with?"

"Only him. And only once."

"Well, that's a relief," she said. "So, were you in trouble as a kid?"

"When I was young, I tried my hardest to be the best kid in the universe and could still never do anything right. So when I hit about sixteen, I gave up trying to be good and started being as bad as possible. I really regret that. I hurt my mother."

"What kind of bad things did you do?"

"Oh, you don't really want to know…"

She smiled. "Oh, I really *do!*"

"I lied. I hustled girls, and not with pure thoughts. I drank too much. Had a couple of fender benders because I was driving too fast. Skipped school to go out to the lake with friends. That kind of thing."

"Steal any cars? Get anyone pregnant? Do hard drugs?"

"Nah."

"Then you weren't really trying," she said with a laugh. "So, if you got punished for little stuff, what did the old man do to you for getting drunk and wrecking cars?"

He smiled as if this was one of his few happy memories. "He almost lost his mind. He threatened to send me to boarding school, but I think we both knew no one would keep me for long while I was on that particular course. I was pretty incorrigible. Plus, I remember it was one of the few times my mother really stood up to him—she said, 'Over my dead body, Jasper!' It was fantastic. But eventually he packed me off to seminary. It didn't work. I quit and went to Seattle where I tried to stay away from Bible studies." He took a drink of beer. "So— were you in trouble a lot?"

She shook her head. "Never. Well, I missed some classes from oversleeping, but I worked late. My one big screwup was getting pregnant. I felt just terrible about that. My gramma was so sweet, but I really felt like I'd let her down. And then when Jason was killed, even though my life was a disaster, I was glad for the baby. Jason was sweet. A good boy. We'd dated since I was about fourteen. I guess in the end, there were just too many hormones between us."

"You must have thought you were in love," Noah said.

"You're damn skippy," she said. "I sure haven't felt that way since. We had it bad. We had big plans, too. Well, probably they wouldn't seem big to you…"

When her voice trailed off, Noah prodded. "What kind of plans?"

"Hmm," she said, thinking. "Jason had this really good job in construction. He poured cement—he made a good living for a nineteen-year-old. He lived at home with his folks, so he had money to burn. But he saved and saved. For us. We were going to get married after I graduated, live in something small and work hard, and then after a few years, we were going to buy a house. Two stories, big yard, nice neighborhood. Not fancy, you know, but real nice. To me it would've been like a castle. Then the first baby a couple of years later… That would have brought me to about today."

"Those sound like nice plans," Noah said.

"He drove the motorcycle most of the time because it was cheap. The only reason I wasn't on the back when that car hit him was because he wouldn't let me ride anymore. Because I was pregnant." She looked down. "You would've liked him."

"He looked out for you the best he could," Noah said. "You must've been real proud of him."

The give-and-take went on through dinner. It didn't surprise Noah at all that Ellie told him anything he wanted to know—she had been that way since the minute they met. She was unflinchingly honest. What surprised him was that *he* was so open. He rarely spoke about his father, and he only talked about Merry with their close mutual friends. "She was the sexiest, funniest girl in Seattle. I was twenty-seven, she was twenty-five, and she was not interested in some Goody Two-shoes who studied religion."

"She *told* you that?" Ellie asked, laughing.

"She did. She said it was her opinion religion got in the way of faith and she thought most religions did more harm than good. So I promised her that I'd teach and counsel. Maybe just get a Ph.D. That way she'd never have to be stuck with a good-goody minister. And she said I would still be a man, and that would be burden enough."

"I *like* her."

"I couldn't resist her. She was maddening. Exciting.

Beautiful. So funny she almost made me forget I was nurturing a private rage against my father."

"When do you suppose you'll get tired of that?"

"I was hoping to be done with it by now. I think I was moving away from that when I found Merry. And when I lost her, I got mad all over again."

"Well, duh," Ellie said. "Noah, losing someone you love is *supposed* to make you mad. First you don't believe it, then you get pissed. Aren't you the one with the big education?"

After more talking, they picked up the dishes and washed and dried them companionably. And as Ellie dried the last pie plate, the towel slipped from her hand and fell to the floor.

"Got it," he said, bending to pick it up. Just as she bent to pick it up.

Both of them were bent at the waist, reaching for the towel. Their faces came so close together, his cheek was nearly touching her cheek, his chin hooked over her shoulder. And when she could have moved away, he grabbed her upper arms in a firm but gentle grasp and said, very softly, "Don't. Don't move for a second." And then slowly, carefully, he straightened with her until they stood, facing each other, his cheek against her cheek. "Be still. For just one minute," he whispered. "Please."

He let his cheek press gently against hers. Noah held her arms, but not tightly. If she wanted to pull back, pull away, she wouldn't have a problem. But she didn't, so he let his eyes gently close and inhaled deeply. She wasn't wearing perfume; she smelled of soap and shampoo and dust and woman, the first woman he'd been this close to in quite a while. Her body was soft against his, though he resisted the temptation to pull her hard against him.

Yet he stood there, unable to break away. He breathed

her in. Her arms remained at her sides, passive, and he just inhaled her. He enjoyed the velvety softness against his cheek; he thought maybe she was far softer and silkier than the average woman. He enjoyed the feeling of the smooth skin of a woman against his rougher skin. Why didn't she pull away? He lifted a hand from her upper arm to her face and placed his palm against her other cheek, just absorbing the sweet, delicate warmth, the texture, the scent that was only her.

At least a minute had passed. Maybe two minutes.

It's just an affectionate hug, he told himself. Not a big deal.

But when he stepped back, he looked into her large brown eyes and said, "I apologize. That was probably inappropriate."

"Probably," she said. "You being my boss and all."

"I won't do that again," he promised. "It's just that—" Words seemed to fail him.

"Just that you wanted to be close to someone?" she supplied.

To you. "I did," he said, relieved that she had an explanation.

"But I let you, Noah. Don't you go thinking you can get away with things."

He shook his head.

"Don't start thinking I'm easy."

He couldn't help but smile at her. She looked about one inch away from biker chick and she'd been through the school of hard knocks, but there was something just plain pure about her. "You haven't been the least bit easy since the minute I met you."

"I think it was all that talk about your wife, Merry," she said. "I know you miss her. And miss being close to a woman in general."

"I doubt that's it," he said. "Merry's been gone five years. I've been close to a woman or two since then."

"Just the same, you should think about it," Ellie said. "You don't want to get your feelings all mixed up. You don't want to start thinking you like me in a certain way when all you're really feeling is lonesome. Which is natural. Easy to understand."

"Maybe *you* should be the counselor."

"I mean, if we're going to work together—"

Noah's good sense took a hike. He put his hands on her narrow waist, pulled her close and covered her mouth with his. A little squeak of surprise escaped her, but it only took her a second to settle against his lips. Her hands slid up onto his shoulders and his tightened around her waist. He tilted his head to a new angle and rocked against her mouth, gently parting her lips. And he groaned in pure pleasure.

Ellie was lost in his kiss; his lips were so strong and soft, his mouth so deep and wet, his arms firm and confident. And, oh, she hadn't been kissed like this in her *life.* He left her lips for just a split second, long enough to look down into her startled eyes, and then he was on her mouth again, pulling her tight against him, bending her back with his hunger. She welcomed his tongue, joined him with hers, and her arms rose to circle his neck. And they rocked together, body to body, mouths together, tongues entwined, breathing coming harder and deeper. She liked this kiss, she thought. But this is not a good thing.

At long last he broke from their kiss, gazing into her eyes, and she asked, "Can you fire me for letting you kiss me? Because you know I need this job."

"No," he said softly. "You can probably sue me. But you'll end up with an old RV and a dog. An expensive dog."

"I don't know what I was thinking. I should never have let you…"

"How can you taste like strawberries when you had brisket, beer and apple pie?" he asked her.

"It's not me, Noah. You've just been lonely…"

He lifted one expressive brow. "Is that so? And what's your excuse?"

"I told you, you're kind of cute, for a minister, and— Oh!"

She was going to have to watch that sarcastic sense of humor, it obviously turned him on. He grabbed her against him again and devoured her once more. And he was delicious. Powerful and starving and passionate. He licked her lips apart and invaded her with his tongue. Then he kissed his way down her neck and was back on her mouth, feeding her a wonderful kiss that wouldn't end. This is not what one expected from a good-goody preacher. Whoa, his chest and arms were so hard against her, his arms like vise grips. His kiss was hot, wet and wonderful, lasting a minute, then two.

Noah tried reciting the Psalms backward, but it was useless. He began to feel a burning lust, the tightness of desire and arousal. And it felt at once shameful and *fabulous.* He'd been with a couple of women the past several years, looking for something solid and satisfying, but no one had stirred him like this in a long, long time. He welcomed the feeling of his natural sexual response. It was real, and really great.

And she knew. She pressed against him, he held her tight, and there was not one secret between them. Finally, reluctantly, he freed her lips.

"Don't even think about it," she said.

He grinned in spite of himself. "Come on, Ellie. You can't make me not think about it."

"I'm not getting mixed up with someone like you. First of all, I'm all wrong for someone like you. Second, I'm clearing out the second I have my kids. Third…" She paused. "I don't need a third. That's good enough. Don't ever do that again."

"I haven't kissed a woman like that in quite a while," he said. "That was nice. Are you angry?" he asked.

"Did I *taste* angry?"

He just smiled. "You tasted *wonderful*. You're right— it's not such a good idea. Well, I mean, it is a good idea. But I see the potential for disaster."

She pulled away and put a hand against her wild curls as if to smooth her hair into place. The hand trembled a bit; he'd never seen her rattled before. "You're just going to get yourself in trouble with the Big Guy, and there's no point in making your life tougher."

"Nah, God's not opposed to kissing. I think employers taking advantage of employees, however, could put a big black mark on the minus side of my chart. But you liked it," he said. "You did. And I liked it. It felt pretty consensual to me."

"I'm not the kind of woman a man like you gets interested in, and we both know that. Eventually that could hurt me. And if you really are a nice guy, hurting me will hurt you."

"Because of that dancing thing?" he asked.

"That dancing thing, and I'm poor, undereducated, strapped with kids and very, very temporary."

"Wait now," he said. "I'm not trying to make an argument for interest, because you might be right—it might be a mistake that could get out of control. But you're smart, no matter how much or little formal education you have. And I don't believe you see your kids as a liability, and you know I don't—I like them. And you won't always be poor, not with your ambition and positive attitude." He smiled gently. "The dancing doesn't matter a damn. I understand about that."

"I don't want to be your bad girl. The one you take chances with for a little walk on the wild side. To break a few rules, have a little sinful fun."

"Ellie, there's not a bad bone in your body. And we both know it."

"That isn't really the point, Your Holiness…"

"Okay, let's be rational. I apologize, I won't do it again, but really—it was just a kiss."

"Not the way you do it," she said.

Ten

Ellie was wrong about one thing; for the first time in years Noah *wasn't* lonely. He now had Ellie.

He hadn't thought he was going to kiss her. He hadn't even seen it coming. It wasn't something he'd been aching to do but, in retrospect, it made sense. They had grown closer, sharing personal things about their lives, and despite Ellie's wisecracking, they had fun together. They depended on each other. He liked her better and trusted her more by the day. She might look and talk like a diamond in the rough, but she had a simple wisdom about her that was addictive. Her honesty alone was alluring. She had a sharp, teasing tongue, but she was kind and genuine. She listened with compassion, with sympathy and not pity, as he ranted about his father. She didn't suffer fools gladly. *Anyone who doesn't go to his daughter-in-law's funeral would be a bastard in my book.*

And there was that other thing that was overdue—strong feelings for a woman, feelings of desire. He was a thirty-five-year-old man with a perfectly healthy libido and throughout his adult life had enjoyed normal feelings of arousal. The past few years had been a bit lightweight in that department. He'd been out with women, even been in some very interesting clinches, but hadn't met anyone that made him crazy with longing. He missed that and needed that in his life.

Noah wasn't a complicated man. He had to admire more than one thing about a woman to desire her. He had to like her, to start with. He had to feel comfortable with her—all that teasing and arguing with Ellie, that was like friendship foreplay to him. Something that had been painfully absent from his life for the past several years—playfulness. He'd let his life get a little too serious. Ellie brought the laughter back to him.

The first time he laid eyes on her, her blatant sexuality had shocked him. She didn't shock him anymore. Either she was playing it down a bit or he was getting used to her. True, she wasn't wearing as much makeup, but why would she for cleaning and painting? But things that normally put him off, he'd begun to find amusing. Kind of cute. So completely Ellie. Like the long fingernails, painted a different shade almost every day, decorated with sparkles. In his opinion she'd gone from a spectacle of womanhood to pop art.

He hadn't felt this alive or happy in years. She not only made him feel again, but made him feel fun again.

But, after he walked her home, he went back to the church, stood in front of the now-dark stained-glass window, looked up and said to himself, *I promise I won't let her down. I'll find a way to be there for her while she recovers the life she has every right to. Amen.*

"George?" Noah said into the phone.

He was answered with a grunt. And then, "God, man! It's midnight!"

"I kissed her. Not a little affectionate peck on the cheek. I tickled her tonsils with my tongue."

"Well now," George said. He sat up in bed and felt around for his glasses. "I can't tell if you're bragging or apologizing."

"This has disaster written all over it."

"Ah. Bragging. No one loves a good disaster like Noah." Then he chuckled. "And now?"

"Now I can't wait to do it again."

"Might want to put that off for a while, boy. Till you get settled down a little."

There were certain things about one another that did not require further explanation. George didn't ask Noah if he cared for her because Noah didn't get involved with women who meant nothing to him. No need for Noah to explain that he was starting to care way too much and it worried him. From the hour of the call alone, George knew that.

"It's probably just some good old-fashioned lust," Noah said.

"Hmm, probably," George agreed.

"Some of the best lust I can remember," Noah said. "Christ above, this is all wrong."

"We both know what's wrong with it, son. Let's take a second to talk about what's right."

"I can't think of anything at the moment. Besides the lust, that is. And that she's incredible. I never thought this would work—I thought it was a charity job, giving her the position to help her get her custody deal worked out. But I couldn't ask for more. And she makes me laugh. She's so sassy. And soft. Did I mention she's soft?"

"Did you coerce her? Harass her? Emotionally blackmail her?" George asked.

"Of course not. I told her she could sue me."

George chuckled. "Well, Noah, what a sweet-talker you are. No wonder the women are just falling at your feet."

"She depends on me and the job."

"Yes, you've explained. Is it likely she's afraid that if she doesn't yield, you or the job will vanish?"

Noah took a breath. "She is afraid of *nothing*. Even when she should be."

"Noah, are you courting her?"

Dead silence hung in the air. And finally he said, "I'm fighting my libido, and for a while tonight it was winning. I don't even know if I'm courting—it's too new. I like her, of course. She intrigues me as much as she annoys me. I admire her, but I admit she's strange to me. I've never known anyone like her. And of course she's entirely the wrong kind of woman for me, in my circumstances."

"Oh, I don't know. Jesus hung out with Mary Magdalene. You don't get more provocative than that."

"Thanks a lot," Noah grumbled.

"I'd better come up there. I was going to wait till you got rid of all the mouse shit, but I'd better come before you create some of your own."

On Monday morning a couple of work crews descended on the church and got right to it. A few men on ladders and scaffolds were scraping old paint off the outside of the church; the sander was running over the sanctuary floor at the same time a man was working on replacing broken windows. In the basement, the concrete walls were being textured, and flooring was due to be delivered along with ceiling panels. There was a plumbing truck outside and Noah heard someone banging on the pipes, looking for leaks. Feeling as if he was just in the way, Noah left Ellie in charge of the phone and went to run errands.

First he went to the Goodwill and grabbed a few second- or third- or fourth-hand jackets and a handful of wool socks—fall was upon them and from what he heard, winter followed fall quickly. He wondered if his congregation, when he had one, would take on some of the needs in the town—castoffs to the poor, Thanksgiving and Christmas baskets, that sort of thing.

Next he went to the nursing home in Fortuna to watch TV with Sal. He hung around for about fifteen minutes of *I Love Lucy* and a little conversation. Sal was grumpy as ever but couldn't disguise the way his eyes lit up when Noah stood in the doorway. Then Noah made a run by the hospital, visiting some young parents who had a seven-year-old in surgery.

He wasn't all that anxious to get back to Virgin River, to the church. He was giving Ellie a wide berth because of the memorable, unforgettable way her lips tasted. If he closed his eyes he could recall it all in amazing detail. But he was very proud of his ability to act natural around her. Neither of them mentioned the kiss; neither of them behaved oddly. They had spent Saturday with the kids together and for all the world's eyes, they were merely casual friends who worked together.

But he thought about her all the time.

Later that afternoon, after the hospital visit, he dropped in on Vanessa. He hadn't called ahead or made an appointment, he just wanted to see how she was holding up. She came to the door with the sound of children yelling and crying at her back. There were dark rings under her eyes and she looked a little unkempt. "How's it going?" he asked.

"Great," she said unenthusiastically. She ran a hand through her hair. "I'm trying to get dinner ready for Paul and those two decided to skip naps. It gets a little wild sometimes."

Noah stepped inside. Both kids were reaching out of the playpen with tear-stained faces. "Have they been crying long?" he asked.

"Oh, on and off the past couple of hours. Both of them are really cranky and tired." She just shook her head.

"Vanni, aren't you getting enough sleep?" he asked.

She just shook her head. "They both sleep through the night. I go to bed with them—I seem to be sleeping a lot. Maybe that's it—maybe I'm oversleeping because I just stay so tired."

"What can I do? Hold a child, stir a pot?"

"Whatever," she said, backing away so he could come in.

Noah went straight to the playpen. He was saying, "Hey now," to the little ones, but he was thinking, Uh-oh. She's sinking. Whether under the strain of two small children or the emotional distress, it was hard to tell at first glance. But something had to be done here. He lifted Mattie out of the playpen first because he was the biggest. And then, when Hannah put her fat little arms around his neck, with his forearm under her bum, he pulled her up. Both children held on to him, one head on each shoulder. He jiggled and talked softly. They quieted at once; they had only needed to be held. They were as tired and frustrated as Vanni.

Vanni had disappeared into the kitchen and Noah just held a couple of armfuls of kids until the crying was under control. And then he said to them, "Well, first things first." And he went down the hall in search of a nursery.

He kept talking in a soft voice while he put Mattie in one of the two cribs in the room and Hannah on the changing table. This was new territory for him. He'd changed a baby or two, but not in a long time. He kept talking while he studied the disposable diapers kept in a diaper caddy that hung on the side of the changing table. There were two stacks in there and he took a smaller one for Hannah. He opened it, located the sticky tabs and held it up. Then he gingerly removed her diaper and said, "Ewww." She giggled at him. "Yeah, I bet you think that's funny. You should see it from my point of view. Hannah, that's disgusting." She giggled again while he looked around for wipes, finding them on a shelf underneath the changing platform. He was making a face that Hannah found hilarious as he gingerly wiped stinky poop off her rosy butt. It took a *lot* of wipes because he was reluctant to get too close.

He got her clean, but her bottom was pink, like maybe she wasn't being changed often enough. And he had completely destroyed a new diaper in the process, tearing the sticky tabs clean off, but he was luckier with the second one, though it seemed to be listing to one side. Mattie was a simpler affair; he wasn't muddy. With a child on each hip and one terrible diaper and one nontoxic, he found Vanni in the kitchen. She turned from the sink and saw the diapers and wrinkled her nose.

"Which one of you had the present for Pastor Kincaid?" she asked, taking the dirty diddies.

"It was madam," he said. He watched as Vanni folded the dirty diaper and deftly taped it closed in a nice, tight, odorless package. "Wow," Noah said. "That was slick."

"Let's put them in the high chairs," she said, taking Mattie and leaving Noah to settle Hannah. "What brings you by, Noah? Checking on me?"

"In a way," he said. "You've been on my mind and I wondered how it was going. I hope I'm not imposing too much. Looks like you could use a hand."

"I could use nine hands," she said, but not much humor seeped through.

Once the kids were settled in high chairs, she put some crackers on their trays and fixed up two sippy cups with juice.

"Hannah's bottom is kind of pink," he said. "Kind of *too* pink."

"I'll take care of that," she said.

Noah pulled a chair out from the kitchen table and sat down. "You could use a little help around here," he said. "Just during the really busy times. Huh? So you can catch up a little, maybe steal a nap. Any friends or family available for that?"

She shrugged and although dinner makings were spread across the island, she poured two cups and sat down with him. "Everyone is willing, but everyone is also far too busy. Shelby's starting school in a few days; she's waited forever for that. Plus, she's planning her wedding and I'm supposed to be helping her. My dad and Muriel are pretty caught up in running two ranches and doing some traveling for Muriel's new movie. Believe me, I couldn't be more pleased about that—I haven't seen my dad this happy in years. Noah, I don't want to impose on anyone. This is our problem. We need to figure it out."

"Might be easier to figure out with a little help."

Vanni just glanced into her coffee cup.

And Noah thought, she *wants* it to be hard, because she's thoroughly pissed off. She's having trouble caring about this infant because Paul brought her home and she's angry with him, with the baby, and mostly with herself. And anger turned inward is depression. And depression can be deadly.

"Did Paul mention that he has crews working on the church now?" he asked her.

She shrugged and said, "I can't remember. He may have mentioned it."

"Well, it's loud, and it's going to stay that way for a couple of weeks, maybe a month. They're scraping the outside of the church, sanding the sanctuary floor, tearing windows out of the frames, that sort of thing. I have this girl working for me now—nice young girl. Ellie Baldwin."

"I think I heard about her," Vanni said.

"Well, I have a million things to do every day that take me out of the church and I leave her to clean, paint, answer the phone, and I think she's about ready to kill me. I'll send her out here to help tomorrow. She'll thank me for it."

"A young girl?" Vanni asked. "Are you sure that's going to help me?"

"She's twenty-five and has children of her own. They're with her ex-husband right now and she really misses them."

"Why are they with her ex-husband?" Vanni wanted to know.

"Reasonable question, before you let her help out with your children. The details aren't really mine to share, but I can assure you she's a wonderful mother. I've spent a couple of days with her and the kids and she's devoted to them. She's brash with me." He laughed. "And nothing but sweet and gentle with the kids. The separation is real hard on her. Maybe this will serve two purposes—give her some kids to cuddle and you a little break. Plus, she cleans like a genie in a bottle."

"Are you sure she wouldn't mind?" Vanni asked.

"Oh, I'm positive she'd welcome it, compared to the crappy work I've had her doing on that old church." And maybe Gramma Baldwin can counsel while she's at it. He smiled secretly.

When Ellie came to the church the next morning, Noah said, "I have a special assignment for you. Today, tomorrow and for as long as you think it's necessary. Some friends of mine have a situation—you know Paul? The builder?"

"Can't miss him," she said. She dug into her tight jeans and pulled out a couple of cotton balls she clearly intended to stuff in her ears.

"Well, a woman he barely knew and whom his wife never met died recently and, guess what? She named Paul as her baby's guardian in her will. Without any warning, with a son of their own only eighteen months old, they inherited a baby girl who is under a year. Vanni is struggling to keep up and they might be getting the best of her. Go out there and help, will you?"

"What should I do?" she asked.

"You'll know what to do. I wrote down some directions for you—they're about ten minutes out of town. And, Ellie? If you can make her laugh, that would be good."

"Sure," she said, grinning. "I'll get right on it. I have a bunch of preacher jokes I haven't tried out yet."

When Ellie rang the bell at Vanni's house, the door was a long time in opening. When Vanni finally answered, she had a little boy on her hip, the sound of a baby fussing behind her, and she was wearing her robe. "Hi, I'm Ellie, Pastor Kincaid's assistant," she said. "Want a hand?"

"You'll be sorry," Vanessa said, turning away from the door.

"Nah, I'll be happy. Your husband is making my life miserable!" Ellie walked in and went immediately in search of the fussy baby. She found her standing in the playpen, reaching out. The second Ellie came into the room, her face lit up in a beautiful smile. She reached for the baby. "Well, my little cupcake. What's your name?"

"That's Hannah, our newcomer," Vanni said. "And this is Matt."

"Hello, Hannah. What a pretty name. Are you wet or hungry or just ornery?"

"She could be wet, but they've had breakfast."

"Then let's try a change," Ellie said. "Where are the diapers?"

"Right down the hall. I could do it if you—"

"Nah, let me. It's been years since I've changed a baby. I kind of miss those early days, difficult as they are." And off she went to carry through. When she returned a few minutes later, Vanni was sitting on the couch, holding Matt, looking pretty down in the dumps. "This one has diaper rash, but you probably knew that."

"I've been putting stuff on her. There's a tube on the changing table."

"Uh-huh, I found it, gave her a good smear."

"Listen, if you have other things to do—"

"My mission, assigned by none other than His Holiness Kincaid, is to see what I can do to help you. I understand Miss Hannah here was a surprise?"

"To put it mildly," Vanni said.

"Well, that's my specialty. Both of mine were surprises. But what luck—they're awesome. Danielle is eight and Trevor is four."

"You don't seem old enough to have an eight-year-old," Vanni said.

"Oh, I'm not." She laughed. "Like I said, I specialize in surprise children. But I've decided to give that up."

"Paul and I were just about to start on one of our own when Hannah showed up."

Ellie frowned. "One of your own?"

"Oh, I guess Noah didn't tell you. I was married to Paul's best friend before. I was pregnant when he was killed in Iraq. And Paul stepped in to be my husband and Matt's father. And, as it turned out, a woman he'd dated before we married died in a car accident and bequeathed that adorable little package to us."

"Well, holy shit," Ellie said. "No wonder you're a little out of sorts! So you're the mother of that one and Paul's the father of—"

"No, Hannah's not his. Sometimes I think it might be easier if she were. But she's not. And even considering Hannah has a father out there somewhere, Paul brought her home."

Ellie nuzzled the little girl. It was anyone's guess what Vanni struggled with most—the fact that she suddenly had two small children, or that one of them was Paul's previous girlfriend's. Did Vanni wonder just how important Hannah's mother was to him? That would be enough to put anyone in a mood. But she said, "Listen, I have an idea. Since everyone is dry and fed, why don't I take over while you enjoy your morning rituals. Take some time. Have a long soak or shower, a primp, even a rest if you're tired. I can handle everything till lunchtime. Or even longer."

"You might find it to be more than you bargained for."

Ellie shrugged. "Or, I could have more fun than I've had cleaning and painting an old church. If I have trouble, I'll come for you. Go on now—this is your big break. Unless—gee, maybe you want to observe me for a while, to be sure I'm okay with the kids?"

"Noah says you're wonderful with kids."

"He did? Well, how about that. I should be—I've had plenty of practice. It's been just me and the kids for a long time."

"I'll go take a shower," Vanni said, without responding to that last comment. She handed off Matt. "If you have problems, holler."

"And take some time for yourself," Ellie said, bouncing a kid on each hip. "I'll juggle for a while."

When Vanni disappeared, Ellie took the kids to the kitchen. Once there, she found the remnants of breakfast on their high-chair trays and the kitchen was a mess—dishes in the sink, the floor sticky, dirty pots on the stove, the newspaper spread out on the table in front of a coffee cup with a ring around the inside. "Well," she said softly to the kids. "Mommy's got issues. But, hey, we can deal. Right?"

Hannah said, "Ma!" and Matt patted Ellie's head.

"You two," Ellie cooed, kissing each cheek. "Could you be any more delicious? Come on, let's settle in. There's stuff to do here."

Once she had them strapped in the high chairs, she cleaned off the trays. She found sippy cups in the sink, scrubbed them and filled them with juice. Then she put a handful of dry Cheerios on each tray and, talking and singing little ditties the whole time, began cleaning the kitchen. There was a thin, sticky coat of kiddie paste over everything, including the floor and high chairs, so when the dishes were loaded, she started the dishwasher, wiped down the stove, table and countertops. In the laundry room off the kitchen she found a bucket, mop and sponge. Also, loads of dirty laundry. "Hmm," she said, thinking. "Well, whoever said 'one thing at a time' didn't know squat." She got a load of kids' clothes going. Back in the kitchen, singing the "ABC" song, "People on the Bus" and "Little Soap," she washed down the high chairs while the kids were in them, stopping occasionally to make faces and noises and tickle. And then, dishwasher and washing machine humming away, she mopped the floor, scooting the high chairs out of the way one at a time.

She flipped the laundry and started another load. And then she took the kids to the great room where a playpen stood ready. She settled both of them, playing with them for just a moment before she left them to grab some Windex and Pledge and rags. If there was one thing a single mother of two had learned pretty well, it was how to make a small house presentable in record time. Well, this was no small house—it was like a castle to Ellie—and brand-new. She knew she would never live in such a house, not unless she won the lottery—which she never played—or fell in love with some rich guy, which was now off the table. But still…

She shined up the glass and wood furniture, found the vacuum in the front-hall closet and, talking to and singing to the kids, she ran it around the room. She glanced at her watch and saw that Vanni had been missing for well over an hour, but it had been time well spent. She was making great progress.

Another hour passed and she had cleaned the kitchen and great room, folded some clothes on the couch while picking up toys that had been pitched out of the playpen. Since she had a couple of stacks of clean baby clothes, she put them in the nursery, rounded up towels and ran a bath.

Ohhh, they loved the bath, so she supervised while they played until the water was cooled. Little Hannah needed that soak on her rosy bottom. Next, clean clothes and a glance at her watch told her it was lunchtime. She took the little ones back to the kitchen. She found baby food in the pantry but, if memory served, there was one thing kids loved universally. "Mac and cheese," she said, grinning at them. It took only minutes in the microwave and then minutes to cool a bit. She managed to put away the clean dishes from the dishwasher, though if Vanni ever found them again, it would be a miracle. When the mac and cheese had cooled down enough, she gave each child a bowl on their tray.

Now, this was where aggressive supervision was required if they were going to get more in their stomachs than on her clean floor. She sat on a chair with a handy rag and helped Matt guide his spoon while she fed Hannah. "I so knew you'd love this," she said to them. "It was a big treat at my house."

There were bottles in the dishwasher. Since she didn't find any powdered formula anywhere, she was left to assume they were now on regular milk. So, she filled a couple of bottles, and with Hannah in her arms and Matt lying on the couch, his legs draped over hers, they relaxed together. Hannah played with Ellie's ponytail that fell over her shoulder and Matt held her finger.

These children needed to be *touched!* They needed kisses and giggles and cooing and pleasant smiles! They needed to feel the love! But their mother was sad, overwhelmed, hurt and exhausted.

Both children passed out with their bottles. Ellie scooted out from under Matt's legs and hefted Hannah into her arms. Matt slept with his mouth open and arms limply splayed outward, totally gone. To his sleeping form she whispered, "Do not roll off this couch or I'll be fired!" Then she took Hannah to her crib and went quickly back for Matt.

Both children were settled and Ellie was folding another load of clothes when Vanni finally appeared. "Well," Ellie said, smiling, "you look like you had a little rest."

"I apologize. I didn't help you at all. I left you high and dry with them."

"Don't apologize, angel-cakes. I was having a nice time. This is a magnificent house you have here. I enjoyed tidying up a bit. Are you hungry? Why don't I fix you some lunch."

"Oh, don't bother. Now that you've done so much and the kids are sleeping, you don't have to stay—"

"I still have things to do, Vanni. After the kids wake up, I'm going to freshen their room. But while they sleep,

I thought I could get you a fresh set of sheets, give your master bath a bit of a fluff and buff, maybe run the vacuum around in there." She smiled happily. "You should take advantage of me while you can."

"Only if you'll have a little lunch with me," Vanni said.

"I'll make us a couple of sandwiches," Ellie said. "How's that?"

While Ellie made the sandwiches, Vanni snuck the clean clothes into the drawers in the nursery. Vanni stripped her own bed and got her sheets washing. Then they sat at the kitchen table together.

"So your children came as surprises?" Vanni asked.

"I think stunned and scared shitless would be more accurate," Ellie said, biting into her sandwich. Vanni laughed in spite of herself. "Believe me, it wasn't funny."

"No, not that. I'm laughing at the way you swear. Must be quite a challenge for Noah."

"Uh-huh. He's talking swear jar in the church. Quarter a curse."

"Mel and Jack have one of those!"

"So I hear. I also heard Mel's taking the town on a cruise in the spring, just on the contents. Really, just so you don't think I'm completely terrible, I never swear in front of children. I don't even slip. I know that sounds far-fetched, but really. When I swear, I do it on purpose."

"Well, at least you've got that going for you." Vanni laughed. "So—the kids?"

"Oh, yeah. I got pregnant with Danielle in high school. My boyfriend was killed in an accident—motorcycle versus car, not his fault." Once again she conveniently left out the fact that she had two children by two different guys, neither of whom married her. She chewed a little more and swallowed. "I was on my own. Well, with my gram's help, but she died when Trevor was two."

"Oh, I'm sorry, Ellie. I'm sorry for the loss of both your boyfriend and your grandmother. Is that the extent of your family?"

"I have a mother somewhere, but she hasn't been around since I was, like, three months old. She drops in once in a while, but she never spends the night. She's pretty much consumed with her own life, which is fine. My mother—she's a real load. She needs taking care of. If she ever got the idea I could do that for her, I'd never get rid of her and she's very self-centered."

Vanni was quiet a moment. "I lost my mother almost six years ago."

Ellie's hand that held the sandwich slowly lowered to the table. "Oh, man. A mother and a husband? Oh, sugar, you've had such a rough time!"

"Same as you," Vanni said softly.

Ellie shrugged. "I miss my gram all the time, but sometimes it's like she's right on my shoulder," she said, patting the place. "I can hear her, feel her. Like she never really left me. She was seventy when she died. She'd been reading in her chair and died with her book in her lap and her glasses on her nose. We slept on the pullout sofa, Danielle on a small daybed and Trevor in the crib, all of us in one room. While I slept and she read, she passed. I found her in the morning. She must have been dead all night, but she went so softly, no one knew she was gone. Funny," she said, "but I dreamt about her that night. I dreamt I was lying on the couch with my head on her lap, on her favorite corduroy jumper, and she was rubbing my head. I was real little when she did that, but it's one of my favorite memories." She looked at Vanni and noticed she had glistening eyes. "Oh, God, I'm sorry. My marching orders were to make you *laugh,* not make you cry!"

"Who told you that?" Vanni asked, wiping her eyes. "To make me laugh?"

"Noah. I asked him what I was supposed to do and he said, 'You'll know what to do.' And added that it would be good if I could make you laugh. Noah thinks I'm a real stitch, but he'd like to shove me under a pew and keep his future congregation from seeing me."

"And why is that?" Vanni asked with a laugh.

"Oh, he hasn't been real specific, but I believe it has to do with my potty mouth, my tattoo, my cleavage and, when I'm not Mommy's helper or Pastor's painter, the way I like to do my hair and makeup. Kind of Dolly Parton." She grinned. "I know it annoys him, but I can't seem to stop."

Vanni reached for her hand and smiled. "Don't. Don't change for anyone, especially a man."

"Ah, we *are* sisters. I thought so." The spin cycle stopped. "I'm going to put those sheets in the dryer, then we can make up the bed together. While they're drying, why don't I go see if your bedroom and bathroom could use a once-over. When I leave today, it's my goal to see that everyone is happy and can relax in a fresh house."

"You're amazing, Ellie. Your grandmother trained you very well."

"Yeah? Well, baby, it's such a great thing to have more than two rooms to clean, it's like you're doing *me* a favor."

The girls talked while they worked on the master bedroom and bath, when Ellie wasn't running the vacuum, at least. They laughed like girlfriends, told sentimental stories about family members, and Ellie even tried on some old pants and tops that Vanni said she'd never fit into again. Vanni was only an inch shorter than Ellie and wore her pants long to compensate for boots, so the fit was perfect.

"Take them," Vanni said. "If you like them, that is. My feelings won't be hurt at all if they're not your style. I mean, I doubt Dolly would like them. I was going to give them to Goodwill, so they're yours if you want them."

"That's so nice, Vanni. I didn't expect anything like this!" She tilted her head. "I think I hear something. That was a good long nap. With any luck, they'll be in good moods tonight. What do you usually do when they wake up, after a change?"

"Snack. Playtime till dinner," she said with a shrug. "Nothing special."

"How about a little cuddle time. Just waking up is awful sweet," Ellie said. "Let's do it."

As Ellie was leaving the master bedroom, Vanni touched her arm. "Um, would you take care of Hannah, please?"

"Sure. I'd like that."

They collected their assigned children, changed them and cuddled them. As Ellie held Hannah close, she said, "So—not really connected to this one yet?"

Vanni took a moment to answer. "That's terrible, I know…"

"It took me a while to feel like Danielle was really my baby. To believe I could love her more than anything, which was what my gram said would happen. Of course, I was just a kid myself. But if it took me a few days even though I'd carried her inside my body and felt every movement, I guess it's natural for it to take you a little while when you didn't have any relationship with her at all before she was suddenly living with you."

"You don't think I'm a terrible person?"

Ellie smiled at her and held Hannah tighter. "Vanni, I barely know you, but I can tell already. There's not one terrible thing about you. Now—what do we have for snacks?"

"Yogurt," Vanni said with a smile. "They love it."

At four o'clock, with the beginnings of supper ready, the house clean, laundry done, children bathed and happy and Vanni looking pretty good, Ellie was saying goodbye. She gave each child a loud smack, making them both laugh. She clutched Vanni's cast-off clothes close, very excited about them since they were a bit more conservative, though it killed her to think she had pleasure from the thought of pleasing Noah. "I'll see you in the morning about eight-thirty," she said to Vanni. "Let's do it the same way—you answer in your bathrobe and I'll take over. You can have the morning all to yourself. And whatever needs doing, I'll do. You can have the afternoon, too, if you need it. Maybe you have shopping or errands or something. Whatever you need."

Vanni's eyes were round with surprise. "I get more than one day of this special treatment?"

Ellie grinned. "Baby, you get the rest of your life if you need it. I think Paul gave Noah a deal on the redo and Noah's so happy I'm not around the church to make his life difficult. See you in the a.m."

Ellie went to the church before going home. She found Noah in his office, and Lucy on the floor behind the desk. She stood in front of the desk, her hands on her hips.

"How'd it go?" he asked.

She frowned at him. "You might've mentioned everything had gone to hell out there."

He stood up and cleared his throat. "A picture's worth a thousand words? Were you able to help?"

"Of course," she said. "But, buddy, that woman needs more than household help. She needs a miracle. Inspiration."

Noah smiled at her. "That's why I sent you, Ellie."

"No, you sent me because you can't clean and you don't have anyone else."

"And that, too," he said. "Going back tomorrow?"

"It'll be a lot of tomorrows before she's good to go," Ellie said. "Do *not* screw up the painting while I'm busy at the Haggertys'."

After Ellie was back in her rented room, after a microwaved burrito and diet cola, she turned on the clock radio for a little music. And then she cried for her own children.

Eleven

The rest of the week was a busy one for Ellie as she reported for duty at Vanessa's house every morning. Given there were two of them to tend the children and keep the house and laundry up to speed, everything went smoothly. Having a full-time babysitter allowed Vanni to run errands, have regular horseback rides for exercise and fresh air and, not least of all, have someone to talk to. It didn't take Vanni any time at all to start looking more rested.

It wasn't long before Vanni asked Ellie, "Now, where are your kids?"

Ellie took a deep breath; up until she lost custody of her children and went to work for a church, it had never occurred to her to lie. She felt she had to protect everyone—her kids, her boss, even herself. But lying was complicated. And painful. "Well, I met Arnie when I was all alone with two little kids, two jobs and very little means of holding it all together. My judgment must have sucked, because I married a real strange guy who was obsessed with controlling me. Talk about changing your appearance for a guy? Vanni—that one wanted me to dress like an old woman and never leave the house. It was so bizarre. Of course, I left him almost right away—we were married less than three months. But Arnie wanted me back. The only way he could figure out how to do that was to take a custody case to court." And she explained the same details she'd given Jo Fitch.

"Ellie, wasn't there help available to you? I don't know—like welfare? Food stamps?"

"Sure," she said. "If there's anything worse than working two jobs with little kids, it's trying to figure out how to live on the 'help.' Do you know what I qualified for? If I worked a job that paid eleven dollars an hour—a real find—I could get an extra two hundred and twenty from the state. You ever try to live on about two thousand a month with two kids? My money was long gone before I even got to things like clothes for them and school supplies. Just keeping a roof over our heads, usually two rooms, gas in the car and insurance, the lights on and a babysitter for Trevor, as well as a sitter for after school and evenings for both of them… Well, I never did get that far. After my gramma died and I didn't have a place to live anymore or a babysitter, I just couldn't do it."

"Didn't your grandmother have a house to leave you when she died?" Vanni asked.

Ellie shrugged. "My gramma had a little tiny house that she'd kept mortgaging over the years. Between the two of us—her retirement benefits and my income from two jobs—we could keep going. But when she was gone, I couldn't make those payments. I had to find something cheap to rent."

"Aw, Ellie. I'm so sorry. And that's how you ended up married to that jackass?"

"That kind of sums it up. I thought Arnie would take care of us. He was so sweet to the kids before we got married, so hard on them the very first day we lived with him.

It was just awful. He was only looking for some people to boss around—I didn't see that till it was too late. He's still looking for control. It's a nightmare for the kids. But, we'll get through it and then we'll move on, legally, and get out of the pastor's hair."

"No, Ellie!"

"It's okay, Vanni. Noah took a real chance on me, just so I'd have a good job to take to court and get my kids back." Vanni didn't know the half of what Noah had taken on—giving a job to a stripper who'd lost her kids? A woman with two kids with two different dads, both times out of wedlock? One dead and one in prison? "I just need my kids."

"You're going to get them back, honey. And if you need my help on that, you just tell me what to do!"

"That's so sweet," Ellie said softly.

"What I want to know," Vanni said, "is how you stay so positive after all you've been through."

Ellie shrugged. "I don't know. I don't take anything for granted. Good stuff doesn't come my way all the time, so when it does—like this job that will get me my kids back, this town, friendship, people like you who can accept me even though I'm a big mess—that means something. And my gramma used to always say, 'Gratitude brings happiness.'"

On Friday, after four full days of togetherness while Ellie played mommy's helper, they were talking about the weekend while the kids had their lunch. "So, does Paul work on Saturdays?" Ellie asked. "That's my day with my kids, so I can't miss it, but if you're going to be up a creek, I can go pick them up and bring them with me. They're fantastic and they'd love playing with the little ones. They're very careful and I'd watch every second. Danielle is so grown up at eight. Trevor's a little clumsy, but I wouldn't let him do anything with the tots that would cause harm. And while everyone's sleeping—I could help with laundry and housework."

Vanni smiled. "You never stop lending a hand, do you?"

"I intend to see my assignment through. I might need a letter of recommendation someday." She sobered. "Seriously, Vanni—I don't want you to be stranded again. I can pick up the kids and—"

"No, no, don't. Just have a nice Saturday with them. I'm all caught up, thanks to you. Maybe Paul will make it a short day."

"Then I'll see you Monday?" Ellie asked, wiping little faces after lunch.

"If Noah says you're not needed at the church," Vanni agreed.

Ellie lifted Hannah out of the high chair. She had fixed two bottles and the women took the kids into the great room, settling in. Ellie held Hannah, and Vanni held Matt.

Ellie cuddled Hannah close. She was a precious little thing, her dark curls so silky and her cheeks so pink. Her eyes glittered with happiness. She held the bottle herself, but Ellie could tell she enjoyed being cuddled. "My gramma used to say, 'Hold them whenever you can, Ellie. Touch and the sound of your voice is everything.' And even now, when my kids are so big, it still seems to matter to them. Another thing she used to say was, 'All you really need to tell them is that you love them no matter what and that you wanted them.' Being wanted is very important in life. I don't think my mother wanted me, but my gramma did, and she told me all the time that I was her blessing, her dream come true."

Ellie sat on the sofa and Vanni in the chair with Mattie. And suddenly Hannah pulled the nipple of the bottle out of her mouth and turned her whole body away from Ellie. She held the bottle with one hand and stretched her other arm out toward Vanni. "Mama!" she said, and smiled. "Mama! Mamamamama…" And then she turned back, put the bottle back in her mouth.

"Well," Ellie said. "You might not be there quite yet, but she is."

Vanni lifted her chin with a sniff, closing her eyes.

"The other thing my gramma used to say, 'You're not happy? Fine. Act happy and see if the right feeling catches up.' And you know what? Sometimes that works."

Vanni was quiet for a long moment, and then very softly she said, "Let's trade."

"Good," Ellie said. She stood with Hannah in her arms, carrying her the short distance over to Vanni. She put the baby on Vanni's knees and lifted the much heavier Mattie in her arms and went back to the sofa.

And Vanni held Hannah. Hannah snuggled close, putting her fingers into Vanni's mouth while she suckled. Then the suction broke with her smile. And without quite letting go of the nipple, she said, "Mama," in a very small, almost relieved voice.

And Vanni began to cry.

Noah was kneeling in the sanctuary on the sanded floor, inspecting some hardwood seams that might need repair. He'd have to ask Paul about replacing the boards before the floor was finished. Lucy was beside him as usual. It was that magic hour, about five o'clock, when the sun caught the stained-glass window and lit it up.

"Pastor?"

He turned at the sound of Ellie's voice. She had never addressed him so.

"I thought you'd like to know about the progress out at the Haggerty house. Everything is spic-and-span, and I think Vanni is warming up to Hannah. I'll go back on

Monday morning, but I feel like they're doing better than when I found them."

Noah took several steps toward her. "Why do you look so tired? Was it real hard work?"

Ellie shook her head. "It was hard on the heart. That baby girl is priceless, she's so wonderful. She needs a mother's love. I think it's getting closer, but it's been a tough adjustment. I guess you knew that or you wouldn't have sent me out there."

"What did you do?" he asked gently, his hand absently wandering to stroke the ponytail that hung over her shoulder.

She shrugged. "Nothing amazing. I cleaned, held the kids, let her talk, talked myself—you know. Like girls do. But when I was leaving today, Vanni was holding Hannah, probably the first time she didn't absolutely have to. She was holding her close, kissing her little head, crying while that amazing child put little fingers in Vanni's mouth and called her mama. I think it's coming together. But, God, it's killing me."

Noah smiled, unsurprised. "Did your grandmother contribute a lot to that evolution?"

"My gramma?"

"You know," he said. "My gramma said this, my gramma said that…"

"Do I do that a lot? I don't even know when I do that."

"It's not a liability, Ellie," he said. "That's why I sent you."

She put her hands on her hips. "Well, how sneaky is *that!* Really, I should be paid better if you're going to have me doing that, and especially if you're not even going to tell me!"

"You should be paid a lot more than I'm paying you," he said with a smile. "But it's what I can afford."

She rolled her eyes. "Why the *hell* can't I ever run into a *rich* man who wants to take advantage of me?"

He just laughed at her.

"Well, this is a fine mess," a deep voice said from behind them. "Much worse looking than I expected. You must be thrilled, Noah."

Noah turned. There, standing at the other end of the empty church, was his best friend and mentor. "George!" He left Ellie and strode toward him. "You didn't say you were coming!"

"Sure I did. I just didn't say when. It comes as no surprise to see you looking happy, surrounded by this disaster."

Noah laughed and embraced the older man in a fierce hug. "God, it's good to see you! How long will you stay?"

"Long enough to get the lay of the land. Now, who is your friend? You shouldn't leave a beautiful woman standing behind like that."

Noah grabbed George's arm and pulled him down what would eventually be an aisle in the church. "George, meet Ellie Baldwin, pastor's assistant. Ellie, meet George Davenport, my best friend and mentor."

A slow smile spread over George's face. He took Ellie's hand, raising the back of her fingers to his lips. He bent and brushed a kiss on them. "Ellie, it's an honor. I retired too soon—I had no idea the assistants would be so beautiful down the road."

"Nice to meet you, Mr...."

"Pastor Davenport," Noah corrected. "Retired, but still a preacher."

She smiled. "A pleasure, Your Worship," she said.

Noah laughed at George's look of surprise. "She doesn't mean it, George. She's extremely disrespectful. And unrepentant."

"Then you'll do penance by sitting through dinner

with us," George said. "I can't wait to try that little place next door, the one Noah's been bragging about. Come, Ellie, stay close to me. I want to know how you like working for this reprobate."

"It's hell, Your Reverence."

George felt he had met the entire town by the time dinner was over, but Jack Sheridan assured him he hadn't come close. "These are pretty much the regulars, though," Jack admitted. That included Jack's wife and two small children, the neighbors who lived nearby, Hope McCrea, who sold Noah the old church. George was introduced to young Rick Sudder and his fiancée, Liz; Rick was recently returned from a tour of duty with the marines in Iraq. Somewhere along the line George learned that Rick had a prosthetic leg, but he never did figure out which one. The lad had a carefree manner and not the slightest limp.

And then there came a story that had half the bar in stitches—it seemed that when Rick was struggling to adjust, the man sitting beside him at the bar, Dan, challenged him to a fight out in the street. Dan, over thirty-five years old, took *off* the prosthetic leg no one knew he had! "It was a circus," Jack said. "But it seemed to turn Rick onto the idea that life could go on."

There were more stories; clearly the folks in town enjoyed sharing their tales with newcomers and strangers. And while they partook of some of the finest stew George had ever tasted, along with the softest, sweetest bread, he was able to get to know Ellie a little bit. Of course, he'd heard all the details that brought her here from Noah, details that Ellie would never know George knew. George was interested in her children and how she was settling into town.

George was captivated by her. She was a pip, as George's father might have said. But what he saw quickly, what he was sure Noah was oblivious to, Ellie was very like Noah's late wife. She was unique, confident, funny and impossibly positive.

Noah and George enjoyed a brandy after dinner while Ellie and Jack had coffee, then both men walked her home to her rented room. And while Noah was walking George back to the RV for the night, he told him about some of the things he had found in the town and surrounding mountains that could use his attention. "If you'll stay a few days, I'll take you out to the vagrants' camp, give you a car tour of some of the more isolated cabins dotting the landscape, take you to Valley Hospital and the nursing home, and to meet the pastor in Grace Valley."

It's a gold mine for Noah, George found himself thinking. *It has everything the young man has ever wanted or needed. A sense of family, strong community ties, not to mention the girl.* But George said nothing about Ellie. What he did ask was, "Someone mentioned Ellie was helping some young mother with her children…?"

Noah explained the situation at length. "That's precisely what we were talking about when you arrived," Noah said. "Ellie seemed drained, not from the work of helping with the kids, but from the ache it gave her to think of an unloved child. I never asked her to keep that confidential, not any part of it. It would be futile, as the whole town knows about Vanessa and Paul. She's a natural, George. A helper by nature. She's armed with all these old sayings her grandmother left her with and they have roots in psychology, but they're all lore. The girl grew up in two rooms with her grandmother; they slept together on a pullout couch her whole life. Then she added two small children to the family and they all worked together to care for one another." He laughed. "Talk about evidence that money can't make you happy."

"Correct," George agreed. "It needn't make you miserable, either. I may be an old fool, but Ellie strikes me as the kind of person who wouldn't be destroyed by a little money. I could be wrong, however. She's very inexperienced."

Noah laughed. "George, if there's one thing Ellie is not, it's inexperienced. Well, maybe with money, but in all other things, she's had way too much experience."

George thought, *He's fighting for his life.* And he smiled at that. No one loved a battle more than Noah! He wasn't your mother's preacher; not a sweet and docile guy, but a warrior. He'd fought his father and his father's shallow television religion for so many years; then went on to fight the injustice and apathy of the world at large. He wanted to bring peace and love to his people, but inevitably he brought courage and muscle. And that part of Noah, the part he constantly resisted, that was the part that made George proudest.

"I'm staying at least a few days," George said. "I'm interested in this place." But what really interested George was Noah *in* this place. With these people. With that *woman.*

The woman was perfect for him. She was one of the people—not some female bred to stand beside a man of the cloth. She would bring laughter, excitement and passion to his life, his work.

On Saturday, Noah took George with him to bring the jackets and some wool socks to the boys in the woods. At George's stubborn insistence, they took a couple of Preacher's pies and two Bibles. The men in the camp sniffed appreciatively of the pies and wrinkled their noses at the Bibles. But, they turned over a few buckets for stools and Noah read to them for a little while. Of the whole camp, there were just a few who enjoyed that, but those few might as well have been a multitude for the way it made Noah feel.

They made the rounds of the nursing home, Valley Hospital and Sunday church in Grace Valley. George, being a fine figure of a seventy-year-old man, garnered the attention of some of the more mature ladies, though even the younger ones were inclined to look his way more than once, something he enjoyed perhaps a bit too much. He was a consummate flirt and flatly admitted he liked women. By the time they left Grace Valley, he was armed with e-mail addresses and promises to stay in touch, and of course to return. "Absolutely," he said. "But by then the Virgin River church will be open and you'll have to attend services there. Noah will entertain you completely."

Later that afternoon, they were prowling around the inside of the Virgin River church, talking about the possibilities in renovation. "Noah, tell me about that stained-glass window," George asked.

"I researched it. This was a poor church when it was constructed and pretty much depleted the funds of the congregation. The population was smaller then— about three hundred. But one member went on a campaign to find something special for the church and wrote to every artist in the world until she found a man willing to donate the window, though he'd probably never attend the church. His name was Josiah Piedmont and his only requirement in the deal was that it never be destroyed. It came to this church in the sixties and Josiah lived in Connecticut at the time. He has since died and left behind amazingly beautiful Christian art in all mediums. When the church was forced to shut down because they couldn't support it anymore, the people in town boarded up that window to keep it safe. Now, times having changed, you can find a Web site for the artist and see where his works are displayed. When I get organized, I'll add this piece to his Web site, with the location. It boiled down to one woman on a mission."

After dinner at Jack's, they indulged in an evening brandy at the bar. "Did you enjoy your tour the past couple of days?" Noah asked George.

"I think you're onto something here, Noah. I like this place. My only disappointment so far is that we didn't gather up Ellie to join us for dinner tonight."

"She deserves a day off, don't you think?"

"I think you like her. And that it's about time," George said.

"Let's not start all that again. I've been around plenty of women," Noah said. His eyes twinkled. "George, who are you seeing these days?"

"Well, let's see. I've been dating around, you might call it. There's a visiting professor at the college I see when she's in town. She travels quite a lot. And a neighbor lady and I like to have dinner in the city. She writes an 'about town' column for the paper and we enjoy some of the best restaurants, all on her tab, but that's not the best part about her. There's a waitress in Tacoma I like, a music teacher out on Bainbridge Island and a professor of veterinary medicine. She's the most trouble and I think I like her best."

Noah's eyes were round. He swallowed. "You're seeing *five* women?"

"Well, on and off. Each one of them is completely irresistible in her own way."

"Don't any of them want more of you than an occasional date? Like a serious relationship?"

George sighed and looked upward. "I'm not opposed to the idea of marrying again, Noah. But, as of this moment, the only woman I'm seeing I would consider is the vet, Sharon. But she's forty-four. I think that might be a tad risky, don't you?" Then he grinned. "Although we do jog together on Sunday mornings. She's keeping up very well."

Noah burst out laughing. This was what he loved about George and always had—he was so unafraid to live life. He held nothing back. "They used to call men like you rogues," Noah said.

"Not men like me," he protested. "I care very much for these ladies. They are, each one, wonderful women. I treat them with genuine affection and respect."

Noah suspected George was sleeping with at least one of them, but he'd never ask. In Noah's younger years, he'd been frivolous where women were concerned and had been intimate with quite a few. When he was about to be ordained, he'd struggled with the chastity issue. He wasn't big on chastity. He didn't think it was so much a sin as a recommendation, and in most cases there was a strong argument for the recommendation. Youth, for example. And there was no argument to support sex with partners you weren't committed to; he could admit he'd been impetuous there. And he couldn't find anything to support adultery—you didn't need a commandment to see how bad that could turn.

For that matter, the Bible was riddled with suggestions that by modern standards were ridiculous. Isolation for menstruating women. No eating of fish without scales or fins; no wearing of linen and wool in the same garment. And there was a lot of stoning. Some were ageless rules that made perfect moral sense even today, others were cultural manifestos of the period.

Still, he had wanted George's take on it, especially if he was about to encourage members of a congregation to stand firm on something that bothered him hardly at all.

George was blasé. "No one knows the Bible better than you, Noah. And you have an impressive knowledge of related studies. There are obvious reasons why things like chastity are enforced even today. To keep women safe, for one thing. To keep men from acting like rutting beasts. To discourage promiscuity, to honor the sanctity of marriage. To keep the act of love holy and virtuous. And to keep children from coming into unblessed unions before the man and woman were prepared to parent them, to feed and protect them."

Noah knew this too well. The reasons for most of the Bible's rules were practical as opposed to arbitrary proof of one's discipline.

"But I suggest making use of the Eleventh Commandment. Moses ran out of stone, but its wisdom has survived the ages. *Take responsibility for your actions.*"

Noah had grinned largely and said, "Now, *that,* I get."

Twelve

On Monday, George and Noah took a hint when they realized they were simply a bother to the workers who were trying to get some real work done in the church. They decided to drive over to Arcata to look at the bird sanctuaries, then they had a nice dinner in Old Town.

By the time they got back to Virgin River it was getting late so George took a book to bed while Noah sat up. He was on the couch with his laptop, trading late-night e-mails with a university friend who had moved to Los Angeles. It was after ten when there was a knock at the RV door. A soft knock. Noah typed, Gotta go. Company.

Noah answered the door and standing there, below him, was Ellie. She was upset; all color was drained from her face.

"I'm sorry, I'm sorry, it's late and you were probably asleep and I'm sorry, but I'm so scared and I don't know what to do."

"I wasn't asleep. Come in," he said, putting out a hand. "What in the world happened?"

"Someone visited Arnie from Child Welfare today,

talked to him, interviewed the kids, and he's furious! He says he knows I'm behind it and he's gonna make me pay. Oh, God, Noah! What if he does something terrible to the kids?"

"Come here," Noah said calmly. He led her to the couch and closed the laptop, pushing it aside. "Just sit down and tell me about it."

"I told him I didn't ask for that, which is the truth, but he was snarling at me, threatening me, telling me that two can play that game. If I bring trouble on him, he'll bring trouble on me."

"Did you call Brie?" Noah asked.

"I did. I have her business number and it went to voice mail, so I left a message. Then I called again and said I was coming here to talk to you, in case she tried to call me back. I feel like I should drive over to Arnie's or something. I'm afraid."

A tear suddenly emerged and he wiped it off her cheek with a thumb. And just at that moment, the door to the bedroom opened and George stood there in his bathrobe. "I'm sorry to intrude. Is there anything I can do?"

"You heard?" Noah asked.

"No, I just heard voices, but it's obvious there's a problem," George said.

"Come in if you like. This is not a secret," Noah said. "Ellie has a problem with her ex and we're going to talk it through."

George just smiled and said, "I think I'll leave you two to work it out."

Noah barely heard him as he was concentrating on Ellie. "I have Brie's home number, if you'd like me to call her."

"Should we?" she asked. "I don't want to be a problem, but I don't know what to do."

"I think this is what Arnie wants, Ellie. He made you

blink. He delivered his vengeance, he scared you. He doesn't know where that Child Welfare worker came from. For all he knows, the judge ordered it. Those social workers are very slick, they know what they're doing. They don't let things slip that might hurt the children."

"He said he doesn't believe the judge did this. What if he calls the judge?"

"If this works the usual way, no one can have an ex parte conversation with the judge—you would have to be present, as well. We'll talk to Brie before the judge is in chambers," Noah said. "It's going to be okay. The problem is proving he threatened you. That's more he-said-she-said."

"Oh. Well. I should tell you, I got one of those thing-amajigs. I taped him. When he started giving me trouble about talking to the kids or picking them up, I went to the electronics store and, even though it pretty much wiped me out, I bought a phone answering machine that could record calls even while I was talking. All I have to do is push a button before I pick up. So I have a tape. But that won't help, will it?"

Noah's face split in a huge grin and he put his palms against her cheeks, gave a laugh and kissed her, quick and hard. "Ha!" he said. He kissed her again. "Ellie, you got him!"

"But I've always heard that if you tape someone when they don't know it, it won't hold up in court…"

"Bull. When attorneys and judges, not to mention law enforcement, are aware that there's a real threat, the tables turn. It makes him the bad guy and you the victim! Any chance he knew what you were doing?"

She shook her head. "Arnie doesn't think I'm smart enough to do anything."

"Ha!" He laughed, grinning. "What are you doing to-morrow?"

"Back to Vanni's, I guess…"

"But first, you go to Brie's office, play her the tape and ask for her help. Now we're done screwing around here—I don't care what she might charge you, we'll work that out. I have a couple of bucks saved. Whatever she can do, hang the cost, get it done. Please?"

"Do you think anything *can* be done?"

"Oh, honey, you're so used to having the deck stacked against you, you stopped believing things can be worked out a long time ago, didn't you? Yes, we can get ahead of this." He pulled her back on the couch, his arm around her, her head on his shoulder. "We'll get everything straightened out. This has gone on long enough—we have to bring it to a close."

She was quiet for a long moment before she said, "We?"

He gave her shoulders a squeeze. "Come on, don't you feel like we're in this together? I *want* to help, Ellie. You got screwed, by Arnie, by the court, all around. You don't deserve this."

She sighed heavily and rested against his shoulder. "I don't understand people like Arnie, Noah. What's the matter with him? Why does he want to hurt me so much?"

"He's a borderline personality," Noah said. "Not exactly insane, he appears to be functional. But he's manipulative, angry, jealous, thinks he's omnipotent, and he's narcissistic."

"Wow. Lotta ten-dollar words there."

"And you know what every one of them means, don't you?" he asked with a smile. "He probably didn't have a happy childhood."

"And so, making sure my kids don't have one, that'll make him feel better?"

"Ironically, no. In fact, he'll probably feel worse and act worse. But he's a bucket of trouble, and he's not going to repent. They're the hardest ones to cure with therapy and counseling. Everything is justified in his mind. His perception is that he acts and feels the way he does because he has to, because other people drive him to it. It's a convoluted way of thinking to people like us who aren't that way."

"You can say that again. And he's missing out on everything good. It doesn't cost you anything to be *nice*."

Noah chuckled. "Gramma Baldwin."

"As a matter of fact."

"What I'd like to understand is you, not him. Him, I get. But you, Ellie. You've had one bad break after another and it doesn't seem to sour you on life. I'm not sure I know how you do that."

She shrugged. "I think about what I have, and what *has* gone right. My kids top the list. Coming here is another perfect example. I hate the circumstances, losing my kids and all, but the town has worked out for me. And if I can just get the kids back, this will have been one of the best times." She tipped her head and looked up at him. She smiled. "I could use more money, however. You're a real cheapskate."

"How much more?" he asked.

"Another two hundred a month would make a difference," she said.

"Fine."

"Fine?" she asked, lifting her arched brows.

"You've earned it. You were right—I didn't believe you could get so much done. I'm impressed. You should be compensated for that. And I realize it's still not enough, but when you work for a church, it's not easy. Wait till we have a congregation and a board of elders running the show. They'll come up with a budget and both our salaries will be hammered out based on what they can afford. In the beginning, it's going to be bleak."

"I won't be here then," she said.

"You might be," he answered. "You're doing a great job. There's no reason to run off till you've thought it through and looked at all the options. At least if you're here, among friends, Arnie will not be able to harass you. He can't get anywhere. And you do have friends here now."

"Noah, I have one room and two kids."

"That's now. You said you'd be comfortable in one room with them. And Jo Fitch likes having you around. Plus, you've somehow tamed Nick. And I'll be honest with you, Ellie—I never thought I'd have such a versatile, energetic, efficient assistant in my life. You should keep the job awhile before you cut and run. Virgin River is a good place to raise your kids. It's a safe place."

"There are problems with this idea."

"Like what?" he asked.

"Don't I have to be a Presbyterian, to work full-time at the church?"

"No," he said. "Not necessary. I'm the one with the calling, you're working for a living. Is that what's worrying you?"

"I can't work for someone who wants to kiss me."

"Oh, that. Well, I think we're doing okay with that. Don't you?"

"No," she said, snuggling closer. "You've been behaving, but it's right there, under the surface, I can feel it. You're dying to do it again."

He laughed. "I am." He put his thumb and finger on her chin and turned her face up toward his. "But I'm not sure I even remember it right." He touched her lips briefly with his. "Pah. Not that great. I can live without it."

She laughed at him. "Funny. That was a decoy, which is the same as a lie, Your Worship."

His eyes grew hot and he put his mouth over hers again, rocking against her lips, licking them open and penetrating with his tongue. She shifted slightly and put her arms around his neck, holding him close, her tongue joining his in play, and she heard him growl deep in his throat, pulling her across his lap, tight against him. And they kissed, and kissed and kissed. His hands roughly massaged her back, her hip, her leg; her fingers locked into his hair and she made a soft moaning sound.

Noah was lost. He could no more stop kissing her than move a mountain. He continued to devour her, groaning as she added her own sweet sounds, pulling at her mouth, drawing her closer, until finally, breathless, he broke away. He took a few breaths, his eyes pinched closed. "Whew, Ellie, I don't know who taught you to kiss, but you don't need any further instruction."

"See, you like that too much," she whispered. "We're headed for trouble."

He chuckled. "You don't hate it, either, I could tell. I have some serious feelings happening here."

"That's another reason for me to leave," she said. "I'm getting out of here before I totally fall for you and end up with a broken heart."

"You don't really like me that much. You call me names."

"I tease. Don't you know anything? Girls tease the boys they like. But before I run for my life, will you please help me get my kids back? Noah, I can't live without my kids. I just can't. It's the one thing that could really break me. Do you get it? You could hurt me, but that could *break* me."

It was like a brick in the head. There was so much more to her than lips, than his desire, than wanting and caring. She had a family, and this situation with her kids was serious business. He would have to be careful here. He ran a knuckle along her cheek. "Yes. I am going to help. Tomorrow, first thing, you go to see Brie with your tape. And now, I'm going to walk you home."

"This is Virgin River, Noah. You don't have to walk me home."

"Your ex-husband is threatening you, promising to get even. I'm going to get you home, make sure you're in safely, and there's no discussion about it."

"You have to promise something," she said.

"Anything," he said before he could stop himself.

"You can't be looking at me like you want to kiss me. And I won't look at you like I want you to. This is a little scary. I can't afford to have anything go wrong before I get the kids."

"Nothing will go wrong, I promise. We're going to get this worked out. Come on," he said, standing and pulling her up. "Because if you stay, I'm going to want to make out all night and I don't think we can take it." He tapped on the door to the bedroom and George opened it altogether too quickly, as if he'd been pressed up against it. Noah smirked at him. "I'm walking Ellie home, and Lucy is staying with you."

"Fine," George said.

"She likes to sleep on the bed," Noah said, nodding at the dog.

Noah held Ellie's hand as he walked her home in the dark. Even though their pace was leisurely and they didn't talk, his mind was racing.

He cared about her so much that his chest ached. No matter how bad things got, she never gave in, so for her to cry signaled disaster and terror for her. He wanted to crush her to him and protect her and keep her safe like no one had been able to do in her life. Her grandmother had given her love and wisdom, but while she'd been devoted, she'd obviously barely kept the wolf from the door. By the time Ellie was a seventeen-year-old mother, it was she who was working to support the family.

But nothing seemed to ruin her; nothing embittered her. She was *grateful* for a horrible job because it allowed her to take care of her children. And she appreciated this job, though it didn't pay her enough to live, because it was a means to an end and would get her children back to her.

She was so tough, yet so vulnerable.

It wasn't pity that drove his desire to hold her close. It was admiration. Respect. Friendship and loyalty…and, if he was honest, undeniable lust.

"Can I ask you a personal question?" he said.

She sighed. "Another one? What now? I told the truth about the lap dances."

"Not that. Did you date much besides Jason and the other guy—I'm sorry I just can't remember his name right now? Like in school? Like between relationships?"

"Noah, I started going with Jason when I was fourteen—he was almost my first boyfriend ever. After Jason, I was a mother who worked two jobs—I didn't have time to date or see guys. That's probably what got me into trouble—a complete lack of experience. I loved Jason with my whole being, I didn't think I'd ever be able to care about anyone again, but then I met Chip at my night job at the convenience store and he was *fun*. He teased Danielle and made her giggle, and he made me laugh and feel wanted. It was the first time I felt like life might turn out okay if I just went with it. After all, being with Chip was better than crying over Jason. But when I told him I was pregnant, he said, forget about it. He wasn't ready to be a father, he didn't want a baby. He told me to get rid of it and we'd think about that again in a few years, if things worked out for us. And right after he said that, he went to jail. I guess you know my decision. I kept Trevor and let Chip go."

"I see," Noah said quietly. "So—no boyfriends," he said. "That seems impossible. Surely men noticed you."

"All the time," she said. "But I was too busy for men. And for the ones who didn't understand the word *no,* I developed a very fast left hook."

He chuckled at her. "Passes," he said.

"That would be the polite term. I swear, men can be so fricking rude! Well, after Chip, I said I'd never be that stupid again. And, in my immature mind, I thought that being practical where Arnie was concerned made so much more sense than letting myself get emotionally stupid and make a big mistake. Shows you what I know."

"Three men? In your life?" he asked.

"Technically, two. Arnie wanted me, for whatever insane reason, but as it turned out, he didn't want to have sex with me."

Noah stopped walking. "What?"

She turned to look at him. "It took me a long time to accept the idea of sleeping with him even if I didn't love him. It turned out that wasn't going to be a problem." She shrugged. "I asked him once what that was about. I didn't want him to change his mind, but I couldn't figure out him wanting a wife so much, but not wanting to have sex. He said his blood pressure medicine interfered, and that it wasn't the most important part of a relationship. Maybe he said that to be nice, maybe I just turned him off…"

"Whew," Noah said. "That makes his possessive behavior even more twisted. I bet it wasn't his blood pressure medicine. I bet it's some other kind—some psychotropic medication. "

"Some what?" she asked.

"Something for a psychiatric condition. In addition to his personality disorder—like depression, bipolar disorder or whatever. The upside to that would be that he's actually *taking* his meds."

"So, you see, there really have been just two men in my life. Are you surprised? Did you think maybe I slept around a lot? Did you think that if a girl ends up as a stripper, it's because she's just a slut? I'm sure that's what most people think."

He shook his head. "That's not why I asked. I just wondered if you've been mostly alone."

"Mostly. Except for friends. I had friends where I worked, sometimes great friends, but it's hard to keep up with friends when you have two kids and two jobs. So, what about you? Until you told me you were married, I took you for a thirty-five-year-old virgin."

"No. I dated a lot. Had some girlfriends who lasted a pretty long time, like six months. Had a lot more I dated for several weeks or a couple of months." He grinned at her and pulled her closer. "There were a few I dated for one night. Before I was clergy, of course. Merry wasn't my first girlfriend, but she was the first woman I wanted to marry."

Ellie smiled. "That's very sweet. I guess you aren't exactly a late bloomer, huh, preach?"

"Nope. I bloomed right on schedule," he said with a smile. "I got an early start, but I didn't get serious for a long time."

"And I got serious too young. It felt real, and I'd bet a million dollars that Jason and I could have lived happily ever after, but there's no getting around it—it was kid love. If Danielle turns fifteen and tells me she's dead in love and can't be away from some young buck, I'll ground her for life."

Noah laughed. "Don't be too surprised if that happens. Lots of wild hormones in youngsters."

They reached the bottom of her steps. "Thanks for the escort—"

"Let me come up," he said. "I want to be sure your room is totally safe."

"Noah, Arnie just called me a half hour ago. No way he could have driven over here and hidden under my bed."

"Okay, point taken. Let me come up anyway. I want to kiss you good-night."

"Listen, I'm bad with men. I seem to make all the wrong choices, which is why I decided it would be best if I gave them up, at least until my kids grow up, move out and own their own real estate. And I'm sure not getting involved with some guy who's just going to chuck me in a couple of weeks because, believe it or not, I'm just not casual about stuff like this. And you're too easy to like, so stop trying to trip me up."

He laughed at her. "Come on, Ellie, it's good you like me. We shouldn't be kissing if you *don't* like me. And I would never chuck you—I'm considerate. Responsible."

"In order for me to even think of going off my man-diet, I need more than considerate and responsible. I want someone who isn't going to die or stick up the night manager or treat me and my kids bad! Or leave! Or let *me* leave! I'm looking for soul-deep, lifetime, unbreakable, unbearable passion. Love to the nth degree. The real thing for once, not some poor excuse for it. And certainly not just consideration. I'm not looking for some polite version of love, but the real thing."

Then she backed away. "No, forget I said that. I don't

even want that—it would just mess up my already messed-up life. Don't make me want you. Now go home and don't press your luck!"

And with that she stormed up the stairs, walked into her room and slammed the door. She crossed her arms over her chest and leaned against the door. That had to be done; he had to be sent away. Life was complicated enough without thinking romance was possible. Especially with someone as perfect as Noah....

There was a soft knock at the door. Ellie rolled her eyes. This was pure hell, being pursued by a good man, a sweet man, a sexy and adorable and very masculine man. Ugh. There was no reason she wouldn't fall right in love with him, and it wasn't going to work out—it wouldn't last. A minister couldn't make a commitment to an ex-stripper who had two kids by two different men. It had to be against some major Presbyterian rules, had to be.

She opened the door with a frown. "What are you doing?"

"Pressing my luck," he said. He walked in, pushed her gently out of the way and closed the door. He put his hands on her waist and pulled her to him, going after her lips at once. It took her exactly two seconds to melt to him, moan, reach her arms around his neck and return the kiss. They kissed as if they'd been at it for years; they both knew when to open, tilt for a deeper fit, press harder, open wider, twine their tongues, breathe hard and deep. "Oh, God, stop," she whispered. "This is too good. And so not going anywhere."

"What if it goes somewhere?" he asked breathlessly.

"Don't build me up for a big letdown," she whispered. "Don't."

He ran a hand along the hair at her temple and looked into her eyes. "I won't do that to you, Ellie. I'm not planning to hurt you—I'm not that kind of man."

She fell into his lips again, kissing him deeply, holding him close, her body pressed up against his. When she broke away, she had tears in her eyes. "You know what my curse is? I can't help but always hope, that's what. I have so wanted someone who's 'not that kind of man.' It's not so bad that I get let down, but it affects my kids, and they're everything to me."

"I know," he said. "I know. I won't hurt you, I won't hurt them. These feelings just keep getting stronger. I feel it, and I can taste it in you."

"Mmm," she hummed, letting her eyes fall closed.

He carefully backed her up against the wall, pressing her there with his body. His aroused body. He placed the palms of his hands on either side of her head and expertly worked her lips, her mouth. Then he slipped to that place just below her ear on her neck. "I want you," he whispered. "I want you so bad my hands shake. My eyes cross."

She put her palms against his cheeks and pushed him back a little. "You've just been lonely," she said.

"That's just it—I haven't been lonely since you came to town. I can't stop thinking about you, feeling you, tasting you, imagining you. I should be stronger than the craving you set up in me, but I'm not. And I'm not just thinking about making love to you once, but making love to you over and over. And I think about how much I want to hear you laugh, how fun it is when you're teasing me. Then I think about our bodies, skin to skin. It's powerful, Ellie. And very real."

"God, Noah, you're confused… You just haven't been with a woman in a long—"

"Ellie, I can be with women anytime I feel like it, but I want to be with *you*. I want to feel you under me. I dream about that." He shifted slightly, pressing himself against her right in that vulnerable place where her legs were joined. He ground against her convincingly and heard a slight whimper escape her even as she held him closer. Tighter. And she moved her hips against him.

"I want to undress you, touch you, kiss you, taste you. And then I want you to taste yourself on my mouth." He kissed her again, hot and strong and long. One hand crept to her clothed breast, kneading it. "I want you hard and hot and deep and fast. And then I want you slow and sweet. I want you to wrap those beautiful long legs around me. I want you under me and on top of me and sitting and standing. I want to see your eyes when pleasure makes you light up. I want to hold you when you come down and try to find your breath. I want everything with you, Ellie. I care about you more than I've cared about a woman in so long, I hardly recognized the feelings. I'm dying for you."

"Oh, God," she whispered, moving against him.

"Tell me," he demanded. "Tell me you feel something for me. I taste it. Tell me *you're* not just lonely."

"Of *course* I feel something, you big dope. Why do you think this scares the holy hell out of me? But I thought you'd be the one with the great control! Besides, we're too different!"

He ran a hand down her bottom, down her thigh and to the back of her knee, lifting her knee to his hip so he could press himself closer.

"But the difference is what's so exciting, so beautiful. Sometimes I remember your last tease and laugh out loud when I'm all alone. I wake up in the middle of the night and I smell your skin, like you're next to me. And I want you. I can't stop how bad I want you. I don't *want* it to stop!"

"Noah," she whispered, her arms around his neck, her mouth open and wet under his. And to her core, she was wet and quivering. He couldn't know how turned on she was, but as he pressed and gyrated, she just fell headlong into pleasure. She was balanced on the brink of orgasm, and no one had removed a stitch of clothing. He pressed harder, moved his hips against her.

"I want to love every piece of you. I want to be inside you. I want our bodies together, to make the two of us into one. I want it all, and I want it hard, soft, anything that will make you happy. I want to hold you, keep you safe, make you scream… I want to make you gasp and tremble and lose control, like I'm losing control. And tip over the edge. And fall." He kissed her again. "And fall," he whispered against her lips. "I want to make you fall in love with me. The way I'm in love with you."

With those words, she tumbled right over that edge and without even getting undressed, experienced a shattering orgasm. She tipped her head back so that it hit the wall, pressed hard against him, put both hands on his butt cheeks to hold him tightly to her, and enjoyed a very beautiful orgasm. Fully clothed, right against the wall. She closed her eyes, bit her lower lip and groaned as unbelievable pleasure washed over her, through her.

Then she let out a long sigh and smiled. She moved her arms over his shoulders, dropped her leg from his hip and laid her head on his chest. She went so limp he had to hold her up.

"Ellie?"

"Hmm," she hummed. "Hmm, be with you in a sec."

He chuckled. "Well, now."

"That was a first," she muttered.

"Not a first orgasm, I hope," he said.

"No. The first time I was talked into it. You sure have a way with words, Noah. I just got too turned on." She took a breath. "I guess you're in the right job. You can talk a person into anything."

He laughed, a deep, gravelly, sexy laugh. He lifted her and carried her to her bed. He put her down carefully and kicked off his shoes to lie down beside her. Her eyes were closed; she was in afterglow. He could kiss her good-night and leave her now and he wouldn't have stirred up too much trouble.

But no, he couldn't. No more than he could summon thunderstorms.

He slowly began to undress her. He unsnapped her jeans, pulled her knit top up and kissed the top of her breasts. He licked her ear, kissed the inside of her elbow, unsnapped her bra.

"Ah," she whispered. "Now the foreplay."

"Well, in your case, I think it's afterplay. But I bet you'll enjoy it."

"Noah, you can talk to me anytime… But don't you have an RV guest?"

"George is asleep. And even if he's not, he wouldn't interfere in my private life. He's a grand proponent of private lives."

"Good…old…George…" And she closed her eyes and let herself be stripped.

Noah's hands were sweet on her body; his kisses were both tender, then not so tender. His touch was soft, then not so soft, causing her to rise off the bed to try to reach him. He was taking his time, though his breathing was becoming ragged and she knew he was struggling to wait for her. He filled his hands and then his mouth with her breasts, drawing on her until she felt she was going to fall over the edge again. He parted her legs gently, and found her slick inner parts.

When he took his clothes off, she found one of his many secrets—a tattoo of his own on his upper left chest.

A fish, of course. Not that religious symbol, but more like a trout leaping out of a river. She ran her fingers over it; she loved it.

He was a talker. "I need you," he whispered. "You're beautiful, Ellie. And soft and sweet. I love the taste of your skin, I'm already addicted to your scent."

She almost laughed out loud when she remembered swearing off men and realized that wasn't going to work for her, not with Noah around. She hadn't felt so much as a twinge of desire since long before Trevor was born; life was too hard and she couldn't even imagine a *man* making it easier. That had been until Noah kissed her, then touched her.

"I can't say no to you," she whispered. "Noah, I didn't think you'd do something like this."

"I didn't think I would, either. At least not yet."

She put her hands against his bare chest and held him back. "Please," she said. "If you do this, when you leave me, don't be all guilty and sorry. Please."

He touched her lips with his finger. "Ellie, I won't be sorry. Didn't you hear me? I'm in love with you."

"No. No, you're not. You're in lust, that's all…"

"That, *too*," he said.

When he reached for his discarded pants and pulled a condom out of his pocket, her eyes widened. "You were planning this?"

"I was *fighting* this, but I knew better than to be stupid. The last thing we need right now is to be in trouble."

Her eyes drifted closed while he suited up. And she said, "I think we're already in trouble, but it's too late. Fill me."

Noah paused above her for just a second, because this was it, this was the moment. There would be no going back; this would bond them. He had certain values that had been set in stone for a long time. He didn't take the act of love lightly. It wasn't recreation, as it had been in his youth. It was more than just a part of life to him, it was a commitment. From this moment, he would belong only to her; he would be hers for as long as she would have him. And he was far past the point of regrets. He just hoped *she* wouldn't be sorry.

He pressed his lips against hers while he entered her slowly. She inhaled sharply, rising against him, bringing him deeper. As soon as he began to move, she surrendered again. Another powerful orgasm shook her, causing her to tremble in his arms. And in a breath, he said her name twice. "Ellie, Ellie…" He held her still and deep, and when she was beginning to relax, he pumped his hips and let go with a deep, sexy groan.

He held himself above her so as not to crush her with his weight and he couldn't even make himself leave her body. "Sweet Ellie," he whispered, brushing her hair out of her face. "I think you're saving my life."

When he began to pull away from her, she tightened her arms around him. "No. Please," she whispered. "Please don't leave me."

"I'm not going to leave you," he said.

"Stay inside me. A little longer. I don't think I've ever felt that way before."

"Sweetheart," he answered, lowering his lips to her neck, her shoulder. "You're heaven."

"And here I thought ministers were probably boring in bed. Are you sure you're a minister?"

His answer was a mere chuckle and a little squeeze.

"And how about the whole waiting-for-marriage thing? I mean, I realize you don't want to marry me, but I thought ministers especially never messed that up. Isn't that a real special rule?"

He put a finger under her chin and lifted it so he could look into her eyes. "I'm just a man, Ellie. I've had to learn to accept that and so will you."

"Do you feel like you failed?" she wanted to know.

"This was not a mistake. This was supposed to happen," he whispered. "Ellie, I'm not going to let you down."

"Hmm. You haven't so far." She laughed softly. "I thought you'd make love in black socks," she said softly. "Badly. I thought you'd do it badly."

"I guess you're okay with it so far…"

"Ohhhh." She sighed. "Oh, Noah."

"Listen, I have to tell you something." Her drowsy eyes opened. "I don't want to push you into anything, take your time about me, but you have to know—I feel pretty strongly about monogamy."

Her eyes widened. "You can't think I'd be with another man! I wasn't even going to be with you! But there is one thing you have to do for me," she said.

"Anything that makes you happy," he promised.

"I want this to be only between us."

"Sure. Of course. It's personal. I agree."

"I don't want anyone around here to know it's like this between us. I just work for you, that's all."

He frowned. "We don't have to share our personal lives with anyone, but we don't have to hide the fact that we care about each other."

"Yeah, we do, Noah. No one can know about this. About us."

"Ellie, why? Are you embarrassed to find yourself attracted to a man who's a minister?"

She laughed a little bit. "No. But no one would ever believe you seduced me. And you did, Noah. You did and I loved it. Not only are you the sexiest minister alive, you might be the sexiest man alive. But people will think I trapped you. They'll think I ruined your purity and dirtied you up. And I don't need that right now."

"Come on, you're wrong…"

"I'm *right*," she said. "No matter how much I try to do the right thing, no matter how determined I am to do the right thing, everything that happens ends up being my fault. And when people around here find out you like me…they're going to think I cast an evil spell on you and made you break your vows."

"Honey, I didn't take a vow of chastity. I didn't promise not to love a woman. I never said I wouldn't have a perfectly normal sex drive. I'm not fifteen, Ellie, I'm thirty-five and I've missed passion. Passion and intimacy, two things that are really healthy for a normal man. Don't argue with a man with seven years of theological training."

"People don't get that about you like I do. They think of you as different. As a *minister*. Please, Noah. Let's just act like I work for you, and that we're casual friends."

"We can do that, if that's what you need. Or we could change the way things have been for you. We could be honest without being indiscreet. We could hold hands, you could let me put my arm around your shoulders, smile at you like you're special. Treat you like the woman of my choice while I enjoy being the man of yours."

"You don't get it, do you, Noah?" she asked, shaking her head. "Don't you see how fragile this is? How much hangs in the balance for both of us? At some point—maybe sooner, maybe later—the people here are going to figure me out. They'll know I come from a dirt-poor background, that the men who gave me my children didn't marry me, that I was a stripper when you hired me. What if they hate me? What if they treat my kids like trash because of me?"

"I won't let anyone—"

"Don't you see it's your future in this town, too? What if they ask themselves what kind of minister you could be if you'd choose a woman like me? Oh, Noah," she said, running her fingers through his thick, dark hair. "We'd get along okay in a bigger town where no one knows us all that well, where I'm not hooked up with the local preacher. But here—you and me? It could ruin us all."

"No," he said, shaking his head. "It's not going to be that way."

She smiled at him. "You're just a fool," she said. "It usually *is* that way."

He gazed into her eyes for a long moment, then he covered her mouth with his for a long, deep, luxurious kiss. He began to grow firm, still inside her. "You're wrong," he whispered. "And it won't work. It will show in my eyes. Everyone will know, even if I never touch your hand."

"Promise me to try, Noah. Please, promise me."

"I'll try, if that's what you want. But, Ellie, one of the best parts of you is that you never have shame. You make your choices, you do your best, and guilt and shame— the two most useless, negative emotions on the books— just aren't part of you."

"I'm not ashamed of loving you, Noah," she said. "I'm afraid. For both of us."

Afraid yet one more thing in her life would go badly? Wouldn't turn out? Would punish her rather than bringing her joy?

Loving him? Was she talking about her feelings or her actions? he wondered. Both, his inner voice told him. She was hardheaded and sure of herself; she wouldn't do anything she didn't want to do. She loved him. And they had come further than they had planned, but she still wouldn't say it. She wouldn't say, *Noah, I love you.*

"I'm going to do everything I can to make sure you're not afraid," he said gently. He pressed his lips against her temple. "But first, I'm going to make love to you again, before I have to start pretending I barely know you." He smiled at her.

"Excellent," she said with a heavy, yielding sigh.

Thirteen

It was after four in the morning when Noah kissed Ellie goodbye and made the walk back to his RV. He saw the lights were on inside and wondered if he'd forgotten to turn them off when he left, but once inside he saw that George was up, sitting at the table with coffee and his laptop open.

George looked up, lifted a brow and gave a half smile, but he didn't say anything. Noah poured himself a cup of coffee and sat across the small table from George. Lucy rose slowly, wandered to Noah and put her head in his lap, looking up at him with those big, sad brown eyes. She looked incredibly sympathetic.

"This is a little awkward," Noah said.

"Because an old man twice your age caught you coming in at almost five in the morning?" He chuckled. "Relax, Noah. You know I approve of you getting on with your life. You're overdue."

Noah took a sip, swallowed and said, "I'm not sure if you're going to approve of how I'm going about it."

"You don't need my approval. I'm happy if you're happy."

"It's not the spending-the-night part," Noah said. "I know you're not going to give me a hard time about that. It's that I'm not sure Ellie is ready for all I'm willing to commit to. And I pushed her anyway."

"What a shame," George said. "Because it's up to you to make sure no one is hurt by your actions."

"I'll do my very best," Noah said. "I haven't felt this way in such a long time, I barely recall how it's supposed to feel. Ellie has a lot of doubts—about me, about everyone I hope to welcome into a church losing all respect for me when they find out I'm in love with her…."

"Obviously not everything is in doubt," George said. "I know you, Noah. You're not careless or impulsive. You plot. You think too much, actually. If I'm right, you left here with her thinking you might spend the night, or at least that you'd try to."

"I was prepared. If it came to that."

"Thank God. Listen, son. I think Ellie surprised you. You weren't ready for a beautiful, bright and sassy young woman to make your world light up. And poor Ellie, she wasn't ready to fall for you. I'd venture a guess that you're not her type at all. Now, while you two work through whatever issues you have, try giving thanks and being happy. Gifts don't come banging at the door every day. In a push-up bra, yet." George peered at Noah. "It is a push-up bra, isn't it?"

"Answering that would be indiscreet," Noah said.

"I suppose," he muttered in disappointment.

"She doesn't want anyone to know about us. Not just that we're intimate, but that we're interested in each other. She doesn't want a whiff of romance to be obvious between us. She said people will blame her, especially after they learn all about her past, which they inevitably will. She believes they'll think she threw her evil web around me and trapped me. But, George, nothing could be further from the truth. There's not a mean or insincere bone in her body. And I was on her like a duck on a june bug." Noah shook his head. "It puts an ache in my chest that she would feel undeserving. God, I'll have to work my whole life to deserve her."

George looked down briefly. "I hate that she should have such self-esteem issues. With you, I'm used to that. But Ellie has too much joy despite her problems to do that to herself."

"What do you mean, with me you're used to that?" Noah demanded.

"You remind me of the man in the flood. The flood swamps his house and he stands on the roof. A boat comes along and he says, 'Don't worry about me, God will take care of me. Go save others.' Not long after, the waters rising, a second boat comes along and he says the same thing. Soon enough, he's perched on top of the chimney and a helicopter lowers a rope. 'Don't worry about me,' he shouts. 'God will take care of me.' Well, of course the silly ass drowns. When he has his first meeting with God, he rails, 'I believed in you, I trusted you, why didn't you save me?' And God says, 'I sent two boats and a helicopter? What more do you want?'"

Noah just stared into his cup. He knew the joke; it came up regularly.

"Struggling is mandatory. Suffering is optional."

Noah knew that, too.

"If God rescued you, if God gave you a gift, do right by it." George got up and refilled his cup. "I talk to you only because you want me to, Noah. Otherwise I wouldn't have said a word and I'm definitely not asking questions. I hope you don't mind that I'm an early riser, because I don't want to stay away. I'm leaving on Wednesday morning as planned, but I want to come back very soon. I want to see how this turns out. Stay out all night as often as you want—I don't care."

"You're disturbed," Noah said.

George laughed at him. "I remember being your age. I believe my wife was leaving me about that time and everything in my life was chaotic. So melodramatic. You're going to like being seventy. Things change, especially where you choose to expend your energy. I probably have as many problems as I ever did, but I wake up every morning thinking all is right with my world. I couldn't seem to do that at thirty-five." George sat down and opened his laptop again. "Get a shower, have another cup of coffee, get right with the world. You're a good man, Noah. You have a good and faithful heart. God isn't mad at you about anything."

When Noah got out of the shower, George had scrambled some eggs for the two of them. It was barely after six when he decided to head for his office in the church, only because it would give him a little quiet time before the work crews arrived and began pounding and whirring.

He wasn't being deliberately quiet when he entered and climbed the stairs, but he'd left Lucy with George, and his entry must not have made a sound. He looked into the sanctuary and saw a most beautiful thing. Ellie knelt before the stained-glass window and, hands folded and looking down, she appeared to be praying. It made him smile to himself—he had so many assumptions about her, so much he took for granted. He leaned in the archway to the sanctuary and just watched. He felt as if he was eavesdropping, though she didn't pray aloud. Her lips moved, however.

A few minutes passed before she raised her eyes and

got to her feet. When she turned and saw him, she jumped and grabbed her heart.

"Sorry," he said. "That was such a beautiful image, I couldn't look away. I didn't know you prayed."

She took a breath to steady herself. "You never asked."

"I never did," he admitted. "Were you brought up in the church?"

"Now and then." She shrugged.

"Any special denomination?"

"All," she said. "My gramma used to think that passage when Jesus said, 'In my Father's house are many rooms,' didn't mean there was a big hotel in heaven. It meant there were lots of different ways to worship. We dropped into different churches for the occasional sermon."

"Interesting. And you weren't confused?"

"We were never at one long enough for confusion to settle in," she said.

"So, this wasn't a special occasion?" he asked.

"Noah, I've spent so much time on my knees, they should be callused. That's figurative—I usually pray in the shower. My gramma taught me that—if you pray naked, you don't try so hard to hide things from God. She said, the Old Testament aside, God is our friend. He had a real short fuse in the Old Testament. Oh, and she also taught me that more important religion happens over the back fence with a good friend than anywhere else, so poo on your seven years of seminary training."

He laughed. "I'd have to agree with that. What else? I live for her sayings."

"I'm afraid Gramma didn't have one for the morning after you spent all night having wild monkey sex with a minister—" she grinned "—that I know of."

He lifted her chin and looked into her beautiful brown

eyes. "Why do you look so rested? I'm exhausted and I look like I worked on a term paper all night."

"I feel fine. Finer than I've felt in a hundred years. I'm going to see Brie when I think she's got her office open. Then I'm off to Vanni's to help her out."

"Were you praying for forgiveness? For trapping me in a secret affair?"

She smiled at him. "I was saying thank-you, for everything. For my gramma and her good years, for my kids, for this little town that's working out. And for you, but don't let it go to your head. Gramma didn't have two nickels to rub together, but she was always grateful. And happy."

"Ellie, I wasn't sure you even believed, much less practiced."

She shook her head. "Noah, everyone prays in a foxhole. I've been in one foxhole or another for the past nine years. I don't even count growing up poor—I just count since Jason died. Gramma always said to trust that things would be as they should be. I just can't figure out why they shouldn't be easier."

He gave her a little kiss. "Did you ever hear the story about the man in the flood?"

After a little private churchgoing, and a little chaste kissing, Ellie's next stop was Brie's office. Brie was incensed by what she heard on Ellie's answering machine tape.

I know you did this, you bitch, and you're not going to get away with it.

What are you talking about, Arnie?

Child Welfare Services paid a visit, while I was at work! Asking a lot of questions, talking to the kids without me present. Got the staff all worked up and curious. I know you—you told those little bastards what to say! But it's not going to work!

I don't know anything about this. Maybe it was something the court wanted...

You're going to pay for this, and pay big. I hate you, you skanky bitch, and I'm going to fix you good. You think losing the kids because you're just a low-life slut was hard? Wait! I'm just getting warmed up!

Brie had to take a couple of deep breaths before she could even respond. And then she said, "I'm going to file a motion at once. We have to revisit the custody issue now, in light of his refusal to let you visit or talk to your children, and his threats, one of which is recorded. Be warned, this will require a court appearance. If the judge doesn't dismiss my motion, he'll schedule a hearing where all parties can be present. The scumball will have a chance to defend himself and level his own accusations. So, tell me now, Ellie—is there anything he's going to bring against you that we should be prepared for?"

Ellie felt the heat rise to her cheeks. She had told Brie the entire story, including her work as a stripper, all in confidence. "I don't think so."

Brie took a breath. "Just lay it on me. Have you been dancing for extra money? Writing bad checks? Missing deadlines to return the kids? Using drugs or getting drunk? Anything you can think of?"

Ellie swallowed. Her voice was very small when she said, "No, nothing."

"Somehow I think there's something. Listen, we have confidentiality, just don't let me be surprised. It's critical that I be prepared for the absolute worst possibility."

She gulped. "The pastor. We have kind of a...thing. I asked him to please not let it show in public. I don't want people thinking I tricked him. And I know some people would think that—but I didn't make the first move. Honest."

"A thing?"

"A very, very new thing. Last night I was upset about the phone call and went to him. He walked me home." She looked away. "He stayed."

"Oh. Well, that's interesting." One corner of Brie's lips turned up with the temptation to smile.

"It's been heading there, I let Noah kiss me."

A slow smile grew on Brie's face. "Is that it?"

"It was a very good kiss. A couple of them, in fact. Believe me, after all I've been through with men, I sure wasn't about to get involved with another one, but I admit it—I wasn't exactly put off. And then... Well, I just couldn't help it. He's so wonderful."

Brie laughed. "Ellie, adult relationships are not against the law. They're not considered indecent. You've been divorced for almost a year and unless you're rolling around in bed under the same roof with your children, where they could see things they're too young to see, you're within your rights to date. You're single, you're young and healthy, and it's not a factor in custody agreements. And if you had to pick someone, gee, a lily-white pastor isn't a bad choice. Just the same, take no chances with that—don't find yourself in a romantic situation with *anyone* while the children are present. We don't want any unnecessary trouble."

"Lawyers have said the judge should never have taken them away from me because of my dancing, since it was legal. I wasn't abusive, neglectful or doing icky things in front of them. The judge should have at least warned me, had me investigated to see if I was a bad mother, not made his decision like that, so fast."

"But that ship has sailed," Brie said. "We could appeal

his decision, and before it got to the court of appeals, not only would the period of your ex-husband's temporary custody be long past, your kids would be in junior high. No, the way to go is to do everything his way, and promptly. It often means kissing some unworthy butt, licking dirty shoes, but the goal is reversing the custody order based on this new information. Or, failing that, getting them out of his house."

"Even though the judge is wrong?" Ellie asked.

"He's wrong, but he's safe. You're not. He could retire before you get an appeal. Trust me, Ellie—we just want this to go away. If the motion is denied, the best thing to do is serve the time, circle the wagons, load court up with solid citizens who can vouch for you and get this over with. Believe me, I know this judge. He goes his own way. We just say, 'Yes, sir, very happy to please you, sir.'"

"But you think it looks promising?"

"The worst-case scenario is ninety days. You're about two-thirds done with it. It could take a couple of weeks to get a hearing. So, we're not asking for much—we're only asking to shorten this temporary-custody ruling by a little bit. Hope for the best. From my point of view, you're making a very reasonable request. You've carried out the judge's wishes to the letter. Nothing says proper job like a pastor's assistant."

"Or pastor's lover?" she asked, looking down.

"Well, I'm not going to bring that up. It's not relevant. Okay? Now, is there anything else you should tell me?"

Ellie shrugged and said, "No matter what names he calls them, the one that hurts the most is bastards. I don't want them called that. That's my fault, not theirs."

"Ellie, you have to be stronger than name-calling. You gave them life. You can rise above a dirty word."

"I know," she said. "I manage to rise above a lot of

things. That one's extra hard. I'm so happy I have them. So sorry there's anything missing from their lives."

From Brie's office, Ellie headed over to Vanni's to play Mommy's helper. Her new friend looked much better than she had when Ellie began this special assistance. Vanni appeared rested and the house was holding up. In what seemed no time at all, it was a whole new scene. Rather than Mommy's helper, she was Mommy's friend. They worked together to tidy the house, caught up on the laundry and got an early start on dinner.

While they each sat at a separate end of the sofa with a load of clean baby clothes to fold between them, they talked. "I haven't held Hannah enough since she first arrived here. I avoided holding her and, when I did, I don't think my heart was in it. Do you think that's going to be a lasting harm to her?"

"I don't really know much about that sort of thing, but my gramma used to always say, 'Children will tell you what they need if you just pay attention.' Hannah isn't even cranky. The only time she cries, she's tired or dirty or hungry or…reaching for you. If you're a little better about things now, you can cuddle more, catch her up. I mean, think about it, Vanni—sometimes mommies are too tired, don't feel good, even get sick and go to the hospital. Sometimes they have to work more than one job."

"I'm afraid she'll never forget, on some subconscious level, that I was cold to her. I'm still not sure I'm committed…"

"I know what you mean. I always worried about that, too."

"About what? Being cold toward your kids?" Vanni asked.

"I wasn't cold, but I was never able to give them enough. I was wrung out. I mean, I had my gramma to watch the kids and I knew she was giving them tons of love. But they need their mother, right? And I worked day and night. By the time I could be with my kids, I was worn out and I just didn't have anything left. I've always wondered if they suffered because of that. But if you knew them…" She smiled wistfully. "They're so amazing. I probably owe it all to my gramma."

Vanni shook out a onesie and folded it. "*You're* pretty amazing," Vanni said. "And I don't think you give yourself enough credit."

"I'm just having one of those emotional days," she said. "I don't have them too often, thank God." But she'd been threatened by her husband, loved by her man, encouraged by her lawyer, depended on by a good friend. And it wasn't even noon.

By September in the mountains, the weather was beginning to cool. Fishing was good, hunting was around the corner and the bar was pretty full at dinnertime. Jack greeted a man he'd never seen before. He gave the bar a wipe and said, "Welcome. How you doing?"

"Great, thanks. Nice place you got here."

"We're proud of it," Jack said. "Passing through?"

"More or less. How about a cola? That too much trouble?"

"Not at all, my friend. I'm Jack."

"And I'm Arnold. Pleased to meet you."

While Jack served up a cola, he noticed that Arnold took a slow look around the bar, taking it in. There were a few couples in the place, three senior ladies occupied one spot near the window, and a couple of tables were pushed together to accommodate Mel, Brie, Paige and the small children, with Mike Valenzuela, Brie's husband the town cop, sitting at the end. Some fishermen played cribbage and shared a pitcher at one end of the bar and at the other end, a solitary man nursed a drink. Arnold was almost turned around on his stool when Walt Booth and Muriel St. Claire came in. Walt, a powerful-looking man with silver hair and black eyebrows, came up to the bar next to Arnold while Muriel wandered over to the table of women. Patrons greeted them both. "Hey, Walt! Hi, Muriel!"

Arnold turned his attention back to the front of the bar and Jack saw him smile. Arnold picked up his cola.

Jack looked at Walt. "Beer, General?"

"Thanks. And a Chardonnay for Muriel. And a take-out from the kitchen, but no hurry on that. When you have a minute."

"You got it," Jack said. And then he was busy at the other end of the bar, producing another pitcher.

Jack noticed Hope McCrea as she came into the bar wearing her standard uniform of big clown glasses, muddy rubber boots and what looked like a trench coat that had seen better days. She sat beside Walt and tapped the counter for her whiskey. Right behind her, Dan Brady arrived wearing his Shady Brady.

"Haven't seen you in a while, Brady," Hope said.

"I've been working on that old house night and day, trying to get it right so it can be sold."

"Oh, yeah? And then what?"

"I'll find another place," he said with a shrug. "General," Dan greeted, leaning around Hope. "How're things?"

"Never better, son. Thanks for asking."

Jack made a quick trip to the kitchen to put in the general's order and was back at the bar quickly. "How you doing, Hope?" he said as he served up the old woman's whiskey. And, "Brady? You avoiding me?"

The man said, "A little bit of you goes a long way." Jack laughed at him.

Then Jack asked Arnold, "Can I interest you in some dinner? Some outstanding corned beef and cabbage tonight with boiled potatoes and apple pie. The apple crop has been great this year."

"That might be nice, thanks. I'll think about it a minute. And what do you know about the church next door?"

"Been boarded up for years," Jack told him. "But we got us a new pastor and he's fixing up the church. Presbyterian. Should be open for business in another month or so. It's been a long time since we've had church in this town. Way before my time, that's for sure."

"Ah. Pastor's name?" Arnold asked.

"Noah Kincaid. You from around here?"

"Not so far away. Thing is, I'm sure that's the church where my wife took a job."

Everyone at the bar seemed to go silent at once. Then finally Jack asked, "Wife?"

"Ellie. Have you seen her around?"

Jack knew only two things about Ellie. She seemed like a nice, genuine girl. And he knew she had difficult custody issues that concerned Noah, but Jack didn't know the particulars. And there was one more thing—for no particular reason, he didn't like this man who said he was her husband. Jack said, "Nice young woman, Ellie. I was under the impression she was unmarried."

Arnold laughed. "Yeah, I suppose that would be her story, that she's not married. She has a long history of that kind of thing, good at stories, my Ellie. She's married and a mother, and the judge gave me the kids. What does that tell you?"

"That someone's not telling the whole truth," Jack

said, and his jaw twitched. He was a *bartender*. He didn't very often read people wrong.

"Well, there you go. I wondered if maybe someone should warn the minister about her. You know, before he gets in too deep. Gets in trouble with the town or his higher-ups because of her."

The silence was deafening. Everyone was listening except the fishermen at the end of the bar, and they were concentrating on their cribbage game.

Jack probably knew Ellie the best of everyone present, but others apparently had their own strong opinions about her. Ellie had been helping Walt's daughter, Vanni, with the babies, and Walt appreciated that. Hope and Dan had met Ellie several times, and Ellie made them laugh. Mel turned in her seat to stare at the man; Jack knew Mel got a kick out of Ellie and liked her, too. By now Brie actually stood up to listen to the exchange. Jack thought Ellie and Brie had met at least once in the bar; possibly Ellie had taken her issues to Brie for legal advice. The look on his little sister's face was venomous. The three little old ladies by the fire? They were all ears, and their legs almost twitched with the desire to bolt to their phones. And then Mike slowly got up from his table and went behind the bar to stand beside Jack.

"And why would Noah have problems?" Jack asked evenly.

Arnold laughed lightly and shook his head. "She's using him and the job to get out of trouble. Penance. Ellie worked in a strip joint. She was hooking. She's a whore. Selling her body and who knows what else. I kicked her out when I figured out what she was doing." He sipped his cola. "I'm divorcing her, of course, but for now I just have to keep the kids away from her. Who knows what all she's into."

The door to the bar opened with a ripple of friendly male laughter, and Noah and his friend George walked in. Without looking at his watch, Jack knew it was time for Lucy's dinner and knew she was leashed out on the porch. Noah and George said a few hellos, and didn't seem to notice that it was morgue quiet in the bar as they grabbed a couple of stools. Noah said, "Hi, Jack," and George said, "My God, something from the kitchen smells incredible."

Noah slowly became aware of the unusual silence that surrounded him and after looking around a little, he spotted Arnold. And, Jack noticed, Arnold smiled and narrowed his eyes.

"What a coincidence," Jack said. "This man here was just explaining, in great detail, why he should warn you off that nice girl Ellie, who's been painting the church and helping Vanni with the babies. Noah, this is—"

"I know who he is," Noah said with deadly calm. "What are you doing here?"

"Checking out this town," he said with an air of innocence. "Seeing where Ellie got her job."

"And making sure everyone in the bar heard him accuse her of some very unsavory things," a female voice said from behind them. It was Brie, and she looked furious. "Untrue things, by the way."

"Is that so?" Arnold said with a laugh. "You married to her? You live with her? I'm telling you, the girl knows how to put on a real good show. You'll believe what she wants you to believe. I have personal knowledge."

"You're not married to her, Mr. Gunterson," Brie said easily. "You should probably go now, before you dig your hole any deeper."

And with a voice as smooth as silk, a half smile on his lips, he faced Brie down and said, "And just who do you think you are, ordering me out?"

Jack's hand came down on the bar hard, clamping over Arnold's wrist, and he glared into the man's eyes. Jack's eyes glittered. Jack hated this kind of cheap, sissy maneuver—trashing the girl to the town behind her back. He might not know exactly what was going on, but he knew this guy was wrong and Ellie was an okay kid. All he was lacking were the facts. "That's my little sister, asshole. And your fifteen minutes of fame are up. You're leaving."

Arnold started to laugh meanly. "Jesus, is she fucking *all* of you?"

Noah's stool scraped back and fell, he stood so abruptly. As if choreographed, as slick as a football play, Dan stopped Noah from mixing it up with Arnold, Walt grabbed Arnold's upper arm and held him firmly, while Jack and Mike came around the bar to escort him out.

Unfortunately, before they could remove him, the door opened and Ellie stood there. She saw Arnold and shock was etched on her features. "Arnie? What are you doing here? Where are the kids?"

"I just thought I should pay a visit, make sure your minister here, and your new friends, knew that they were cozying up to a prostitute. A stripper, a druggie, a whore."

"What?" she said, stunned. "What on earth?"

Arnold just laughed. "Your stories are just getting worse and worse, Ellie. You shouldn't have lied to all these good people."

"But that's not true, you know that's not true. Arnie, who's watching the *kids?*"

"I have them handled," he said. "No thanks to you."

"That's all," Jack said, gripping one arm while Mike grabbed the other. "You're all done here." They walked him out of the bar and down the porch steps. "Just in case you're wondering, you shouldn't show your face around here again," Jack said. "It could be bad for you."

"Are you threatening me?" Arnold asked.

"Nah," Mike said. "Promising."

In the bar, Ellie looked around and found all eyes on her. Panic immediately set in—would they believe what Arnie had told them? Brie said, "Ellie, come here. Right now." Brie grabbed her hand, and with Ellie in tow, immediately bolted for the kitchen phone to call the police. "This is just a hunch, but from what you told me about Arnold's isolationism, the kids might have been left alone, unsupervised. What's the address?"

Ellie gasped. She put her hand over her open mouth.

"Ellie? The address?" Brie asked.

Ellie recited it and Brie reported the children as abandoned. She requested that the police check the house. "They're four and eight," Brie told the dispatcher. "I'm Brie Valenzuela, a friend of their mother's."

The second Brie hung up the phone, Ellie grabbed it and dialed Arnie's house. There was no answer, but that meant nothing. Arnie could have demanded they not answer the phone, as he had when they all lived together. But what if it was something far worse? After letting it ring too many times, she hung up and fell into Brie's arms, sobbing. "God, what has he done…what has he done?"

"He's trying a little damage control, but it backfired on him. When we get a hearing, the judge will hear about that, too. Before we get that far, he *was* lying, wasn't he, Ellie?"

"Of course he was lying! I worked in a strip club, you know that. A clean club—the boss was always on the lookout for funny business. Most of the women who danced there were single mothers, doing it for the money. I swear to God!" She ran a hand through her hair. "I have to get to my phone, in case they call me!" And with that, she ran out the back door and down the street.

Ellie didn't even notice Jo and Nick sitting on their front porch as she ran past until Jo called her name. Ellie stopped for just a second, made a sound of despair and then hurried on to her apartment. She tried calling from her own phone, but she knew Arnie didn't have caller ID. At least he hadn't when Ellie lived with him; he didn't want the phone answered, period.

There was no answer. Again.

Ellie paced, but it wasn't very long before there was a tapping on the door and Jo popped it open without being invited in. "Sweetheart," Jo said. "What's the matter?"

Ellie quickly ran down what had just happened in the bar. Then she added, "Jo, that bar I told you I worked in? It was a strip club and yes, I danced. But I swear to God, I never took drugs or worked as a prostitute! I promise you! And if I don't talk to my kids real soon, I'm going to Arnie's and if I have to tear the doors and windows off the place, I'm going to be sure my kids are—" She stopped as the phone rang and she snatched it up. "Hello?"

"Mama?"

"Oh, baby, where are you?" Ellie asked Danielle.

"I'm here," she said. "I'm at Arnie's house."

"Are you all right?"

"I think so," she said. "He said we could have supper when he comes back."

"Danny, are you alone? You and Trevor?"

"Uh-huh. The phone's been ringing and ringing, but he said don't answer the phone and if it was him, playing a trick, maybe we wouldn't get supper."

"All right, sweetheart, I want you to listen to me. You're not supposed to be left alone, so a police officer is coming to check on you. Ask who's at the door and if he says it's the police, you can let him in. Just so he can be sure everything is okay."

"We can't, Mama," she said.

"Of course you can, honey. It's okay."

"No, Mama, the door is *locked!*"

"It's okay for you to unlock it for the police, honey. In fact, I'll stay on the phone with you until they get there."

Over her shoulder, Ellie noticed that Jo had taken up the pacing. Nick came into the apartment, a look of concern on his face. There were pounding footfalls on the stairs and Noah appeared in the doorway.

"But, Mama, we can't reach the lock!" Danielle said.

Ellie sighed. "Pull a chair over, Danny. It's okay. But wait until the police—"

"Mama! It's locked on the *outside!*"

Ellie was speechless. She had to shake herself. "Danielle, Mommy's coming right now. It will take me a while, but I'm coming right now. I love you."

"Mommy," she said. "I'm being afraid."

"And I'm coming right now. Jo Ellen is here and she's going to talk to you while I'm on my way. You just stay on the phone with Jo and everything is going to be okay."

"Bye," she said. "Bye, Mommy."

Ellie took a breath and, with her hand over the mouthpiece so Danielle wouldn't hear her, she looked at Jo, Nick and Noah. Her voice was softer than usual; deadly soft. "He locked them in," she said. "The door is locked on the outside. They can't get out. They're trapped." Then she handed off the phone to Jo, grabbed her purse, lunged out of the upstairs apartment and fled down the stairs. Noah was on her heels, moving fast to keep up with her.

When she hit the bottom, Noah caught her. "Whoa," he said. "Want me to drive?"

She wrenched free and literally dove for the car, throwing herself behind the wheel, digging frantically in her purse for keys. The passenger door opened and Noah jumped inside as she started the ignition. "I grew up on these mountain roads. Buckle up and hang on!"

Deputy Stan Pierce pulled up to the address he'd been given and, as he walked to the front door, he scowled. He couldn't make it out from the curb, but as he got closer he could see that right inside the screen door, bolting the door closed from the outside, was a padlock. A *padlock.* Like an ordinary lock a firefighter could just release wasn't enough? Like a dead bolt with a key they could turn on the inside wouldn't do the trick? He opened the screen, pulled on the lock and felt a groan escape. He knocked on the door.

A very small voice asked, "Who's there, please?"

"I'm a police officer. Are your parents at home?"

"No. Just me and Trevor. Arnie went on an errand."

"All right, I'm going to get this door open. It's going to make a noise, but don't be worried. It'll just take a minute."

Pierce went back to his car, opened the trunk and pulled out a crowbar. He radioed his dispatcher that he'd need a social worker from Child Welfare Services, but in the meantime he was going to open the house and look around inside. Rather than trying to cut the lock, he pried the whole contraption off the door and frame. Screws fell to the ground; the padlock bounced on the walk and into the bushes.

He pushed the door open gently. The house was dark inside because the blinds and curtains were drawn. In the light from the open doorway he could see two young children sitting on the sofa in a sparsely furnished living room. "Hi," he said. "I'm Deputy Pierce from the sheriff's department." He got closer and crouched to get to their level, sitting on the heel of his boot. "How long have you been by yourselves?"

The little girl shrugged. "Since right after school. Arnie's the principal of our school."

"Ah," Stan said. "You call your dad Arnie?"

"He's not our dad," the girl said, slipping an arm around her brother, pulling him close to her. "He was our stepdad for a little while."

"I see. Do you know where I can find him now?"

She shook her head.

"What's your name, honey?" Pierce asked.

"Danielle," she said, tightening her arm protectively around her brother. "This is Trevor."

"Nice to meet you. Do you mind if I look around a little bit?"

Again, she just shook her head.

So Stan did a quick inventory. Most situations like this were real easy to figure out. If the house was filthy, the kids thin and hungry and the food in short supply, it was a no-brainer. This was a little weird. The house was immaculate, even the kids' beds were made up. It was dark; all the blinds were closed, very little food in the fridge… Absolutely no clutter. With two little kids? No clutter? He checked the back door—another padlock. The locks… This was just plain scary.

He went into the kitchen to call his sergeant and explain the situation. "The kids seem to be okay, but I have a real bad feeling. The scene is too controlled, the blinds all closed, the doors locked from the outside and it's creepy clean—no toys or anything lying around. The kids are weird, just sitting on the couch like they were told to stay put. They're clean, but scared. My kids? If we were out of the house for a couple of hours, they'd have the place torn apart. You know? I want to bring 'em in, get CWS involved. Something about this is too off. Well, the locks—right there we're looking at some serious endangerment. Neglect and endanger—" He stopped and listened. "Okay, I'm bringing them in."

He went back to the front room. He crouched again. "Kids, I want you to go find a couple of things to take on a possible overnight. A toothbrush. Pajamas. Clean clothes to put on in the morning. Anything special like a teddy bear or blanket or pillow you can't be away from. Maybe a book or toy that's special. Can you do that? Do you need my help? I have kids—I could help."

Silent, Danielle shook her head. She got up from the couch very stoically, and pulled her brother along behind her. They went to their bedroom and Stan just stood up and sighed. They'd done this before. Packed their own bags.

While the kids were in their rooms, a car pulled up out front. Stan went to the doorway and was standing there when a big man got out of his dark SUV and came to the door. "What's going on? Where are my kids?"

"They're packing up a bag, Mr....?"

"Arnold Gunterson. Packing a bag for *what?*"

"I'm taking them to the police department, sir. We have a big problem with the locks on the outside of the doors, trapping the children inside, unsupervised." Stan shook his head. "You can meet us at the sheriff's department and talk to the social worker from Child Welfare Services. I'm not going to cite you right now, but—"

"This is my house, my kids—what business is this of yours?" he asked hotly.

"It's neglect and endangerment, Mr. Gunterson. You can't leave minor children alone in a building, locked in and trapped."

"They weren't *trapped*," he growled. "I had to make sure they didn't open the door for anyone dangerous!"

Deputy Pierce lifted an eyebrow and tilted his head. "Would that include firefighters and paramedics? Mr. Gunterson?"

"Okay, fine—not a good idea. That won't happen again."

"We're going to the sheriff's department substation. I'll have to write up a report," Pierce said. "You can meet us there. Give you time to make up your story." Pierce stepped aside so he could escort the kids to his patrol car.

It was impossible to ignore—both kids backed up when they spotted Gunterson.

"Okay, look, Deputy," Arnie said. "I apologize. I can see where you're coming from here, that wasn't such a good idea. I give you my word, I'll be much more careful. We've been through a lot, the kids and me, and I just wanted to be sure they were safe from their crazy mother. That's all. I—"

"You can explain all this at the station, Mr. Gunterson," Stan said. "I'll take the kids in the squad car and you can meet us there." Stan put a big hand on Danielle's shoulder and urged the kids around their stepdad.

"This is a mistake," Arnie said. "Let them be, you're scaring them. You want a report? I'll bring them!"

"I don't think so, sir," Pierce said, urging the kids toward his vehicle.

A silver PT Cruiser rushed up to the house, screeched to a stop and a woman jumped out of the driver's side. Both kids immediately shot across the lawn to her, yelling, "Mama!" She fell to her knees and caught them, holding them. A man got out of the same car and came around the front to approach Stan, his hand out.

"Reverend Noah Kincaid, Officer. Are the kids all right?"

"They seem to be okay, but as I was explaining to the gentleman here, I'm taking them to the station. I'd like them to sit down with someone, talk about what went on here, and while they're doing that I'll write up a report. You call it in? Kids left unsupervised?"

"I believe it was a friend of their mother's," he said.

"Do they have to go with you?" Noah asked.

"I'm afraid so," Stan said, knowing he had some kind of big-time domestic situation on his hands. The husband and wife calling the cops on each other, the reverend showing up for ballast. If it weren't for the weird house and the locks and the nervousness of the kids, he might assume the wife was playing out some vengeance on the husband. "That Mrs. Gunterson, there?" Stan asked.

"No, sir," Noah answered. "She's Ellie Baldwin. The kids are Danielle and Trevor Baldwin. Miss Baldwin hasn't been married to Mr. Gunterson for about a year. They were only married a couple of months. It's a long story."

Stan snorted. It always was. "Well, there will be plenty of time. Let's gather up these kids. You can all come to the station while we figure out what's next." Then, under his breath, he said, "My sergeant's gonna be thrilled...."

"I'll follow you, Officer," Arnie said. "I'm sure we can straighten this out without too much confusion." And with that, the big man strode stoically and confidently to his SUV.

Fourteen

Thank God for Noah, Ellie thought. She was angry enough to kill, but on the way to the sheriff's substation, he talked her off the ledge. He emphasized that she had to stay calm and try her hardest not to act out. "Arnold will be cool. He'll do what he can to appear to be the sane, stable one, to smooth things over—he's obviously good at it. Don't let yourself get sucked in."

And of course, that was exactly what happened. While Ellie and Arnie were separated from the kids, Arnie finagled a moment alone with the sergeant in charge. After hearing what Arnie had to say to the locals at Jack's, Ellie could only imagine. And he'd been in there a long time. "I guess that whole ex parte thing doesn't apply to sheriff's deputies," Ellie muttered.

"It's a little substation, but you can bet the sergeant has dealt with this before, Ellie," Noah said. "Let him do his job."

"I'm worried about the kids," she said softly. "They've been in that back office awhile now."

"But it was the right thing to do," Noah said. "Giving permission for them to talk to the social worker alone—

that was smart. Arnie couldn't prevent that happening without bringing some suspicion on himself. Danielle will tell her how it is at that house. And that whole business with the lock—that's sick. The guy is seriously twisted."

A giant tear ran down her cheek. "Oh, Noah, this is all my fault. What was I thinking, getting mixed up with him? Look what I've done to my kids!"

"Hang on, kiddo. This is a bad time for a meltdown."

She looked at him with such remorse, such despair, her eyes all liquid, her voice so soft, so unlike Ellie. "It wasn't too much of a sacrifice for me, you know? I get by any way I can. If Arnie could give them a good home, I could manage. I thought I was making a good decision for my family. I thought—"

"Stop, baby," he said, pulling her against him, holding her. "It's going to be all right."

"Noah, what's wrong with me? I shouldn't have—"

"Ellie, stop. You were doing the best you could."

She was shaking her head. "I should have put more energy into keeping us independent. On our own. At least we could trust each other."

He lifted her chin and looked into her frightened, wet eyes. "Nothing like this is ever going to happen to you again, Ellie. I'll make sure of it. I don't know how yet, but I'll find a way."

"But, Noah, that's not what—"

"Ellie!"

She was cut off by her name being called. She turned to see Jo Fitch rushing toward her, Nick close on her heels.

"What are you doing here?" Ellie asked, giving the wet on her cheeks a nervous swipe.

"I knew you'd end up here. Honey, are they all right?"

She nodded. "But I don't know what's going to happen next. Arnie's with the sergeant and I'm out here and the kids are—"

The sergeant's office door opened and Arnie came out. He walked toward the front door, paused to glare at Ellie, then exited the building. "Oh, God," Ellie said. "Was that a good sign? Or bad?"

"He left without the kids," Noah said, an arm around her shoulders. "So far, I'd call that good."

"Noah," she said softly. "This is killing me."

The woman from Child Welfare Services came from the room where she'd been interviewing the kids. She held a couple of thin files in her arms and approached Ellie. "Mrs. Baldwin, I—"

"Miss," Ellie said. "Miss Baldwin. Ellie would be even better. Are they doing all right? The kids?"

"They seem to be holding up just fine—but after I make a couple of phone calls, I'll need your help to talk to them. They're not going back to Mr. Gunterson's house tonight, but because of the court order, I have to locate some emergency foster care for them. Hopefully we can keep them together, depending on what's available. But I can't make any promises about that."

"Please," she said pitifully. "Can't I take them with me? At least until we can see the judge again? My lawyer filed something, asking for another court date. Soon."

"I'm a licensed foster parent," Jo Fitch said abruptly. "I was a foster-care provider and kept up my license. It's been a few years, but I know these children. And what's more important, they know me."

"And your relationship to the family?"

"Ellie has been renting the furnished room over our garage since she's been working for Pastor Kincaid. It's on the same property as the house, but it's not attached. And we have two extra bedrooms. On some of Ellie's Saturdays with the kids, they spent the day with Nick and I, baking, painting, reading. I think they'd feel safe there— and their mother's nearby. Listen," Jo said to the social worker, "all custody orders aside, this is a fine young woman, a wonderful mother. Believe me, I've been around the block with parents whose kids were in the system and I know what I'm talking about."

"We had a total of nineteen," Nick said, stepping forward, slipping an arm around Jo's shoulders.

"Oh, God," Ellie prayed. "Please. I could tuck them in. I could have meals with them. And with Jo, I know they'd be safe."

The social worker looked down while she considered this. She looked up and said, "You understand, the foster parent is in charge? Even if they're right next door, even if you have access to them, the foster parent has the last word."

"That's not a problem," Ellie assured her. "I won't interfere. As long as they're safe, I won't interfere."

"Well, let's go back to the office and check your credentials," she said to Jo. "Just so we don't muck up the procedure and make it worse on these kids, I'll get a judge on the phone. It shouldn't take long. Then if everything is in order, you can take them home. Since you haven't provided foster care in a while, expect a few unscheduled visits."

"By all means," Jo said, following behind the social worker.

A half hour later they were under way, herding the kids into the sheriff's substation parking lot. And there, leaning against his big black SUV, was Arnie. He was glowering at them. It brought Ellie up short with a gasp.

Noah grabbed her upper arm and whispered in her ear, "Say nothing. Absolute silence. Let's get these kids away from here with Jo and Nick."

"Right," she said. She quickly settled Trevor into his

seat belt while Jo made sure Danielle was fastened in. And as they pulled away, Ellie leaned against Noah and gave a huge sigh of relief.

Ellie's relief was short-lived. Noah took the keys from her hand and drove, despite her protest that she was just fine. And they'd no sooner cleared the parking lot of the sheriff's substation when the headlights of that big, black SUV beamed through the PT Cruiser's windows, nearly blinding Noah as they hit the rearview mirror. The roar of the engine was loud; Arnie was driving within inches of the back fender.

"What the hell is he doing?" Ellie said, turning to look into the glare.

"Harassing. Don't turn around. Don't look at him."

"Noah, turn around. Go back to the sheriff's department."

"Uh-uh," he said, pulling up to a Stop sign. "Not yet. I want him with us, not with Jo and Nick and the kids." He sat at the Stop sign for far longer than necessary while Arnie revved his engine. Then he pulled away slowly. "I thought maybe he'd get out, charge the car, pick a fight. I'm a little surprised. Happy, but surprised."

"I'm not. Noah, he's going to get us going up the mountain. He'll rear-end us right off the road, down the side."

"No, that's not going to happen." He adjusted the mirror to get rid of the glare. Then he took a couple of turns, stopped a couple more times and lingered, staying in town. "Eyes front, Ellie. We're not going to engage him. Um—does Arnie have guns?"

"He said he did, but that they were locked up safe. I never saw them. He didn't take time to go in the house before following the deputy to the station. Unless he has one in the car…" She slid down in the seat as Noah drove through a motel parking lot, back out onto the main street, the SUV close on his tail.

"Are you sure he never hit you or the kids? While you were with him?"

She shook her head. "Sometimes he looked like he was going to either explode or coldcock me, but he didn't. He brooded. Pouted. Grumbled and accused and demanded, but he was never physical."

"He's a powder keg," Noah said.

"He's so close! How does he manage to keep from hitting us with his car?" she asked. "Pray, Noah. Really."

Noah laughed softly and thought—two boats and a helicopter, and made yet another right turn, that big SUV inches from his bumper. There were only a few Stop signs in town and he slowed down as he approached the only light while it was green. He purposely caught the end of the yellow and forced Arnie to run a red light. "Where's a cop when you need one?" he muttered.

"What are you doing? Giving me a tour?"

"Giving Jo, Nick and the kids a good head start," he said. He glanced at the console clock. "You know what? This is a good little car, Ellie. She's got some zip."

"She doesn't have the zip of eight cylinders and all that weight. And she's got a lot of miles on her."

"Yeah, but she's maneuverable. I like that in a car." He turned a couple more times, drove through an alley and a parking lot, then pulled right into the parking lot of the sheriff's substation again, right up to the front door, in a No Parking zone. "You go in and ask for advice. I'll ask Arnie what we can do to help him."

"Oh, Noah…"

"Quick now," he said, putting the PT Cruiser in Park, and getting out.

But of course the second he approached the driver's

door, Arnie put his SUV in Reverse and left the parking lot. He left nice and easy.

Twenty minutes later, Noah and Ellie had a highway patrol escort up Highway 36 into the mountains and hadn't gone far when they passed a black SUV parked by the side of the road, waiting. The SUV was facing the direction of Virgin River. When they passed en route to Virgin River, the SUV made a U-turn in the middle of the road and headed out.

Ellie laughed and clapped her hands. "Ha! That worked!"

Noah was quiet for a long moment. "Ellie, that guy is scaring me," Noah finally said. "And I'm fearless."

By the time Ellie and Noah got to the Fitch household, the kids were sitting at the kitchen table with Nick, having ice cream. They both jumped up and ran to Ellie, hugging her so hard she had to peel them off. "Hey now," she said, laughing nervously. "Looks like you have an ice-cream party going on here."

"They had a sandwich first," Jo said. "I thought some ice cream, bath and bed, in that order. I think these two have had a little too much excitement for one night."

"I agree," Ellie said. "How about it, you two? Finish up here. Would you like me to take care of baths?" she asked Jo.

"Mama, I have my *own* bath," Danielle said.

"Of course you do," Jo agreed. "And guess what? There are two tubs in this house, one in the hall and one off my bedroom. While your mom makes sure Trevor gets clean behind the ears, you'll have your own bath. We'll put bubbles in the tub…"

"I want bubbles," Trevor said to Ellie.

"Bubbles for you, too," Jo said. "Then bed. You don't

have to go right to sleep, but you have to get comfortable, quiet, and slow down a little. All right?"

While both kids agreed, Ellie mouthed *thank you* to Jo. And Jo just smiled.

"Nick, do you have a phone in your den that I could use for a private call?" Noah asked.

"Sure, Pastor. You know the way?"

"I do, thanks. I won't be a minute."

Twenty minutes later, while Ellie was settling her kids in their beds, Noah was having coffee in the kitchen with Jo and Nick. "Okay, here's our situation. Arnie followed Ellie and I for a while after we left the station. He was dangerously close to her car, until I circled back to the station and they helped me out with a CHP escort up the hill. I made a call to the California Highway Patrol and the sheriff's department from your den, Nick. Arnie's a loose cannon and I can't guess what he's thinking. Be sure the doors are locked here tonight. You probably haven't bothered to do that in years...."

"Never had to worry about that before," Nick said. "But we have precious cargo in the house. We'll make sure they're safe. I'll even check the windows."

"Jo, no way they go to Arnie's private school in the morning. I don't know how the CWS system works, but if you have to take Danielle to some school, it can't be that one. I'm going to talk to Ellie about having Brie Valenzuela get a temporary restraining order. Check with whoever supervises you about how to handle school. And keep sharp—I'm worried about Arnie's behavior."

"You should mention this to Mike V," Jo said. "Do you think Ellie should spend the night here tonight?"

"You can run that by her. Nick, is the phone line to that apartment accessible? Should someone have a desire to cut it and leave Ellie without a phone, is it possible?"

Nick shook his head. "It runs underground and through the inside of the garage walls. It's safe, unless someone broke into the garage—and I'll be sure those doors are locked also."

"If she wants to stay in her room, I'll make sure she gets in safely. She'll have the phone if she has a problem. I'm not letting anything happen to her—she's the best assistant I've ever had." He smiled. "And I'll take your advice and mention this situation to Mike Valenzuela. You're right—he should be in the loop."

"We're going to be all right," Jo said. "We'll stick together and keep them all safe. That girl—she means a lot to me. So do the kids."

"I know," Noah said. "Listen, do you have a can of soup?"

"Sure. Why?"

"Ellie hasn't eaten anything. She should keep her strength up. I think she has a battle ahead."

"I can sure do that," Jo said, going to the pantry.

It was ten in the evening before Ellie had finally eaten something, knowing her kids were safe and sound asleep. Noah walked her to her apartment and when he followed her up the stairs, she didn't protest. Instead, she unlocked the door and left it open for him to enter behind her.

"Are you sure you feel all right here tonight?" Noah asked her. "If you'd like me to, I can stay."

She shook her head and smiled. "Didn't you say George is leaving in the morning? You should be home tonight, Noah. I'll be fine."

He pulled her gently forward and held her against him. "You've had a grueling day. You must be exhausted."

"The most important things are taken care of," she

said, leaning her head against his shoulder. "Noah, this could have been so much worse. At his worst, Arnie wasn't that scary." She took a breath. "You just have no idea how relieved I am that they're right next door to me, safe and asleep."

"Did you know Jo was a licensed foster parent?"

"I did," she answered. "But it never occurred to me it could benefit us in any way."

"You need to lock your door tonight, Ellie...."

"Oh, believe me!"

"Maybe pull the trunk in front of it, or something."

"Noah!" She laughed. "Try not to wig out on me now. The lock is good and if I hear a sound, I'll call you. I'll call Nick and Jo, too. Do you think after Arnie struck out with the sheriff and highway patrol tonight, he'd come around here and try something?"

"I don't know," he admitted. "I think he's crazy."

"No thinking about it, Noah, Arnie's nuts. I'll lock the door."

"Good." He ran a hand up and down her back. "I'm impressed, Ellie. It was an emotional, scary day, but you kept your head."

She laughed softly. "I came real close to losing it a couple of times. If you hadn't been there, who knows..."

"Anything you need to talk about before I go?"

"You mean, like the fact that Arnie told everyone at the bar that I was a stripper, that I was a hooker and drug addict?" Ellie pulled back and looked up into his eyes. "Noah, sometimes people are just waiting to believe the worst. I can't do anything about that. But the people who know me, the people who I consider my new friends, they know I'm not like that. All I've really cared about since the second I got here was getting my kids back. Arnie's just full of jealous shit, that's all."

He smiled at her. "*Shit*'s not even on the cusp—it's full-out swearing."

"But I'm not in front of your church people or the kids and you're all grown up. Let's not worry about things we can't—" She stopped suddenly and her eyes grew round. "Oh, Noah, I'm sorry! You must be worried about how this will look for you, starting a new church! It could be bad for you because you hired me and helped me so much."

He shook his head. "Aw, people have found plenty of reasons to judge me. I've made a lot of waves in the church—I've got a rebellious nature. I can't worry about things like gossip. It would take precious time away from important work. No, I was only worried about how you were holding up under that slander."

"What in the world could anyone say about you? You're the most Goody Two-shoes guy I've ever been around. And for sure the most straitlaced guy I've ever been involved with." Then she grinned. "Except for sex, but I won't tell. What could anyone be judgmental about?"

"Oh, you'd be surprised. I hate my very well-known, saintly father. I was wild in my youth and wasn't even married in the church. There are about a hundred things I did before hiring a stripper as my assistant. And that turned out to be the smartest thing I ever did. Now, would you do something for me before I kiss you good-night?"

"What do you need, Noah?"

"I need you to look behind the shower curtain and under the bed. Then lock me out and put the trunk against the door."

"Noah, did you have monsters under the bed when you were little?"

He touched her nose. "No. Because I checked."

* * *

It was the smell of coffee and the sound of shuffling coming from the RV's bedroom that first woke Noah early the next morning. Then it was a cold, wet nose right on his temple. Whoever made up that old wives' tale that if a dog's nose was wet and cold, it was healthy, would be pleased to know Lucy was fine. He sat up on the couch and threw the blanket back. Then he watched the coffeepot perk. He glanced at his watch: 5:30 a.m. "Want a trip out back?" he asked Lucy. She went straight for the door. Noah stood outside his RV in his boxers while Lucy had her morning constitutional.

When the coffee was done, he grabbed himself a cup and sat back down on the sofa, trying to get his morning bearings. George appeared in the bedroom doorway, dressed, perky and grinning.

"Well, good morning," George said cheerfully.

Noah made a face. "If we had married, it wouldn't have worked," Noah grumbled. "What in God's name gets you up so damn early?"

George laughed. "I don't know what it is—when I was younger, I liked sleeping through the sunrise, liked staying up late. Somewhere along the line, that changed. I might be a lot happier in the morning if someone didn't take up most of the bed," he said, peering at Lucy. "Why does she have to sleep across the bed?" He shook his head. "So tell me—is everyone safe and sound?"

"Perfectly," Noah said. Since George had been asleep when Noah got back from Ellie's the night before, he explained all about Jo showing up at the sheriff's department, Arnie following them, and all the rest of the drama from the night before. "So—the best of a bad situation, the kids are in Jo's house and Ellie is able to see them all the time. And, better still, the Child Welfare worker isn't likely to let them go back to Arnie's house. The judge shouldn't have any excuse to undo this small victory, but I'll go ahead and cross my fingers on that. This is all good for Ellie, as long as Arnie doesn't try anything bizarre, or scary. She's going to lock her door and be careful."

"But she's all right?" George asked while he poured himself a cup of coffee.

"George, it's a miracle that nutcase didn't hurt her or the kids. He's off balance. I don't know what's wrong with him, exactly. But he's one mixed-up dude."

"As long as Ellie and the kids are all right now," George said.

"She seems to be okay—maybe more worried about the effect all those lies Arnie was spreading at Jack's will have on my reputation. And I could care less about that as long as I can take care of her and the kids." He smiled to himself. "Hercules Baldwin."

"Huh?" George asked.

"Never mind. So, you're up at the crack of dawn, ready to head out?"

"For now," George said. "When's the church going to be ready?"

Noah shrugged. "Soon. It had better be—we have a wedding coming up. Probably my debut and inauguration of the church. I'm sure I could wrangle you an invitation."

"That would be great, Noah. Now, how about breakfast at Jack's? I don't feel like cooking for you today."

"You're on. I'll buy."

Ellie was up early, dressed and at Jo's back kitchen door before the kids were even awake. Ellie tapped very softly on the door, not wishing to disturb the house. Jo was up, however, having coffee in the kitchen while reading the newspaper.

"I thought I'd see you bright and early," Jo said. "How'd you sleep?"

"A little too lightly," Ellie said. "But, there were no suspicious noises and I just couldn't wait to see the kids this morning. Is it okay? That I'm here?"

"It's more than okay. Get yourself coffee and I'll go jostle them. They should get up for breakfast. I'm going to drive Danielle over to Valley Elementary School and enroll her; I'll take Trevor along. I'm going to make sure they know never to release her to her stepfather. There's a school bus, but until things are all calmed down, I'll drive her and pick her up."

"I'll give you money for gas," Ellie said.

Jo put a hand on Ellie's arm and looked into her eyes. "That's the least of our worries right now. Emergency foster care usually lasts forty-eight hours or less, but I suggest we leave things as they are until your hearing. With your consent, and if your lawyer doesn't protest, I think your caseworker would go along with that. For right now, let's just make sure they feel comfortable here, and that they can make this adjustment. I think the last couple of months have been real hard on them. I'm going to see if I can line up some counseling for them through CWS. And how about you? Is there anything you need to help you cope?"

Ellie actually got tears in her eyes. Since her grandmother, no one had ever worried about whether she was handling things all right. And she couldn't remember anyone ever asking whether she could use some professional help. There hadn't been any available, for that matter. Her load, always heavy, belonged to her alone. She hadn't thought there was another option.

Ellie put her hand against Jo's soft cheek and smiled just as a big fat tear rolled down her cheek. "I'm so sorry I lied to you. About the club. About…"

"Shh," Jo said. "First of all, you had to protect yourself and your kids. Second, you didn't do anything wrong, working at that club. Let it go. Immediately."

"I'm so sorry…"

"Ellie, that doesn't matter at all in how I feel about you. I care about you and the kids and it has nothing to do with your previous job. It has only to do with the kind of human being you are. Now—should I line up some counseling for you?"

Ellie sniffed back a tear. "I have everything I need, Jo."

"Ellie, this is not a sacrifice for me," Jo said softly, pressing her own hand against Ellie's. "This makes me happy. I feel good with you and the kids around. I feel useful. Connected. Let's lean on each other."

"I don't want to take advantage…"

"We've been over that," Jo said. "It's not like that. Now, do you want to wake your kids or shall I?"

Ellie pulled her hand back. "No, you do it. It's your house, you're their foster mother. I'm right here if they ever need me, but I'd like them to understand that you're calling the shots here. I want them to trust you. Like I do."

"You're such a good girl," Jo whispered. "If I'd actually had a daughter of my own, I doubt I could have brought one up so fine."

Ellie helped Jo with the breakfast, talked with Danielle about another new school and washed up the dishes while Jo helped them dress. All the kids had to wear were the clothes in their backpacks, so Jo decided that she would arrange to go to Arnie's house with an escort to pack up their belongings.

"Is there anything I can do about that?" Ellie asked.

"Yes, you can give me his work phone number. And then, stay out of it. You really can't be involved with him at all, not in the least way. I'll make sure Nick comes home from work early to supervise the kids while I go over there. I'll take Nick's SUV."

"He doesn't have to come home early," Ellie said. "I could—"

"Ellie, you can be here with them whenever you want to be, as far as I'm concerned, but you have to let me act as guardian for the moment. I can't rely on you to parent right now. Let's do this by the book."

"Yes. Right," she relented. "Get a very big escort."

"I've done this before, sweetheart. It's been a while, but my foster kids tended to come from some very scary places. Usually with only the clothes on their backs."

That was a thought that stayed with Ellie as she went off to work at the church. She thought about her own kids, sure, but it weighed even more heavily on her mind that too many kids grew up hard. She'd lived from hand to mouth with her grandmother, but they'd always managed. She'd had friends who hadn't managed as well, some of whom were in the system, but they hadn't had a Jo or a Nick. The ones she knew were placed in crowded homes where living was tough. It wasn't unusual for them to be tossed in with a group of kids with an established pecking order and have to defend themselves or suffer abuse from either other foster kids or even the parents. Foster care was a big, scary monster among her crowd while she was growing up.

It was not a pretty, clean house like the Fitches', with an experienced, kind couple prepared to give their hearts as well as their space.

By the time she got to the church, Noah was waiting in his office and the construction crew was already starting to work. Noah stood and went to her immediately, giving her a brief embrace and kiss on the cheek. "Good, you're all right. You must not have had any problems last night."

She laughed at him. "I bet you're glad you didn't hire Mrs. Nagel. Wouldn't she be a sourpuss to kiss? Everything is fine or I would have called you. What's on your schedule?"

"I have calls to make. You?" he asked.

"You're the boss. But if it's no big deal, I'd like to stay in town, in case Jo needs something to do with the kids. I think Vanni's doing fine with her babies, but I'll call her, explain what's going on and be sure she can do without me for a couple of days. I'll start painting your office if you like."

"The noise is going to make you crazy."

"Nah. I'm about as crazy as I'm going to get. Is George gone?"

Noah nodded. "But he'll be back when the church is open."

"Go on then. Go do your pastor thing. I'll paint and answer the phone and be close by in case Jo needs me for the kids. She's not going to need me, though. She's got this situation wired—she knows *exactly* what to do."

"You okay with that, kiddo?" he asked.

"Yeah," she said in a breath. "I can't believe what a break it is—having someone like her fill the bill. I don't think all the court motions in the world could have worked out better. Sometimes I end up being so goddamn lucky."

His lips quirked up and he shook his head.

"I guess you wouldn't have exactly put it like that, huh?" she asked.

He leaned forward and gave her cheek a kiss. "No, I might not have. But I know you didn't mean any disrespect. Remember, I'm the guy who saw you on your knees."

"Who'd'a believed it would finally pay off, huh?" She grinned widely.

"I'm going to get out of here before I do something crazy and get caught by a construction worker or something. I'll call to check in from time to time, make sure you're doing okay and there aren't any new developments. Call Brie first thing and ask for a restraining order. Arnie isn't worth trusting."

Ellie was back at the Fitch house before Jo had returned from fetching clothes for the kids from Arnie's. Nick was in charge. The kids were watching a little afternoon TV and he was in the kitchen. "Jo told me to get started on dinner. I'm not trusted with anything more complicated than peeling potatoes and carrots," he said.

"Would you like me to take over?" she asked.

"I'm almost done here. I expect her any minute. And she said no more than an hour on the TV, so I have my eye on the clock."

"Nick, this is wonderful of you—watching out for my kids like this. I owe you an apology. That first day I met you, when I wanted to rent that room, I made some assumptions about you that were wrong. You haven't been anything but respectful to me. I'm sorry I was so rude."

He stood at the sink, peeling carrots. He glanced over his shoulder. "No apology necessary, Ellie. Your assumption wasn't far off base. I've done some real dumb-ass things in this little town. I should be the one to go around apologizing, not you. But you and your kids are completely safe here. I'd never let anything happen to them. And, my God, it is good to see Jo so happy."

She took a step toward him and spoke to his back. "Then why?" she asked. "Why did you get yourself that terrible reputation? I can tell you're crazy about Jo. You'd be lost without her, I know you would."

"You're right. And I don't know why. Lonely, maybe.

Cross because I wasn't getting my way? A couple of times I thought maybe Jo would be jealous and—" He shrugged. "It really doesn't matter. It's been a long time since I did anything as stupid as make a pass, and that's when I almost came up against Jack Sheridan. Whew," he said, shaking his head. "That was years ago, and if Mel hadn't put me straight right quick, Jack would have killed me. That was before they were together, you know. But Mel was already his woman in his eyes." He glanced over his shoulder again and smiled sheepishly at Ellie. "You're old enough to know this, Ellie. Men can be very stupid."

She took another step toward him. She put a hand on his shoulder. "Nick, listen to me. Don't waste another minute. This thing with Jo has gone on too long. Fix it."

He looked down. "I wish I knew how."

"Beg," she said. "Ask her forgiveness. Say you were stupid and wrong and that you need her. And, for gosh sakes, tell her how much you love her. It shows all over you when you're within ten feet of her. The two of you have already wasted so much time."

"It might not make any difference, you know. Jo might not want things back the way they were."

"You have two choices, Nick. You can find out, or you can go on like this and never know." She grinned at him. "By the way, I didn't have a boyfriend, six-five or otherwise, and the only judge I know is my worst nightmare."

He grinned back. "I know."

Fifteen

Vanni was doing much better at keeping up with two little ones and a house, thanks to Ellie's help. She'd even gotten pretty adept at putting two toddlers in car seats and carting them off for shopping errands. Her days were a bit more tiring, of course; there was no way to minimize the work involved, nor the amount of cleaning and laundry. And diapers? She was up to her eyeballs in diapers without the energy to begin potty training Matt. But Ellie promised to be back—she had just needed two or three days in town so she could be available to her own kids. Just one day of help from Ellie would probably put Vanni right again.

Much of the time lately, when Vanni was in the same room, the kids were set free. If Vanni wasn't exactly doting on Hannah, little Matt certainly was. Hannah followed him around—he, toddling; she, crawling at top speed and pulling herself up to a standing position on any piece of furniture that she could reach. Matt would bring her toys; she would offer hers to him. It was when Vanni noticed Hannah taking a couple of tentative steps from her spot leaning against the coffee table that Vanni realized she would be a year old in a month.

Her first birthday.

When Matt was taking first steps, Vanni and Paul and anyone else within shouting distance would be coaching him, reaching out hands for him, praising him, taking movies. But Hannah was doing it on her own.

Was this because she was the second child, or because she was Terri's child? Vanni asked herself.

When Matt was about to have his first birthday, Vanni and Paul and Walt were planning a wonderful big birthday celebration to include all their friends. But, with some shame, Vanni realized she was going to have to look at the documents that came along with Hannah to find out her exact date of birth.

"Mama!" Hannah said triumphantly. Then she went splat on her diaper-cushioned butt and laughed.

"Yes," Vanni said, smiling at her, "you're walking! Big girl!"

Thankfully the doorbell interrupted her thoughts and she went to answer it. It was a UPS delivery, a very large box addressed to Mr. and Mrs. Haggerty. She signed for it and brought it into the great room where the children played. She put the box on the floor in front of the couch and sat down. "What do you think we have?" she said to the kids, who migrated nearer, curious. She opened the box and found a letter on the top of the Bubble Wrap. "Hmm, a surprise, I think," she said. She opened the letter and read:

Dear Mr. and Mrs. Haggerty,
Mr. Hanson told me you hadn't made a decision about Hannah yet, but I thought maybe you could take care of these things. I have nowhere to store them and I don't want to lose track of them. They belong to Hannah. If you decide she's going to be

adopted by someone else, please be sure her new family gets them. I'm in a nursing home now, my MS is pretty serious, so the nurse is writing this for me. I know it's a lot to ask, since I haven't done anything to help out, but if you or her new family can ever work it out, I would sure love a chance to see Hannah.

Thank you for taking care of her.

Roberta Bradford

"Wow," Vanni whispered. She put the letter down and pulled aside the Bubble Wrap to reveal a box full of pictures. The one on top was an eight-by-ten framed picture of a baby that looked *exactly* like Hannah. She removed it and beneath it were a couple of shoe boxes full of snapshots. She fanned through a few and caught shots of Terri at a birthday party, Terri as a pudgy two-year-old in a bikini, grinning that big, huge-eyed grin, all dark curls. Terri with people Vanni would never know and Terri sitting on the same woman's lap a lot—that must be her mother in younger, healthier times.

Beneath the shoe boxes, a treasure trove. While Hannah hung on her knees and Matt tried to grab at the things Vanni removed from the box, Vanni pulled out picture after picture—school pictures, those cute toothless, pigtail pictures, pubescent shots of what Vanni had always referred to as the "big-teeth" age. Terri in braces, Terri in dance class, Terri helping someone wash a car. And then there were prom pictures and winter-dance formals and the homecoming game with Terri right out in front, a trim and beautiful high school cheerleader who could not have imagined her life would be cut short at the age of thirty, leaving a baby behind.

Vanni tried looking through the pictures though her eyes clouded with tears. She simultaneously kept rescuing photos from Matt's eager little hands. Finally, frustrated, she leaned Hannah against the couch and picked Matt up. She found his favorite blanket with the satin binding and snuggled it to him, putting him down in the playpen. It wasn't exactly nap time, but when the blanket came out, it meant quiet time. He did a little insulted fussing before his thumb found his mouth and he nestled down.

She went back to the sofa and lifted Hannah onto her lap. She continued to sift through the pictures, showing them to Hannah, saying, "Hannah's mama, see?" Hannah didn't grab or fuss, but leaned against Vanni and just looked as each picture was pulled out. And then there was a framed wedding picture. Terri had been married? Vanni didn't know that. Obviously she hadn't been married while Paul dated her, and if she'd been married afterward, Hannah would have had a stepfather. She looked very young in the picture; she must have been divorced before Paul met her.

There were several albums that Vanni pulled out and stacked on the couch, one of them a wedding album.

Beneath the albums was a smaller box. Inside, carefully preserved, were several items. A white, lacy christening gown wrapped in tissue paper, a silver cup and spoon, badly tarnished, a couple of rattles, a pink knitted baby sweater with a hood and matching mittens. And inside more tissue paper, a floppy, sorely used stuffed puppy with one eye. "Oh, Hannah," Vanni said. "Oh, Hannah, Mama's puppy."

"Bah-bah," Hannah said, hitting the stuffed toy.

"Sweet puppy," Vanni choked out, pressing the toy to Hannah and holding her tight. Vanni rocked Hannah back and forth, tears running down her cheeks.

Hannah settled back against Vanni and looked up at

her face. She put a pudgy little hand against Vanni's cheek and said, "Mama."

"Yes, my little angel," Vanni said with a sniff. "I'm going to be your mama. Yes. Mama loves you."

By the time Vanni had given the kids lunch and settled them in their cribs for afternoon naps, she had everything from that box spread across the dining-room table. Then she called Jack. "Can you give me Rick Sudder's phone number?"

"Sure," Jack said in some confusion. "You all right, Vanni?"

"I'll be okay—it's just real important that I talk to him right away and I don't know when he works or goes to school, or anything."

"Well, he and Liz just moved into their own place in Eureka near the college. It's a little dump, but they think it's the frickin' Taj Mahal. He has classes three days a week, works for Paul on Tuesdays and Thursdays and some Saturdays, so he'd be in Eureka today. I have no idea of his class schedule and I don't know if they have an answering machine. Here's the apartment number," he said, reeling it off. "But, hey—he's got that cell phone I gave him when he was in the hospital. He gets no reception in Virgin River, but it works fine in Eureka. Whether he carries it or stuffed it in the back of some drawer—"

"Jack!"

"Yeah, okay. Here's the number," he said, reciting it. "You sure you're okay, Vanni?"

"I'll be fine, thanks."

Vanni immediately dialed the apartment number and of course, there was no answer and no machine. Then she tried the cell phone and it went directly to voice mail. "Rick, it's Vanni Haggerty. God, I hope you actually carry that cell phone so you get this message. I really need to talk to you the second you get this. Nothing's wrong, Rick, but it's real important. Please call."

While Vanni waited, she continued looking through the dozens of snapshots and pictures. She had put Hannah to bed with the stuffed puppy. If she didn't hear from Rick by early evening, she would call his grandmother, Lydie Sudder. But really she'd rather—

The phone rang and she grabbed for it. "Hi, Vanni, it's Rick. Is everything okay? You sounded a little—"

"Freaked out?" she asked with a nervous laugh. "Rick, you know we have Hannah with us now, right?"

"I heard that, yeah. Paul said he was living in some kind of day-care center."

She laughed, but there were tears in her throat. "Yeah, that's a true statement. Listen, Rick, I hope this doesn't make you uncomfortable, but there aren't too many people I can ask. I know your parents were killed when you were really young…"

"Car accident," he said. "I was two."

"Like Hannah's mother, but she's not even a year yet. What I want to know—did you cry for your parents? Did you grieve? Did you miss them? Want them? Feel like something was missing out of your life?"

Silence answered her while he thought. "I don't know if I cried for them when my grandma first brought me home to Virgin River—you'd have to ask her. But growing up? Vanni, I don't remember them at all. Sometimes, when I look at the old pictures, I think I remember them a little bit, but really, I don't have a single true memory of them. I hate that."

She sighed. "But how could you help it? If you can't remember, you can't remember."

"I had a lot of questions, growing up. And I had some

pictures. Not a lot of pictures. First of all, my gram didn't take a lot of pictures of my dad when he was growing up. They were kind of poor, picture taking wasn't a big thing. My mom had hardly any family—her folks died when she was real young, and no one knows what happened to pictures of her, if there were any. But there were pictures of them with me when I was a baby, and I had my gram to answer questions about my dad's growing-up years. And she said they were real in love and happy to be having a baby."

Terri wanted her baby, Vanni remembered. "I'm trying to understand what Hannah will need," she said, almost more to herself than to Rick.

"She doing okay?" Rick asked.

"She's doing great. She has no idea all she lost," Vanni said.

"Well, there's one thing I remember from growing up. My gram was so great to me—I couldn't ask for more. I never knew my grandpa, but my gram took good care of me. And I had Jack. Then Preacher. But there was one thing… I always wished I could have had a mom and a dad, like other kids. You know—a regular family. But, hey, accidents happen to families. I had the next best thing. I have to say, there wasn't anything about my growing up I'd call bad. But a regular family… That would have been good."

What if Paul and I were killed in an accident like Rick's parents? Like Terri Bradford had been? Who would take care of little Matt? Matt was luckier than Hannah—his paternal grandparents were alive and well, Vanni's father a young sixty-two and her brother, Tom, twelve years younger and devoted to Mattie. Paul's parents and brothers considered Mattie their own. There were many people to keep Mattie's parents alive for him, to assure him he was loved and wanted, to be sure he knew the details of his ancestry.

Vanni was quiet for a minute. Then she said, "She's going to have a regular family. A ton of pictures of her mom and details about her life, her family, so she knows what she needs to know about herself." And she will never doubt, Vanni vowed, that she has a loving home.

Paul should have shot straight home after he was finished supervising work on the church, but, gee—Jack's Bar was right there. He knew that Ellie had family stuff going on and hadn't been to his house to help Vanni and, frankly, his house with a tired wife and two wild little kids wasn't exactly a relaxing place most days. So he clapped Noah on the back and said, "Let me buy you a beer, pal. I need one and it probably wouldn't kill you."

"Wouldn't kill me, that's for sure," Noah said.

They walked out of the church and across the street and Paul said, "So, there was a big deal going on at Jack's last night and I missed the whole thing. Ellie's ex showed up and spewed a whole lot of bad trash about her being a stripper and stuff, and the whole thing ended with her kids living with Jo and Nick Fitch."

"How do you know all that already?" Noah asked.

"Well, I could've found out from Jack, but I was still home this morning when Ellie called Vanni. That true?"

"What part?" Noah asked.

"The kids are with Jo and Nick now?" Paul asked.

"That's a fact," Noah said. "Turns out Jo and Nick are certified foster parents, though they haven't had any kids in a few years. And the social worker from Child Welfare was up a creek—had a court order saying the kids were to be with the stepfather, and that turned out to be a bad choice. So it was a solution. And a good one for Ellie."

"Wow. And it's true? She's a stripper?"

Noah stopped walking and looked at Paul. "No. She's a pastor's assistant."

"Right," Paul said, losing that boyish grin the second he saw the angry tic in Noah's jaw. "Okay, my bad. That wouldn't do so much for you. Sorry."

Noah started walking again. "Sure makes life interesting, though," he said. "And all this has made Ellie's life a challenge, to say the least."

"And all that other stuff? Vanni says that other things he said—like about drugs and stuff—"

"Not a kernel of truth to it," Noah said.

Both men walked up to the bar and Jack was right there. "Paul," Jack said, "what's going on out at your place?"

Paul shrugged and shook his head. "Same old stuff, far as I know."

"Vanni called here earlier. She was looking for Rick's phone number and she sounded a little…frazzled or something."

"Rick's number? Why?" Paul asked.

"She didn't say, just that it was important and she was in a big hurry. I asked her if she was all right and she said she'd be fine."

Paul turned questioning eyes to Noah. "Hey, I don't have the first idea," Noah said.

Paul didn't think about it long. He turned on his heel and without saying goodbye, he darted out of the bar, jumped in his truck and drove home. All the way there he was saying to himself, *Please let it not be any more nuts than usual.*

When he walked into the house, he could hear Vanni talking to the kids in the kitchen and the sound of little fists and little spoons banging on high-chair trays. There was a huge mess scattered around the dining room. A box sat beside the table and there were smaller boxes and pictures and stuff everywhere. And of course the great room was strewn with baby gear and toys. On some bizarre instinct, he peeked into the master bedroom. He saw a couple of suitcases on the bed. And he thought, *This isn't happening to me.*

He went to the kitchen. "Hi, honey," he said tentatively.

"Oh, Paul, you're home!" she said. She didn't look as though she was leaving him.

"Have you been cleaning out closets or something?"

"No. Will you turn on the oven, please? Three-fifty. I've got a frozen lasagna to put in there. I hope you're not starving, because I've been really busy."

He turned on the oven. "Vanni, are you leaving me?"

She laughed at him. "For a few days. I'm taking the kids to Grants Pass. I've already talked to your mom and she's going to help me with them and watch Matt for me. I could've called the Rutledges," she said, speaking of little Matt's biological grandparents. "But frankly, I'm not up to explaining Hannah to Carol just now. What I have to do is take Hannah to see her grandmother—I don't know how sick she is. What if she doesn't have long to live? What if I miss a chance to ask her questions about Hannah's mother? There are things Hannah is going to need to know." Vanni was rambling, talking more to herself than to Paul, it seemed. "There doesn't appear to be family Terri was close to while growing up. I don't dare waste a second. I'm afraid to even wait till the weekend. I'm going to pack tonight after the kids are in bed and leave right after breakfast."

Paul was really sorry he hadn't had that beer. It felt as if the ground was moving under his feet, things were shifting so quickly. He reached into the refrigerator and pulled out a bottled beer, popped the top and sat down at the kitchen table. Vanni was trying to referee dinner, two kids in two high chairs with Matt pretty adept at getting the food from his bowl to his mouth, while Hannah was just barely getting the occasional spoonful there. Her hands sure worked good, though.

"Hannah took steps today, Paul. All by herself. Didn't you, sweetheart?" she said to the baby. "Such a big girl." Then to Paul, "Her first birthday is coming up in just a month and we haven't even talked about it. I got the digital camera out and took a few shots of her standing, but I want a movie camera. Right away. The digital will do a two-minute movie and that's not good enough. I don't care what usually happens—the second child in this house isn't going to have an invisible childhood just because I'm really busy. Maybe I'll pick one up on my way into Grants Pass so I can get some movies of Hannah with her grandma."

Paul took a big slug of beer. Then he said, "Um, Vanni? I'm a little behind here, sweetheart."

She turned and looked at him. "I'm sorry, darling. My head is spinning. I've been thinking so hard today, about everything. Hannah's grandma, Terri's mom, sent a big box full of memorabilia. Pictures of Terri, her cup and spoon, her stuffed puppy… Terri's whole life fit in a box and her mother's very sick with MS. I need to bring Hannah to see her right away."

"Jack said you were trying to find Rick today.…?"

"Oh, that. Uh-huh. I had to find out from Rick how he felt growing up, with his parents gone since he was a baby. He said he had his grandma to answer his questions about his mom and dad. If I don't find out as much as I can about Terri while her mother is able to tell me, I won't be able to answer Hannah's questions when she's older."

"Oh," Paul said dumbly, thunderstruck and afraid to ask anything more.

"I asked Rick if he felt he missed out on anything and he said, not really—his grandma was great. But there was one thing he said—it would have been nice to have had a regular family. A mom and a dad. Paul, I want Hannah to have a mom and a dad who love her. I have to get to work on that!"

Paul felt his eyes sting. "We're keeping her?" he asked softly.

"As my friend Ellie would say, you're damn skippy."

Paul swallowed hard, afraid he might burst into tears. He took a drink of his beer and set it down. He cleared his throat. "I'll take a couple of days off, take you to Grants Pass…"

She focused on Paul. "Are you sure? I know you need to work. You have so many projects. And if we're going to have a houseful of kids, you're going to have to make a decent living."

"I'll call Dan Brady," Paul said. "He loves it when I leave him in charge. I don't want you to have to do this alone."

Vanni got a little teary. "I looked through those pictures, Paul. And I realized that if I didn't act soon, a real important part of Hannah's babyhood could be lost. I don't want her to have one month of her life without a mom and dad who adore her. While we're in Grants Pass, we should give Mr. Hanson a call and tell him to get our paperwork going. Unless you have reservations."

He shook his head. "No. I'm good with the idea. It's all up to you."

"Well, I had a lot of things to consider. But I thought about it just a little too long. Hannah calls me Mama. And she is *not* going to lose another mama. Not this precious girl. We need to get on the road first thing in the morning."

He swallowed down his emotion. "Sure. Of course." Filled with relief, his heart bursting with pride in his wife, with respect for her generosity and compassion, all he could do was get up from his chair and put a soft kiss on her brow. "Want me to do baths while you cook lasagna?"

"That would be good," she said. "And please, don't forget the hard-to-get places—neck wrinkles, backs of ears, between toes. Your mother checks those things."

He laughed a little emotionally. "She does, huh?" And he thought how lucky he was to have a mom like that. And now both Hannah and Matt would have one like that, too. Fussy. Committed.

Noah was researching Arnold Gunterson again. Besides his age and current address the only thing Ellie could tell him was that Arnie said he grew up in Southern California. Noah found nothing to match. Nothing *anywhere.* In fact, his house was owned by a woman—he must be renting it. Noah even bit the bullet and plunked down a credit-card number to a couple of online-search companies and there was still nothing. Funny enough, he could look himself and George up on Google and get way too much information on a couple of relatively dull Presbyterian ministers.

Yet the only thing he could find on Arnold Gunterson was his marriage to and divorce from Ellie Baldwin, which was less than two years old. He wasn't even pulling up Arnie's current address or place of employment. And the Brightway Private Elementary School gave the bios for the board of directors, but only the names of the teaching staff and director.

There was something so eerie and sinister about those locks on the outside of the door, about the way he'd followed them, about his threats. Noah had a gut feeling there was a lot more to Arnie than met the eye. Upon researching, there was in fact *less* information than he expected.

But—as the principal of a private elementary school, there would have to be information available to the parents of prospective students, not to mention fingerprinting, which was required in almost all states. He would have a résumé; he would list his credentials and the universities from which he received them. There would probably be framed degrees on the walls and a packet of information for prospective students and their parents that outlined policies. Clearly, Arnold would not happily give any information to someone like Noah or Brie. Nor could Mel or Jack, Jo or Nick, or anyone who Arnold might have seen before visit the school and inquire.

Noah knew he needed more information.

He decided to get a few chores done to keep his hands busy while he was thinking. That old faded blue pickup he drove had been misfiring and sputtering a bit lately, so he went outside and got under the hood. Before long he found himself changing the points and plugs, cleaning off the battery, adding water to the radiator.

Jack wandered out of the bar and, as men will do, got his head under the hood, as well, lending a hand. While this was going on, Noah was thinking out loud, complaining about the lack of information he had on Arnold Gunterson and his inability to think of a way to get more.

"Wait a minute," Jack finally said. "I know someone Arnold hasn't seen before, and they happen to have an elementary-school-aged son."

Before the afternoon was over Jack and Noah were talking to John and Paige Middleton about visiting a private school in Redway to discuss enrolling their son, Christopher. And to see what they could learn about the school and its director.

Sixteen

It seemed to Ellie that people were just a bit uncomfortable around her, as if they'd love to ask for the details about all that trash Arnie had spewed. Of course, she had explained to Vanessa and Jo Ellen immediately what parts were true, and what were just malicious attempts to make her look horrible. It was the vast number of people she didn't know well that she imagined were looking at her strangely. Perhaps judgmentally. Perhaps thinking less of Noah because of her. There wasn't much she could do about it, but it bothered her.

If it weren't for that nagging worry, Ellie wouldn't have a care in the world. She went home from her work at the church, showered off the paint and grime, and went to Jo's to be with her kids. They were sitting at the kitchen table while Jo prepared dinner. Jo was asking Danielle spelling words for her upcoming test and Trevor was coloring.

"Can I help, Jo?" Ellie asked.

"After we finish our spelling, you can set the table. Danielle will help. Danielle, tell Mommy about your school."

"It's nice, Mama," she said. "And I wish I could ride the bus, but Jo said not till we get more comfortable."

"I would have to agree with that," Ellie said. "Did you like the teacher?"

"Her name's Mrs. Spencer, and she's not even as old as you, Mama. And guess what? She says I'm a little bit ahead in the class. I took a couple of tests for her and she was very happy with me."

"Wonderful. Did you make any friends?"

"Just the hello-goodbye friends. You know—the kind who are nice to you, but they have other, better friends. I kind of had to eat my lunch alone."

Ellie's heart ached. "Kind of?" she asked. She noticed that Jo smiled over her shoulder at Ellie.

"I went to a table by myself and then some other kids sat there, too. Except they were already together. So I was with them, but by myself."

"Tomorrow Danielle is going to take some extra cookies in her lunch," Jo said. "Sometimes if you have something to share, it gets conversation going."

"There's one boy in my class who's in trouble all the time. I think he's one of them hyperactive boys. He sits in the hall a lot when he makes Mrs. Spencer's head hurt."

"Why do you think that? That he's hyperactive?"

"Mrs. Spencer said, 'Joshua, did your mother remember your medicine this morning?' and he said he wasn't sure. And, Mama, he's a wiggle worm and he makes a mess and picks his boogers."

"Ew," Ellie said. "Goodness." She saw Jo's shoulders shake with laughter.

"I don't sit by him," Danielle said. "But I like Mrs. Spencer. Mama, do you think I'll be in that class very long?"

Oh, God, Ellie thought. She's already worrying about

moving again. "I don't know, honey. We're going to have to take it one day at a time."

"Danielle, help your mother set the table and we'll run through the spelling words one more time before bed," Jo said. "How does that sound?"

"Good," she said, putting her notebook aside.

"Set the table for five," Jo said. "We'll just eat in the kitchen tonight. And remember place mats."

When dinner was done, Ellie got her kids ready for bed, then went back to the kitchen to help clean up dishes. Then back to the bathrooms to make sure they were cleaned up, tubs scoured, sinks wiped out, towels hung. And before long the house had quieted down, with only the sound of the TV in Nick's den.

Jo came back to the kitchen after kisses good-night and got down a couple of mugs. "Will a cup of coffee keep you up?" she asked Ellie.

"Not if I just stick to one," she said.

"Good. Let's talk. I can feel the rough edges, Ellie. You're worried about taking advantage of me, about eating my food and straining the space in my house. I want you to let that go. I asked for this arrangement because, selfishly, all my life I have wanted to have family around. And even though we're not related by blood, we've become good friends. Please, don't be in a hurry to leave as some favor to me."

"This will be resolved soon, Jo. The judge isn't going to have any excuse to keep me from having custody…"

"I know," Jo said. "But nothing has to change, Ellie. Even Nick is happy with our situation. Can't you tell? I'm certainly not going to pressure you to stay—it's your life and your family. But, if you're okay with this—"

"Jo, I can't let you feed us, shelter us, drive my kids around forever. It would be irresponsible of me."

"Fine," Jo said. "Pay your rent on time. Go to the grocery store sometimes. Help with chores, just like you've been doing. Earn your keep. But what we have here is a safe environment for you and the kids, comfortable living conditions, and you even have a little privacy with that room over the garage—a single woman your age should have a little privacy now and then. Ellie, you're not a burden. You fill a place in my life that's been empty for a long time."

"You know we can't live like this forever."

"If things work out for you, even if you don't live in my house, we might be in the same town for a long time. I might be able to meet the school bus while you're working. We might shop together, have tea on the porch, and I'd love to teach you to quilt, if you're interested. My mother was a master quilter. And have you ever canned? Because the fruits and vegetables from the farmers' markets and roadside stands in this part of the country are just incredible. I'll show you how. Oh!" Jo said, noticing a tear on Ellie's cheek. "I'm being too pushy, aren't I?"

Ellie shook her head. "I don't deserve you," she said in a whisper. "I think you're the best friend I've ever had. At least since my gramma…"

Jo shrugged. "Honey, you're my only shot at something that resembles a daughter and grandchildren. And I intend to nurture the opportunity. I'm just saying—this is your home for as long as you want it."

Ellie hugged Jo good-night at the front door and went to her room—the room she loved. She took a book with her—a romance novel that Jo thought she might enjoy. She put on her comfy boxers and T-shirt, propped herself up in her double bed with the firm mattress and read for a couple of hours, feeling completely decadent and self-indulgent. And relaxed.

There was a soft knock at the door and she glanced at the time on the bedside clock radio; it was after ten. She opened the door and smiled at Noah.

"Never do that again," he said sternly. "We don't really know how far we can trust Arnold." And then he brushed past her to enter.

"I knew it was you, Noah," she said, closing the door. "I could hear Lucy panting."

"You *thought* you knew it was me. It could have been Arnold panting. I don't think it would take much to say, 'Who's there?' before you open the door."

"I can do that," she said, smiling. Lucy made herself comfortable at the foot of the bed on the corner of the area rug. "What are you doing here, Noah?" she whispered.

"You going to make me say it?" he asked, and couldn't suppress a smile against her lips. "I'm here to make that kind of love you like, when it's a little wild and out of control, which is just how I feel when I'm close to you. Out of control. Desperate. Famished. Starving for you."

"Okay," she said in a breath, her eyelids dropping closed. She leaned into him. "Only if you have protection...."

"Of course, sweetheart. I wouldn't put you at risk." He kissed her deeply, licking her lips apart to let him inside. "Why aren't you on the pill?"

"Hmm. Because I gave up men...."

He chuckled, low in his throat. "How's that working out for you...?"

"I was fine until you. You've messed up a lot of my plans."

"You played hell on mine, too," he groaned, lifting her T-shirt over her head, tossing it and steering her toward the bed. He eased her back and kneeled over her, kicking off his shoes and tugging at her boxers. She didn't even think about resisting him, but rather lifted her hips so he could slide them down. "I guess we both have to be flexible."

She laughed at him, reaching for him. "Flexible? Come here. I just can't resist you." She pulled him down and tugged his shirt out of his trousers and he finished the job, tossing it aside. Her hands were on his belt buckle. Then the button. Then the zipper. Then inside, causing him to draw in his breath sharply.

As her hands ran down his hips, pushing his pants down so he could kick them free, he fell on her, taking her mouth almost savagely. "You. Taste. Wonderful," he said. "The best thing about going crazy wanting you is the way you want me right back. This feels so right…" He scrambled through his pants pockets for a condom. "I crave you, and I love the feeling." And that fast, he was inside her, buried deep in her, moaning with the pleasure it gave him.

"And I love you," she said softly.

He was utterly still. Even his breathing stopped for a moment. He knew he was unresponsive for too long, then he gently lowered his lips to hers and in a solemn whisper he said, "I love you, too, with my whole heart. I wondered if you were ever going to say it."

"I don't know if loving me is one of your smarter moves," she whispered. "It's like trouble follows me wherever I go."

"Not anymore, Ellie. From now on, it'll only be the good stuff. For the rest of our lives together, only the good stuff."

"Right now I'll try to concentrate on good stuff for one more day, maybe one more week. I'm afraid to think any further ahead than that."

"I understand, but I want you to know that I'm thinking lots further. And, honey, I don't see any dark clouds. Maybe pretty soon you'll forget to be afraid…."

She smiled and pulled his lips back down to hers, wrapped her legs around his waist and moved against him in a powerful way that had him gasping for breath and groaning with desire. Her eyes were opened enough to watch the clenching of his jaw as he held himself back, waiting for her. And the wait was not long; she exploded into pleasure so blinding, her back arched beneath him and she threw her head back, baring her throat.

He put soft kisses on her neck and shoulder while she shuddered. And then, his movements slow and luxurious, he joined her. And then he stayed with her until the wee hours of the morning.

Once Vanessa and Paul got to Grants Pass and could leave little Matt with Paul's mom, they were off to the nursing home. Vanessa put Hannah's cutest outfit on her along with her new high-top sneakers—good ballast for those early steps. When they got to the nursing home, they left the box of pictures in the car. Vanni carried Hannah on her hip. Hannah clutched the stuffed puppy that had been Terri's. Vanni, a woman on a mission, went directly to the receptionist and asked if someone could direct her to Roberta Bradford. A nurse's aide was called to the front and when she arrived, she reached a hand out to shake Vanni's. "This is a good thing you're doing, Mr. and Mrs. Haggerty," she said.

"Hannah and her grandmother need this time," Vanni said.

"You have no idea," the aide replied. "We've all been so concerned about her since the loss of her daughter. Come with me. She's been waiting in the lunchroom."

Vanni followed along. There were a few elderly people

playing cards, some watching soap operas on TV. Over by the window, in a wheelchair, was an attractive woman in her midsixties; she looked across the room at them.

Vanni walked toward Roberta, Paul following closely. When she was right in front of her, Vanni said, "Mrs. Bradford?"

A couple of large tears ran under her thick glasses and down her cheeks. She reached trembling hands toward them and said in a soft voice, "My God, thank you for bringing her. It's like a trip into the past. Hannah looks just like her. My sweet little Terri."

And Vanni was reminded, not for the first time, that the loss of a child is probably the most brutal loss of all, no matter that child's age.

A couple of days later when Noah went to the bar for breakfast, Paige came out from the kitchen with a file folder containing some papers. It contained information from her visit with Arnold Gunterson at the private elementary school. "I found him likable," she said. "This is a guy who padlocked his unsupervised children into a house and I found him likable? What's going on with him?"

"That's what I'd like to know," Noah said. "Not only the padlock deal, but he followed Ellie and I at a deadly pace—we were in her little PT Cruiser and he was in a huge, black SUV with darkened windows. There were only inches between us. No telling what he's capable of."

"The scariest thing is, I'd put my son in his school in a second. The only good news is, John didn't like him, almost on sight."

"But why?" Noah asked.

"The handshake, he said. First of all, it was too firm, and second, it was a politician's shake—Gunterson used two hands and squeezed John's hand real hard. Who would dare do that to John? What if he squeezed back? And John said that while Gunterson smiled, his pupils shrank to pinpoints. So, look through this stuff. It's all yours. I hope it tells you something."

"I can't thank you enough, Paige. We have to figure this out, get ahead of him, for Ellie's sake."

"Didn't you tell me Ellie said he came from Southern California?" Paige asked.

"That's what she said, yeah."

"Well, not this Arnold Gunterson. He came from Maine."

"Maine?" Noah repeated. *"Maine?"*

"Yeah," Paige said. "Think he could've gotten any farther from home? You know, every time I hear some news story about a creep who's hurt or molested a kid, he or she's in a position to work with kids and they were *supposed* to be fingerprinted, but they weren't. Do you think maybe it's possible that this guy should have been checked out and wasn't? Because he can be convincing?"

"I'll look into that," Noah said.

"Well, go get 'em, Noah."

Noah looked at his watch—it was only noon, which meant 3:00 p.m. on the East Coast. He looked through Paige's collected papers and notes. Then he called the private university in Maine where Arnold Gunterson had obtained his degree in early-childhood education. He was directed to the office of the dean.

"Hi, my name is Reverend Noah Kincaid of the Virgin River Presbyterian Church in California. I'm looking at a private elementary school in Redway, California, for some children in our church, and the director and principal is a graduate of your college. I just want to verify that, if it's not too much trouble."

"No trouble at all, Reverend," the woman on the line said. "We're a small school. The name?"

"Man by the name of Arnold Gunterson," Noah said.

"Yes, he's a graduate with an advanced degree in clinical psychology. He specializes in children's art psychology."

"Wow," Noah said. "You looked that up fast."

She laughed. "I'm afraid you must have the wrong Arnold Gunterson. Dr. Gunterson is still here, teaching."

Noah felt ice dash through his veins. "Will you check and see if there was, by chance, another Arnold Gunterson who graduated with a degree in early-childhood education?"

"Dr. Gunterson is an old friend, Reverend. I'd know if there had been another student in his field with his name. Did the man you're researching graduate more than thirty years ago? Because that's how long I've been here, as well as Dr. Gunterson. We're both sixty-two and I'm thinking of retirement, but he'll never stop. Now, who is this man?"

Noah sighed. "Obviously not who I think he is. You might want to give my number to Dr. Gunterson and have him call me. He might be the victim of identity theft."

While he waited for a call back, Noah did an Internet search of a couple of the private schools Arnie had listed on his résumé and found that they'd closed. One of them was an Arizona school and there was an article in an Arizona newspaper archives online. Small private schools are very hard to keep going. A regular infusion of money was required—high tuition, lots of fund-raising and often corporate sponsors. There was no shame in having worked for an accredited private school that couldn't keep the doors open. And this particular Arizona school had a successful fifteen-year history. And no one around to answer questions about teachers who had worked there years ago.

Could Arnie have convinced the current board of this new school of his positive role at the old school and his grief over its closure?

Noah immediately told Ellie what he'd learned—or not learned—about Arnold Gunterson. That night after her kids were tucked in at Jo's, he showed up at her apartment with Lucy in tow, as usual. She was confused by his information, but not surprised. Of course, after the things Arnie had done, it hadn't come as a shock that he was a liar. "But why?" she asked Noah. "What does he hope to get by doing that?"

"There's no innocence in this, Ellie. There's no reason to take on a false identity without a motive. We'll take this information to Brie at once. You have to tell Jo and Nick and be extra careful until the facts are in. Okay?"

"Of course!" she said.

"If he calls you or comes around here, get away from him fast and don't tell him what you've found out," Noah said. "Promise?"

"You can bet on it. The shitbag," she said. "Oh, there was another swearword, not even on the cusp, even though he is definitely a shitbag." She smiled at him. "I bet you've just about had it with me, huh?"

He pulled her close. "I've had it with you, all right. And not enough of it, either."

"Oh, Noah," she whispered. "I think you're insatiable."

"I want to spend the night with you, but I don't have to. If you'd rather be alone...."

She smiled at him and snuggled into his embrace. "I love it when you stay, but I think you'd better go. I feel like I'm playing with fire every time I let you talk me into bed. I don't want to become too dependent on you. And

I don't want the whole town to know we're sleeping together. I have children to think about."

"Are you cutting me off?" he asked nervously.

She smiled at him. "Did you just *whine?*" She chuckled at him. "Noah, much as I love cuddling up to you, I don't want your new town, your future congregation, to think the worst of you."

"I'm not worried about that. I think I'd get a standing ovation for finding you. But, to ease your mind and your reputation, I'll be very discreet," he said.

"That's about half the problem… There are also children to think about…"

"We'll be very cautious there, sweetheart. They're your top priority, which makes them mine also."

Then he pulled out his secret weapon. He kissed her. Hard and deep. He pulled her against him and it took her less than fifteen seconds to melt into him and fully enjoy his arousal. When he released her lips, she said, "You are a very bad boy and no one with an ounce of sanity would take you for a minister."

"Could I be taken for a man who wants the woman he loves?"

"Yeah, you qualify," she said. She melted to him again. And he stayed. Again.

Brie Valenzuela listened very patiently while Noah laid out what he'd learned about Arnold Gunterson, Ellie with him while he did so. Brie asked for the pages he held. When he was finished, she asked, "Have you heard from Dr. Gunterson in Maine?"

"I talked to him early this morning. He took a year's sabbatical to research and finish his dissertation right about the time Arnie was settling into his new school, so if anyone from the school board tried to check his credentials, they would only learn that he was a graduate working on his Ph.D. Dr. Gunterson can't imagine who would do something like this to him."

"I'll call Dr. Gunterson," Brie said. "Now, listen. No more amateur sleuthing. Stay away from Arnie and his school, keep the kids away from him. If you see him around here, call me at once. I'll take it from here. I've already filed a motion for a temporary restraining order. I'm going to talk to the district attorney about this, but more importantly, I'm going to ask Mike to speak to the sheriff about a possible fraud and identity theft.

"Here's what I want from you, Ellie. Vanessa is out of town with the little ones right now, but she'll be back next week. I want you to pay a call on her and ask her a favor. Ask her to dress you for court. Borrow something from her, something conservative and appealing, and be ready. Vanni will know exactly what to do—she's the best. And you two are almost the same size.

"Beyond that, stay alert and cautious. And hear me when I say this—no more investigating. If you make one little slip, he might find out what you're doing and it could spoil everything."

"Spoil what?" Ellie asked.

"There are very few reasons for identity theft, Ellie. One is to profit from the victim's bank accounts. The other is to hide who you *really* are because who you really are is not lawful. Since Dr. Gunterson never suspected his identity was borrowed, I assume there was no theft. I bet our Arnie has priors. He's done something wrong somewhere and needs to be someone else. And if he's hiding, he's probably hiding from the police. And if he's hiding from the police, there are probably warrants. And if there are warrants, I believe it would serve our purpose to let him be arrested." Brie lifted an eyebrow. "Hmm?"

"Wow," Ellie said. "I should have *known*. If he's nothing but a criminal, shouldn't I have *known*?"

Brie shook her head. "I can't answer that one for you, Ellie. I spent years in the district attorney's office in Sacramento, prosecuting crimes like this. I met a lot of very intelligent women who were victimized by manipulative men, as well as perfectly sharp men taken for a wild ride by clever, dishonest women. It's a con, and you were at a vulnerable time in your life. Cons can smell that a mile away. Sadly, it's common in the world of criminal law."

"Can we get beyond this?" Ellie asked. "I can't even think about my kids dealing with this in the years to come!"

"I think, if we get law enforcement help in handling this, we have a good shot at resolving the situation. If you see him or hear from him, call me at once. I'll give you the house number." She leaned over her desk and scribbled on the back of a business card. "I wrote down Mike's pager number, as well. Your next call is 911. Got that?"

"Got it." Ellie took the card.

"Now," Brie said, relaxing visibly. "Don't you have a church to finish, and a wedding to organize for Shelby and Luke? All sorts of really important things to get done?"

"We do," Ellie said with a smile.

"Then do them. If I learn anything at all about your ex-husband, I'll let you know." She smiled. "You just have to hunker down for a little while longer. I'll do everything I can think of to get this business behind you."

By the time the weekend arrived, Vanessa, Paul and the kids had been in Grants Pass for three days. While Vanni had daily visits with Roberta Bradford at the nursing home, Paul spent a lot of time with his father and brothers at the corporate headquarters of Haggerty Construction. Additionally, they had a couple of meetings with Scott Hanson about adoption. That legal transaction was typically an expensive affair, but because Terri Bradford had worked for Scott and because the Hanson family happened to be quite fond of little Hannah, they were getting a good deal. The Haggertys would be charged just the filing costs. And the Hansons asked to see Hannah whenever it was convenient.

The good news was that Roberta Bradford was not lingering at death's door. She was disabled and her condition would not improve, but if she could avoid illness and infections, she'd be around awhile. Long enough to have many visits with her granddaughter and supply information about their family.

Paul had spent most of the day out with his brothers, looking over some of their building projects, and when he went back to his mother's house he found her in the kitchen, kneading dough.

"Hi, Mom."

"Sweetheart," she said, lifting her flour-covered hands. "Be very quiet. Vanessa and the babies are exhausted. All this running around, visiting, working things out... they're shot. They're napping."

"And you're baking?"

"I bake off stress," she said. "And the weather turned cool at last—I love it when the leaves have turned and I can use the oven and fireplace again. It's been just beautiful here."

"What stress are you baking off?" he asked. "Have we been too much for you this visit? Two little kids?"

"Don't be silly, I love having the babies," she said, kneading. "I just want everything to go smoothly for you and Vanni, and for the children. I want Hannah to be content. And..." She paused for a moment. "And I want you to get one of your own, like you and Vanni were planning, and yet I don't want Vanni to be overwhelmed. This thing you've taken on—it's a huge undertaking. And I'm so proud of you both."

He grinned at his mother. "It's going to be a houseful. And me and Vanni? We're not that young. Not as young as you and Dad were."

"Yes, but we were young and dumb and poor. At least you're not poor. You should've seen how we lived in the beginning. And every time your father walked by the bedroom door, I was pregnant again."

He chuckled and went to his mother, putting his arms around her despite the fact that her hands were messy with flour. "Thank you for helping, Mom. This was so sudden, Vanni's need to make this trip. I could see her warming up to Hannah, but it was overnight that she made her decision."

Marianne smiled at him. "She must have wanted to kill you for bringing an old girlfriend's baby home."

"Pretty much," Paul said. "Mom, I liked Terri, but it wasn't out of affection for her that I took Hannah home. Have you held that little girl? Let her put her arms around your neck? Who, in their right mind, could have left her behind?"

Marianne put her hand against Paul's cheek, leaving a trail of flour there. "You're a good boy, Paul. I don't know where you got it, but you're a good boy."

He laughed at her. "I know where I got it. I'm going to look in on my family, if that's okay."

"They're napping together in your room. The kids were a little overtired and fussy and Vanni wanted them close."

"I'll be right back."

He went up the stairs to the largest guest room, the one

he shared with his wife. There was a smaller room right next to it for the kids and there were two cribs there. The door to the bedroom was ajar an inch or so and Paul pushed it open. Vanni had the kids on the bed with her. She was lying on her back with Matt curled up against her on one side and Hannah on the other, both of them sleeping with their mouths open. Vanni was sound asleep, but there was the smallest smile on her lips. She had her arms around them, holding them close, one of Marianne's afghans pulled over them.

And Paul fell in love all over again.

Seventeen

The first of October brought a very hectic schedule of events for the Virgin River Presbyterian Church, beginning with the delivery of the kitchen appliances. Next came Noah's personal shipment, which was stored in the newly finished basement. In that shipment, the piano arrived and as soon as it was tuned, Ellie couldn't wait to try it out. Her out-of-practice attempts, accompanied by the occasional muffled curse, could be heard all over the church, causing Noah to laugh to himself.

Timing was on their side; Paul was finishing up in the sanctuary just as the pews were delivered for installation. New desks, a conference table and chairs, bookcases and filing cabinets for the upstairs offices were delivered, which meant a lot of sorting, organizing and file building. Ellie loved organizing. This work would barely be finished in time for the MacIntyre-Riordan wedding less than a week later.

Needless to say, both Noah and Ellie were extremely busy and, in the midst of this, Brie reported that the end of that first week of October, after almost exactly ninety days since her children were removed from her care,

Ellie would finally get her court date. "I need a brief meeting with you, Ellie," Brie said. "My office, tomorrow sometime. Call when you're on your way."

"Sure. Everything okay?"

"I'm going to brief you on the hearing and some other details."

When Ellie told Noah, he said, "It's almost over, Ellie. This can only go one way for you."

Ellie had quite a few questions for the man who was creeping into her bed night after night, questions she was not planning to ask. *What should we do about us?* was first on her list. When he said he loved her forever, that he loved her with his whole heart, that her children were his priority, too, was that a suggestion that they marry? There was no way she'd ask him. And waiting to see what Noah would do next was almost as hard as waiting for her children to be legally returned to her.

Noah was managing to keep up with everything despite the increased activity in the church. He had a couple of counseling sessions with Vanni and Paul while they waited for their adoption paperwork to be filed and found them to be coping better all the time. Ellie was still giving Vanni a hand a couple of mornings a week, for which Vanni was enormously grateful. He'd meet with Shelby and Luke and Father Demetrius from Arcata to discuss the particulars of their wedding service. Noah managed to get over to visit his friends in the woods. As well, he was kept busy with a couple of elderly women in town who appreciated being looked in on now and then.

Ellie sat in a chair facing Brie's desk, listening to her lawyer's briefing on the hearing that would take place.

"All set with a conservative outfit to wear to court?" Brie asked.

"Uh-huh. Vanni hooked me up."

"I believe the judge will decide to make this whole thing go away before he comes under public criticism for the corners he cut with his last decision. An attorney ad litem has been assigned to the children, protecting their interests, and I don't expect your ex-husband to make an appearance. Based on his 'incident' with locking the children in the house, I suspect he's done with this particular mischief."

"Really? You think?" Ellie asked hopefully.

"There have been a few developments, Ellie. I phoned Dr. Arnold Gunterson of the University of Maine. The poor man was understandably upset and confused by anyone's desire to use his name and credentials, but when I explained the circumstances of the custody situation, the locking of the children in the house, it jogged his memory. It seems a former student from almost twenty years back had some real issues in that same area. He was a very troubled young man. As he was growing up, his parents disciplined him by locking him in the cellar or the closet. A cellar during a Maine winter, Dr. Gunterson explained, can be brutal."

"Oh, God," Ellie said. She scooted forward in her chair. "The basement," she said, remembering. "Once, only a few days into our marriage, Arnie said something at dinnertime… He said that bad children were locked in the basement. I really freaked out at that comment. I pitched a fit. I unloaded on him, told him that if he ever tried anything like that on my children, I'd have him behind bars. And if he ever *said* anything like that again, we'd be gone. It was one of the only times he ever backed down without a fight. He said it was just talk—he'd never do anything like that. I'd almost forgotten…"

"The student Dr. Gunterson remembers is named Robert Beck," Brie said. "Dr. Gunterson imagines he was studying psychology to see if he could get a handle on what damage had been done to him, growing up. He was obsessed with Dr. Gunterson, a kind of hero worship that ended just shy of stalking. Beck taught young children for a short time in Maine, but was terminated for treating the kids too harshly. He got in trouble for locking one child in the closet in his classroom. He spent some time in a psychiatric hospital, and that was the last Dr. Gunterson heard about him. A little further checking turned up some minor scrapes with the law. Our sheriff's department will arrest him for fraud and identity theft, but whether there's any extradition remains to be seen.

"I have no idea how long he's been using a second identity as Arnold Gunterson," Brie went on. "I don't know if it's been months or years. He was hard to trace because he got his driver's license and vehicle registration in his legal name, rented his house and took his job using his false identity. Frankly, Dr. Gunterson would like to have sole use of his identity, but he's not anxious to see Beck again."

"After we got married I realized he was weird," Ellie said. She swallowed. "Turns out he was once a frightened child. An abused, frightened child." She shook her head sadly.

"Treating people the way he'd been treated. I can't tell you how often that's the case," Brie said.

"Yes, Noah said as much. He said that mistreating my kids wouldn't bring Arnie relief, it would make his life more miserable, but that probably wouldn't matter. Oh, Brie, thank God my kids weren't hurt any worse than they were!"

Brie was writing something down on a piece of paper. "I'm sure they're getting along fine, now that they're reassured you're near and they're safe. Just the same, make an appointment with this counselor. Get them evaluated. No point in borrowing trouble. And I'll see you in court at nine o'clock Friday morning."

Ellie stood. "Are you sure he won't give me any more trouble about custody? Because no matter what a judge says, I can't let my kids be alone with him. Not ever."

"He's going to be arrested before court on Friday, Ellie. He might make bail, but he's not taking on custodianship of any minor children. I can almost guarantee that."

"Thank you," Ellie said softly. "Really, thank you isn't enough, but… It may take me a while, but I'll make sure you're paid for your work."

"Sure. Whenever," Brie said. "Thing is, I have a daughter. Before long I'm going to be looking for a good school. Right after this custody case is finished, I'm going hunting. I want to know why none of the teachers or directors at that private school were fingerprinted. Then I'm going to find out if all the employees of the rest of our county's schools have had the required background checks. For that, Ellie, we owe you. And the price you could have paid is way too high."

When she got back to town, Ellie checked at the Fitch house, but no one was home. It wasn't quite time for Nick to be home after work and Jo often ran errands after collecting Danielle from school. She walked down the street and saw the carpenters who'd been tasked with installing pews loading up their trucks, finished for the day, and Noah's old truck was gone. But unless Noah said otherwise, he would be home in time to be sure Lucy had her dinner. Ellie went in the side door and up the stairs to the sanctuary.

Ah, it was looking good. Just a little spit and polish, the accoutrements like kneeler, pulpit and baptistery in place and it would be absolutely beautiful for Saturday's wedding. Ellie had offered to join Vanni, Shelby and some other women in decorating the pews with flowers. A florist from Grace Valley would bring a truckful and, while the women concentrated on the pews, she would adorn the front of the church. The church would be barely done and Noah would have his debut. Ellie sat in the front pew and imagined it. Her eyes were drawn to the stained-glass window. The peace in his eyes comforted her. Calmed her.

There was a voice from the back of the church. A deep, familiar voice. "You have to give me a chance." A man she'd known only as Arnie spoke.

She stood and turned toward him. He was standing at the back of the church, a big, homely, unhappy man. "Robert? Or is it Bob?" she asked.

"I never hurt them," he said. "I took good care of them, Ellie," he said.

"You locked them in your house! And you scared me that night you followed me in your big SUV!" She wrinkled her brow. "Where'd you park that big thing? I didn't see it outside."

"Ellie, if you'll just cooperate for once, I can make this right. All I ever wanted my whole life was to do a good job with a family. Do it right. Be respected. Maybe I shouldn't have followed you, but—"

"Maybe?"

"You were with him. You weren't supposed to be with him. You're *mine.*"

"We're divorced! We've been divorced over a year!"

"I never accepted that. Marriage is forever," he said with a shrug. "That wasn't part of the plan, wasn't what we agreed. I let myself get mad about the way things went. You know me—I don't often get mad."

"You get mad *all* the time!" she said hotly. "You get mad, you threaten, you harass and badger! You punish!"

"No, no, no," he said. "I just try to keep things on track, that's all. You know."

He took a step toward her and she said loudly, "What's your *name?* Is it Robert? Is it Bob? What?"

He stopped in the aisle. "No," he said, shaking his head. "I haven't been Robert in a long time and I've been better off for it. Listen, just listen to me for once, if I apologize to the professor, all this will be over. We can pick up where we—"

"Pick up what? We were never even really married! Why in the world do you want me at all? We never even… You know what we never did! And you know you can't be around children! You hate children!"

"I don't," he said, shaking his head, taking another step. "I wasn't mean to them, Ellie," he said, taking another step toward her. "I was strict and I didn't mollycoddle 'em, but I didn't mistreat them. I mean, that business with the house locks—really, I did that so no one could get in and hurt them."

"They cried every night, you wouldn't let them talk to me on the phone, they were scared and lonely—" She backed away a step. "Arnie, you need to see someone. You need help and I can't give it to you. And even if I could, I wouldn't take the job."

"You don't understand about the help," he said, appearing frustrated. "The help doesn't work. I take medicine for depression, but it's not good. As long as things are calm, I'm just fine."

"I've got news for you, Arnie—things can't always be calm."

"They *can*," he insisted. "Look, you're just upset, that's all. Mad about what I said in that bar. That won't matter, Ellie. We'll just start over. You'll see. We'll apologize to everyone, you'll just say it was a misunderstanding and we'll just—"

"No," she said calmly and firmly. "You're on your own, Arnie or Robert or whoever you are. If you're smart, you'll get a lawyer, tell him you have problems and need some help. You probably won't go to jail that way. And, for sure, you should talk to someone about, you know, the stuff you went through."

"What do you mean?" he asked, stepping toward her, scowling down at her.

"Whatever happened to you that makes you want to control people, that makes you depressed, makes you want to lock up little children," she said, backing away.

"You don't know what you're saying. All I want to do is make it up to you," he said. "You know, I liked you. I really did. I could take care of you. And them. It was really easy to see you needed someone like me— someone who could take charge and take care of you. You admitted it yourself—you just couldn't do it."

"Certainly you no longer have any kind of job," she said to him. "What am I saying? I don't care if you're president of General Motors! No, Arnie. Never. No way. Be smart—get a lawyer, get some help. It has *nothing* to do with me."

He made a growling sound and moved toward her, taking three quick steps.

"Stop!" Noah shouted from the side doorway into the sanctuary. "Don't take another step. Back away from her. I mean it!"

Arnie stopped. He grinned at Noah. "You again?"

Ellie skittered to stand beside Noah and Lucy. Noah

slipped his arm around her waist, pulled her against him and said, "Ellie gave you excellent advice. Find a lawyer to help you. Get some help for yourself. You're done here."

"This is about me and Ellie," he said. "It has nothing to do with you."

"Nothing there anymore, Arnie," Noah said. "Move on. Before this gets any more complicated for you."

The man gave a short laugh and moved quickly toward them. He reached out to grab Ellie by the wrist. Noah's hand gripped Arnie's forearm instantly, so the three of them were locked together. And Lucy lost it. Without warning, she snarled and lunged, sinking her teeth right into Arnie's leg. With a howl of pain, Arnie kicked the dog off his leg and sent her skidding and yelping into a nearby pew.

In the melee, Noah lost his hold on Arnie, but Arnie continued to grip Ellie's wrist. Ellie twisted her wrist sharply toward his thumb rather than fingers, breaking the hold. And then she kneed him hard in the groin. With a grunt, he doubled over for just a moment.

Noah stepped between Arnie and Ellie, grabbed Arnie's arm and twisted it behind his back. "Ellie, get out of here," he growled. Then, with Arnie's arm as leverage, he marched him back down the church aisle toward the front entrance. As Noah pushed him toward the exit, he informed him, "You ever go near her again and I can't be responsible for my own actions. You have no claim on Ellie, as if you ever did, and I intend to keep her safe from the likes of you. The sheriff has been called and until he gets here—"

The front entrance to the sanctuary opened and Jack and Preacher stood there. "Right here, Noah. We got him," Preacher said, as they stepped forward, taking one arm each, dragging him toward the door. Noah was

Arnie's equal in height, though trimmer, but these two at six-two and six-four with shoulders like door frames, dwarfed him. Arnie moaned with each step, no doubt still hurting from that shot to the testicles. "Sheriff's deputy, Henry Depardeau, should be here in ten minutes," Jack said.

Noah turned back into the church and saw Ellie on her knees in front of Lucy. Lucy was alert, but down on her belly. When Noah came toward her, she looked up at him and gave a wag of her tail, but she didn't get up.

"I think she's just stunned, Noah," Ellie said. "After her accident, maybe you shouldn't chance it. Maybe you should take her to the vet, just to be sure."

Noah knelt in front of Lucy, gently petting her head. "Remind me never to get into a fight with either of you girls," he said. "Want to come with me?" he asked Ellie.

"I have to see my kids," she said, shaking her head. "I stopped by Jo's and they weren't there. I came here looking for you, to tell you all about Arnie. Brie has a ton of information on him. He must have seen me come in here. Noah, did you hear the way he was talking? He just wanted to do it all over again. He said we could start over and this would all go away. He said I was *his*."

"Yeah, well, he's delusional," Noah said. He stood up and pulled gently on Lucy's collar. "You gonna stand, girl?" Slowly, Lucy got up, then started wagging and panting. "I think she's all right. But I'll take her over to Nathaniel anyway." He looked at Ellie, who seemed to be staring at Lucy, but not seeing her. "Ellie? Forget him, he's crazy." She didn't respond. "Are you in shock?" Noah asked her.

She lifted her gaze to his face. "Hmm? No. No, just thinking. Take Lucy, Noah. I'm going to check on my kids. I have to tell Jo about court."

"Sure," he said. He leaned toward her and gave her a peck on the cheek. "I'll see you later, then." He looked at her closely, frowning. She was completely pensive, which was unlike Ellie. "Ellie, what is it?"

"Hmm. Sorry. Thinking."

So Ellie went to the Fitch house and found everyone there—Nick was in his den, reading the newspaper while the kids had their one hour of after-school TV in the same room. Jo was in the kitchen, working on dinner. Ellie stepped right in without needing to be asked, getting out the salad makings and going to work on it. While Jo seared meat and cleaned and cut vegetables, Ellie worked on their salad and told Jo all the news of the day. At the end of a softly told tale, she said, "I don't think the kids need to know about court on Friday morning—it will just stress them out. They've already had a short meeting with their attorney, which didn't seem to upset them, and they don't have to be in court. Better to tell them when it's over, I think. I mean, if I thought there was some reason to prepare them for the worst, I'd do that," Ellie said. "It will be so nice to tell them when it's over. That we're a family again."

"I'll come to court right after I drop Danielle at school. Nick is going to take the morning off to keep an eye on Trevor. I haven't exactly taken a poll, but I understand a number of friends will be there—Jack and Mel, Preacher and Paige, Vanni, her father the general. Maybe Shelby and Luke…"

"Oh, get out!" Ellie said. "They don't have time for that. There's a wedding happening on Saturday. They have family from out of town coming, and lots to do. And don't they have Friday-night rehearsal and a dinner? And I'm helping to decorate Saturday morning…"

Jo covered Ellie's hand and smiled. "Sweetheart, getting

your custody resolved is just as important. And your friends are committed to that. We'll get everything done."

"I can't believe it. I was afraid people around here would think the worst of me after what Arnie said."

"I don't think so," Jo said, shaking her head.

"They really plan to go to Eureka for this?"

"Don't argue," Jo said. "It's not a good idea to take chances at this point."

"I guess you're right," Ellie said. Ellie took a deep breath and smiled. "There's a lot to do between now and Saturday night. This is the opening of the church, a wedding the whole town has been looking forward to, and before we can see that all done, I have to go to court. I might be a little tense."

"Well, take it easy, honey. We're going to be fine. I'm sure of it."

By the time Noah got out to Nate Jensen's stable and veterinary office, the sun was lowering in the sky, and Lucy seemed to be moving around just fine. But since he'd come this far, Noah decided to proceed with the visit. The vet office attached to the stable was locked, so he went to the house and knocked on the back door. He saw Nate and a woman in the kitchen, apparently having a drink and snack at the breakfast bar; Nate answered the door.

"Hey, Noah," he said, popping the last bit of a cracker into his mouth.

"I'm sorry to bother you, Nate. Something came up with Lucy and I thought I'd better have you check her out." Suddenly a chorus of barking came from inside the house and three fluffy, black-and-white dogs with pointy ears came racing into the kitchen. "Whoa," Noah said.

"Winkin, Blinkin and Nod," Nate said with a laugh. "Mostly border collie, we think."

"Donner, Dasher and Blitzen," the woman said, joining them at the back door. "We call them Don, Dash and Blitz. Hi, I'm Annie, Nate's fiancée." She put out her hand. "I've heard about you. Nice to finally meet you."

"The feeling's mutual," Noah said. "We had an incident. I got into a little altercation in the church. It wasn't serious, but a man and I locked horns, grabbed each other, and Lucy bit him."

"Lucy?" Nate said, looking down at the dog. "Even-tempered Lucy?"

The three almost full-grown pups were busy sniffing her and she was standing stock-still, letting them. The pups were dancing around a bit, whining, stumbling over each other, crowding Lucy.

"The situation must have made her nervous," Noah said. "Anyway, she latched on to the guy's leg and the guy kicked her off, throwing her into a pew. She couldn't get right up and—"

But Nate wasn't really listening. He crouched near Lucy, in the midst of a throng of prancing pups. And then Lucy got down on her belly and the pups laid down, as well. They continued to sniff while Lucy started to smell and lick them. One of the pups rolled over on his back and Lucy went to work on his closed eyes.

"Isn't that something, the way she does that?" Noah asked. "Do all female dogs just take over the cleanup on instinct? I thought only cats did that. I've seen her do that to another dog in town."

Nate looked up from his crouched position. "Comet? Christopher's pup?"

"Yeah. How'd you know?"

Nate stood up and grabbed Annie's hand. "Silas was training Lucy and she was coming along just great. But Silas also had ranch dogs that roamed pretty free—he kept cows and other livestock. A couple of 'em were border collies. I think if Lucy got friendly with another border collie, these might be her pups."

"You're kidding, right?" Noah said. "But she was in an accident. When would she have had pups?"

Nate was shaking his head. "Jack Sheridan found a box of abandoned puppies under the Christmas tree last December. They were too little to be weaned; it was a surprise they survived the cold. I put them at about three weeks old. They had to be eyedropper fed and kept warm." He chuckled unhappily. "I wouldn't put it past old Silas. He wasn't the type to have a litter of eight in his house or likely to go to any trouble to place them. I'm kind of surprised he didn't drown 'em."

"Come on," Noah said. "You think it's possible?"

The three adults stood around, looking down at Lucy and a big pile of playful pups. Even though they were almost as big as she was, they certainly acted like puppies. Lucy seemed to be on the bottom of the pile, and very content, snarling an occasional warning, nudging them, licking them, pushing them around with her snout.

"The town named them after the reindeer. There were four females in the litter—Dancer, Prancer, Vixen and Cupid. I got these guys because they were left over." Nate connected with Noah's eyes. "Lucy wasn't trying to find her way home," he said. "She was trying to get back to her kids."

Eighteen

At the Fitch house, after the children had been settled in bed and Ellie had gone to her apartment, Nick wandered into the kitchen where Jo was brewing a cup of tea. "Think I could have one of those?" he asked.

"You hate tea," she said.

"Just the same, could I? And sit with you a minute?"

"Sure," she said, totally confused. "But *tea?*"

"Want me to get it myself?" he asked. "I'd be glad to. You wait on me too much anyway."

She went for a cup and saucer, put a tea bag in it and poured boiling water from the kettle. "I just do what I'm expected to do."

He let that go a beat, until he was busily dunking the tea bag. "You do way more than what's expected. What you're doing for Danielle and Trevor, for example. If those kids didn't have you, life just wouldn't be fun for them right now. For that matter, if Ellie didn't have you in her corner, I hate to think…"

"You should give yourself a lot of credit, too, Nick," Jo said.

He took a courage-building breath. "We're not a bad

team, despite all. Jo Ellen, I'd like to say I'm sorry. I'd like to apologize to you for my mistakes, but as it turns out, there are too many to count. I could start right now and still not be done by next Tuesday. But in my gut, I'm aware of every mistake I ever made, and I'm sorry. I love you and I'm sorry."

"Nick?" she questioned, dumbfounded.

"Seems like the turning point for us had to do with the adoption issue, but I don't kid myself that that was all that was wrong between us. I bungled a lot of things, and somewhere along the line, I lost you." He reached across the table to take her hand. At first she jumped, almost pulling her hand away. But then she thought better of it and let him hold it. "Can you ever accept my apology? I'm just not a very smart guy. I knew I was making mistake after mistake, but it was like I was helpless. Once you went to your own room, I wanted to pull you back to me. But instead, out of hurt pride, I pushed you further away. God, what I'd give to undo that, to be able to change course."

"I know why you didn't want to adopt children," Jo said. "I never could accept it, but at least I knew your reasons. But what possible reason could you have for making passes at women? For making me a laughingstock?"

He shrugged and looked down. "Lord, I don't have a reason. I was always looking for attention, I guess. Wanted you to think you had some competition, maybe. But you weren't a laughingstock—it was you the town respected. I heard them say it—what is she doing with that idiot? Why does she stay with him? They knew why I stayed, even though it looked like I wasn't satisfied in marriage. Because, Jo Ellen, there's not a better wife in this town than you. You take better care of me and our home than any woman ever could. But even though you made sure I was never without a good meal or a sewed on button or a perfect house, our days of hugs and kisses have been over for decades. You know everything I like and don't like, know everything about me, even though we hardly ever have a real conversation. I miss you, Jo Ellen."

Jo felt the moisture rise in her eyes. "This is so sudden…"

"It probably seems like it. If you only knew how many times I wanted to bring it up, and didn't know where to start."

"And why now, Nick?"

"Because, Jo Ellen, seeing you with Ellie and the kids, I realize it's not too late for us. It might be too late to adopt children, but… I'd like it if we get to keep Ellie and the kids as part of our family from now on. But even if that's not possible for some reason, it's pretty obvious we can make it our mission to have family. We can get involved in community stuff to do with children—they're always begging for volunteers for everything. Make A Wish, Special Olympics, Parks and Rec, Little League, everything. We got us a new church in town—we can help out there. I bet there are single parents everywhere in this county that could use a hand…"

Jo started to laugh and squeezed his hand. "Don't you dare volunteer us for anything without talking to me first."

"I promise," he said. "Jo Ellen, honey, can we start over? We used to have something pretty special, you and me. I don't think it's too late for that."

"Ah. I think I know what you want. Pretty sneaky."

"Huh? What?" he asked.

"Bedroom stuff," she said. "That's what this is all about."

"Oh, phooey," he scoffed. "That's not what I'm after. I just want some good feelings to go with the great way we manage this marriage. Know what I mean?" He leaned toward her. "I want to hug. I want a kiss on the cheek sometimes. I want to help with the dishes and talk about our days." Then he got a twinkle in his eye. "But, if I remember, we did have that bedroom stuff pretty well figured out."

"Nick!" she said with a laugh.

"We did," he said, grinning.

"I'm going to have to think about this a little bit. You took me by surprise."

"Think about this, Jo Ellen," he said, taking both her hands across the table. An unaccustomed dark stain rose up on his cheeks, like a youth looking for romantic courage. "We're going to a fancy wedding on Saturday. In our brand-new church. We could hold hands while they say their vows and we could silently say ours to each other. Nothing official, no big announcement, but a private renewal for you and me. A new start. If you can forgive me for everything I did to screw us up, that is."

She was quiet a minute. "I'm sorry, too," she said. "And my list is long, too."

"You have nothing to be sorry for, sweetheart," Nick said softly. "I just want a chance to live the rest of our marriage in love again, like we used to be. Like I've been all this time."

"Do you really mean that?"

"Really. Will you think about it?"

"I will," she said. And by the way she said that, he knew she wasn't going to say no. He could see relief in her eyes that matched the relief he was feeling in his heart.

"Whew," he said. "Think I'll have a brandy. Want one?"

"What about your tea?"

"I hate tea," he said. Then he smiled at her.

Noah couldn't wait to tell Ellie about what Nate Jensen suspected—that Lucy was the mother of eight pups left under the Virgin River Christmas tree eight months ago. He had to be patient, however. It wouldn't do to go bursting in on the Fitch household. And he'd be sure to run it by Ellie before sharing this story with the kids. It made him grin, though, knowing how the kids would enjoy it.

But he didn't have to wait to tell Jack and Preacher. He leashed Lucy to the porch rail for her dinner, went inside for his own and said, "Wait till you hear this...."

When Noah repeated the story, Jack said, "No way! I never even knew Lucy before you brought her back to life! 'Course, I never knew Silas, either. His ranch was on the other side of the valley. Heard about the wreck, but—"

Jack turned and banged on the wall, bringing Preacher out from the kitchen. And when Preacher heard the story, he said, "No way! Lucy? Two of 'em didn't get the border collie markings, just the long hair and pointy ears, but those pups could definitely belong to Lucy. Well, Noah, isn't that just unbelievable? I'm going to have to look that up on the computer, see what I can find out about breeding, about mother dogs being reunited with their pups after a long separation." And with that, he turned and went back to the kitchen.

Jack grinned. "That's going to keep him busy for days. He won't stop till he knows everything." Jack leaned close. "Noah, Henry Depardeau took your man Arnie away. Said he'd broken some laws in another state and that he's not going to make quick bail."

"Good," Noah said. "Because Ellie has her custody hearing on Friday morning."

"I know," Jack said. "It got leaked. Me and Preach, we're closing up shop and heading for Eureka with our wives. I think we'll have a good showing for her. I know it doesn't really count for the judge's decision, but it'll make Ellie feel good."

Noah was touched. "That's nice, Jack. She'll appreciate that."

When the light tapping came at her door, Ellie didn't have to ask who was there. Arnie was tucked away in jail and it was Noah's usual visiting hour, which he liked to stretch out till dawn. When he walked in, Lucy by his side, Ellie said, "Oh, thank God, she's all right."

"Better than all right," Noah said, taking off his jacket and tossing it in her chair. "Wait till you hear this. It turns out that little Christopher Middleton's dog, Comet, and seven other pups that were abandoned in the cold of last Christmas, left to freeze, rescued by the town, are probably Lucy's pups. Taken from her too early. She might have been trying to find her way back to them. That's what Nate Jensen thinks could have happened."

Ellie knelt in front of the dog and began to massage her neck and jowls with loving hands. "Is that a fact, my dear girl? Good for you."

"Isn't that remarkable?" Noah said.

Ellie shrugged. "It is if you don't know much about women and mothers," Ellie said.

"Are you doing all right?" Noah asked. "When I left you earlier, you were kind of strange. Preoccupied."

She stood up. "I'm real edgy. Facing that custody hearing, even though Brie said it can only go one way, is bigger than I am. I thought it could only go one way the last time, and look what happened. It's going to be a long night, getting ready for court."

"I'll help you pass the time," Noah said, reaching for her. He pulled her against him and sighed. "The church will be done, the Booth and Riordan families have all arrived for the wedding, George is coming tomorrow…"

"Everything right on schedule," Ellie said. "Just like we planned." She pulled back and looked into his eyes. "When I tricked you into giving me this job, I said I'd get out of your hair the minute I had custody again. It would free you up to get a real pastor's assistant."

He chuckled. "The joke was on me. I couldn't have found a better pastor's assistant if I tried."

"Or at least a more accommodating one," she teased. "I doubt you'd have snuggled up to Mrs. Nagel this well. Noah, I can stick to the deal. If I do get through this hearing and get my kids, I won't owe anybody as much as I owe you. If you hadn't given me a chance, it wouldn't have worked at all."

"I told you," he said. "I gave you my word, my commitment, that I'd stand by you, wouldn't let you down. I'll love you forever, never let you down, stay with you from now on. I couldn't have made love to you under any other terms. It's not just some notion of mine, Ellie, but part of who I am. When I make promises like that, I don't back out. No matter what."

She tilted her head, peering at him. "That's really something, Noah. You must have great willpower. God must be so proud of you."

"I'm pretty sure I fall short more often than make him proud." He gave her a little kiss. "I'm sure you made similar promises…"

She shook her head. "I'm sorry to say, I'm not as devout as you. I wasn't thinking of promises or commitments at all—just that I loved you. Really, I tried not to. I thought it might complicate both our lives. But

I hadn't felt anything like that in such a long time, I just gave in."

"I'm not sorry you did," he said, smiling. "You'll see, Ellie. It's going to work out for us. And you can have the pastor's assistant's job for as long as you want."

She was quiet for a moment, then she said, "Why, Noah, you might be the most generous man I know...."

Early on Friday morning, Ellie dressed very carefully in the nice pantsuit and conservative pumps Vanessa had loaned her. She straightened her hair so it wouldn't be wild and wore light makeup. Her nails were shortened and done in a clear polish. And her stomach was upside down.

She walked down to the church and used her key to go in the front entrance rather than the side door she usually used. She walked up the steps to the wide foyer and pushed open the double doors to the sanctuary. Then she walked slowly down the aisle.

The October sun was barely rising above the tall trees at 7:00 a.m., but the inside of the sanctuary was resplendent in shining hardwood, glittering altar accoutrements, including the gold candelabra and cross she had polished herself. She and Noah had worked until past eleven a couple of nights, making sure all was ready for the wedding rehearsal that would take place late Friday afternoon. She had spent hours the day before making sure every last speck of workman's dust was wiped from the floor and pews. Tomorrow morning Shelby and her family would attach floral arrangements to the end of each pew for the afternoon ceremony. Ellie had promised to help. Shelby and Luke had decided on 5:00 p.m. to exchange their vows.

Ellie was so proud she could burst. She'd helped make all this happen. She'd worked *hard*. She gave thanks every morning that she'd had the chance. "Little melo-dramatic of you, messing with my motherhood to force me into the position," she said to the holy stained-glass image before her. "I know—I can't be sure that was your idea. But I can let that go if you just settle down on the big life lessons. Really, I'm so damn tired. Gimme a break, couldja?"

"Ready?" a voice said. Noah stood in the hall door that led to his office. He was wearing a very sharp dark suit, blinding-white shirt and royal-blue tie. It brought out the sheen in his black hair, which had finally been trimmed, and his magnificent blue eyes glittered.

"Whoa," she said, stunned. "I didn't even know you had good clothes! That's amazing—you look so hand-some," she said. "If this minister business doesn't work out for you, you could be a model."

"You worried I'm going to fall on my face?" he asked. "I've actually done this before, you know. I know how to get people married. Only once, but I've even been complimented on my performance. And you look pretty—"

The sound of a door opening and feet on the stairs cut him off, quieted them. Then Brie was standing beside Noah. "Morning," she said. "Everyone ready?"

Ellie's stomach took another flip. "Ready," she said.

It was a long ride to the Eureka courthouse. Noah made small talk while he drove Ellie's car. He told the story of Lucy and the pups yet again. He explained to Brie who George was and that he'd be in town by early afternoon; George wasn't about to miss the very first service Noah performed in the new church. Noah wouldn't leak the secret vows Shelby and Luke had agreed on but said, from what he'd heard, the rehearsal dinner party that would take place at Walt Booth's house would be one gala night. And the wedding reception would take place in Walt's pasture under tenting and complete with linen, crystal, space heaters and a dance floor. It would put the Taj Mahal to shame. "I doubt any president has done it better," Noah said cheerfully.

Ellie wished he'd just shut up. She was a wreck. A sick worried wreck.

When they pulled into Eureka, Brie said, "Ellie, we've already talked about this, but one more time—the judge has had all the paperwork pertaining to your case for over a week—the motion, the temporary restraining order, arrest report, paperwork from Child Welfare Services, the letter from Reverend Kincaid verifying your employment—everything. He may have all he needs for a decision. Or, he might have a few questions for you. Answer honestly and politely. And, Ellie, no matter what happens, hold your emotions in check. By all means, your temper. If we hit a bad patch and things don't go well—a very very remote possibility—please let me handle it. For your own good."

"I will," she said quietly.

Brie repeated all this several times in very soft tones while they waited right outside the courtroom doors until the bailiff called Ellie's name. And while they waited, familiar faces began to appear. Her friends and neighbors—Jack and Mel, Preacher and Paige, Vanni and Paul, Walt and Muriel. Even Hope McCrea. Of course, Jo Fitch arrived before they were called. All Ellie could do was smile tremulously and nod. Yes, she told someone in a uniform, they were all approved to be present in her closed hearing. Closed because it involved juveniles.

When the double doors opened to admit them to the courtroom, her eyes focused on the dais where that blasted judge would sit. She was so oblivious to her surroundings, she didn't even hear all her friends behind her. She followed Brie to the front, Noah walking behind them. The judge came in and the bailiff ordered them to *all rise*. The case was announced. The judge said good-morning. Ellie shook inside.

"Miss Baldwin, what kind of arrangements have you made for housing for yourself and the children?"

She cleared her throat. "I'm not making any immediate changes, Your Honor. Mr. and Mrs. Fitch have invited us to stay on their property until I can save a little money and look for something. The kids are very happy there and we each have our own bedroom. I have breakfast and dinner with them every day. I put them to bed at night."

"Hmm," he said, flipping through the documents. "Very generous. Are Mr. and Mrs. Fitch here?"

"I'm here, Your Honor," Jo Ellen said from behind Ellie. "Mr. Fitch is with Miss Baldwin's four-year-old, Trevor. Trevor doesn't attend school yet."

That's when Ellie turned and really took notice of the encouraging faces in the courtroom. Shelby and Luke were there, even though Luke's entire family was in town for the wedding. Mike Valenzuela had arrived.

"This works for you, Mrs. Fitch? Because part of the recommendation of the court is adequate housing."

"Ellie is like a daughter to me, her children like grandchildren. Nothing could make me happier."

"Once the order of custody is changed, the minor children won't be in foster care," he pointed out. "There will be no stipend for—"

"I'll be paying additional rent, Your Honor," Ellie said. "I wouldn't take advantage. Jo's been so… I mean, Mrs. Fitch has been so wonderful to us."

"Well then, I'd say we're done here. Do a good job with these children, Miss Baldwin. I don't want to see you again."

It burned on her tongue to say she probably wouldn't see him again as long as she was working in a church, but thankfully he banged his gavel, closing the case. And rather than words coming to her tongue, tears came to her eyes and she lost it. She put her face in her hands and just cried. She felt arms around her; Brie hugging her. She heard a loud murmur go up from behind her—subdued cheers from her new friends. She felt strong arms grab her by the shoulders, turn her, embrace her. "You did it, honey," Noah whispered. "You did it. It's over." And she put her face against that beautiful dark suit and wept.

Ellie knew she had been wound too tight for the hearing, but she had no idea how much energy had bled out of her with the decision. She was weak as a kitten as she accepted congratulatory embraces from her friends. Out on the courthouse steps, there was a mood of victory, which she tearfully and meekly accepted.

"Come out to the house, meet the Riordan clan and my little brother," Vanni invited. "Before all the wedding stuff officially starts."

"First we're going to pick up Danielle from school," Jo said, pulling Ellie against her. "We'll meet Nick and Trevor for lunch and tell the kids that the whole thing is fixed, they have their mother back. Noah? Will you join us?"

"Of course," he said. "Then I'm back to town to meet George."

Ellie just nodded numbly. But she snagged Brie's sleeve and asked, "He can't change his mind, can he?"

Brie smiled. "We're done with this, Ellie. And I'll watch the proceedings involving Arnie to make sure he's out of your hair. I'll let you know how that goes when something happens there, but don't even worry about it. I'd say that's over, as well."

As Ellie walked with Noah to her car, he took her hand in his. "I'm so proud of you, Ellie. You never gave up. Meet Hercules Baldwin." Then he grinned.

Because Danielle and Trevor were so comfortably ensconced in Jo and Nick's house, Ellie was pretty sure the impact of the ruling was lost on them. They had already moved on, emotionally. Once children feel safe, they can relax. All they wanted to be sure about was that they didn't have to pack a bag and that they didn't have to live with Arnie again. Beyond that, Danielle wanted to get back to school in time for her spelling contest—she was sure she was ahead of the class. And she wondered how soon she could start riding the bus to school. Nick had promised Trevor a PlayStation tournament if he ate his vegetables and had a little afternoon nap. With things so settled, Jo urged Ellie to go on to Vanessa's house.

It was that visit that gave Ellie her second wind. She'd been to Vanni's so many times to help out, finding her friend collapsing under the weight of two babies and a lot of emotional baggage, but all that had changed. Her house was full of people "staying clear of the general's house while caterers set up for tonight's party." Vanni grabbed her by the hand, led her around, introducing her to people, including Luke's visiting family.

She was embraced by Maureen Riordan, Luke's redhaired, green-eyed mother who held a contented Hannah on her hip. The general almost broke Ellie in half with his bear hug, then introduced her to his son, Tom, home from West Point for the wedding. Muriel kissed her cheek and pressed a glass of wine in her hand. Then there were the Riordan men, of whom Luke was the eldest. Next in line, Colin, just back from an assignment in Iraq in the Blackhawk. Then came Aiden, a very handsome navy doctor who bent elegantly over her hand. Before that introduction could even be complete, she was embraced by good-looking, playful Sean, who said, "Thank God above—I was afraid there'd be no beautiful women to dance with at the wedding!" And finally the baby of the family, Patrick, on leave from a naval aircraft carrier stationed in the Gulf where he flew fighters. She learned they ranged in age from thirty-one to thirty-nine, all single, Luke soon to be off the market.

When she could catch her breath, she whispered to Vanni, "Oh my God, would you look at these men? You should have warned me!"

Vanni laughed. "Nice eye candy for the unattached female," she said. "Know any?"

Ellie just smiled. But she had a fantastic time, honored to be a part of the wedding party and their afternoon of reunion and celebration. Those present were all included in the party following the rehearsal, but Shelby and Luke had decided on only one attendant each. Shelby's matron of honor would be Vanessa, and Sean would stand up with Luke. Shelby's uncle Walt would give her away and from what Ellie heard around the house that afternoon, the rest of the Riordan boys planned to drink just enough to keep from getting some famous ear twist from their feisty red-haired mother.

Late in the afternoon, Vanessa snagged her arm and said, "Come with me just one second." She pulled Ellie to her bedroom and closed the door. "My timing might not be the best, but before this crowd descended on us, I had to do some cleaning and clearing. I went through the clothes that aren't horribly out-of-date and put some aside for you. Keep what you want and give the overflow to Goodwill. There could be a pair of jeans or sweater in there you can use."

"Oh, Vanni, you shouldn't have. Really," Ellie said.

"I should be sending your firstborn to college, for all the help you gave me. But keep this in perspective here—we're talking hand-me-downs. I just hope I'm not insulting you. These things may not be what you like. By the way—you look gorgeous today." She grinned. "Did I mention I can't fit into that suit anymore? It's yours."

Ellie plucked at her borrowed slacks. "But you will again…"

"No, I won't. I'm planning to get pregnant. Just give me a chance to potty train little Matt, the most obstinate of male children. I swear, he likes sitting in poop. But, I have to get down to one in diapers before I take another plunge." She smiled. She beamed. "You have no idea how happy it makes Paul to think about actually fathering one of his own. Men, huh? How predictable are their egos? If they had to push 'em out, it would be a whole different…"

"Hannah looks so happy," Ellie said.

Vanni's voice softened and she smiled sweetly. "We're doing fine, Ellie. Thank you. We should have our adoption final in a few months, but she's already ours. We're moving ahead." Then she opened the door to her walk-in closet and there stood some packed suitcases. "The luggage is old and is going the way of Goodwill also, so I just put the clothes in them. Really, my feelings won't be affected if you reject them all. I'm going to have a couple of the boys load the stuff in the back of your car for you."

George had a hard time believing how beautiful the church had turned out, from the perfect white paint on the outside to the rich, shiny hardwood finish on the inside. Noah and George stood at the sanctuary entrance to take in the full view. Lucy sat patiently between them. "Have any of the town people seen the finished product, or are you making them all wait for the official unveiling?" he asked.

"Just about everyone in Virgin River has tromped through here at one time or another," Noah said. "I learned it's a favorite pastime around here—when Paul's building a house, especially for someone local, whole families get in their cars, drive to the building site and do regular walk-throughs, commenting on the structure, choice of stone or wood, paint color. Mel Sheridan says it's all part of being in each other's affairs at all times. But—Ellie and I barely finished the final cleanup, so you're among the first to see it like this." Noah looked at his watch. "Where is she? I thought she'd be down here to say hello by now. And she's helping with the music for the rehearsal."

"How much help?" George asked dubiously.

Noah laughed. "Poor girl, she really wanted to play for them. Once the piano arrived and was tuned, she got right on it. But I guess Ellie's been away from the piano a little longer than she thought—it was pretty rough. Not to mention the language this old church had to endure. We decided together that it wasn't right that Shelby would have to stop walking down the aisle suddenly when the pianist hit a bad note and muttered 'shit' loud enough for an entire congregation to hear."

George laughed loudly at that. His laughter echoed in the empty church.

"We're going with some wedding CDs. Preacher loaned us a real nice stereo setup so the music is piped in—it's fantastic. Once things slow down a little, I'll get a unit up and running and find some speakers for the high corners in here," he said, pointing around the sanctuary ceiling.

"It must feel good, Noah. You've worked hard. Did a fine job."

"Ellie worked hard, too," he said proudly.

"She must be so relieved," George said. "Church is finished, kids safely back with her, crazy ex-husband gone."

Noah looked at his watch again. "I haven't even had time to talk to her since we got back from Eureka. She spent the afternoon out at Vanessa's, being introduced to the bride and groom's visiting families. They're all so grateful to her for her help, not just with this wedding stuff, but to Vanni while she was overwhelmed with the little ones. Ellie…" He chuckled, shaking his head. "She can be so in your face one second and the next, utterly oblivious. She doesn't even realize what a good neighbor she's been to these people."

George grinned. "I take it you have that relationship ironed out now…."

Noah laughed again. "God had to send me four boats, two helicopters and several flotation devices. But I don't feel so bad—Ellie hasn't found it much easier."

"I hope you proposed. At least told her you'd be a worthless failure without her…."

"I told her—" Noah stopped. He looked at George in silence for a moment. "I told her I'd made a commitment to love her forever and would never let her down. She said she thought I was real *ethical.*"

George smirked and shook his head. "Why, Noah, I bet that just swept her off her feet. She must be out shopping for a trousseau as we speak."

"Crap," Noah muttered. "I'll get that straightened out tonight. I'll steal her away from the rehearsal party and make sure—"

He was cut off at the sound of people entering the church, laughter accompanying them. The Booth and Riordan parties entered from the front of the church, just those partaking in the ceremony, to keep things simple. The group included Walt, Vanni and Shelby; Luke, Sean, Maureen and two ushers—Tom Booth and Aiden Riordan. Noah shook hands, bussed the lady's cheeks and made introductions. The bride and groom and their attendants wandered to the front of the church, murmuring in awe at how beautiful it finished up, Shelby pointing out where the flowers would go.

"Let's get this over with," Walt blustered to Noah. "They're setting up some mighty fine-looking food back at the house and those Riordans are circling like starving dogs. I'd like to get back there while they're still sober enough to make the toasts."

Noah looked at his watch yet again. "Let's give Ellie another minute—she's helping with the music tonight. Tomorrow is a no-brainer, she can just start the CD and—"

"You sure she's coming, Noah?" Walt asked. "I saw her wrangling a couple of big suitcases down the stairs…"

"You saw her *what?*"

"When we were driving into town, past the Fitch house. She was on the stairs with a big suitcase—one still on top, one already sitting behind her car. I thought maybe she was…"

"Oh, God, no," Noah said. "George, handle this for a few minutes. Lucy, *stay!*" And then he bolted out the side door and ran down the street like the seat of his pants was on fire. Or like he might be losing the love of his life.

When he got to the Fitch house, he saw exactly what Walt had described—a big suitcase sitting beside the open hatch of her PT Cruiser and the door to her apartment standing open. He took the steps two at a time. When he got to the top of the stairs and looked inside, his heart stopped. There she stood, beside her bed, an open suitcase sitting amidst several neatly folded piles of clothing ready to be packed.

"Ellie! *No!*" He rushed to her. "God, *no!* You can't be leaving me! Don't!" He grabbed her face and covered her mouth in a hard, desperate kiss. Her eyes flew open in stunned disbelief; she stopped breathing. He released her mouth but not her face, which he held in his hands, his fingers threaded into her hair. "You can't go, Ellie, you can't. Don't you know how much I love you? God, I'd be nothing without you. I never thought I'd get to feel like this again, but you brought me back to life. You took the loneliness away and brought laughter back into my life. Ellie, you're everything to me— I can't make it without you. If you leave, I don't know what I'll—"

She just stared at him, a slight smile on her face. "Really? You don't say."

"Listen, I know I'm not a good romantic, I know that. I realized just a little while ago that I— Oh, hell, I told you how responsible I was, not how much you light up my life. I told you about my vow and how I could stick to it, not how life without you would be all gray and sad and awful. I didn't tell you everything you mean to me. I promised myself I'd take care of that tonight, for sure. I was almost too late."

"Tell me now," she said.

"Now?" he asked, dropping his hands from her face.

"Right now," she insisted.

"But I haven't prepared!"

"I know. That's the whole idea," she said. "I'm listening."

He cleared his throat. "Ellie. Dammit, you saved my life. I was a wallowing, pathetic, self-pitying—" He stopped talking at the sound of her soft laughter. "You're not supposed to laugh at my attempts to be romantic."

"Noah, that wasn't romantic. That made me wonder what I ever saw in you. Start over."

He grabbed her face in his hands again. "I want to be with you forever. I want to lie beside you every night, holding you close, whispering to you that I love you more than anything in the world, that you turned my whole world upside down just when it needed to be turned upside down. I want to make forever promises to you out loud, in front of God, and I want you to promise to be my woman, my wife, my one and only love, my best friend and my conscience. You're never easy, Ellie, but you're sure never boring…"

"I don't know about that last part," she commented.

"God, I love you so much. If I lost you, I don't know what I'd do. I'd go after you, that's what I'd do. I'd find a way to get you back. You know we're perfect together. I know you feel it because I can feel you feel it." He grinned roguishly. "We sure fit together perfect, don't you think? You told me you loved me—tell me again."

"I love you, Noah. I tried not to. I usually screw up love situations. But, apparently, we have that in common." She grinned. "A good start."

"You won't leave me?"

"Why would I leave you? I adore you. And unless I'm completely stupid, you just asked me to marry you."

"I did. We should give the kids some time to get used to the idea. And we should find a house that can hold us, but as soon as we can work out the details, we should get married."

"Okay," she said. "Am I late for rehearsal?"

"We were waiting for you," he explained. "Then Walt said he saw you struggling with luggage and thought maybe you weren't coming, that you were leaving."

She laughed a bit. "Noah, these are Vanni's hand-me-downs. I thought I had time to unpack them before the rehearsal."

He was shocked silent for a moment, absorbing this, then he grabbed her and kissed her hard. And he said, "I have a feeling I bit off more than I can chew with you."

"No question about that, Your Holiness."

The church was decorated in fall floral arrangements. The ribbons that held turning leaves, dark yellow roses, coral tulips and red calla lilies together were brown, orange, yellow and red. Two big sprays at the front of the church tied the whole look together. The decorations were an amazing complement to the shining dark wood of the pews.

Ellie's role in the ceremony was small but important. When everyone was ready, she pressed Play on the stereo, then went back to sit beside Paul Haggerty so she could hang on to Hannah. The priest and Noah entered from the right, standing together at the front of the church. Luke and Sean Riordan entered from the left. Vanessa came down the aisle and, Hannah, standing in Ellie's lap, raised a fat little hand and yelled, "Mama!"

Vanni beamed at her and blew her a kiss as she passed.

Ellie glanced over her shoulder to smile at her children, seated with Jo and Nick. As she did so, she noticed that Jo and Nick were holding hands and it gave her a lift in her heart.

Right behind Vanni was Shelby, her glorious long hair pulled back and held away from her face with a few small flowers and flowing down her back to her waist. She looked so petite next to her towering uncle Walt; so radiant as he passed her hand into Luke's.

Noah began the ceremony. "Dearly beloved, we are gathered together here in the sight of God—and in the face of this company—to join together this man and this woman in holy matrimony, which is commended to be honorable among all men and therefore—is not by any— to be entered into unadvisedly or lightly—but reverently, discreetly, advisedly and solemnly. Into this holy estate these two persons present now come to be joined."

The priest was next with his part. "Marriage is the union of husband and wife in heart, body and mind. It is intended for their mutual joy—and for the help and comfort given one another in prosperity and adversity. But more importantly—it is a means through which a stable and loving environment may be attained."

Next the reading of 1 Corinthians 13, which they also shared, reading every other verse, beginning with Noah. "If I speak in the tongues of men and of angels, but have not love, I am only a resounding gong or clanging cymbal…"

"Love is patient, love is kind. It does not envy, it does not boast, it is not proud," said the priest.

"Love never fails," said Noah, nearly completing the verse.

And then the priest finished with, "And now these three remain: faith, hope and love. But the greatest of these is love."

Ellie watched Noah with admiration in her eyes, but Noah didn't watch Ellie—he was busy. He focused on the couple before him, on the priest beside him. They presented the bride and groom their candles and they lit a unity candle together. He was so at ease, at peace before his own congregation. He was so beautiful. His smile was filled with joy and love; his eyes glowed. He spoke to the bride and groom softly, so softly no one but the couple could hear. He chuckled at something Luke said.

"There is no wedding sermon today," Noah said. "The bride and groom have decided that the exchange of their vows will provide their message, after which Father Demetrius and I will have the honor of pronouncing them husband and wife. Shelby? Luke?"

Shelby handed off her bouquet and faced Luke, taking both his hands in hers. And she began: "Luke, I love you. I promise that each day I have you in my life, I will show you my love."

Noah's eyes drifted to Ellie's and a smile played about his lips as the bride and groom spoke.

"Shelby, I love you. In each day of our lives together, I will show my love. And where there is injury, I will pardon without hesitation."

"Where there is doubt, Luke, I will have faith in you."

"In times of despair, you will be my hope."

"In times of darkness, I will find my light in you."

"When there is sadness, let me bring you joy."

"Luke, I will not so much seek to be consoled as to console."

"I will seek to understand, not just to be understood."

"I will love, not just crave love."

"I pledge you my heart, my life."

"And I pledge mine to you."

"I, Luke Riordan, take you, Shelby MacIntyre, to be wife, my best friend, my lover, my partner, the head of my family and other half of my heart. Forever." He slid a ring on her finger.

Shelby slid a ring onto his finger. "I, Shelby MacIntyre, take you, Luke Riordan, to be my husband, best friend, lover, partner, head of my family and other half of my heart. Forever."

"With God's blessing," Noah said. "Father Demetrius and I pronounce you husband and wife."

The priest made the sign of the cross over them and invited them to seal their vows with a kiss.

As their lips met, the setting sun shone through the stained-glass window behind them, casting a glow over them. Ellie looked over their heads to Noah's eyes and smiled. The shine in his eyes lit her to the marrow in her bones.

He was home. And she was home with him. Forever.